Advance Praise for T

"Niezen delivers immersive imagery and engaging dialogue, both of which highlight the realism of the story. Well-researched and masterfully told, this powerful tale about war crimes pulls no punches." –***Kirkus Reviews***

"An outstanding novel—the tension buildup was masterful! An astounding achievement from a brilliant author. I loved it!"

–Jonas Saul, author of the *Sarah Roberts* series

Praise for *Truth and Indignation*

"...a tremendous step forward from a scholarly human rights culture that has been overly awed by the truth commission phenomenon and far too slow in probing beneath the surfaces."

–Human Rights Quarterly

"Niezen opts for a clinical remove from the moral content of the story, in order to observe the TRC more critically. There was an easier book to write, but *Truth and Indignation* is more nuanced, more challenging, and as a result more stimulating."

–Literary Review of Canada

"A rare combination of intellectual poetry and absolutely necessary social science."

–Mark Goodale, University of Lausanne

"A brilliant book!"

–Rhoda E. Howard-Hassmann, Wilfrid Laurier University

"Niezen pushes the boundaries of our understanding of what the Truth and Reconciliation Commission can and should mean."

–Joanna Quinn, Centre for Transitional Justice and Post-Conflict Reconstruction, Western University

To Sarah

THE MEMORY SEEKER

RONALD NIEZEN

16 Feb 2023

Black Rose Writing | Texas

The author grants the final approval for this literary material.

First printing

This is a work of fiction. Names, characters, businesses, places, events, and incidents are either the products of the author's imagination or used in a fictitious manner. Any resemblance to actual persons, living or dead, or actual events is purely coincidental.

ISBN: 978-1-68513-140-1
PUBLISHED BY BLACK ROSE WRITING
www.blackrosewriting.com

Printed in the United States of America
Suggested Retail Price (SRP) $22.95

The Memory Seeker is printed in Baskerville

*As a planet-friendly publisher, Black Rose Writing does its best to eliminate unnecessary waste to reduce paper usage and energy costs, while never compromising the reading experience. As a result, the final word count vs. page count may not meet common expectations.

THE MEMORY SEEKER

“It is impossible for the person who secretly [commits a crime] to feel confident that he will remain undiscovered, even if he has already escaped ten thousand times; for right to the end of his life, he is never sure he will not be detected.”

–Epicurus, *Principal Doctrines*

CHAPTER 1: NORA

Peter Dekker willed himself to stop ravaging his fingernails, but it didn't always work—one little moment of abstraction, and he'd find himself with a piece of skin or the edge of a nail between his teeth. He was new to the job, and wasn't used to horrors captured on video, not whole days of them anyway. There were breathing exercises that were supposed to help. Now and then he looked out at the Scheveningen forest through the building's trapezoidal, bombproof, light-bending, espionage-resistant windows. The view wasn't always relaxing, no fault of the forest. The windows themselves, with all their security-oriented genius, evoked images of the bombs and bullets they were designed to stop.

Rashbinder, with three months more experience than Peter, ranked the videos in quarts of blood, a three-quart image or a five, now and then into the tens and twenties. Dark humor to steel the soul. Objectively, the blood-measure didn't always work. It amazed Peter, the things humans could inflict on one another without breaking the skin.

If Nora were here with him, it'd be easier. She was on the other side of the Channel, finishing her fellowship with another month to go before the end of Lent Term. Until then, they'd make do with weekend visits. With her Friday afternoons and Monday mornings free for quick flights, they'd have two whole days together at a time—if he could pull himself away from the screens. They took on a life of their own, those screens, as though possessed by demons. Which, if you considered the complex algorithms driving the search engines, they actually were.

His first assignment as a new hire at the International Criminal Court in The Hague was to gather evidence of war crimes from videos posted to social media. First, he had to learn about how the online platforms worked, the different sources of satellite imagery; how Russian search engines did pretty a decent job of facial recognition; how you could geolocate an image with something as simple as a minaret, an irrigation ditch, the shape of a mountain in the distance, or even a contrail from a jet matched against flight logs. Then there was metadata analysis, looking for signs of fakery, things like shadows not lining up consistently in different parts of the image or the time stamp being out of sync with the hands on someone's watch. It was a crash course on how to acquire god-like powers from behind a desk. There was no end of tools and techniques.

His supervisor, Evan, was a good teacher. Peter hadn't trusted him at first. The British public-school accent clashed with his jeans and Asics in a way that made him seem an imposter. Not that a sweater with college colors and a bow tie would've been much better. Evan had gained Peter's trust by letting him explore on his own, flounder for a while, suffer psychologically from repeated viewing, then with a few clicks of the mouse reveal a solution, or the way toward one.

For the sake of his sanity, with his mind over-filled with the imagery of violence, Peter needed to switch to something else. He caught up on events in Mali, starting with the documents that made the gears of an investigation grind forward. The language of the reports was peppered with acronyms that forced him to flip back and forth between the main text and the list of abbreviations: AIG for Armed Islamic Group, GSPC for Groupe Salafiste pour la Prédication et le Combat, and RCP, for Regiment of Paratrooper Commandos. No real need to read beyond the list to get a sense of the mess he was trying to unravel. He skimmed through a document dated January 2013, released just a few months previously, until he found a passage that he marked with a line and asterisk in the margin:

> The Prosecutor alleges that there is a reasonable basis to believe that the following crimes have been committed in Mali: *war crimes,* including murder; mutilation, cruel treatment and torture; intentionally directing attacks against protected objects; the passing of sentences and the carrying out of executions without previous judgement pronounced by a regularly constituted court; pillaging; and rape.

It was the bloodless language of a court-ordered investigation at the behest of a country soaked in blood. Measurable in quarts.

He recognized in these few lines the reason he'd been hired: not so much for his skills in digital investigation, but his field experience. Or the combination. The way it might be put to use in an investigation was still unknown—at least to him. The Court was built on layers of secrecy, regimes of access. Access to the building via the handprint readers next to revolving doors would get you only so far. He wasn't in the room where his assignment—his fate—had been decided. That information was being carried in other, more eminent, heads.

He wondered when it would wend its way down to him.

* * *

Peter had a temporary, tiny apartment he'd booked online through Airbnb, at least until he could find something better. The bedroom doubled as a living room. Next to the fold-out bed, a nightstand served equally well as a coffee table. A miniature television screen was mounted on the wall above a dresser. Next to the main room was a kitchenette with a two-burner stovetop and an oven barely big enough for a casserole dish. The bathroom was a miracle of design, with the toilet, sink, and shower somehow assembled into the space of a closet. For all the intelligence of the design, his long-limbed body just didn't fit in the space. The bruises on his shins accumulated, the early ones faded to yellow, the fresh ones in blue.

He had enough clothes for a week. The rest of his things were on their way, presumably to arrive in two weeks, or what a woman from the "house removals" company in Cambridge referred to as "a fortnight." This introduced the problem of laundry. It would have to wait. In a pinch, there was always the option of hand washing in the bathroom sink, even if it meant doing one or two pairs of underwear at a time.

These minor problems were made more present in his mind by Nora's imminent arrival. True, she was Dutch, a people of small, tidy apartments, one stacked on the other, but she was accustomed to better. Her father was a retired insurance executive who dedicated much of his time to golf and the creation of new gin-and-tonic recipes. As far as stereotypes went, Nora wasn't categorizable by national type, even with her north-European strawberry blond hair. She'd spent a good part of her teenage years in a winter home in Spain, on the Mediterranean near the Costa Dorada. No matter what the possible sources Nora's self, it didn't include acceptance of tiny apartments as a necessary condition of life.

As a partial solution, Peter bought flowers and put them on the dresser, blocking the TV screen.

Nora arrived via RyanAir, Gatwick to Schiphol, and insisted on taking the train from Amsterdam to The Hague. Peter spotted her white cane first as she came up the escalator from the platforms. She'd be able to see—with some difficulty—in the interior of the station, away from bright outdoor light. It was impressive, the way people in a hurry parted around her. She held the cane close, hanging it down from the handle like a Knight Templar with a sword, her backpack slung over one shoulder; no other luggage. She smiled brightly when Peter called her name, then navigated toward the direction of his voice, scanned her ticket, and passed through the gate closest to him. They hugged, kissed quickly, lips touching, and turned their attentions to the queue for a taxi. She held his hand in the back seat, interlaced delicately in his. There was a trace of sweat in her palm that he caressed with his finger.

The taxi had to navigate construction closures and one-way streets. The amount of time it took to arrive at the Airbnb explained the Dutch preference for bicycles. Before Peter opened the door to the apartment, he offered his prepared excuses: “It’s really tiny. Hardly enough room for me. I hope you don’t mind.”

“But *schatje*,” Nora said, “I’m not here for the apartment. I’m here to be with you.” He opened the door, and her face fell. “You’re right,” she added. “It feels small.”

“It’s just for a few days,” Peter said. “I tried to brighten it up.” He put Nora’s bag in a corner, out of the way.

Nora approached the shelf with the vase. “You got flowers.” She put her nose to the bouquet. “Chrysanthemums. And lilies. Lovely.”

“There’s wine, already opened to breathe. And I pre-ordered Indonesian. It should get here in a half hour.”

“You thought of everything.”

But in truth, Peter hadn’t thought of everything. Or if he had, he then banished some of his darker imaginings. He didn’t know how to tell Nora about what his job entailed, where it was taking him. He hadn’t thought of a way to say how different he felt after just a few days at his new job, as though returned from a tour of the underworld and make believing everything in this world was the same.

* * *

The next morning, Peter woke before dawn, stared at the ceiling, and listened to Nora’s breathing. Once he was sure he wouldn’t get back to sleep, he eased out of bed, moving carefully, still feeling the injuries to his shins. He prepared the moka pot quietly and took it off the heat just before it sputtered. Back in bed with his coffee, he opened his laptop and dimmed the brightness, but Nora stirred as soon as he began to type.

“*Schatje*, what are you doing? It feels early.”

Peter closed his laptop and leaned it against the nightstand. “Sorry. I’ve been awake for a while. Thought I’d do a bit of work.”

“But it’s Saturday,” Nora protested. “You’re awake because you’re working too much. How is turning on your computer going to help with your sleep?”

"You're right." Peter settled deeper under the covers.

Nora ran her hands over Peter's face, with fingertips accustomed to reading the textures of the world, and discovered a small pimple. "Hmm. What's this?"

Peter felt the side of his temple where her touch had just been. "I think it's a pimple. A small one."

Nora went into the bathroom, and returned with a square of toilet paper, then quickly dispatched the offending whitehead between her fingernails, squeezing the pus until it bled. She felt his skin for others, and discovered one on the side of his nostril. She took her work seriously.

"Okay," Nora said once her hand had done a thorough, caressing search. "All better."

"What's the matter with a few little pimples?"

"I don't like them. They feel like they don't belong."

"Thank goodness I'm not a teenager anymore."

In partial apology, Nora planted a kiss on his temple.

"My turn," Peter said. He left the bed and returned from the bathroom with a pair of tweezers. "Sit still."

"What're you doing?" Nora looked apprehensive.

"The hair above your lip."

"What hair?"

"Just one, a dark one. You probably can't see it. Sit still."

She turned her face as he isolated the hair, placed it carefully in the tweezers, and pulled.

"Ow! *Dat doet pijn*!"

"This'll make it better." Peter kissed her on the mouth, giving more attention than usual to her upper lip.

"Hmm. Okay."

Peter pulled another hair, a smaller one, and this time she said nothing, just turned her mouth for the reward. They kissed and depilated and soon the tweezers were forgotten. He could feel her turn inward, responding to him with sureness, as though her body were able to take in and understand everything about him.

Later, Nora felt her lip and said, "Do you think I'm beautiful now? With the hairs gone?"

"Yes. You were beautiful before, too."

"Wait." She went into the bathroom, following an inspiration. Peter heard the shower running.

She came out shrouded in steam and wrapped in a towel with her hands together above her head.

"Look." She had shaved her armpits.

"Very nice," Peter said. She came closer and he kissed the tender skin and tasted the blood coming from a group of small bleeding nicks. "You hurt yourself."

"Mmm. It doesn't hurt and you're still making it feel better." Nora turned her face toward him and they kissed. Then she nestled into his shoulder.

Peter stared toward the bouquet in front of the television, then up at the stucco ceiling. He focused on a stain that might've been an insect of some sort and waited to see whether it moved. It stayed in place, a lifeless blot.

After meditating for a moment, he said, "Was this the right move?"

"What do you mean? This apartment? This city?"

"This job," Peter clarified. "For us, I mean. The being apart. The travel to see each other."

"Oh, that. But your fellowship at Cambridge was almost over anyway. There was a good chance you'd have found something in America. This way, you won't be too far."

"I suppose," Peter admitted.

"And it's really great for you. A super move."

"You think so?"

"Really. It's what you were born to do."

"What do you mean?" Peter was at once curious and gratified. He couldn't think of another time someone had cared enough about him to express insight into his character.

"I mean, you can't stand bullies," Nora explained. "And this is a job where you get to go after them."

Peter thought about that. "If they don't get to me first," he said.

***

They spent the weekend together exploring The Hague, just as Peter had anticipated. Nora was happy to join him in a walking tour of the city. They circled the outskirts of the Nooreinde Palace and looked up at the equestrian statue of William of Orange. Then they walked as far as the Peace Palace, the landmark headquarters of the International Court of Justice, where states litigated, ideally before assembling their armies. Nora was unimpressed by the famous edifice with its ornate clock tower and spires, and was drawn instead to the wishing tree at the main entrance, with its thousands of slips of paper inscribed with visitors' prayers for peace, blossoms that never gave way to fruit.

"Look how many." Nora ran her hands over them, from one sheaf to the other, felt them flutter between her fingers. "I wonder how many have been answered."

Peter understood that the answer to Nora's question was *likely none*, but kept the thought to himself. "It goes to show how much hope there is in the world," he said.

It was the right thing to say. Nora put her head against his shoulder and drew herself closer.

***

The weekend passed quickly. Back from the rail station after Nora left for Cambridge, Peter found himself alone in his temporary one-bedroom. He went to splash his face and found his razor clogged with her hairs. Immediately after he dropped it in the garbage, he had an instant of regret, as though discarding something essential, of her. During the time they'd been together that weekend, she'd taken him out of himself. Now, with her flight back to London just off the ground, he was already going back in. Back to his drive and obsession. Back to the screens. Back to the demon-haunted images.

The flowers on the dresser were starting to turn.

He stared at the screen of his iPhone on the nightstand and sighed, went to the kitchenette to make coffee, then came back with his cup and stared at the phone again before he picked it up quickly and pressed the number.

"Hi Dad."

"Oh, halloo, Pieter." His father, Arie, sometimes pronounced his name the Dutch way, with a long "ie." He did it more often as he got older.

"It's been a while since we talked. I have a couple of things to tell you. Some news."

"Oh, good. I have news, too," Arie announced.

"You first."

"My stamp collection won second." Arie sounded proud.

"That's wonderful, Dad. Congratulations."

"It should have won first. I had every Dutch stamp with a ship since 1945."

"I'm sure it was a fine display," Peter said, politely.

"It got beat by Peterson and his bumble bees from all over."

"Well, I'm sure it was a great event. Congrats, again."

"*Ja*."

"So, about my news—"

"Peterson's bees were easier," Arie interjected. "He just had to collect bee stamps from all over the place. I needed to have every one from the Netherlands. None missing. Some were hard to get."

"So, Dad, I've met someone—"

"I mean," Arie continued, "if I just collected ships from anywhere, that would be easy, right?"

"Dad, I've taken a job as a war crimes investigator at the Hague." Peter spoke more forcefully than he intended. There was a pause. "Are you there?"

Arie returned, "I can't keep track of all the different things you do."

"I know, I haven't had a steady career. But now I landed something great. I'll be investigating war crimes."

"War crimes?"

"Yes."

"What war crimes? In a war, people do anything." Arie's voice had become serious.

"There are things you can't do, Dad. I'll be investigating them."

"Well, well. Pieter, the war detective."

"I thought you might like to know."

"Oh, yes. Good to know."

"I've also met someone. You'd like her. Her name is Nora."

"Nora?"

"Nora Waterman. Her family's from Eindhoven."

"A Catholic?" Arie's inflection betrayed a prejudice cultivated over centuries.

"Yes, well, not really. A Christmas and Easter Catholic."

"Well, that's okay, I suppose."

"I thought you'd like to know that, too. This is important for me."

"Yes, yes." There was a pause. "So, what war are you investigating?" Arie asked, interested this time.

"I don't have my assignment yet, but I think it'll be the civil war in Mali."

"Oh, that's nice."

"Nice?"

"It's very nice that you're investigating a war in Mali. Nice that you've met a Catholic girl. Very nice."

"I'm glad you appreciate it," Peter said. He wished it were true.

"Oh, *ja*. I've got to go. It was nice hearing from you."

"Yes. Good talking to you, too. Congrats again with your second place."

"Peterson won first. With his bees. Bye."

"Bye."

Peter looked at his phone, then put it on the nightstand, at the end of his reach.

CHAPTER 2: ESSEN WAF, WAF

Peter was reminded of the existence of his aunt who lived in The Hague from an unlikely source: his uncle Jan on his mother's side, who mentioned her over the phone. Peter, feeling the emptiness of the apartment, had called to let him know about his new job, maybe arrange a visit. Jan offered no congratulations and no invitation to get together. Instead, he said without hesitation, "You have an aunt living there."

"Which aunt?"

"Julia. Your dad's younger sister."

"That's right," Peter said. "I remember hearing about her from my mother."

"They argued about something a long time ago," Jan said. "I have no idea what about."

"How do you know her?"

Jan's answer involved a story that took over the rest of the conversation. As a teenager, Jan had been infatuated with Aunt Julia. *Smoorverliefd*, he put it, smothered with love. She always made her entrance to Sunday services with precise timing. Never too early so as to lack an audience. Never so late that she caused offense. She always wore impeccable clothes—the latest fashion, probably copied expertly on her sewing machine because there was no way anyone could afford *that*. The money she saved went toward her shoes, which were black with heels that pushed the bounds of decorum. Every week, Jan waited for her to walk the aisle to her usual place. Back straight and somehow graceful, she was a challenge to the church women who, with their stiff, buttoned-up clothes and equally rigid ideas, had forgotten the movement of their bodies. Something about the way she carried herself made her a counter-reformer, a dissident.

This, at least, was what Peter pieced together from the conversation.

Jan put things more directly. "How do you say it in English?" he asked at one point. "She was hot." He laughed so hard Peter had to hold the phone away from his ear.

Jan had followed her life ever since. He'd gleaned a piece of information here, a fragment of gossip there. "Her husband died years ago," he said. "We got on well. His name was Askar or Amsel or something like that. A heavy smoker. Cigars, so what do you expect?"

"I'm sure it was still a terrible loss."

"Yes, but the really terrible loss was the girls. She lost them more recently. A tragedy, really. Trage*dies*, more than one. One died in a car crash. The other lung cancer. Fast, out of nowhere. Went to the brain. Nobody should die like that."

"That's too bad."

"She lives in The Hague where your job is," Jan said. "Might be lonely. You should look her up. Hang on, I've got the number somewhere."

Peter took down the number and spent all that evening mulling over the fact that his father had a sister he'd never talked about. Cancelled out of existence by a conspiracy of silence. His mother must've been in on it, too, with only a snippet here and there. It wasn't exactly a lie. Nobody had told an explicit falsehood. But it felt that way. No, it was worse, more like a betrayal. It felt to Peter like an affront to his sense of who he was and where he came from. They had created and cultivated an information void. The lack of prior knowledge of his Aunt Julia put everything out of kilter in Peter's origin story. His parents had taken advantage of their conditions of immigration to reinvent themselves—and their two children, unbeknownst to them. Peter would have to tell his sister Emma. They could no longer trust what they'd been told about themselves.

Peter called his long-lost Aunt Julia the next morning after an internal debate about the best time. How late do people that age sleep? His father was usually up at the crack of dawn. Maybe she was different.

He decided on nine-thirty and watched the time pass on his phone until nine-twenty-eight and couldn't wait any longer.

The answer came on the third ring. "*Hallo met* Julia."

"Hello. Is this Julia Dekker?"

"No, this is Julia Olsen. Who, may I ask, is speaking?"

For a moment, Peter was thrown off by the name Olsen. His Uncle Jan must've been mistaken and given him a wrong number. Peter's confusion deepened with her switch to English. Perfectly accented. Polite. Could it really be a blood relative of his?

He meant to excuse himself and end the call, but instead heard himself say, "This is Peter Dekker."

There was a long silence. Peter checked his phone to see that the connection was still there. The call-timer on his phone was still turning over the seconds.

"Oh, Peter!" Aunt Julia finally exclaimed.

Recognition. The way she said his name was as though she'd known him his whole life. The beginning of a new story of himself suddenly fell into place.

There was nothing out of the ordinary about the conversation that followed. Of course, it would be lovely to meet. How about tea on Sunday? Aunt Julia sounded genuinely happy to hear from him. There was a lilt in her voice that came from something other than the flow of words.

***

Sunday came and Peter was eager to meet his aunt. He carried the image of the young churchwoman with him when he pressed the intercom to Aunt Julia's apartment. She buzzed him in without saying a word. The lobby was tiled with Italian marble. Mailboxes in a neat row with embossed nametags. Permanent, solid. He opened the metal gate to the ancient elevator, art deco era, and closed it behind him. The buttons were recessed from years of use. Except for a faint background smell of old iron and disinfectant, everything was impeccable and odorless. He pressed the button for the seventh floor. The elevator lurched before the ascent.

Aunt Julia was in her eighties, sparrow-like. She greeted him with a smile that revealed a distinctly receding eyetooth, a feature missing from Jan's description of her. Funny how things like that get left out. But there was also truth in what Jan had said. She was an elegant, older woman, coiffed with a short cut that needed regular maintenance, impeccably dressed for comfort with an off-white cashmere sweater and tailored slacks. A pair of turquoise studs in her ears matched her blue eyes.

"Peter! *Welkom*!" He bent down to her level and they kissed once on each cheek.

The apartment was decorated around the themes of family and country. A wall of framed photos in the dining room was arranged top to bottom in what looked like temporal order—old black-and-white family portraits at the top, men stern, women stiff, children dressed with symbols of their station in life, boys with wool shorts and high socks, girls with oversized bows in their hair. Farther down the wall were more recent color photos, a mix of studio portraits and mementos of family vacations, including one of Peter as a teenager petting a baby moose. His mother must've sent it at some point. He'd forgotten it completely.

Peter peered into the adjacent living room. It was prolifically decorated with porcelain, *Delfts blauw*, spilling over from a glass-doored buffet onto a shelf with no other apparent purpose than to display vases, and from there to plates hung on the walls. They depicted historic buildings, landscapes with windmills, farmers with cows, fields of tulips, barges—self-stereotyping as a unifying theme. Even the floor-to-ceiling bookshelf was decorated with ceramic figurines, of dogs and cats and a boy and girl wearing traditional clothing, placed on separate shelves, their union incomplete. Looking through the wide entryway, he could see hardcover history books about this city or that, the sort of volume carried in better second-hand shops. They were familiar from his parent's bookshelf. They'd be full of glossy black-and-white photos. The text would explain details like when and in what circumstances this bakery opened or the historic moment that a mayor, decorated with his ribbons of office, welcomed a dignitary. The books looked well used, with frayed and faded covers.

"Some of these are in Swedish," Peter noted.

"Danish," Aunt Julia corrected. "Aksel was Danish. Those are his."

Peter felt himself blush, not because of being unable to tell the difference between Swedish and Danish, but because he knew his family so incompletely.

They were interrupted by a shout from somewhere in the living room.

"Waf, waf!"

Peter took a few steps toward the room to get a better look. All the chairs in the living room were empty. The sound seemed spectral, coming from nowhere. Peter looked to Aunt Julia for a response, but she seemed not to notice and continued looking toward the bookshelf.

"Waf, waf!"

"You have someone else visiting?"

"Oh, pardon me. That's Toen. He probably wants you to say hello."

Peter stepped farther into the living room. Just around the corner was a large cage with part of a dead tree fixed to the base. Perched on the end of one limb was a parrot, grey with red tail feathers. It looked at Peter sideways with one eye, a black dot of a pupil in a cream-colored iris.

"Waf, waf!"

"What an amazing, beautiful bird."

"An African grey. Would you like to give him a peanut?" Aunt Julia didn't wait for an answer. She disappeared into the kitchen and returned with a single peanut in its shell. "Just one. We don't want to spoil him."

Toen bobbed his head in anticipation. Peter offered the peanut through the bars of the cage. Toen took it gingerly in its beak, passed it to one foot, deftly opened it, and removed one peanut, allowing the other half to fall to the bottom. As it ate the peanut, it made sounds of appreciation that to Peter sounded like, "uh, huh."

"I've had him close to twenty years, since not long before Aksel died. Raised him from a chick. He's still young. They sometimes live longer than their owners." She opened the cage and Toen walked up her arm, one foot following the other, to perch on her shoulder. It rubbed affectionately against her ear.

"Why does he like to say 'waf, waf'? Did you train him to bark like a dog?"

Julia smiled faintly. "That's a story in itself." She returned Toen to his cage and covered him with a blanket, made to size.

"*Welterusten, Toentje*. Night, Night."

She turned to Peter. "Now while Toen has a nap, we can have a nice cup of tea."

Aunt Julia led Peter into the kitchen and pulled a chair from the table, angling it toward him as an invitation to sit. Peter sat and watched while she made tea, moving nimbly in the kitchen. She served it with teacups and saucers and a collection of small silver spoons. The spoons' stems depicted churches and windmills. Peter looked for something different and found one with a profile of a young Queen Wilhelmina. He stirred the tea and felt her embossed profile on his thumb.

Aunt Julia saw Peter looking at the photo gallery on the kitchen wall and stood to point out a pretty girl wearing an oversized hair ribbon. "This is me," she said. "And this is Corine, the one who died young." She paused. "Here's your Uncle Joop, who passed away just about twenty years ago, around the same time as Aksel." Her finger hovered indecisively. "And this is your father."

Peter wouldn't have recognized him without Aunt Julia's help. His black hair was there, combed neatly to the side with a slight sheen of pomade. His chin receded slightly, a feature he'd covered with a goatee ever since he was able to grow one. Here, the beardless chin wasn't so much weak as featureless. There was nothing in the image to suggest one quality of character or another. Just a young man with dark eyes looking straight at the camera.

Aunt Julia interrupted Peter's thoughts. "So, you have a new job. You're doing research."

"Yes, I do research. On war crimes. At the ICC, the International Criminal Court."

"That's very excellent. Very good for you."

Peter took a moment to interpret "very good for you" as an offer of congratulations.

"Thank you."

"I lived through a war."

"Yes, a very terrible war. I learned about the German occupation mostly from my mother."

"And your father not." She said it as a statement.

"My father just had nightmares about it. Never stories."

"I see." She took a sip from her tea. "I have stories."

"I'm sure you do."

"My mind is not as clear as it once was . . ."

"You seem—"

"And my English."

"But your English is perfect!"

She smiled, accepting the compliment. "I learned with Aksel. And *from* him. He was better with languages than me. When we met, English was the only language we both spoke. Each of us with a little from school. Not much practice."

"How did you meet?"

"Ooh, not romantic at all. In a café. He was in Zwolle on holiday. We were the only ones sitting by ourselves. He was one table over facing my direction. He looked at me and said, 'it must've been hard growing up here.' It was unexpected. And true. I liked that. We started to talk and he sat at my table. After a week, he decided to quit his job."

"That was fast. And *very* romantic."

She looked at Peter over the rim of her cup, took a sip, and put down the cup measuredly. "The war had this effect on us. Even when it was over. You had to live while you could."

Aunt Julia then talked about Aksel. About the time they had first met. The family scandal. How she argued with her Uncle Hero, her mother's older brother, who objected to the marriage. Aksel was an older man. Not even a *Nederlander*. She told her uncle, an elder in the church, to show her where in the Bible it says you can't marry a Dane. As she spoke, Aunt Julia spent longer moments staring ahead, her blue eyes looking somewhere past Peter's shoulder.

He felt uncomfortable, wanting to fill the silence. "I'd like to hear the story."

"What story?"

"The one about your parrot, Toen. Why he says 'waf waf.'"

"Oh, *that*. I had completely forgotten."

"I'm curious."

"Well, all right." Aunt Julia stared into her empty teacup. "We used to tell a joke," she began. "Well, not a joke, really. In those days you could get killed or sent to the Oranjehotel or Westerbork, the prison camp, if you weren't careful. The joke was about the Waffen SS, the elite military division of the Nazi party. They were the ones everybody was afraid of, real nasty, committed Nazis. And they recruited from the young men here, *Nederlanders*. Let them join as volunteers. So, very simply, instead of Waffen SS, we used to call them *essen, waf waf*. In German, *essen* means to eat and *waf waf* is the sound a dog makes. Our history teacher taught us that. A wonderful man. I forget his name. I used to know it." She stared ahead, her blue eyes wide open, moving, thinking.

"And that's the thing you taught your parrot?"

She turned back to Peter. "Well, I was starting to, but Toen only learned the *waf waf* part. Essen is a little harder for a parrot, I suppose."

"That's very impressive all the same."

Aunt Julia seemed not to hear the compliment. She poured herself more tea, then held her cup suspended just above the saucer, deep in thought. "Ach. What was his name? I thought of him as old, but he couldn't've been much more than thirty. He would start every class with a joke about the Nazis, which kept us all in good spirits. Or he did, until somebody denounced him. Nobody knows who."

"That must've made it hard to have friends. People you could trust."

"Yes. And it was even harder after they picked me as a witness to testify against him. Some saw me as a traitor. But I really had no clue what any of it meant. They must've picked me because of my rickets." She paused, without apparently realizing that invoking the disease from malnutrition raised more questions than it answered.

"Why because of rickets?"

"Well, I suppose because it kept me from growing and made me look young for my age."

"I see."

"They put me in the witness box. I was so scared of the prosecutor with his little round glasses. When he leaned toward me, I couldn't remember anything and they had to let my teacher go."

"That seems odd. Did the Nazis actually give him a fair trial?"

"Oh, no! Never! They didn't give up that easily." Then she fell silent, looking into her tea. Her eyes suddenly lit up. "Meijer! Now I remember!"

"There, you see? Clear as a bell."

"He came back to the classroom for a while, but he wasn't the same. He would come and go straight to the lesson. No stories. No laughter. He seemed just, well, *sad*. And probably for a reason. The German prosecutors interviewed every child in the class and picked the three best witnesses. They prepared them with what to say. No surprise then that the second trial went better for them. The day after it was over, we had a new teacher. She had swollen ankles and was grumpy. I can't remember anything else about her."

"That's awful."

She sighed deeply. "The Nazis executed so many hundreds. They went in stages. First to the Oranjehotel, our name for the Prison the Nazis took over, the *Polizeigefängnis*. Then a trial before a judge. The same sort of trial my teacher had. Rigged. For show. What do you call them? Show trials. From there, some went to Westerbork. Some to factories. Others on the train to camps in Germany. The ones who went to the camps usually never came back."

"What do you think happened to your teacher?"

"Well, he might've been sent to Germany. Otherwise, if they thought he was in the resistance, he would've been executed here in the dunes, at a place called Waalsdorpervlakte. That was where the Nazis took people they were worried about. The Waffen SS usually did the executions." She took a sip from her tea. Impassive. Matter of fact. "I could show you the memorial there if you're interested."

"I'd like that," Peter said politely. The happy anticipation of visiting an execution site sat awkwardly. He found it hard to dismiss the image of the teacher, Meijer, facing the firing squad. Hands tied together behind a post, throat dry, pulse racing. Waiting for the order to shoot. Peter felt his own pulse quicken. His teacup shook in his hand. He put it down, a little too quickly so it clattered.

Then he asked himself, how will I ever be able to investigate war crimes if Aunt Julia's story gets to me like that?

CHAPTER 3: THE ASSIGNMENT

After his first week of onboarding, Peter was already feeling the emotional weight of the material he was sifting through. Images of torture, killing, burning villages, the worst of human depravity. Now and then, there was something worse. Happy perpetrators staring straight into the cameras. It was the most damning form of evidence—it directly connected individuals to their crimes—but there was still something dark about it, beyond the violence. In some videos it was the sadistic pleasure the perpetrators were taking, as though the suffering they inflicted was an experience of play. In other clips they clearly expressed pride in their acts of atrocity, the muzzles of their rifles held inches away from the base of a prisoner's skull, a look to the camera. Pulling the trigger. See? See what I'm doing? There was defiance in those looks, too. Come get me, you bastards. I dare you to try.

Peter's explorations went in every direction he could think of. Far beyond the ICC's video archive, beyond even the clips he found on social media depicting the destruction of Timbuktu's heritage sites. He looked for background information, things that weren't necessarily useful, but informed him about the conflict. One image posted to Getty Images by a photojournalist told him a great deal. It showed a cache of weapons the French forces had recovered from a cave in the central Sahara, laid out on a tarp like a picnic. Everything neatly arranged, with weapons systems matched with ammunition. Peter called Evan over to look.

"Whaddya think?"

"Whoa." Evan studied the screen intently. "Here you've got what looks like a Russian AT-14 Spriggan anti-tank missile system. This is a rocket-propelled grenade launcher made by the Korean company Daewoo. Here you've got some good old-fashioned Soviet-era anti-personnel fragmentation mines from the 60s. Plus an international collection of assault rifles from Italy, China, Germany." He paused briefly. "Oh, and, look. This is important. Here you've got your basic homemade IED roadside bomb. High tech and low."

Peter was more impressed by Evan's knowledge than the weapons themselves. "And the benefactors who got them all this stuff? How'd they get it?"

"Libya," Evan said without hesitation. "Well, not Libya exactly. The fall of Gaddafi. The chaos. The security failure."

Peter looked again at the cache on the screen. "And now it all finds its way into the desert. To the benefit of Al-Qaida and Ansar Eddine."

Evan nodded. "Yup. So now more military expenditure to keep the lid down. Malians, French, Americans. All feeding the beast."

"The arms manufacturers."

"Them."

Peter tapped on another monitor on his desk, then regretted the fingerprint smudge. "I'm also going to YouTube and a few other platforms to see if there's anything we missed, related to the ones in the archive."

"Good. Super." Evan sounded upbeat. "Don't forget to record every keystroke when you do that. Screenshots of every page. Chain of custody. Judges will need to know exactly where, when, who, what, why. Everything about how we got the clip."

"Of course," Peter reassured him. He wanted to put his experience on display. "I also don't want to lose anything, so I'm downloading anything else that might be remotely interesting."

"Good. Great." Evan looked at the computer screen and back to Peter.

Peter lowered his head and took a deep breath. "There are a few other videos in the archive that are harder to watch."

"Ah, right, those." Evan's face darkened. "Let's talk about those another time. Stick mainly with the UNESCO sites. That's another case."

* * *

The next day, Peter had been the first to arrive and hadn't left his desk for hours. He needed a break, not just to look through the bombproof glass, but to move his legs.

Olga was back from a few days of working at home and caring for her four-year-old daughter. She glanced up from her screen for the briefest instant as Peter walked by. The movement dislodged a strand of blond hair, which she tucked back behind her ear. They'd been introduced with first names. Her badge said Olga Podporska. Polish. That would account for her dogged persistence in investigating Russian bombings of schools and hospitals in Syria.

Peter continued to saunter down the aisle toward Rashbinder's desk. He'd been away on assignment in London. "Morning, Rash," Peter said.

Rashbinder accepted his nickname with good humor. His angular face and his eyes flitting over the screen gave him the look of a secretary bird prowling for snakes. Peter hadn't been able to read his last name, which began with an S and took up half a line on his ID card.

"Morning, Peter," Rash said. "Except it's not morning."

"What time is it?" Peter looked at his watch, almost panic stricken. It was twelve fifteen. "Oh, shit. What the hell happened?"

Rash laughed sympathetically. "Happens to everyone."

Evan overheard this exchange and suggested the four of them stop whatever they were doing and get some lunch. The surrounding neighborhood was bereft of cafés and restaurants, which limited their choice. A taxi to downtown was still possible, but took too much time. They agreed grudgingly on the café downstairs. Anyhow, they were drawn more by having a conversation away from their desks than the allure of the cuisine, which tended toward the simple and unseasoned. They stood in line together with their trays, each assessing the food on display while the server waited for their selection. Haddock or pork chops. Steamed beans or sauerkraut. The server lightly tapped the handle of a slotted spoon in the palm of one hand. They each chose the haddock and beans, paid separately, then fanned out in search of a table. Evan found one near the windows.

"This is nice," Olga said, settling into her chair.

"Interesting that none of us eats pork," Rash observed.

"I was vegan for three years. Just started eating fish again recently," Olga said. "Since coming here."

Evan poked at his breaded haddock with his fork and chose instead to stab a green bean. "I hear that during the Special Tribunal for Sierra Leone, Charles Taylor complained that the food at the detention centre was inedible. Was ready to starve himself in protest."

"Didn't he know that prisoners in detention are allowed to order groceries and cook whatever they want?" Peter was eager to contribute something he'd learned.

"Must be that last part stopped him," Olga said. "He probably couldn't imagine cooking for himself."

"Maybe he just missed having human on the menu," Rash said.

"Ugh. That's disgusting." Olga screwed up her face in distaste.

"Yeah, but kinda true," Evan said. "Wasn't one of the claims against him that he ordered his men to eat the dead soldiers of the rebels?"

"Right," Rash added. "A basic tactic. Strike fear in the enemy. Interrupt the care of the departed soul. Just with a cannibalistic twist."

"Well, it's twisted all right," Olga said.

"It doesn't mean that he ate human flesh himself," Evan said. "It was to test the fidelity of his men. Make *them* afraid, too."

"Ah, yes, the war crime of vicarious anthropophagy," Peter remarked. They were silent for a moment.

Rash took a bite of haddock and said, with his mouth full, "Funny thing, I watched part of the trial from behind the glass. Taylor was sitting only a few feet away, with his back to the gallery. Without the glass you could've reached out and touched him. Dressed in white robes and one of those white African cap thingies. Smiled nicely, without being too creepy. Which was actually unbelievably creepy. He was super polite to the judges, saying all the right things. Your Honor this, Your Honor that. Very smooth. Made it hard to imagine him doing those horrible things."

"And yet he did," Peter said, "do those things."

"The ones who are well-mannered are the most dangerous," Olga said.

"There you go," Evan said. "A lot of us have this mistaken idea that something has to be visibly wrong with someone to commit a mass crime. But they're usually ordinary. Nothing special."

"I'm not so sure," Rash said. "I bet if you were there when he was giving the orders to eat the corpses, you'd see something very, very wrong."

"Even more when his men obeyed," Olga said.

"I wonder how they ate them, raw or cooked," Rash remarked. He stabbed at his last piece of haddock. "Maybe a bit of seasoning. Rosemary would go well."

"Gawd," Evan said. "Can't we talk about something lighter? What's wrong with us? We look at horror on our screens all day, and all we can talk about at lunch is cannibalism."

They stared down at their plates.

"How about AFC Ajax this year, eh? Scoring some pretty goals, what?" Rash joked.

Peter's phone rang. "Looks like Mr. Ferman wants to see me." He stood to leave.

"Good luck," the other three said, almost in unison.

***

Peter leaned down to look through a window in Mr. Ferman's office, the one that gave the best view of the forest between the ICC building and the dunes. He thought he saw the sail of a kite surfer appear for an instant over the crest of a hill, someone out there on the North Sea catching some lift. Mr. Ferman was seated at his desk looking down at an iPad. There was a monitor in one corner, but his desk was otherwise clear. Not even a notepad or pen.

"Please sit down," he said.

Peter sat and shifted his knees sideways to avoid hitting the front of the desk. He'd done some background research on his boss, against which he compared the man in front of him. Norwegian, with a slight accent, even though his name was German. Dark hair, grey at the temples. It showed on him more than on Peter. Somewhere mid-fifties. Served as an officer in the Norwegian military, which might explain the erect posture, even as he leaned over his desk. Impeccably pressed suit. Nothing fancy, off the rack. Even his eyes, blue-grey with hooded lids, suggested an upper echelon military background. How did that happen? Did officer training somehow select for people with raptorial eyes? Now Investigation Division head at the ICC. The change of career wasn't explained by anything online. Probably a roundabout route through military intelligence.

"Please excuse me," Mr. Ferman said, looking down at his iPad. "I had to miss your interview. It must appear you're having another one with me here." He laughed, without dissipating Peter's sense of being under scrutiny.

"That's quite all right. I understand things get busy. Travel, and so on."

Mr. Ferman looked up, acknowledging Peter's reply, then back to the iPad. "So, you came to us from Cambridge. A fellowship at St. John's."

"Yes, that's right."

"And got your highest degree from McGill. A while ago, I see. An MA in anthropology. Nine months of fieldwork in Mali."

"Yes."

"And in between McGill and Cambridge, quite a lot of experience in the NGO world."

"Mostly human rights organizations. Interviews with witnesses, some work on mass graves when they needed another pair of hands, that kind of thing."

"Yes, of course. Let's talk a little about what you'll be doing for us."

Peter felt relieved to have the focus turn away from him. "I'd like that."

"Do you have thoughts about that already?" Ferman asked.

Peter had a sense the question wasn't meant sincerely. Ferman wasn't really asking for his input. "If I had to guess," he replied, "I'd say I'll be working on something that has to do with my experience in West Africa." He omitted the fact that Evan had already started him on the case archive.

Ferman nodded. "Yes. Not just that, but yes. I expect your experience there will be valuable to our investigation. You also have some computer skills, it seems."

"Well, a little. I'm not a programmer. And in online investigations, Evan is—"

"But you do have some knowledge of intelligence databases and investigation management systems."

"Well, yes. Some . . ."

"The thing that will be quite valuable to us is the combination." Ferman said. "The field experience in northern Mali *and* the skills in online investigation." Peter opened his mouth to say something, but Ferman cut him short. "Or at least familiar enough with it to get by, right?"

"Yes, of course."

"You see, what we're doing here is building a file. More than that. I look at it as a prosecutorial campaign. We want an indictment, and beyond that a conviction. We just got Lubanga on the use of child soldiers in the Congo last year. We've spent nearly a billion dollars in ten years, with just that one shitty conviction to show for it, if you'll excuse my language."

Peter puffed out his cheeks sympathetically.

"We badly need more wins," Mr. Ferman continued. "And to get those, the evidence has to be solid. Actually, more than that. Impeccable. We're bringing powerful actors to account. The standards of proof in this court are very high. We eventually want to go after people with real power. Maybe even heads of state, not just rebels."

"And the best way for me to contribute is?"

"Linkage evidence. Making connections between online and in the field."

"I see."

"A video doesn't mean a dammed thing if we can't show where it comes from. A lot of the evidence we have comes from YouTube and footage shot by a few intrepid journalists. It seems pretty solid if you look at what's in them, but judges aren't your average viewer. They're going to ask questions. The defense will try to poke holes in it. They'll want to know who held the camera, when, why, and so on."

"Of course."

"I'm sure you've already read your job description. Do you mind if I read something from it?"

"Please do."

Mr. Ferman held up his iPad like an actor declaiming his lines during rehearsal. "Candidate must have experience in conducting fact-finding activities, in complex and large-scale cases, involving personal interaction with victims, witnesses and criminal suspects, in a multicultural context, and/or placed in conflict or post-conflict areas." He put the iPad back on his desk. "Does that sound about right?"

Peter nodded. "That does seem to fit."

Ferman continued declaiming, but from his thoughts. "We want our next prosecution to be based on digital visual evidence. It's never really been done and I think it has promise. But we also have to go beyond, with old fashioned interviews. Know what else people witnessed, before and after the events posted online. That sort of thing."

"Which is where my anthropology background comes in," Peter chimed in.

"Exactly," Ferman confirmed. "We have to meet people on the ground, get statements from them. Take our own images of the sites before too much time passes. Complete the file."

"So my assignment will be to get that all important linkage evidence."

"Yes. Well, no, not quite. We have an NGO working on it already. Justice Global, France and their regional branch in Mali. So, we have people on the ground, locals. And we have the people in France offering direction. But we still need someone to go down there who represents the Court."

"Down there, meaning . . .?"

"Mali. Bamako."

These words unleashed in Peter a year of sights and sounds and smells. Minarets and a luxury hotel tower rising above the skyline. The call to prayer over loudspeakers. *Bashees,* modified Peugeot pickups crowded with passengers weaving in and out of street traffic. A man at the street side checking the fuel level of his motorcycle with a lit match, peering into the tank. The sound and smell of kerosene-fuelled *mobilettes* with pedals to help the under-powered motor on hills and through sand. Women walking gracefully with baskets on their heads, the contents a mystery to marketgoers until they slung their loads to street level. Street hawkers selling everything portable. Cigarettes, by the pack or one off. *Pilbe! Pilbe! Pilbe!* Batteries, made in China, affordable even to the poor. Street dogs, ears bitten halfway down by flies, darting through peoples' legs. Lepers gathered outside the bank, snapping the stumps of their fingers above their begging bowls. A preteen boy sleeping with beatific calm on top of a narrow wall, his arm for a pillow.

"Ah. Super." Peter had half expected a field assignment, but not right away. He did his best to conceal his surprise. There was worry in his immediate reaction, too. Not just about the obvious dangers of travel to Mali only a few months after the liberation of the north, but the sudden displacement, the separation, shipped out before he'd had a chance to settle in.

"When?" he asked.

Ferman smiled, showing even, white teeth. "Is next week too soon?

CHAPTER 4: THE DUNES

From the rear side window of the taxi, Peter saw Aunt Julia already standing at the curbside. It was a windy day with a prediction of rain. Aunt Julia wore a tan Burberry trench coat, perfect for the weather. Peter got out, bent down to greet her with a kiss on each cheek, and helped her into the taxi. She allowed his help into the car, but once there, shed any sign of frailty by confidently giving the driver directions to the Oude Waalsdorperweg.

They soon arrived at a turnout. Peter and Aunt Julia had a brief contest over who would pay the driver. Aunt Julia insisted more persuasively. Even before he got out of the cab, Peter heard gunshots, not the ragged volleys a gunfight, but the regular reports of a shooting range. It puzzled Peter why his aged aunt, who otherwise had proclivities toward pacifism, would want to take him to a military facility. He paid the driver, got out, and went to help Aunt Julia exit the cab.

"What's all that noise?" Peter asked on opening the cab door. "It sounds like World War Three."

Aunt Julia clung tightly to his arm as she got to her feet, but once standing, brushed her arm lightly, dismissing his help. "A what-do-you-call-it, a *schietbaan*, for people who like to hunt birds. They come here on the weekends." Peter must've made an odd expression because she added, "That's got nothing to do with us. We're going somewhere else."

They walked along a well-groomed trail that wound its way past a soccer pitch and through a sparsely wooded park. Aunt Julia stopped when they reached a set of five stone markers at a bend in the trail.

"The names of the victims. One for every year of the occupation. A few victims are still unidentified."

They didn't remain there long. Aunt Julia continued along the path, driven by purpose. They arrived at a terraced path leading up a hill. It was blocked by a low-lying rope, on which hung a sign in the universal, wasp-and-snake colors of danger, black with a yellow border and lettering that read, *Verboden Toegang*—access prohibited. Aunt Julia casually stepped over it, reached a hand back to encourage Peter to do the same, and took his arm as they climbed the path to the top of a rise. A wind blowing in from the North Sea bent the pines and tufts of grass and blew sand into their eyes. They turned their backs against the onslaught. A chrysanthemum blew between Peter's feet, got hung up on some grass, then tumbled down the path at the edge of the hill. They paused and prepared themselves to continue their walk. Each placed a hand over their eyes to protect themselves from the glass-like shards of that whipped around them. In a few moments they arrived at low wall, the height of Aunt Julia's knees, engraved with the years 1941-1945. There were wilted flowers at the base. Behind the wall, on a grassy slope, were four iron crosses. They stood silent as they contemplated the memorial. The background sound of shotguns firing made it easier to imagine the scene as an execution site. It was almost too much.

Peter broke the silence with a question: "People here remember the executions with the Christian symbol of the cross?"

Aunt Julia turned her head and raised her eyes to him. "These are execution posts, where they tied the prisoners before they were shot." Just after she said the word "shot," someone in the distance fired at a clay pigeon. Aunt Julia blinked.

"Ah."

"The survivors used to bring wooden ones when they first gathered here. These brass ones came later. There's a ceremony every year on May

Fourth. People come to lay flowers and, in the evening, they ring the Bourdon Bell." Aunt Julia glanced toward the opposite side of the knoll.

Peter hadn't noticed the other part of the memorial partly obscured by wind-blown scrub and low pines.

"It takes five men to make it ring," Aunt Julia said. "You can hear it all the way to the other side of the city."

Peter leaned against the wind as he walked over to the bell. It was connected to a pivot-wheel, almost as visually arresting as the bell itself, like a church bell without a church. The clapper wasn't perfectly round, the shape of it interrupted by a half-round grommet on one side through which a chain had been passed, the other end of which was wrapped around a support beam and locked. The chain and its attachments were elaborate, like shackles on a prisoner.

The wind made it impossible to appreciate the view. They followed a pathway down from the memorial. Aunt Julia gripped Peter's arm and hesitated with each terraced step. Even in her caution, she carried herself with confidence and self-possession.

The path levelled out to a sparse forest of oak and pine trees where they found an empty bench. The wind swayed the crowns of the trees without reaching the bench where they sat. The clouds passed so quickly overhead it seemed as though time itself was accelerated by the North Sea wind. The rain predicted for the afternoon hadn't yet arrived. They were bothered only by the occasional pine needles dislodged by the wind.

Aunt Julia brushed the sand and pine needles out of her hair. "Much better here."

They sat quietly while she stared straight ahead. Peter didn't want to interrupt her thoughts, but the silence was long enough for him to feel restless. He began to pick one of his fingernails and stopped himself.

After a while, Aunt Julia said, "That hilltop we just saw was also a place of vengeance."

"What do you mean?"

"Well, after the war, the top German Nazis went to Nuremberg, but we had our own mess to clean up. Dutch collaborators. Some people will try to tell you the sympathizers came from the southern towns next to

Germany, as though there was some sort of contamination that seeped across the border, but that's nonsense. The truth is, the NSB, the Dutch fascist party, got its start in Utrecht, right in the heart of the country."

"They were executed by firing squad, too?"

"Yes, yes." Aunt Julia seemed content to leave it at that.

Peter wanted to know more. "So, what happened? Who were they?"

"Too many to remember them all."

"But some must've been more important than others."

"Oh yes. Anton Mussert and Max Blokzijl were big news back then."

"They were collaborators?"

"More than that," Aunt Julia said. "Mussert was the head of state under the Nazis. He wanted power of his own, but he was never anything other than a puppet. It must've been torture for him, being so close to power but never truly getting it, the poor dear."

"You mean like a wannabe Mussolini?"

"Exactly. He put the offices of the Dutch fascists right next to the parliament building where he could look across and see the Nazis govern the country. He never got through the door. And that, of course, was his defense after the war. 'I was under the occupation just like everybody else,' he said. The poor, misunderstood patriot."

"But the new Dutch government would have given him a fair trial, right?"

"He had his day in court," Aunt Julia said. "Well, two actually. He saw it as another chance to spew his nonsense. 'I had nothing to do with the Nazis,' blah, blah, blah. 'I wanted no part of the occupation, aside from realizing my dream,' blah, blah. He and his higher up loyalists, something like forty of them, were charged with high treason. They all used this argument one way or another, every one of them. Again and again. It didn't do them any good. They all went to the firing squad up there." She looked in the direction of the path they had just followed down from the memorial.

"You mean the same place where the resistance fighters were executed?"

"The same place," Aunt Julia confirmed. "The same way."

"You mentioned another one, Max something."

"Blokzijl."

"Right, what about him?"

"He was the propaganda minister. Our very own Goebbels. He actually had a fairly original argument on his way to the dune. When he had his chance to speak, he claimed the Dutch were in his debt because he aroused in them the spirit of resistance against the German occupiers. He tried to create another reality. A complete fantasy. I suppose he thought the most ridiculous lie might actually save his skin."

"I gather it didn't."

"Oh no, heavens. He was actually the first to go. I can tell you why. He was the tongue, the voice. He started off as a singer who sang patriotic songs, an entertainer. Everybody loved him. Then he joined the fascist party and became a mouthpiece of Nazi propaganda. I suppose a lot of us felt betrayed."

"You mean his fame as an entertainer before the war was a promise he broke."

"Not just that. Under the occupation he got more and more power. How do you say that? Shot up the ranks. He had control of all the Dutch press, the radio, too. Everything we were allowed to hear or read. People felt his abuse of power every day. More than with Mussert. The fascists shoved it down our throats."

"If I follow what you're saying, that means there was other information circulating that wasn't legal."

"Yes, yes. Of course." Aunt Julia sounded almost offended by Peter's lack of basic knowledge about Dutch war history. "Some people printed leaflets. Usually making fun of the Nazis. And then there was Radio Oranje out of London. That was more serious, with news of the war. It was strictly forbidden for us to listen, but there were always people who did. You could just tune in. The ones who risked their necks by listening would tell others what they heard."

"But Blok . . . whatever." Peter gave up trying to remember his name.

Julia didn't fill in his memory. Instead, she said, "Better to not remember."

"Okay. But with that amount of control, he must've recruited some people to the Nazis."

"He did. Quite a few. He spewed all kinds of hate against the British and Jews. Lots of people believed . . ." She broke off to gather her thoughts. "He was a *real* Nazi," she continued. "An apologist who felt he had nothing to apologize for. As soon as the German occupation fell, he was arrested. A quick trial. Then off to the dunes. No funeral afterwards. No one shed a tear."

"Except some of the ones he converted to Nazism," Peter said. "They must've been sorry to see him executed."

Aunt Julia focused her gaze on Peter. "No. Not even them."

It occurred to Peter that there was purpose in the way Aunt Julia had arranged their tour of the dunes. It began with the simple story of the execution site. A place of Nazi atrocity, the horror. But then she added the story about the forty or so Nazi collaborators who were executed there the same way. Maybe she wanted him to know there was a during and an *after* to the war, with the after sometimes messier. She was his self-appointed guide to truths that had taken her years of struggle and reflection to acquire. He sensed from her eagerness to talk that the tour wasn't over.

As if on cue, Aunt Julia rose to her feet and said, "There's something else I want to show you. Shall we take a nice long walk?"

They crossed a gate next to a cattle grate and continued on a sandy path away from the memorial. After they had walked for a while, Aunt Julia stopped, took a flip phone from her purse and dialled a number, peering closely at the keys. Peter gathered from the conversation that it was the taxi company. "Yes, Pompstationsweg in twenty minutes. Yes, in front of the Scheveningen prison. That's right. Good bye."

"You called to have a cab ready for us in twenty minutes?"

"Yes."

"And before then we're going to see a prison?" Peter was thrown off stride by the distinctly Dutch feature—a result of land shortage—of unusual things in proximity. Of course, there would be a shooting club next to a war memorial, not far from a prison.

"I thought this might interest you," Aunt Julia replied. "It has to do with your work."

"I see." Peter guessed her intent. "The UN Detention Unit attached to the ICC. Where they hold people being tried for war crimes."

"When I was young, we called it the Oranjehotel, the orange hotel. The Nazis took over an old prison and held people there before they decided what to do with them. They called it the *Polizeigefängnis*, the police prison."

"You mean where they held the resistance fighters who were then executed on the dunes?"

"Not only them."

"And then collaborators after the war," Peter guessed.

"Right."

"And that's the same prison that the ICC is using today for war criminals?"

"Exactly," Aunt Julia confirmed. "Well, a part of it. I used to be a member of an organization called the Oranjehotel Foundation. We tried to save it, but they tore most of it down."

"Let me get this straight. The ICC took over a Nazi prison?"

"Well, yes, but of course it changed hands several times before that. And the UN Detention Unit part has been totally renovated. They even built a two-kilometre underground tunnel to the new court building where you work.

"Do you mean to tell me the prisoners at the International Criminal Court are driven to their trials underground?" Through the trees Peter could see the prison they were talking about. An old building came into view, complete with the parapets and ramparts of a castle.

They walked around the outside wall of the building, complete with the barbed wire and security cameras of a prison, until they came to a dark wooden door with an arched lintel. Next to it was a large metal plaque bolted into the brick, with an inscription:

1940 - 1945
Gedenk hun laatste gang
Door deze lage poort
Hun leven
Voor vrijheid en voor recht gegeven
Zet hun strijd voort
Antoine Denzer

Peter translated as he read: "Remember their last course through this low gate. They gave their lives for freedom and justice. Their struggle continues."

"This part of the Oranjehotel we managed to save," Julia said. "We don't have to go in if you don't want to." Without waiting for him to answer, Aunt Julia led Peter farther around the building and through the main door.

A woman with grey hair stacked in a bun greeted them from behind a counter with a cash register. "Ah, *hallo* Mevrouw Olsen."

"Hallo." Aunt Julia was already walking and staring ahead, without introducing Peter. On his way past, Peter and the woman exchanged smiles.

"No charge, as usual," the woman shouted after Aunt Julia.

True to the name of the prison, the steel cell doors and walls were painted orange. They were the only visitors and their footsteps echoed hollowly in the corridor. Aunt Julia led Peter to a cell with an open door.

"This one we managed to save. Doodencel 601, a death cell. It was one of several in a wing called the *D-gang* for those waiting for execution."

"Death row," Peter muttered to himself.

Aunt Julia entered without hesitation, as though she lived there. Peter followed, bending to avoid hitting his head on the doorway. The cell was only as wide as the narrow pine bed that took up the length of the far wall. There were two corner shelves above the bed, one with a tin cup, the other a wash basin. The only other furniture was a plain wooden chair and a small table with a water jug. Inscriptions had been scratched into the plaster walls near the bed with an assortment of names and dates, a guide to morse code, the Lord's Prayer, and days scored in groups of seven lines instead of the usual five. For luck? Marking the weeks? Peter mentally translated the words, scratched in block letters. *My scale of justice is Marieke, I will always be true. Wim*.

"We think over two hundred members of the resistance came through the *D-gang* before they were executed," Aunt Julia said.

"Resistance fighters?"

"Mostly."

Peter turned to read the inscriptions on the other wall and noticed an area of plaster that was smooth. "What was here?"

"Ah. Peter the investigator." Aunt Julia smiled appreciatively. "I thought you might find something that isn't in the brochures."

"What do you mean? Was something plastered over?"

"That's the part of the wall where some collaborators made their marks. It was covered over in 1946, I think. When the special tribunals were finished."

"So the collaborators were held here, too?"

"Yes, during their trials. Some were given prison sentences. Forty were executed."

"And when they were in this cell, they didn't know which it would be. Prison or the firing squad."

"Right. Except some were let go, too."

"Of course."

They turned back to look at the marked wall and stood quietly, reading the names and messages for a second and third time.

Peter eventually thought out loud., "I wonder what the collaborators wrote."

"I don't wonder," Aunt Julia was quick to reply.

"Why not?"

Standing next to her, Peter saw her blue eyes move quickly back and forth, thinking. "We all had choices," she said. "The ones who were in the resistance chose self-sacrifice. The collaborators went the other way. And we don't want to hear from them. We don't even want to know their names."

"But shouldn't we still want to know what they wrote on the walls? To fight evil, you have to know it."

"To fight evil, you have to silence it," she said. She took hold of his elbow with a surprisingly strong grip and led him out of the cell.

They stood in the corridor looking down the row of cell doors. A young couple passed them on their way to cell 601 holding hands. The sound of their laughter echoed through the building. Aunt Julia watched them, frowning.

She turned to Peter. "I have something else to show you."

From her purse, she brought out a bundle of photographs, and flipped through them. "This one." She handed it to Peter. "These are pictures of the wall markings in the other cells on *D-gang* before the demolition."

Peter furrowed his brow in concentration. The photo was small and the markings difficult to read. "What are you showing me?"

"Look here. Look closely." With a manicured fingernail she indicated the bottom corner of the wall.

There, Peter saw the real reason Aunt Julia had brought him to this place. Scratched into the plaster in small block capitals was his family name, DEKKER.

"But that's my name! What's it doing here?"

"That's what I'd like to know."

"Was someone in my family executed in the dunes?"

"I don't think so. Dekker isn't in the list. It could be one of the unknown victims, but I doubt it."

"Was it a collaborator then? Someone arrested after the war?"

"I have a suspicion. It will take me a while to explain."

Aunt Julia's phone rang and she struggled to find it in her purse and open it to answer. The taxi was waiting outside.

CHAPTER 5: DINNER WITH JULIA

Nora reached for the magnifying strip beside the bed and scanned Peter's face the way she would read a book. She moved it slowly, taking her time. Instead of letters magnified by the lens, there was beard stubble. If he didn't shave every day, he'd be one of those guys with beards down to their chests. She could see the hair at the base of his neck where he stopped shaving and his chest hair took over like an army massed at the border. There was some grey at his temples and the rest his hair had flecks, hard to see, even with the magnifier, disguised as they were by the sandy color. He looked young for his age.

He had open nostrils with hair coming out. Hair was sprouting from his ears, too. She should tell him it was time for a trim. He was normally diligent about that sort of thing, going for the scissors and tweezers before things got out of control. Something was distracting him—his new job, maybe. At least his eyebrows were even. With the magnifier she could see the blunt ends of his cut hairs.

A brown eye with green next to the iris appeared in the magnification strip and blinked.

"What're you doing?" Peter asked.

"I'm looking at you. Up close."

"That's nice," Peter said. "What do you see?"

"I see a handsome man with a huge brown eye. Like a cyclops." She shifted the magnifier so that both eyes appeared in it. The image she'd created was cartoonish, with two oversized eyes in an expression of surprise. She put the magnifier back on the bedside table.

"That's better. I prefer you this way." She stroked the stubble on his cheek against the grain.

"What way is that?"

"Hmm. As you really are."

Peter swung his legs over the side of the bed and pulled the blinds open. The morning light filled the room with an intense glare.

"Aah. Too bright!" Nora pulled the covers over her head.

"Sorry! I wasn't thinking."

From under the cover, she could feel the light dim as he lowered the blind. She peered out. Her face was framed as though she wore a nun's habit.

"Better," she said.

He came back to the bed and tucked a strand of her hair behind her ear and kissed her forehead. Then he disappeared through the door. It took a while for his footsteps to reach the kitchen. There was a feeling of space. Such a contrast with the cramped Airbnb rental. She could hear his moka pot boiling, followed by the smell of coffee. He liked it strong. Funny, he didn't ask how *she* liked it. Less strong, but his way would do.

Peter returned carrying a tray and announced, "Coffee with rusks, jam, and cheese, thinly sliced."

"Oh, you're sweet, *schatje*."

"I won't be able to have this for a while."

They sat silently, sipping coffee. Peter spread jam on a rusk. He used too much pressure with the knife so that it fragmented and spread crumbs across the covers.

"Shit," he said. He was grateful the jam stayed on his plate and didn't stain the white duvet.

"I know," she said. She offered sympathy not for the exploded rusk and its crumbs, but whatever lay behind it.

Peter corralled the crumbs with the edge of his hand. "Should I quit?" He let the question sit while he gathered the fragments of rusk with his fingertips and transferred them to his plate. "If I resign now, they can hire someone else."

Nora answered without hesitation, "I think you should go. I'll stay here. How do you say it? With the cowboys and Indians?"

Peter looked at her quizzically. "I haven't the faintest idea what you're talking about."

"Oh, I remember," Nora said, feeling proud. "Holding down the fort."

Peter laughed.

"I shall hold down the fort for my brave, brave Guppy while he goes adventuring." She smiled at him with her eyes over the rim of her cup.

"Guppy? Who are you calling a guppy?" Peter sounded playfully incensed, but there was a slight edge.

"It's my new name for you, Guppy. I just saw you with two big eyes, like one of those little fishies."

"That takes me down a peg or two."

"Well, that's as it should be." Nora caressed the stubble on his cheek.

"You just can't. Guppies was the name of my swim group when I was five and we learned to blow bubbles under the water."

She laughed. "I can just picture you with your little friends. No idea why that would be a problem for you, but look at it this way. Guppy also goes with G. P., the initials of Grote Pier."

"And who, pray tell, is Grote Pier?" he asked.

"You haven't heard about Grote Pier? Your parents never told you where you come from?"

"Nope. My past is a mystery, even to me."

"It means big Pier, like Peter." Nora sat straight in the bed. "Grote Pier was a warrior and pirate who led the Frisians in a rebellion against the Hollanders. He was something like seven feet tall. People say he could lift an adult horse above his head, plough his fields without an ox, pulling the plough himself. That sort of thing."

"Well, then, that sounds okay. Kinda goes a bit far the other way, but fine."

"I thought you said your grandmother was Frisian. Aunt Julia's mother. So, that's you too. Guppy to me means the little baby Guppytje and the mighty rebel winning freedom for his people. Guppy."

"Well, then. That takes care of me. Now I need to think of a nickname for you."

"Nothing mean, please." She raised her lips to him.

"I promise." He kissed her. Then moved his mouth like a fish. She shrieked and pulled the covers over both of them. A plate fell on the floor, but, judging by the clatter, didn't break.

They'd tend to the crumbs later.

***

That afternoon Nora and Peter went shopping to prepare for having Aunt Julia over for dinner. When Peter called to inquire, Aunt Julia reported that she had neither allergies nor preferences, "just anything at all would be lovely." Which actually made things more difficult. What would an older woman from a generation inclined toward conservative food tastes want for dinner? Peter suggested *boerenkool stampot*, kale, potatoes and farmer's sausage done together in a pressure cooker—his favorite as a child. He would pile the slurry of kale and potatoes into a volcano shape and put butter in the crater.

Nora demurred. Too peasanty. Too rustic.

With Nora holding Peter's arm, they made an initial foray through the market. On the way, Peter described what looked fresh and what not. Dessert was the easiest: A small dark-chocolate cake decorated with strawberries and a dusting of icing sugar. Nora followed her nose and found a flower shop. She was drawn to a scented bouquet with an abundance of hyacinth.

They still couldn't decide on a main course. Something about choosing which animal to eat put her off. She expressed it through indecision.

Peter went into the butcher shop while Nora waited at the corner.

***

That evening, when Aunt Julia came through the door, the scents of the flowers and the lamb and mint sauce cooking already filled the apartment. “Ooh, *wat een lekkere geur*!” she said, and breathed deeply. She was wearing a close-fitting robin’s egg blue dress with half sleeves.

Nora stepped forward and they kissed on each cheek. She felt the sleeve of Aunt Julia’s dress. Cashmere? Angora?

“You’re the first in the family to meet Nora,” Peter said. “We wanted to thank you properly for helping us find this apartment. It’s beautiful. Amazing, really. It saved us so much trouble.”

Aunt Julia wandered languidly through the apartment. She put her nose in the flowers and stood for a while before the tall French windows in the living room to take in the view. At the spare bedroom, she lingered in the doorway. “This was Annie’s room. Our firstborn.” She paused. “Now it is just me.”

Peter put his arm around her, crossing the threshold of familiarity. “I didn’t know you used to live here. I thought it was an investment property.”

“Investment, yes. We invested a lot.”

“We’re very grateful,” Nora said.

“Yes,” Peter added. “Without it, who knows where we’d be living. One of the first websites Google came up when I started looking was, The Living Hell of Finding an Apartment in The Hague.”

“I’m so glad I could help.” Aunt Julia eased herself into a wing chair. Nora noticed the surety of her movements. There’s a way a guest sits for the first time in a new place, and that wasn’t it. These were her furnishings, still in the house.

During the meal, Aunt Julia led the conversation. She asked about Peter’s new job, about Nora’s research at Cambridge. Nora offered a description of her research topic—women, the printing press, and sacred writing in the late Middle Ages—in response to which, Aunt Julia said simply, “So clever you must be!”

Aunt Julia asked Peter what it was like in Canada. "Growing up in Canada," was how she put it, as though Peter was just now out of adolescence. Peter matched her questions, politeness for politeness. He talked about how he especially missed the mountains and trees. Everything in the Netherlands was cultivated, every square inch ploughed or planted or paved or given over to some purpose or other for the common good. No offense, but it was starting to drive him crazy. There was something deep in the Dutch soul, this need for domestication and order. "I remember Oma coming to visit when I was something like six or seven years old," he said. "She spent almost her whole time pulling up dandelions from the lawn. It clearly gave her great satisfaction."

Aunt Julia laughed. "That sounds like Ma."

Peter continued with his memory. "I called her Oma hair-to-the-bum because she went through this amazing transformation when she took her hairpins out. Her hair fell down past her waist. She became another person entirely."

Aunt Julia laughed hard and poured herself wine. "Oh, dear heavens. That was Ma. You don't know the half of it."

"What do you mean?" Nora asked.

"She was two different people, hair up and hair down," Aunt Julia explained. "Up she was organized, in control, got things done. Down was her soft side. Bedtime stories, prayers, and goodnight kisses. Until I was a teenager."

"With her hair up, I'm sure it wasn't just about dandelions in the grass," Peter said.

Nora noticed a particular tone to Peter's voice when he got curious, something like an interrogator feigning friendliness. A determined, goal-directed interest.

"Hair up she could do anything," Aunt Julia said. "I mean, anything acceptable for a woman to do. I grew up in The Hague, but then we moved to a farm near Zwolle in the middle of the war, and somehow or other she knew how to do everything there, too, milk the cows, churn the butter, slaughter the hens and geese, pluck and dress them, everything."

"So she lived on a farm as a girl?" Nora asked.

"She must've, for a time. Interesting how there are holes. Either I don't remember or she never really talked about it."

"She raised the four of you by herself for a long time, after your father died." Peter had a tendency to put questions as statements, his way of being surer of himself than he really was.

"My father died when I was six." Aunt Julia sipped her wine thoughtfully. "Bleeding ulcers." She shuddered at an unspoken memory. "Ma inherited his pension from the police. We lived simply, but didn't lack anything that I can remember. Not until the Hunger Winter."

"That happened before the war?" Peter asked. "Your father dying, I mean."

Nora was surprised Peter knew so little about his own family. Didn't they tell stories? Was nothing handed down?

"Just before the war, yes." Aunt Julia paused deep in thought. "I wonder what Pa would've done if he'd lived."

"Do you think he would've been in the resistance?" Peter asked this on his way to the kitchen. He came back with a bottle of merlot, cracked the screw-top lid, and filled Aunt Julia's glass first, before Nora's and his own.

Aunt Julia took a while to formulate an answer. "I have a feeling he might've ended up on that hill we went to the other day," she said. "In front of a firing squad. Done something terribly brave and foolish. Oma was more careful. She was the strategist."

"The persistent uprooter. The slayer of dandelions," Nora added.

Aunt Julia smiled. "That's right. The hair-to-the-bum uprooter."

Peter remained serious. "That means my father would've been around fourteen when your dad died. He would've taken over as the head of the household, at least symbolically, even at that young age."

Aunt Julia's eyes flashed for an instant. "That certainly describes how Ma treated him."

Nora tried to steer the topic elsewhere. "It really is amazing how much things have changed in just a generation or two. We went from a church-led patriarchy to one of the most liberal countries in Europe in just a few short years."

"That's right," Peter chimed in. "From a Nazi occupation to The Hague as the epicenter of global justice."

Aunt Julia ignored their attempts at diversion. "Ma fawned over him. It made everything worse."

"Worse in what way?" Peter surrendered.

After a few weeks with Peter in The Netherlands, Nora already noticed a pattern. Whenever he was with people who knew his father, the topic of conversation almost invariably turned him, Arie this and Arie that. Was that some sort of charisma? Are people instinctively drawn to narcissists who interrupt normal ways of thinking?

Julia's eyes moved back and forth in concentration as she pondered her reply. Just when the silence became uncomfortable, she said, "Worse in the sense that both his ego and his insecurity got inflated at the same time. Let's just say, he was too young to have that attention and that responsibility." Her voice was crisp, with an edge.

Nora wondered what lay behind the words, "let's just say." They acted at once as a contraction and a postponement. A placeholder with an implicit promise of return.

"My, there are so many memories here in this apartment." Aunt Julia said this with a weary sigh.

"Time for dessert." Peter stood businesslike to get cake, cookies, and coffee.

Nora cleared the plates.

From the dining room, Aunt Julia called to them for a *zwak bekertje*, which, Nora noted, presented a problem for Peter, who had no way to brew weak coffee. She watched him plug in the kettle to dilute the coffee he made with the moka pot, the little Italian coffee maker he took everywhere with him. Even with the cup half filled with hot water, it was black as ink. He poured some out, wiped the cup with a dishrag, and added more water.

After the cake ("just a tiny sliver, please, *dankjewel*") and coffee, Aunt Julia's eyes drooped. "I think I had a little too much wine."

"Ooh, you look tired, Aunt Julia. Let me call you a taxi," Peter offered.

"No," Nora interjected. "I'll make up the couch."

The couch, it turned out, was a cleverly designed sofa bed. Peter pulled it out, ignoring Aunt Julia's half-hearted protestations. Nora opened and closed doors in different parts of the apartment until she found the linen closet. Nora and Peter spread the sheets in an efficient collaboration. Peter found a thick duvet in the top shelf of the closet, where only he could reach.

"But I'm still wearing my dress!" Aunt Julia protested.

"True, but I sleep in a T-shirt and underwear," Nora said. "I've nothing to lend you. Here, we can loosen you here." Nora undid the zip, unhooked Aunt Julia's bra strap and did the zip back up. "And do take off those shoes."

The shoes fell to the hardwood floor with a sound that suggested quality. She slipped out of her panty hose without help. "So nice, being tucked in like this." Aunt Julia's voice was muffled, the duvet tucked over her mouth. "Not since I was a girl."

Nora obliged with a kiss on her forehead. "We're so happy to have you here."

Aunt Julia opened her eyes wide as though the kiss stirred her awake, like a child with a last compelling thought before lights out.

"Funny thing about that dandelion story from Peter," she said. "It's really very odd. Ma never told me she went to Canada. I wonder how she kept it from me."

CHAPTER 6: BAMAKO

Peter waited to check in at the Hotel Concorde in Bamako, Mali. Ahead of him was a balding man with strings of hair combed backward, wearing a rumpled suit. Fresh creases. Must've worn it on his flight. From snippets of conversation between the man and the clerk, Peter learned that he was French, from Paris, and in Bamako for business. "Oh yes, I've been here to this wonderful hotel many times before," the man said. During a lull, while the clerk typed, he turned to stare toward the far side of the lobby.

Peter followed his gaze. Two women sat on the edge of a fountain, the centrepiece of the lobby. One was tall, with subtle makeup, long tresses down her back and a sequined purse. The other was shorter, with close-cropped curly hair, heavily made up, a small red clutch purse. They looked back at the Frenchman, coquettishly.

Peter stepped up to the desk as soon as the Frenchman was done. As the clerk tapped at his keyboard, Peter watched the man roll his luggage to the elevators. The two women, as if on cue, stood and followed.

"Just her," the Frenchman said to the short one. Then he took the tall woman by the elbow and disappeared with her into the elevator.

***

The next morning at breakfast, Peter chose a table next to a window that gave a view onto a kidney-shaped pool. The shadows were long, the water was still, and there was no one in the reclining chairs. That would change toward evening, Peter knew, when there'd be sunbathers ordering elaborate cocktails, offending the sensibilities of the waiters with their nudity and lavish spending.

He ordered a simple breakfast of coffee and a brioche.

From where he sat, Peter had a view of the double kitchen doors and a side room, an alcove for private meetings. A voice drew his attention and he recognized the Frenchman—the john from the hotel desk who'd picked up the tressed hooker—at a table in the alcove, wearing the same rumpled jacket from the day before. The Frenchman put out a cigarette in his leftover fried potatoes. He talked animatedly with a woman wearing an indigo blue headscarf and a man with a white turban worn the Tuareg way, but with the cloth under his chin instead of across his mouth. Peter heard the word "Timbuktu" repeated several times.

Peter suspected this to be Yves Vautour, his liaison from Justice Global, but waited before introducing himself.

A tall waiter wearing a bow tie came out through the kitchen doors. He paused at an empty table just outside the door and set down a tray with a cup of tea and two espressos. He sipped from one of the espressos and gave it a look of satisfaction, then carefully wiped the rim of the cup with the corner of a towel and carried the tray to the table in the alcove. Peter mentally made a bet with himself and won. The waiter carefully placed the espresso he'd just tasted in front of the Frenchman, with the other espresso going to the man in the turban, and the tea to the woman.

Peter picked up his coffee and brioche and carried it to their table. "Good morning," he said. "You must be Yves Vautour. I'm Peter Dekker."

"Ah, the famous Peter Dekker. We've been expecting you." Yves turned to the man with the turban. "This is Goma Ag Ahmed."

"Ag Amellal," Goma corrected.

"Yes, okay." Vautour dismissed his error without apology. "And this is Kella Ult Ralli. Did I get that right?"

"Pleased to meet you." Kella lowered her eyes in a reflex of modesty.

"We were just talking about the research," Vautour said.

It wasn't clear to Peter why Vautour avoided the word, investigation. Not wanting to draw attention, probably. Discretion. Ultimately, it might be about their security.

Vautour opened a briefcase and brought out a sheaf of papers. "There are the questionnaires we'll be working from. We'll use these to take the preliminary notes. The official witness statement that we put together later will have a number. No names. No identities."

"Seems reasonable enough." Peter looked over the forms.

"Yes, well, it follows the reason of desperate men who lost a war and will do anything to keep their freedom. The insurgents set up their own police force that had complete power over the people in the town. That's gone now, but they want it back."

"They want to keep their wives," Kella added. "The girls they forced from their families."

Goma nodded. "The witnesses have as much courage as the men fighting in the field."

Vautour leafed through the witness statements and tapped one of them. "This one here, for example. Walking with her husband and seven-year-old daughter. Two Islamic policemen stop them, even though the woman is fully covered as per the new dress code, with gloves covering her hands and socks on her feet. Husband is not recognized as a member of any occupation group and is suspected of having fought for the Malian army. The policemen put handcuffs on him and are leading him away, presumably to be shot. The seven-year-old girl bites the leg of one of the policemen. He strikes her with the butt of his Kalashnikov and opens a gash in her head. The mother screams at the policemen, so she's arrested and taken to the women's prison, together with the daughter. The prison was formerly the Banque Malienne de Solidarité. She is held in the ATM room for two days where she is raped, in front of the daughter, before being given eighty lashes and released. The husband was never seen again. This is testimony from the woman in question."

They all fell silent as they stared at the witness report. Vautour drummed his fingers on the report, an act of banality to dissipate its power.

"I assume this is not an isolated incident," Peter said. "That there are others."

"Oh, yes, plenty. Probably hundreds."

"But my assignment concerns the shrines," Peter wanted to confirm. "The destruction of UNESCO property."

Vautour opened his palms in a gesture of resignation. "*Alors,* we have to start somewhere."

Kella raised her eyes toward Peter. "Just don't forget, the people are cultural heritage, too."

Goma nodded.

"I mean, sure the cultural treasures are important," Kella continued. "But the books didn't suffer in their burning."

Vautour closed the file folder. "*Bien sûr, bien sûr*. But, as Peter can explain, the case for the destruction of property is the most straightforward. Isn't that right, Peter?"

"Well, we do have quite a lot of visual evidence. We just need to authenticate it, tighten things up with context."

Kella slouched in her chair with her arms crossed. "Of course. Even videos can't be trusted. How can we possibly believe the women who say they were raped in prison?"

Vautour gathered his files and put them back in his briefcase. "The desecration of property case does not mean we don't collect other kinds of testimony. We move forward. We'll put together the sexual violence cases eventually."

There was a long silence in which Kella unfolded her arms and stirred milk into her tea.

"So, I have a question and forgive me if it seems naïve," Peter said.

"Go on." Vautour prompted.

"Why didn't everyone just leave? Get away before the jihadists took over the town?"

Goma shifted in his chair. "Let me explain this to you. Quite a few did leave. Some went to stay with relatives. The refugee camps in Burkina Faso and Mauritania are still full. Some had elders in their families who couldn't travel, so they stayed with them. But not everyone could get away on time. It happened fast. The poor are always left behind."

"I see." Peter was suddenly acutely aware of the insignificance of his impact on the world. He'd felt something like this once before, when he worked for an aid organization at a refugee camp, with row upon row of conical huts filled with people displaced by drought. He had a sense then—and again now—of futility, the loneliness of standing against a too-powerful force of destruction.

Vautour turned to Peter. "We were thinking it would be a good idea for you to go to Timbuktu, the three of you. Meet the team, talk to people there, get a sense of what it was like under the occupation. Get the images you need of the destroyed shrines, or whatever. Jump in with both feet."

"That's an interesting idea," Peter said. "And the security situation? Are you sure it's safe?"

"Oh, as a white person, you'll have a million-dollar bounty on your head." Vautour laughed showing his molars and stopped short when he saw Peter's serious expression. "No, I'm sure it'll be fine. From what I've heard, the French military and the UN Peacekeepers have everything secured, regular checkpoints on all the roads. And, anyway, we're flying you in on a charter. Nothing to worry about. Isn't that right, Goma?"

Goma shrugged.

"Don't you think, Kella?"

"The rebels' families are still there, but the fighters are gone," Kella said.

"There, you see? Safe," Vautour said.

"Good. I'll be sure to run it by—"

"Oh, no need. I've already spoken with Mr. Ferman. Everything's set. We booked a plane for tomorrow."

Peter thought about the stinger missiles he'd seen in the photo of the confiscated armaments. It gave him a knot in the pit of his stomach. He'd be flying above a region where the Malian army and the French were still battling insurgents. What's the point having all those weapons if you're not going to use them?

***

Peter went for a walk that afternoon. His legs were still stiff from the coach-class flight, Paris-to-Bamako. As soon as he exited the hotel, the heat of the afternoon hit him like a wall. A group of boys quickly gathered. "*Toubabu! toubabu! Donne moi cinq francs.*" He hadn't yet bought anything and had no change to give. He strode quickly and they dispersed, discouraged by his pace. The iron-rich red sand soon covered his sandals and feet as far as his ankles and stood out against his untanned skin. He dodged bicycles, *mobilettes*, donkeys, dogs, and sheep led by leashes, all crowded along the street sides, leaving the centre of the broken pavement for cars, trucks and motorcycles to jockey for position. He walked in the direction of the City Centre Market. Every street on the outskirts of the market had a designated profession. The silversmiths gathered cross-legged under awnings, each with their own small pit of coals in front of them, smoke accumulating into a thin blue haze under the awning. Their bellows, anvils, and tools were laid out in front of their feet as they hammered out silver jewelry decorated with turquoise or amber. The ding, ding, ding was musical, without quite forming into a rhythm. Peter picked out an ebony and silver collar necklace and, in the haggling, paid the artisan his second price.

A girl wearing a wraparound skirt stood quietly nearby looking down at the ground, one hand at her elbow, the other held out, palm open. Peter thought of the girl from the witness report who had bitten the policeman. He gave her the fifty francs he had just received in change. She beamed at the unexpected gift and walked away holding the bill tightly. Peter knew she'd never understand why he did that.

The meat market carried a different sound, the dull thud of machetes on flesh and bone, flies swarming on strips of meat hung for customers to inspect. The air was full of the smell of blood. Farther along the street, the blood smell mingled with ripe mangoes.

He stopped at the blanket of a street vendor selling cow-hide flip flops. They were made with wide soles like camel's feet, ideal for walking in the sand. He tried a few on until he found the right size and paid the vendor his first price. He felt generous, wanting in some small way to make up for the horror of Vautour's dossier.

His shopping complete, Peter quickened his pace and circled back to the hotel, his shirt already sticking to his back.

In contrast with the afternoon heat outside, his room was uncomfortably cold. The air conditioner didn't respond to any efforts at adjustment. He called the reception desk and the man who answered told him they'd send someone up right away to look at it. *Tout de suit, Monsieur.*

No one came. Peter surrendered, put on another layer of clothes and crawled under the bedcovers.

He tried calling Nora's number. The line dropped. He tried again a minute later. No connection.

He texted:

Going to Timbuktu tomorrow. Everything arranged.

Three dots appeared, showing her reply was coming. Then they disappeared.

Peter typed again:

Flying tomorrow at—

Before he could finish, her answer appeared:

Is that safe? Will you be okay?

Everyone tells me things there are okay.

I'm worried.

I'm worried too. That means I won't take risks.

Peter couldn't think how in particular he would avoid risks. The whole point of a stinger missile or roadside bomb is the unexpected.

I'm proud of you, she wrote.

Thanks. I'm proud of you too.

Text me when you get there. Make it all worth it.

I will. I'll do my best

CHAPTER 7: FIREWOOD

Nora kept her eyes closed as she surfaced from a deep sleep. She couldn't remember what her dream was about. It was gone, but left a sense of separation. It matched a feeling of melancholy, the sense that Peter was in some ways with her and in other ways beyond reach. It was strange waking up in his apartment. Well, Aunt Julia's apartment, but where Peter had left traces, his smell in the sheets, making her aware of his absence.

Maybe that's where the feeling of a dream came from.

The apartment had a feeling of space. The walls weren't too close, but still there, not so much as walls, but a presence, without intruding. She flexed her toes and sensed the room. So few apartments in the Netherlands felt open and protected like this. There was no way Peter was paying market value for it. It was so very kind of Aunt Julia to rent it to him for a fraction of what it was worth. What was the saying in English? Something to do with paying for a song. Bought it for a song, that's it. Except he didn't even buy it.

The sounds of the city coming to life were different here than in Cambridge. The first thing she noticed was an absence: no turtle dove cooing in a reassuring way like she always heard first thing from the garden in Cambridge. Here, the bird sounds were from sparrows, crows, and seagulls. And the traffic was just as urban as the birds. There was a bus route somewhere nearby, a noisy garbage pickup, then the background hum of traffic as the city awoke. It came faintly at first, intermittent, and slowly got louder, more uniform, like someone turning up the volume. A highway not far away.

There were sounds from within the apartment building, too. It was an older building with thick walls, but noise still traveled between the flats. The man upstairs took his morning piss in a way that resonated in the toilet bowl. He must be tall. There was a child somewhere. Where? The little running footsteps were coming from above, a room somewhere on the far side. Nice to hear a child. Good there's life in the building.

She opened her eyes, looking toward the ceiling. The day was overcast. She'd be able to see outside as she found her way in an unfamiliar city, at least to navigate. The signage would be another matter. Little things like store hours, holidays, specials of the day, help wanted, posters for lost cats, sticker graffiti—these went by her as shapes and colors, but not as messages. And for a time at least, she'd be adrift, missing the undergrowth of signs, unsure of herself, having to learn in other ways. She was attuned to other signs and signals, things other people missed, shapes, sounds, smells. The feeling of colors.

She sat up in bed, gathering and girding herself, assembling her equipment. Her phone was on the righthand corner of the bedside table where she usually left it. Her glasses were in their case next to it. But the magnifier wasn't where it belonged. Where could she have put it?

She swung her feet off the bed and felt across the table surface, almost spilling a water glass. Not there. She put on her glasses to widen the search. The magnifier must be in the living room. She felt hurried, but knew that moving quickly in a new place would lead to collisions with furniture or half-open doors. She slowed her breath and tied her hair into a ponytail from an elastic she kept on her wrist, then walked to the living room. The magnification strip was on the coffee table where she'd left it the night before, next to a book she'd never seen before, about the liberation of the Netherlands at the end of the war.

Peter had done some research on his Dutch ancestry before he left for Africa, it seemed.

* * *

The time approached for a two-hour slot Nora had booked at the Rare Manuscripts Room at the University of Scheveningen. She waited for the driver to confirm his arrival by text, then took the stairs down.

She entered the Reading Room through a heavy oak door. A receptionist rose to his feet, as though expecting her. He had a full head of dark hair and heavy-rimmed glasses. The two-tiered desk he stood behind gave her the feeling she was checking into a hotel.

"Can I see some identification?" he said, confirming the hotel feeling. She half expected him to give her a door key and wish her a pleasant stay.

She gave him her faculty card from Cambridge University.

He was unimpressed. "Do you have any state issued identification?" He sighed audibly.

She handed him her passport.

She felt his hostility, as though something about *her* had set him off. He made no comment about the—surely unusual—combination of a Dutch passport with a Cambridge University ID, no friendly comment like, "How are you finding it there?" or "Things may be different there, but at least the weather's the same." He remained focused on the documents and making sure of her identity. She wasn't carrying her cane. Did he notice something else about her?

He looked up. "May I please have your address in the Netherlands."

She only had Peter's apartment, and had to look for it on her phone. She held the phone close to her face and sensed the receptionist's impatience as she scrolled through her messages to find the one with Peter's address.

"Here it is." She held the phone for him to see.

His hands were quick on the keyboard. She could tell he was done entering the address in the library's client database by the extra force he put on the final keystroke.

"You're all set. Here is a pair of gloves." He held out two surgical gloves. "To keep the oil from your fingers from damaging the paper, you must wear these at all times in the reading room. The computers are for ordering your material. You may only read at the main table. You may only write notes with the pencils provided. Needless to say, under no circumstances are you permitted to write marginal notes on the manuscripts. By that I mean produce indentations on the manuscripts through your notepaper. That includes Post-it Notes. Any questions?"

Nora didn't have any questions.

"Good."

She entered the reading room through a heavy glass door with a bold-lettered, **QUIET PLEASE**, sign. There was a scattering of people seated around a large wood table as far from one another as possible, as though fearful of contagion. Computer workstations were set up around the perimeter. Nora found a workstation in a corner of the room, away from the windows. She lowered the brightness on the monitor, but couldn't figure out how to increase the font size. The library was using an old operating system. By way of a solution, she put her magnification strip on the monitor with her left hand and scrolled with the mouse using her right.

It took her over an hour before she found something interesting—a rare set of instructions by a German printer, Jan de Bos, to one of his Dutch apprentices, dated from the mid-sixteenth century. She used a pencil from a box on her desk to fill in an order form and left the room to hand it to the receptionist.

"You just put it here." He nodded toward a tray on the reception desk marked *Bestellingen*—Orders. "It should take ten to twenty minutes."

How strange that you need to leave the room to submit a book order, she thought. So the staff don't have to come into the reading room, no doubt. But it means more traffic through the door. A culture of administrative narcissism. Nora went back to her desk and continued looking for material in the library holdings. Out of curiosity, she set the timer on her phone to see how long it took them to get the manuscript to her.

A woman with quiet footsteps approached her desk at fourteen minutes and twenty seconds. "I'll leave this for you at the reading table."

Not bad, Nora thought. They're efficient here.

The manuscript was in good condition. She put on the gloves provided, then cleaned her magnifying strip with the same cloth she used for her glasses. The title page gave her the peculiar feeling of going back in time, a sense of discovery. How could people want vacations in the tropics when other kinds of destination are so close at hand? Despite the paper browned with age, despite the dark patches like moles and sunspots on aged skin, it spoke to her as though printed yesterday. Yet, so very different. It was written in German Gothic Fraktur. She took a moment to adjust to the long "s" of the typescript looking like "f" and the capital "I" and "J" being indistinguishable.

The librarian approached her. "Excuse me, but you're not permitted to touch the page with anything except your gloved hands."

Nora took the magnification strip off the page and held it up. "You mean this? But I need it to read. I'm visually impaired."

"I'm very sorry, but we have strict rules."

"I understand the need for rules to protect the manuscripts, but, look, I cleaned it and I'm being very careful. There has to be an exception."

"Rules are rules." The woman folded her arms in the classic gesture of rigidity.

Nora felt her chest tighten and throat constrict with anger. "When I say there *has* to be an exception, I mean that literally. There are also rules that require you to accommodate persons with disabilities. Have you heard of the Act on Equal Treatment of Disabled and Chronically Ill People?" It came into effect in 2003. Do you know about the Convention on the Rights of Persons with Disabilities? It came into effect in 2008. In the Netherlands, we have a commitment to rights."

"Please lower your voice. That may well be, but I'm afraid we have no procedures in place to deal with exceptions."

"Well, that's self-evident," Nora said. "If there was a procedure in place to deal with an exception, it would no longer be an exception, would it? An exception means you use your discretion. So use your discretion. Let me read."

"I'm going to have to ask you to leave."

Nora felt the woman's shape move closer. She tightened her grip on the magnification strip. "What's your name? I'd like to speak with your boss."

"I'm the one in charge. If you have a complaint, you can write to the administration."

Nora stood. Her chair made a scraping sound on the floor. "I think I'm done here."

"Shhh!" someone said.

* * *

That afternoon, still with the emotional aftertaste of her encounter at the reading room, Nora took a taxi to Aunt Julia's apartment in the city center. The button panel was close to the main door. Nora pressed the numbers for the apartment. The door buzzed without an exchange of words over the intercom. It seemed almost rude. Maybe one of those things that happens with age. Her steps sounded hollow in the wide entryway. The elevator smelled like old iron. She closed the cage, found the buttons and pressed seven. It lurched to a start, throwing her off balance. It stopped just as abruptly, but this time she was ready for it. When she slid open the door, a voice came from down the hall.

"*Goedemorgen*, Nora."

They greeted each other at the doorway. Julia smelled faintly of lavender. The apartment smelled like coffee and boiled eggs.

"You made breakfast. That's very kind."

There was a squawk from the adjoining room.

"That's my bird, Toen. He hears you and wants attention. He can be quite a nuisance sometimes."

"That's all right. I heard all about him from Peter. I've been looking forward to meeting him."

Toen's head bobbed as they approached the cage.

"Well, I'd better take him out. We won't get a moment's peace otherwise." Julia opened the cage. Toen hopped out and climbed up her arm, one foot following the other, until he reached her shoulder. He rubbed his head against her ear. "He feels safe here on my shoulder. Now you can gently reach out to him."

"He won't bite?"

"Oh, heavens no. He's a sweetheart."

Nora slowly extended her hand toward the parrot. He made a cooing and clicking sound almost simultaneously. She touched the feathers on his head with the back of her index finger. They were softer than she had expected.

"Good," Julia said. "Now we can have some breakfast. I'm quite sure Toen will be a complete pest."

Over coffee and eggs, Nora told Aunt Julia about her experience in the rare manuscripts reading room. It still rankled the next day.

Aunt Julia nodded thoughtfully. "If you always follow the rules, you don't survive."

"I'm sure you have some experience with that."

Aunt Julia replied with the story of a woman who denounced her husband as a member of resistance, knowing that it would get him killed. She was prosecuted for murder after the war, but eventually released. "A terrible decision," she concluded. "Not only were the laws under the Nazis wrong, some people used them as murder weapons."

Something about the story made Nora uncomfortable. She shifted in her chair and said, "I don't really see how that's an example of not following the rules to survive. The woman who did that was acting *within* the law. The law of Nazi Germany."

"*Precies*. It was her obligation to disobey. Not use evil laws for her own ends."

"I see," Nora said. "That must mean that for you, German laws were meant to be broken. Provided you didn't get caught." Nora sipped her coffee louder than she meant.

"Provided you didn't get caught." Aunt Julia repeated Nora's words as though rehearsing what she was about to say. "I got caught once."

Then she fell silent. She concentrated on buttering a piece of toast.

"You can't just say that and then not tell me more." Nora put her cup down expectantly.

"Well, let me give you a short version then."

"Good. Great." This was more than politeness. Nora was in the mood for a story.

"There was a pretty desperate situation toward the end of the war. For a while we had enough to eat. For heat, we just wore lots of clothes and blankets in the house. You could see your breath, but we were okay. For cooking, though, there was a shortage of wood. We started by sacrificing some furniture, an old chest and some chairs in the attic. It broke my heart to see some of that furniture go. We'd had them for as long as I could remember. It was like a little piece of me getting cut up and thrown in the stove. Then things got more serious."

Julia stood and went to a cupboard. Toen squawked. She returned to the table with a bag of peanuts in their shells. She removed one and held it out to Toen. He took it with one foot and dropped the pieces of shell on Julia's shoulder and down the front of her sweater. She paid no attention to the mess.

"We once had beautiful big elm trees that made a canopy over the street, and it was sad to see them go."

Julia gave Toen another peanut. More shell fragments accumulated on her clothes. She brushed them distractedly down to the floor.

Hand-feeding the bird must be her way of calming herself, thought Nora.

"It was sad in a different way from the furniture. I couldn't say which hurt more. Just different. The furniture was a personal loss. The elms, well that was more . . . a calamity. I cried over that. People just cut the trees up. They started with the lower limbs, then men climbed up with ropes and saws. When only the highest branches were left, some men took the trees down and people scrambled over them, even women, with axes and saws. There was no system, and people argued, saying 'this is mine, it's in front of my house,' and others saying they had no rights, the trees were on city property. Sometimes I woke up to the sound of shouting because someone came to take wood in the middle of the night and got caught. People burned the wood without giving it time to dry out, still full of sap. When people were cooking, the smoke was thick in the air.

Pretty soon the trees were all gone, even the stumps dug up from the ground. The holes left behind looked like bombs had gone off. With the trees gone, there was more light coming in through the windows, but it wasn't cheerful. It felt somehow unprotected."

"Is this what led you to break the Nazi laws?" Against her better judgment, Nora felt herself wanting the story to move on, get to the point.

"I was just getting to that," Aunt Julia said. "When the trees were nearly gone, my mother got the bold idea of sending me and Corine up to the SS headquarters to steal some wood. There was an estate the Nazis took over that used to be owned by a Jewish banker. Or a builder, I'm not sure which. The main thing is, it was a fabulous home with spires and leaded windows and—the best part as far as the Nazis were concerned—a Jewish owner. That made it convenient for them to confiscate. To steal. It had a wooded area that was fenced off, one of the only semi-wild places left in the city. Ma dressed us up in our Sunday clothes to look like we were just out of church with bows in our hair and shiny black shoes. She told us to look for branches on the ground broken off from a storm, go in quickly and get what we could on the wagon. I was thirteen, but not very tall, so I looked younger. Corine was seven. Very cute. Off we went with our wagon. We had a carpenter's saw hidden under a blanket. There was a wire fence at the estate and signs that said *Achtung!* and *Eintritt Verboten* with a gap, hidden because people closed it up again. Ma told me where it would be. We stood there for a long time, thinking about what might happen if we were caught versus what Ma would say if we went home with no wood. I prepared myself to get in and get out quickly. We made our way through the fence. I remember I tore my dress on a wire sticking out. That tear was like a sign that things weren't going right.

"People must've been there before us because there were no branches on the ground. Not a twig. But I didn't want to go home with nothing, so I got a better idea. I found a big, low-hanging branch on an oak tree. A dead branch, ready to burn. It was pretty hard work cutting and I was making some progress, but then my saw got stuck. I made the mistake of cutting from underneath because that was the only way I could reach. The weight of the branch came down on the saw, and there was nothing I could do to get it out. I was struggling with it, trying to wriggle it back and forth, but it wasn't moving. I didn't see the two German soldiers at the fence, until one of them yelled, '*Halt*!' I was thinking 'what now?' They said '*Komen sie hier! Sofort!*' They had rifles and shiny boots. Corine and I looked at each other not knowing what to do. They could've done anything to me. We were a few hundred metres from the SS headquarters and they could've marched us in and who knows. Also, I wasn't born yesterday. I had a pretty good idea what the soldiers could've done to me, taking me a little further into the woods.

"We walked over to the fence, following the soldier's order. There was nowhere for us to run, not in our Sunday dresses. One spoke a little Dutch and said, 'What are you doing? Don't you know you're not supposed to be in there?' I told him I was trying to get just a little bit of wood. Then I told a really good lie. A masterpiece. I said we had a baby brother at home who was sick and if we didn't get him some warmth, we worried he might die. I cried real tears. Corine picked up the cue and started crying, too, with little, shaking sobs. The soldiers' expression softened and they looked at each other and one said, '*Warte*'—wait. They climbed through the fence and went over to the tree where the saw was stuck. One lifted the branch while the other one pulled it out, just like that. And then they kept going, sawing away at the branch, making it look easy. In no time, they'd cut up the whole thing and loaded the wagon full. Then they put the saw in and covered the load with the blanket we brought. They carried the wagon with its load through the fence all the way to the street. Then the soldier held the handle of the wagon toward me and said, 'Be careful that nobody sees what you've got on your way home.' And they were back on their way marching down the street laughing to one another, one with his hand on the other's shoulder. Probably their mood was lifted by their good deed of the day. I was worried they'd offer to pull the wagon and follow us back to the house, maybe check up on the baby brother whose existence I'd invented. I guess they had other things to do. Anyway, that's what happened."

"That's quite a story," Nora said. "Have you ever thought about writing it down?"

"Bah, can you imagine? Me a writer? Who'd be interested in such a thing?"

"Well, *I'm* interested. And I'm sure there are plenty of other people who'd like to read your stories."

"*Ja,* Nora, you're interested because of Peter. But everyone who lived through the war has a story. I was just a girl."

"Well, I think what you have to say is amazing and I'd like to hear more."

Julia gave a dismissive snort.

Toen made the same sound from her shoulder.

"And besides," Nora went on, "we need to hear these stories before the people who remember them are all gone."

Julia gave Nora a steady look with an arched eyebrow.

"I mean . . . well, you know, I don't mean now, but sometime soon," Nora tried to recover from her gaffe.

Julia smiled slightly, with just one corner of her mouth. "Okay then. Let me tell you more. Just a little. This makes me tired."

She poured herself another cup of coffee, so measuredly it seemed the liquid slowed as it fell from the spout. She took a sip, leaned back in her chair, and closed her eyes. Then she opened them and stared straight ahead as she spoke.

"After that near disaster in the woods at the SS headquarters, Ma had another idea. There was a coal depot by the rail station. The coal was used to run the trains, and there was always coal being shovelled and carted and some of it dropped and lay there a while before it got tidied up. Or *picked* up by whoever got there first.

"I had running pants, dark blue, the kind with an elastic at the ankle. Ma turned the pockets inside out and used her scissors and a stitch ripper to open them up. She spent so much of her time to sewing things together and mending holes, it must've been hard for her to cut those pockets open. But she did a proper job, making a seam to keep it from fraying. Everything done right. Except, thinking about it now, it would've been better to leave it alone, just a hole in the pocket, in case I was caught. A carefully sewn hole in the pocket and coal at the bottom of my trousers might've been hard to explain. No matter. You see? I can't tell a story. I already let you know that I wouldn't get caught."

"No, no. I'm listening. Please go on."

"Like before with the firewood at the estate, Ma told me how to get the coal. First, wait for a time when there were no soldiers or railwaymen around. Then take just a few pieces of coal at a time, drop them through the holes in my pockets and let them fall to the bottom of my pants. Not too many or it would show. Brave girl. A kiss on the forehead.

"It turned out, it worked pretty well. I went there just about every day. I'd come home and change out of my pants. My ankles would be all black from the coal and we'd have to wash my pants. I was almost keeping up with the needs of the household, and never got caught. Only once did a railway worker see me putting a piece of coal in my pocket. He looked surprised and opened his mouth like he was going to say something, but he didn't. Instead, he turned his back and looked toward the track as though I didn't exist."

"Where were the men all this time? What were they doing?"

Aunt Julia put her cup down sharply. "I don't really know for sure. I was just ten when the war started and they didn't tell me anything. I do know my brother Joop had an automatic pistol. He didn't show it around. He wore it in the small of his back, tucked into his belt. I caught him cleaning it in his bedroom once. His door was open a crack and I put my head in. He shouted at me and slammed the door."

"How do you know whether he wore it when he went out? Wasn't that risky?"

"I tried to see if he was wearing it tucked in his belt by giving him a hug at the door. Wasn't hard to miss. It was almost always there. I think he knew that *I knew* he was working for the resistance. Sometimes there'd be visitors and they'd have long conversations at the kitchen table, very serious. About what, I don't really know." Aunt Julia paused, staring straight ahead. Toen rubbed his head against the side of her neck. "Isn't it interesting that Ma was always there?" she said.

CHAPTER 8: THE WAY NORTH

The pilot was a French expat whose love of flying came from the stories told by the great aviation writer Antoine de Saint Exupéry. He revealed this to Peter with the easy familiarity of a chat over beers while he loaded luggage into the rear compartment. Goma and Kella had already climbed into the plane. Peter waited as long as he could before he followed them. His knees didn't respond well to the cramped space in economy class flights. He imagined it would be the same or worse in a chartered plane. When the engine revved for takeoff, Peter regretted that he'd forgotten to bring earplugs. Not so much forgotten as overlooked the possibility that his travel might entail a flight in an unpressurized twin-engine Piper.

Peter sat near the back so he could straighten his legs into the aisle without getting in anyone's way. Only once they were aloft did he notice a ragged hole in the middle of the aisle floor that allowed him a view of the dry plain dotted with shrubs that passed below. It was a wonder no one had put their foot through it. Then again, who's to say they hadn't? He settled in for the five-hour flight to Timbuktu, lulled by the oscillating noise from the propellors.

He woke suddenly when the pilot slid open the folding cockpit door with a bang. He tapped the microphone on his headset, getting no result from the intercom, then pushed the microphone aside and announced at the top of his voice that they would be making an unscheduled landing in Mopti.

Goma and Kella took the information in stride and stayed settled in their seats. Peter wanted to know more.

"What do you think it is?" he shouted to Goma.

Goma shrugged.

"It could be anything," Kella said, unhelpfully.

Peter stood and bent his head and shoulder forward, taking care to avoid the hole in the floor. There was barely enough room for him to stand hunched over before having to go on all fours. The plane hit a pocket of turbulence and he grabbed the back of a seat to keep his balance. The cockpit door was still open.

"Why are we landing in Mopti?" he shouted.

"Sandstorm." The pilot pressed forward lightly on the control column to start a descent, then glanced toward him. "Better get back to your seat." The amiability from before the flight was gone.

Peter looked ahead through the cockpit window. A blue sky stretched in front of them with the tops of nimbus clouds on the horizon. He felt the slope of the plane's descent in his walk to the back and used the seats to both steady himself and push himself forward. Goma and Kella were asleep on opposite sides of the aisle and only stirred when the wheels touched the tarmac, as though being in the air was their sole opportunity for peace.

As they left the plane, Peter told Goma what the pilot had said about a coming sandstorm. Goma looked toward the sky. The clouds seemed a lot closer than they did from the air.

"I think maybe we should go inside," Goma said.

Kella said something to Goma in Tamashek that to Peter sounded like "*tazikkay n tenere.*" Her voice lifted at the end. A question. Goma shook his head no and answered with "*agaladous.*" She clicked her tongue and looked at the sky.

The doors to the airport lobby were locked. Peter peered through the glass doors with both hands cupped against his temples to block the reflection. No one was inside.

Goma called him. "Look!"

A churning wall of sand had already engulfed the town and was sweeping across the plain toward them.

"Inside, quick!" The hangar doors were all locked. They clambered into the plane and closed the door just as the sand-wall hit, plunging them in darkness. The plane rocked on its suspension with the sudden force of the wind.

"*Merde*!" the pilot said.

"*Al-Hamd ul-Allah*," Goma said.

Kella was silent.

They all coughed.

"The hole!" Peter shouted. He took off his shirt and used it to block the sand from entering the plane. The pilot switched on the cabin lights, illuminating a fine, flourlike powder that swirled through the cabin like a ribbon dance. Nothing like beach sand, Peter thought. More insidious. It stuck to his shirtless torso and made a dark streak where the sweat ran.

"And now?" Peter asked.

"We wait," the pilot said. He went into the cockpit and came back with a handful of paper tissues. "Here. Use these."

Peter saw that Goma had pulled his turban tightly across his face, with just his eyes visible. Kella had done the same with her scarf.

"Thanks." He took the tissues and pressed them over his mouth and nose. His eyes watered from the dust.

Over the next few hours, the atmosphere outside the plane went from dark brown, to red, to orange, to yellow. The air inside was stifling, like a dust-filled sauna.

Eventually, the pilot looked through the window and gave the signal Peter had been waiting for: "It should be okay now."

The pilot opened the door, with no difference in the air—the concentration of dust outside was the same as in the plane. Peter recovered his shirt and shook it out on the way down the steps to the tarmac. The sand that came off was fine, like brown flour. He buttoned it on and felt it cling to his skin.

Goma lit a cigarette. Peter must have given him a quizzical look, as though to ask how he could possibly add smoke to the dust that was already in his lungs. Goma shrugged, smiled and inhaled deeply.

"No more flying today, *désolé,*" the pilot said. "Even this amount of sand in the air will kill the engine." He looked up at the sky where the disk of the sun hung like a dirty plate. "Good thing we didn't fly into that," he added.

* * *

Mopti was nothing like Peter's memory of it. The lack of fit between memory and perception was like a change of scene just before a dream spins off into surrealism. Two decades earlier he was a thirty-something, starry-eyed grad student, encouraged in his ambitions by French academic advisers who wanted data from northern Mali, but not the hard travel to acquire it. The hotel in Mopti was then a place of indulgence, a luxury before the privations of his low-budget travel to the north. He remembered the bustling café of the Hotel l'Hirondelle where they were now staying, the din of voices, the cooking-meat smell from a kitchen grill, waiters moving athletically with their trays, an elderly Frenchwoman unable to prevent her Pomeranian from barking at the lizards that freely roamed the interior.

This morning, he, Goma, and Kella were the only diners. Even the lizards had deserted the place.

Yves Vautour was a disembodied voice over Peter's iPhone in the middle of the breakfast table at the Hotel l'Hirondelle. The restaurant was empty except for a waiter at the bar polishing glasses and occasionally glancing in their direction, curious. Vautour asked for no input from Peter, Goma, or Kella during the impromptu meeting, just relayed practicalities. The driver for their overland trip would be Ibrahim, a former UN Peacekeeper from Chad and three-year veteran of the peacekeeping mission in the western Sahara. They were lucky to find him on short notice. There'd be military checkpoints set up along the dirt road at regular intervals, so everyone should have their papers ready.

"Lucky you, a free vacation to Timbuktu." Vautour laughed loud enough over the phone to make the waiter throw a judgmental look in their direction.

The same discomforting, dreamlike feeling with which the day began struck Peter later that morning at the fuel station and transit stop. It had once bustled with travelers and drivers waiting for their vans to fill with customers before departing. Street hawkers had wandered with trays strapped behind their necks like cigarette girls. They sold everything a traveler might need while waiting to start a journey: Lipton tea bags, sachets of instant coffee, sugar, cigarettes, tissues, little bags of dried dates, and high calorie famine-relief biscuits, courtesy of the Government of the Netherlands and diverted into a small-commerce black market. Now, in Peter's pre-nightmare, the transit stop was empty except for a few people sitting in the shade of an acacia tree. No sunburned couples pausing over tourist trinkets. Gone were the adventure-tourists driving diesel Land Rovers with extra fuel in jerrycans strapped to the roof, compelled by a form of madness to make a mark on the world by gathering the crumbs of adventure left by the early explorers. Gone too were the fashionable European and American women unwittingly offending puritan sensibilities with their bare arms and midriffs and too-short skirts. Somehow the place wasn't nearly as interesting without them. Without the interruption of their offensiveness.

Ibrahim arrived a half hour late. He raised a cloud of dust by braking the Toyota Land Cruiser too hard in the sand, descended athletically, and shook hands with each of them in turn, starting with Peter. Then he apologized, not for his lateness, but for the Land Cruiser with its dents, chipped paint, and cracked windshield. Its only armour was a grill attached on the front to protect the headlights from rocks on the road. But he pointed to its defects lightly, with an undercurrent of optimism. As though by a preordained order of things, Goma and Peter climbed in the back and Kella went to the front passenger seat with a small duffel bag, no bigger than a generously sized purse, at her feet.

Despite Vautour's assurance over the phone of a regular military presence, once they were waved through the main checkpoint at the outskirts of Mopti, they found themselves on an empty dirt road. Ibrahim did what he could to find the smoothest part of the roadway. He was good at it, but the graders with their heavy plough blades hadn't been at work levelling the surface in a while and it was impossible to avoid washboards and potholes. Peter soon succumbed to the boredom of the road, mesmerized by the passing scrubland dotted with thorn bushes. He found the corner of a fingernail, only to have it torn away from between his teeth by a sudden lurch as the truck hit a protruding rock.

Ibrahim's solution to his boredom was to talk, with Peter as his main audience. Goma and Kella stayed quiet while Ibrahim shifted between watching the road and turning to Peter over his shoulder. He prefaced everything with a smile. His relaxed manner was in contrast to the seriousness of his subject matter, but somehow it didn't come across as inauthentic. According to what he had learned from other peacekeepers, the Al-Qaida and Ansar Eddine forces had been driven out of Timbuktu a few months previously, but there was no telling when or where they might show up. They were still mobile, still armed with light weapons from Libya, spirited away during the chaos of the revolution. As Ibrahim understood it, the whole fruitless, directionless war that created the emptiness on this road had not been started not by religious ideology, nor by a drive to independence, but by weapons, pure and simple. "It used to be, you got weapons to win a war," he said. "Here the weapons just flooded in, and people had to figure out reasons to fight." He jerked the wheel to avoid a pothole. "*That's* why none of it makes any sense."

Goma opened one eye, then the other. "It makes sense to me. They're hyenas." He closed his eyes again to put an end to the conversation.

The approach to the city announced itself by increasing numbers of burned-out husks of cars and trucks along the roadside, like insects after a fumigation. Some vehicles were on their sides or upside-down, exposing their wheel assemblies and undercarriages. Most were sprayed with bullet holes. On a few, the tires were gone altogether, blown or burned off, leaving only empty wheel assemblies.

Within the town limits, there was little sign of the occupation or the chaos of battle. The outbuildings were made of mud-brick *banco* and windows with metal shutters hinged at the top. The shutters were all closed. Maybe the sandstorm had passed through here on its way south and people hadn't yet opened things up again. They drove along a wider sandy boulevard with a decrepit fuel station and what looked to be government buildings that stood out with their concrete and glass windows.

Goma sat upright. "It's been two years since I was here," he said, his face turned toward the window.

"Here's the Banque Malien de Solidarité," Ibrahim said. It was a nondescript two storey concrete structure with no tree anywhere nearby to give it shade.

Peter remembered the detail about the women's prison from the testimony Vautour had read over breakfast a few days previously. As they drove by slowly, he noted the door of the ATM room, the "nightmare cell."

They skirted the old part of the city, with many of its streets built for camels and foot traffic, too narrow for vehicles. Ibrahim looked across to Kella. She stared straight ahead for a while, then gave directions. "Right here. Keep going. Left here. Here, stop." They arrived at the mud-brick wall surrounding a flat roofed main building. When the truck door slammed, Peter could hear shrieks of women's voices from inside the compound. "Kella! Kella! Kella!"

The first to arrive through the gate opening were children, who gathered around her, clutched at the folds of her *boubou*, grabbed her hands, and pulled her through the gate. Peter noticed for the first time that the small duffel bag slung over her shoulder was her only luggage. She smiled back at them, her eyes sparkling with tears, unable to wave with her hands captured by the children.

Peter waved from the back of the truck and said, to himself more than anyone in particular, "She travels light."

"She has everything she needs right here," Goma said.

* * *

They pulled up to a windowless house, not fully recognizable as a house, at least not from the outside, a two-storey brownish grey wall of cement bricks joined to the neighboring houses with a confused combination of mud and mortar, and rising a storey higher, like a rampart. The only thing to show there was a dwelling on the other side was a sheet metal door. "You'll be staying here," Goma said. "Nothing is open anywhere. No tourists." It was a statement of fact more than an invitation.

"And Ibrahim?"

"Ibrahim has friends." Goma slapped Ibrahim on the shoulder to demonstrate his inclusion among them.

With these words, Peter felt the sting of his limited network. He resisted the urge to take out his phone and call Nora. Better to be polite to his new host.

They said good-bye to Ibrahim, who sped off in a cloud of dust. Goma pulled a key out of a side pocket of his bag, an exaggerated comic-book-dungeon-sized key that rattled proportionately in the lock. Peter glimpsed a sandy courtyard centered with a date palm, but only briefly because Goma ushered him up a narrow flight of stairs, open to the sky, that led to a walled patio. There, they reclined on straw-filled cushions on the rooftop of Goma's family home. Night had fallen. There were no stars and the half-moon rising over the horizon was dirty orange. The dust from the sandstorm had still not cleared. There was a rhythmic thud, thud, thud of two mortars and pestles from the courtyard below. Peter imagined the women holding pestles nearly their own height, lifting with both hands and releasing them with a slight bending and straightening of the knees, letting gravity do the work. He heard them clap as they released the pestles before catching them again. A woman's voice began singing.

"They're happy to be home," Goma had somehow intuited Peter's train of thought.

"Your family was away?"

"They're servants," Goma replied, corrected him, "But happy to be home all the same. We were among the lucky ones. We were able to move to Bamako. My father came back last week. He'll be joining us soon. This is his house. You'll have it to yourself while you're here. My father wants me at his other place."

"Your father has two houses?"

"Three."

"A man of substance."

"Wealth will get you only so far," Goma said. "During the occupation this place was taken over by Muhammad Moussa, the head of the *Hesbah*, the so-called moral brigades." He raised his head as though sniffing the air. "I can still feel their presence here."

"You mean the ones who enforced their interpretation of Sharia law."

"Exactly." Goma pulled at a corner of the cushion that Peter was leaning on. "Look what they did to our cushions."

Peter sat up to look at it. The cushion's design depicted two peacocks in indigo blue on a white background. Peter noticed that the peacocks' heads had been sewn over with black thread, with a concentration of stitching covering the eyes. "Why would they do that?"

"I can only imagine the contortions of logic," Goma said. "Or illogic. They believe it is *haram* to depict any living thing in art. It means you are taking God's powers of creation for yourself. At some point they must've had a long discussion here about these cushions."

"I see."

"They wanted to use them because the floor is uncomfortable otherwise, but they had these idolatrous images to deal with."

"So they had them covered with needle and thread?" There was something disturbing about the painstaking needlework someone had applied to the peacock design. Peter couldn't understand the thinking behind it. And where the motives of small things are unfathomable, nothing in anyone's behavior can be predicted. What he felt, but couldn't quite see, was the insecurity of being an unsocialized stranger in a world of possible violence.

"They must've decided at some point that the eyes were the window into the soul," Goma explained. "Once you cover that part, the pillows are permitted."

There was a shuffling sound on the concrete stairs leading to the roof.

"Ah, there he is!" Goma nearly shouted. He embraced the old man before he had even reached the top of the stairs. Peter stood and waited to be introduced. He felt awkward as Goma and his father greeted each other in Tamashek, punctuated by *al-Hamd ul-Illah*. The old man's labored breathing grew steady with Goma's hands on his shoulders.

Goma turned with his arm draped around his father's neck. "Mr. Peter, this is my father Amellal." When they shook hands, Peter felt the man's hands were bony but the skin smooth. A man of means, with no need of physical labor.

"*Un plaisir*," Peter said.

"*Très heureux de vous accueillir*," Amellal said, greeting Peter in perfect French. He reached an arm down to the floor for support and sat heavily.

It soon became clear that Amellal's French was limited, his words of welcome spoken from habitual use. With Goma translating, Amellal talked in Tamashek about the meeting he had just had with a group of traders, the *commerçants* who ran transport between Timbuktu and Bamako. No one had wanted to bring anything into the town while it was occupied and patrolled by the Islamic police and the Hesbah. They knew the town was in crisis, but the risk was too great. Only a few traders kept up their activity. The economy shifted to pillage. The militants were in control of the town and took whatever they wanted, from anyone, anywhere. One small trader, a petit *commerçant*, had picked up a bag of rice that had fallen off the back of a truck driven by a militant who had just raided a storeroom. He—not the militant—was charged with theft in the Sharia Court. His sentence? He was strapped to a chair and his hand amputated with a machete. It was done in the market, with townspeople forced to watch. That happened around six months into the occupation. After that, nobody wanted to bring anything up from the south. The town was close to famine before the French drove them out. Now the *commerçants* were picking up the pieces. Getting the trucks moving again.

"*They* were the thieves. Not that poor man. What they did here has nothing to do with Islam," Amellal said in French, looking straight at Peter. His voice shook in anger. "Now, *Inshallah*, we will have our revenge."

***

Peter called Nora to let her know he'd arrived in Timbuktu. She answered right away and peppered him with questions. How is it there? Is there any sign of militants? Is it safe? Who are you working with?

He told her that the only incident on the way had been a sandstorm. The pilot was excellent. Goma and Kella are wonderful colleagues. He was staying at Goma's house. Goma and his family were very kind. They'd had lamb couscous this evening. A celebration in his honor. It was the first time they'd prepared that meal since the town was liberated. The town seemed quiet as they drove in. He thought about telling her about the remains of vehicles on the roadside, then decided against it. "Tomorrow, we start work," he said. "We'll be visiting the destroyed mausoleums."

"I'll be busy, too. I'm going to see Julia."

"Wow, that's great! I knew you'd like her."

"I miss you. I'm so happy you got there safely. I'm thinking of you."

"I miss you, too."

"*Kusjes.*"

"Kisses."

Peter stared at the phone in his hand, wondering who, if anyone, to call next. He thought of Aunt Julia. Then, without navigating to his contact list, he dialled a number that was deep in his memory, that hadn't changed over the decades since he was a child, the same number he had given to friends in high school, the number he first gave out as a legal person, for things like opening a bank account or filling out a college application.

The answer came on the fifth ring. "Hallo."

"Hi, Dad."

"Oh! Hallo Pieter!"

"Guess where I'm calling from."

"Yes, thank you for calling."

"No, Dad. Guess where I'm calling *from*."

"I have no idea where you go these days."

"Timbuktu. I'm calling from Timbuktu."

"Tim-buk-*too*!"

"Yes, Dad."

"Timbukt*oo,* Timbukt*oo.* Hold on."

Peter heard footsteps, then rummaging.

"Dad. Dad?"

The footsteps returned.

"I have a poem for you."

"Dad, I—"

"I'm going to read it now. It goes like this: A man from Timbukt*oo,* found an elephant's wang in his stew. Said the waiter, 'don't shout, or wave it about, or the others will want one too'. Ha! Ha! Ha!"

"Dad, I—"

"That's called a limer-*ick.*"

"Yes."

"I found it in a book of limer-*icks.*"

"Yes, you did."

"I have a nice book here, with limer-*icks.* Some are very funny. Here's another one—"

"Dad, I wanted to ask you something. Something important. About the war."

"Is Timbuktu even a place?"

"Yes, it really is a place. Believe me."

"What the hell're you doing there?"

"That's a long story. For work. Remember, I told you I'm a war crimes investigator? I'm here investigating. Listen, Dad, I wanted to ask you something about the war. It's because of something I learned from Aunt Julia."

There was a long silence.

"Dad? Are you there?"

"What did that woman tell you? You shouldn't be talking to her."

"Dad, she found our name carved in the wall of a prison cell. At the Oranjehotel. Before it was renovated. Do you know anything about that?"

"I don't know anything about that. It must've been a distant relation. Someone with the same name."

"I hope we can talk more about all this sometime."

"Better to forget."

The line dropped. Peter tried calling again, but there was no answer.

CHAPTER 9: MOFFENHOREN

Toen squawked from his cage in the living room, excited by the sounds of Nora's arrival. "Hallo Toentje, it's me," Nora called as she hung her coat on a peg. Toen squawked louder and beat his wings against the bars.

Aunt Julia went to console the bird. She made cooing and clicking sounds from the living room, as though putting a baby to bed, and returned with the walk of someone who took pleasure in efficiency, a task completed. "I covered the cage. That should quiet him for a while." She pulled a chair out from the kitchen table.

Nora sat in the offered chair and put her iPhone in the centre of the table. "It's really no trouble. He doesn't make much noise at all."

Aunt Julia sat brusquely and patted her hair to put it in place, as though preparing for a photo shoot instead of a recorded conversation. "Well, now. What was it you wanted to talk about again?"

"I thought we'd talk about your family. For Peter. Maybe in English so it's easier for him to understand. He seems to know so little. I thought it'd be a nice surprise for him."

"Family! Good heavens. Well, I'm not sure where to begin."

"Why don't you talk about your *Moeder*. Peter met her as a child, after all. Remember? Oma hair-to-the-bum? Why don't we start where he already has a connection?"

"*Moeder*, Ma . . . okay. Hmm."

"Here." Nora reached to unlock the phone. "I'll start recording. You just talk as though we're chatting at the kitchen table. Which we are."

Aunt Julia stood abruptly. "Let's go for a little walk. I've been in the house too long and it's a beautiful day."

"We can walk, but I'll have to hold your arm." Nora reached into her purse for her cane and wraparound sunglasses. Just a few moments ago, she'd had difficulty in the bright April sunlight. The cab driver had kindly helped her find the door to the apartment.

"Excellent!" Aunt Julia sounded enthused at the prospect of guiding Nora.

Nora unfurled her cane. "Off we go, then."

***

On the street, Aunt Julia held Nora's arm firmly, and warned her about every step and obstacle that couldn't be skirted. She took the challenge seriously, as a new experience. Only once did she fail to note a broken part of the sidewalk that caught the front edge of Nora's shoe.

In the narrow, shop-lined streets of the old city, Nora could keep note of passersby and bicycles as shapes to be avoided, but once they were in car traffic, she needed more of Aunt Julia's help. The intersections where buses cars, trams, and bicycles intermingled were too much for her to handle, even in the best of conditions. The cyclists were the worst. Nora could make out the red-brown asphalt of designated bike paths easily enough, but the cyclists were difficult to make out as they hurtled around corners and rang their bells to scatter the unwary. On this bright day when she would normally stay indoors, she had to put her trust in this elegant old woman, presumably with fading senses, and hope for the best.

Aunt Julia explained they were approaching the Blossom Café, near the International Court of Justice. A good place to take Peter when he came back. "Lots of lawyers and officials in the neighborhood to make him feel at home," Aunt Julia said, leaving Nora unsure if her remark was caring or mildly sarcastic. No reason it couldn't be both.

On their entry to the café, the din of conversation quieted for a moment, then picked up again. There was a background noise of conversation were the sounds of keyboards, a convection oven, a milk frother, and people using cutlery on stoneware plates. Nora's eyes didn't adjust to the interior, filled as it was with bright light from the windows along Anna Paulownastraat. "This is nice, but I wonder if there's somewhere else we might try," she proposed.

Aunt Julia, in her new role as guide, steered Nora back to the door. "I know just the place."

The Café Victoria, on a quiet street a few blocks away was a better choice. A long bar with an assortment of beer taps led into a dark interior. A bartender, sporting a blonde Van Dyke beard and moustache, busied himself washing glasses behind the counter and greeted the women as they found their way to an isolated corner in the back. It occurred to Nora that with his stylish beard, the bartender might've come straight from a painting by Rembrandt or Franz Hals.

Once they'd settled in their corner table, the bartender approached. Aunt Julia ordered a cappuccino for Nora and tea for herself, then called him back and added a salad to her order.

Nora found the choice of café interesting. It was youthful for Aunt Julia, not quite her style. No delicate bone china or waiters with napkins. There'd be no one in this neighborhood she knew. It was off-hours, quiet. She could say anything here and it would disappear into the ether.

Nora held her iPhone close to her face and scrolled through the icons looking for the record function.

"*Nee*. No need for that. I'll just talk," Aunt Julia said.

Nora put the iPhone back in her purse. "Sure. Of course." Then she added, "But wouldn't it be good for Peter for us to record some of his family history?"

"When you record it, it isn't *family* history anymore. It's anyone's. You never know where your words will go."

"True enough," Nora conceded. Her career as a historian was based on documents preserved far beyond their intended use. "But what possible harm could there be for *anyone* to hear what you experienced? Don't we still need a record of what happened during the occupation?"

"Goodness gracious, what could possibly be left to say that hasn't already been said? Again, and again, and again." Then Aunt Julia relented. "But all right, if you must."

"Here goes." Nora put on her best broadcasting voice, as though recording a podcast. "We wanted to hear something about your experience during the war. Let's start with the part that's nicest to remember: the liberation."

Aunt Julia took so long to gather her thoughts that Nora pressed pause and waited. Finally, Aunt Julia came to herself and looked at Nora as she spoke. Nora navigated back into the phone and found the button to record.

"When you see pictures of the liberation in the history books," Aunt Julia began, "it's all about smiles and flag waving and hugging Canadian soldiers and that sort of thing, which is one part of it, true. There were some happy, happy people. *I* was happy. I remember being with the crowds dancing in the street, hugging each other, hugging the Canadian soldiers. For a teenage girl, that was some real fun. The Dominee would've shamed us from the pulpit if he knew what we were up to. Which is exactly what made it fun. But there were also people going through other things, exhaustion, shock, trauma."

This wasn't the happy narrative of liberation that Nora expected. She squirmed in her chair.

"And what were we supposed to do with all those who chose to collaborate?" Aunt Julia continued. "What about the little boys who joined the Youth and paraded and gave Nazi salutes and came of age in the occupation? What about the girls who fell in love with the Germans? What about the NSBers, the German loyalists? What were they thinking? What about the ones who denounced Jews?

"Then there were the others, sometimes their neighbors, who risked their lives to protect the Jews. What was going through their minds? Everything was mixed up. There was confusion, fear and the urge for revenge. There were people who just showed up dead on the sidewalk with a bullet in their heads. It was easy to say they were Nazi traitors and the killing was an act of revenge, but things weren't always that clear. It could've been a convenient theft, a jealous husband, or a business rival. Never an investigation. Who was there to do it? The Germans destroyed everything and the liberating army had its own concerns. Where would they get the resources to investigate? So, just a quick burial. The chaos left openings for people to act on all the hatreds and jealousies they'd been holding in under the occupation."

Nora watched Aunt Julia unfold her napkin and adjust her knife and fork next to her plate following her unspoken criteria of things-in-place. When she seemed satisfied that her cutlery and thoughts were in order, she went on. "This part was different from the happy couples-kissing images of the liberation you see in all the picture books. I know so, because I was there. I saw it. Part of it, anyway. Of course, I was young, and you can't know what's going on in everyone's heads, but I could feel the confusion. The fear. The shame. The fury."

"I see. That sounds different from—"

"The collaborators were lucky so many of us were hungry and exhausted at the end that winter. People were completely worn out, no energy left to kill their Nazi sympathizer neighbors."

"But some did?" Nora asked.

Aunt Julia didn't answer right away. She thought for a moment about what to say. "Most of the attention in the first months after the liberation went to the higher ups. The greater the crime, the more attention was paid to the form of the trial. The bigwigs got a process, with lawyers for the prosecution and a defense and witnesses and the whole thing."

"Well, that seems—"

Aunt Julia lifted her eyes and fixed Nora with an intense look. "Does any of this surprise you? Nobody really talks about how we dealt with things after the war. I know, you probably have this idea of us Dutch people being all about order and reason and process. And some of that's true. The resistance was ready for this moment. They were organized. They knew who they were after. They started with the easy ones, I mean literally the easy ones, the *moffenhoeren*, the kraut whores. They—"

"Sorry to interrupt, but did your mother have anything to say about that? Wasn't she an important figure in the resistance?" Nora was genuinely curious, but also meant to break things up. Better to not let Aunt Julia dominate the conversation too one-sidedly.

Aunt Julia gaze became vacant, glazed over in thought. Finally, she said, "Not as important as all that. The men were the ones who did all the political work, if you see what I mean."

"I know exactly what you mean," Nora said. "She was important, but limited in what she could do. She had to influence things indirectly."

"*Precies*! Except there's more to it than that. Things were also decentralized. Out of anyone's control. All through the occupation, there were people who collected information, even risking their lives for it. Ordinary people. Especially people who were good at making lists. Accountants. Bureaucrats. Stuck at home with nothing to do, they looked out their windows and made their lists. Saw the girls flirting and laughing. Made a note. Followed up with inquiries. 'Who was that girl I saw on such-and-such street with the German soldier yesterday?' 'What did she look like?' But most of the time they knew her already. Watched her grow up. Sometimes there was jealously involved. Why does she like that handsome German—and not me? A list is more than a list. They're artefacts of passion. Right after the liberation, I mean within hours, the lists came out. They were shared among Resistance Council leaders. With the Germans gone, the different resistance groups got together and formed the Binnenlandse Strijdkrachten, the interior armed forces."

Aunt Julia paused for thought, then continued. "Funny, but now that I think of it, there was a fairly clear divide, the women accused sex crimes, the men of political crimes. Usually, the men got away with a public apology. Swearing allegiance to Queen Wilhelmina or the flag or both. No haircuts. No tar. The Nazi NSB party came to stand for '*niet zo* (or so) *bedoeld*' or 'I didn't mean it.' They were paraded to the square at the city hall with their hands in the air, sometimes alongside the girls. Made to give their confession. Most of the time, these were just stupid kids attracted by the uniform. It fed into the whole ideology, the ego inflation. You did up those buttons and it made you a different person.

"The resistance members all got together with the lists—now with no Germans to be afraid of—and the girls were rounded up and taken to the plaza in front of city hall. Lord knows what happened to them before they got there. When you call someone a Nazi whore, it gives you permission to do anything. You start with the label that makes people not human, just like the Nazis did. At the chosen time, they were taken out of the basements where they'd been locked up and marched to the people's court at gunpoint with their hands behind their heads. A member of the Resistance Council presided, as though it was an actual hearing. But it was really all about public shaming. Just like in medieval times. You know, the sort of thing you do research on, Nora, except without the stocks and the witch burnings. The tribunal *was* the punishment. The Resistance Council sent someone there to watch or preside just to make sure it didn't get out of hand, but mostly it was just an organized mob."

"Did you ever see one of these tribunals? Nora asked. "Were you ever there?"

The question seemed to startle Aunt Julia. Before she could reply, the bartender came with their tea and coffee and told Aunt Julia that her salad was on its way. Aunt Julia thanked him and languidly put the tea in the pot to steep. This done, she continued talking, now with her memories in order.

"This is what happened. I went to one of these meetings out of curiosity. I didn't intend to stay long. Just have a look, see what all the fuss was about. And there was Arie."

"Arie?"

"My eldest brother. Peter's father. Presiding."

"Of course. What a shock that must've been."

"He never told me he'd be doing this. I guess it just fell to him. Maybe he volunteered at the last minute. Anyway, he was clearly enjoying himself. He tried to make it theatrical, but he laughed too much, like a bad comedian. 'Look who we have here, a young woman with a taste for Germans. Yum! Ha! Ha!' That sort of thing. I didn't stay long. I couldn't. Just one case, if you want to call it that. The accused was a girl with eyes, so, so light, and her hair dark, hanging down in waves past her shoulders.

Arie asked, 'Who knows her?' and someone said, 'I do!' and the next question was, 'Did you see her with a German?' and the answer that came from somewhere in the crowd was, 'Yes!' and from someone else, 'She's a whore!' and farther back in the crowd, 'She's carrying that Moff's baby.' And that was enough. Case closed. There were cheers when the hair came off. People spat on her and called her things that I don't want to repeat. A bucket of tar was passed forward. She was expressionless when her hair came off. Arie grinned as he applied the brush, covering her ears, down to the shoulders of her fine wool coat, ruining it. No, come to think of it, she was just really sad-looking. When Arie brushed the tar over the rough stubble and the bleeding nicks on her head, she sobbed, and that set the crowd off even more. 'Hoorah!' 'More!' 'You missed a spot!' And Arie looked at them for encouragement. When the job was done to his satisfaction he said, 'There you go, all ready to go out whoring again. Good luck finding a German to fuck. Ha! Ha!' And she walked through the crowd, holding her arms in close, hugging herself for the comfort she couldn't find from anyone else."

"Did you ever tell Arie about what you saw?"

"Of course! Later, at the dinner table, I mentioned it. Arie just said, 'I did them a favor' and wouldn't say more. I couldn't understand. This was the man who just a few months earlier had his arm around the shoulder of an SS officer singing patriotic German songs."

"Are you saying that Arie fraternized with German officers?"

"Well, yes. That's another story, but yes. I saw him. To my mind, what he did cozying up to those men was much, much worse than the women acting on the impulses of love with an ordinary German soldier. And yet, here he was, feeling good about himself for what he did to those poor girls."

"That makes me wonder how he treated Peter. As a father."

Aunt Julia followed her own train of thought. "Some people have no direction of their own. They turn with the wind. They act on their advantage in the moment. I have this feeling that if the family didn't put Arie into the resistance, he would've been one of those who put on an

NSB uniform and later had to make their confessions in the public square."

"If that's so, do you think it's possible he ever worked for the Germans? I mean as an informer?"

Either Aunt Julia didn't want to answer or other memories crowded out the question. She ignored it and continued. "The next day on my way to shop for food I passed three young women with their hair still on, so before their public judgment. They stood close together, holding a big sign that said, *I am a traitor*. I couldn't help wondering whether this, too, was the work of Arie. Maybe not. There were lots of people involved. You see, the idea was to get the shame into their heads."

"Shame is part of the aftermath almost everywhere," Nora observed. "It's part of the curriculum of mass killing." She left unspoken the fact that she saw the same thing in her work on the late Middle Ages: A public spectacle to impose power, restore a sense of order. Shame and an excruciating death for the accused. In the Netherlands after the war, it wasn't about the people walking by and reading the sign that said, *I am a traitor*. The words were pointed outward toward the passersby. But their *real* sense, their *real* purpose and intent, was going the other way, to the ones holding the sign. The women, the *moffenhoren*, were supposed to understand who *they* were in a different way: *I am a traitor*. And they were supposed to know that *everyone else* knew that about them. The whole world could see them. Could see that part of them that was a traitor.

Aunt Julia tapped the table to get Nora's attention. "Some killed themselves while their hair was still short. I don't know how many. Nobody kept records."

Nora stopped recording. She wanted to say something to Aunt Julia, but couldn't find her way past a swirl of questions—why was Arie Dekker friendly with the Germans and then a sadist toward the women? Was he a collaborator? What was it like for Peter, growing up with that man as his father?—which eventually formed into one: Who is Arie Dekker?

CHAPTER 10: SIDI MAHMOUD

From their place on the rooftop, Peter could see the old part of the city, a treeless jumble of mudbrick and concrete-block rooftops. Some *banco* walls of family compounds had eroded from last year's rain and crumbled into the narrow passageways, perhaps a sign the owners had fled.

The sun sat low on the horizon. With the effects of the sandstorm now dissipated, the sun did its work through a thin, yellow-brown haze. Light and shadow covered the ancient city and sent shimmers from the distant surface of the Niger. The burning breath of harmattan wind tapered down, a signal of changing seasons. There was a promise of good things in the shadows and light. Soon, the rains would come. The Niger would slowly swell with the seed of rain. Boats would rise and float, now able to make the journey north. The first would struggle to find the open waterway and occasionally run aground on sandbars. They would meander their way, the pilot looking for the deepest channels and the crew helping, leaning over the bow to peer into the water, feeling their way with depth-measuring poles. The boats would bring precious cargo, abundance beyond the desultory offerings of dry-season trucks: sacks of rice, pots of ghee butter, and fruit from the south, untasted for months, bananas, mangoes, and succulent tree-ripened oranges.

Goma made tea on the rooftop terrace. He fanned a handful of coals to life with a scrap of cardboard while Peter stood in reverie as he looked out over the rooftop wall. The coals glowed, nestled in a bent-wire basket made from recycled radial tires. A small enamel pot sat on the coals. Two glasses, slightly larger than shot glasses, waited for the pouring. Beside them sat a bowl of dates.

"I thought we should start with the shrines and mausoleums," Peter said. "Get some images of destruction."

The coals hissed as tea boiled out the spout. Goma reached for the handle and burned the tips of his fingers.

"Aaaw!"

It surprised Peter that someone who expertly made tea the same way three times a day could still burn his fingers.

Goma shook his hand in the air, tore a corner from the cardboard he'd used to fan the coals, and folded it as a potholder. He skillfully poured a thin stream, holding the teapot a full metre above the glass. It made loose foam on top of the dark tea. Then he opened the potlid and poured the tea in to boil more. The first serving had to be black. Peter remembered this ritual, enacted many times when he lived with the Tuaregs as a student. The main thing was, it had to be well boiled, strong.

"Yes. We could go to the shrines," Goma said. "Maybe start with Sidi Mahmoud."

Peter had committed to memory an inventory of the shrines destroyed by the Ansar Eddine during the occupation. "Right. The shrine that some thought could bring rain. Maybe the most important of the UNESCO sites." He wanted Goma to know he had done his homework.

Goma nodded. "We could also talk to some people."

"Who, for instance? The people who shot the videos? Do you know who they are?"

"I'll introduce you," Goma said, leaving things vague.

Peter sat on a cushion opposite Goma and took a date from the bowl. With the date already in his mouth, he wondered what to do with the pit. He had eaten plenty of dates in the desert, but never faced date-eating manners on the rooftop of someone's home. It might be rude to put the pit on the floor or back in the bowl of dates. Spitting it over the wall was out of the question. Goma watched him closely and slid the piece of cardboard with the torn corner toward him. Peter spat the pit discreetly into his palm and deposited it on the cardboard.

Goma added sugar to the boiling tea. He poured it back and forth between the pot and a glass until it was foamy. Then he slid the glass to Peter, indicating it was ready.

Peter savoured the loud harmony of sugar and tea tannins. It had been years since he'd last been served a concentrated, caffeinated glass of tea like this. He'd missed it.

Goma added more water to the pot. He slurped his tea loudly, holding the glass gingerly with his burnt fingers. "I've got someone in mind," he said. "Would you like to meet a marabout? Not just one of those who makes gris-gris to bring health, find love, success on exams, stuff like that. The one I mean is a great man."

"How could I say no to that?"

Goma took a date from the bowl, chewed it a few times and spat the pit vigorously over the rooftop wall into the street. He turned to look back at Peter and smiled.

Peter laughed quietly, unsure how to take Goma's lesson in date-eating manners. His unfamiliarity with the day-to-day felt like having his status reduced to that of an honorary child. Albeit one who towered over everyone else.

Ibrahim shouted a greeting from the main entrance. It was time to start work. Peter went into his room and tied the mosquito net above his mattress to keep any insects from finding their way in during the day. He exchanged his cowhide sandals for running shoes. There might be thorns long enough to stab through the sole in the sand around the ruins. He shook the shoes upside down just in case a scorpion or, worse, a viper decided his shoe was a nice refuge. Satisfied that his shoes held no tenants, he put them on and tied the laces. He then slathered on a thick application of sunscreen. The air was dry, and his skin would crack and burn without it. He crouched over his camera bag and switched on the Leica to double check the batteries, then swung the bag over his shoulder and hurried down the stairs.

Goma had already left.

Peter was almost out the door when he felt an urgent, stabbing need to defecate. Maybe the strong tea was the cause of his discomfort. The toilet was a second-storey outhouse with a concrete floor, *banco* walls and an open doorway facing away from the stairs. There was a rectangular hole in the middle of the floor, next to it a plastic water jug shaped like a tea pot and a bar of soap with lengthways cracks.

He dropped his pants and crouched over the hole. A good thing he'd kept up with his yoga. He heard the stool drop into the pit with a damp thud a second after his bowels released. He felt nauseated. A cockroach the size of a man's thumb crawled out of the hole between his feet. Peter leapt up with his pants and underwear tight across his knees. The cockroach scampered across the floor to a corner in the wall. He calmed himself. Just a roach. He'd seen these before. He sat back down on his haunches. The rest of his shit came out as yellow foam. Not a good sign. He rinsed using the water jug, soaping his anus with his left hand and rinsing again. The sound of the water falling came back dully from the bottom of the pit like heavy raindrops in a bog.

If he was going to have diarrhea, he'd have to take something to stop it. He found his medical kit in his bag in the bedroom and brought out the Imodium. The directions said one pill. He took two.

His thermos was nearly empty. Where did Goma's family keep the water? They had been good hosts, with tea regularly offered, but he hadn't noted where the water came from. He went room to room and finally found a cistern under the stairs where the floor and walls were sheltered from sun and dust. The porous low-fired clay sweated imperceptibly, just enough to cool the water inside. Peter took off the lid and peered in to dip the ladle. His reflection came back as a dark shape, deformed by the moving surface of the water. The drops that spilled from his thermos sounded hollow, a pool in a wet cavern.

The horn of the Land Cruiser sounded from the street. Peter tightened the lid of the thermos, hurried out of the house, and turned the histrionic key in the lock. He had barely closed the rear door of the Land Cruiser when Ibrahim started the motor and drove off like a getaway driver at a heist.

"Why don't we start with Sidi Mahmoud?" Goma said to Ibrahim, while bouncing in the front seat. He had to shout over the roar of the engine.

They stopped at a UN peacekeeper's checkpoint (one of three in the immediate neighborhood, according to Ibrahim), supported by a 50-caliber machine gun atop a white VAB armored personnel carrier marked 'U.N.' on each side and front and back. A peacekeeper recognized Ibrahim, exchanged a few pleasantries, checked their passports all the same, but in a perfunctory way, and waved them through. After driving a short distance, they arrived at the pile of rubble that had once been the Sidi Mahmoud shrine.

Peter scanned the rooftops of the surrounding buildings and surveyed the scene. The light was perfect, the shadows just long enough to make the broken mud-bricks stand out. They were in the northern part of the city where the buildings were not as tightly spaced. On the perimeter of the graveyard were a few spindly acacias and thorn bushes with the lower leaves thinned by goats. The gravestones were unadorned rocks, red-brown shale dug into the ground as markers. They were for loved ones to mourn for a while, but meant to be eventually forgotten. Remembrance would be in stories, passed through the generations. An open area on the opposite side of the ruin had once served as a prayer ground to honor the saint, but equally to honor life and the living, to supplicate for blessings. Above all, though, the prayers were to bring rain, which the jihadists considered a mortal sin. UNESCO recognized the site for its illustrious history, something that, for the officials in Paris, made it the heritage of the world. There were tourists who flocked for the heritage label and the mystique of the city's history as a place of learning, kept secret from Europe for centuries. To them, there was a romantic appeal to the blue men of the desert—so called because of the indigo dyes they put in their clothes that transferred sun-protective staining to the skin. But, to those who understood, the real significance of the shrine was for the people who lived here, as a source of benediction, of sacred power, a focal point for hope in an insecure world.

From the websites Peter had studied at his desk in The Hague, the mausoleum had once been an unadorned, windowless rectangular block, two metres high and four metres long. Its only purpose was to house the remains of the great sixteenth century Berber scholar Sidi Mahmoud Ben Amar. He imagined the tourists who once flocked here and wondered what must've gone through their minds coming all this way only to find a mud-brick box as a major attraction. How many would have been curious? How many would have understood? From their perspective, whatever weird thing the awesome nomads did was cool. If they wanted to worship a box with a dead person inside, 'I wanna see that'.

Now Peter stood in front of its ruin. He remembered seeing it intact during his stay in Timbuktu years ago. If anything, there was more emotion in the rubble than when the bricks were in place. There was sorrow in it, maybe something like members of his own family must've felt when the Nazis looted their museums and destroyed all the 'decadent' art. Except the Nazis made a few bonfires for show and kept most treasures for themselves. They stole jewelry, ceramics, works by Pieter Breugel the Elder, Gustav Klimt, and Max Beckman, and others. They took things that appealed to the narrow taste of their failed-artist Fuhrer. They took over a half million pieces, many never recovered. The Nazis had the gall to call the military division in charge of the looting the Kunstschutz, the "art protectors." Was their desecration in any way comparable to the destruction of the shrines in Mali? In a way, the Nazis had a specific vision of their civilization, stole what they liked, and destroyed the rest. It was a different sort of crime than the wholesale destruction of religious relics by iconoclasts. The holier the saint, and the more people prayed to him, the readier they were to violate his tomb.

What made the shrines so important to Ansar Eddine that they had to pull them down? What did they stand to gain if there was nothing to steal? What made the pick- and axe-wielders in the videos so energized before fatigue set in?

No doubt they started by taking out the bones and scattering them in the desert. That would disperse the saints' sacred power. Otherwise, the worshippers would just build another mud-brick box to keep them in.

Did the jihadists believe the magic of the shrine didn't exist, or just that it was wrong? Probably that it was wrong, polytheism. Not from the one God, which meant the bones still had power. The saint was alive to his worshippers. If that were so, it would make the crime of destroying this heritage something different entirely, not a war crime against property, but more like the kidnapping and murder of a sacred being. What went through the minds of the desecrators when they drove to the desert with the bones? Did the spirit of Sidi Mahmoud whisper to them? Promise revenge? Maybe, as with so many kidnappings, they would've felt pleasure in domination. They would've minimized the saint's importance, his accomplishments, as a salve to their own sense of insignificance.

The broken walls differed from the bones they once protected. They were just a ruin. Or were they? Was there once magic in this pile of dirt? The clips from *France 24* and *Al-Jazeera* showed the mausoleum's dismantling done with gusto, with picks, axes, and sledgehammers. Now it was a pile of rubble and dirt, the color of the sand on which it was built. The smooth tree-trunk-beams that once held up the roof lay haphazardly alongside the rubble. With the wind and rain of the coming season, everything would soon merge with the earth.

Peter slung his bag off his shoulder. The first step would be to get measurements. While Goma held the tape at the edge of the rubble pile, Peter paced out to the perimeter, looking for the farthest scattered pieces of broken brick. He cracked opened the spine of a new hardcover notebook and jotted down the measurements. Then, realizing he needed more context, he sought the shade of an acacia tree and sat. Goma wound up the tape measure while Peter sketched a detailed aerial view of the scene, with the measurement figures assigned to lines showing where they were taken. When he finished and looked up, he saw Goma and Ibrahim leaning on the Land Cruiser, smoking.

Peter took out the Leica and set it up on a unipod, extending the telescoping pole as far as it could go to keep from having to bend over too far. He started with panoramic images to capture the scene as a whole. He shouted to Goma and Ibrahim to move out of one of his shots. Ibrahim backed the Land Cruiser down the street and Goma followed on foot. Peter took the wide shot he had set up and checked the viewfinder to make sure it had worked. With a resolution of twenty million megapixels, he could zoom in and the clarity seemed to stay the same. He then took the camera off the unipod and moved closer to the ruin, getting images from different angles. He looked for marks on the broken mud brick made by a pick and eventually found one in an ideal location close to the ground. A 90-degree ruler placed next to the hole in the brick would give the dimensions. It would at least give forensics something to work with, match the mark with the likely tool. Linkage data. It would connect the scene on the ground with the video they had in the evidence archive. Confirm for the court that the videos weren't faked, protection against the possibility of a luddite judge who'd never seen this sort of evidence before. He nudged the ruler into just the right place and took the picture with the camera propped on his knee. He looked at the image in the viewfinder. Whoever swung that pick couldn't have known someone would come here before the next rains to gather evidence for a trial in The Hague.

* * *

The plan for the afternoon was for Ibrahim to drive the women to their various interviews to spare them the walking they'd been doing through the sandy streets. Kella had called early that morning to make the request. Goma had the volume on his phone up enough so Peter could hear. She'd been persuasive. Why should the men have a driver and the women not? What was so special about this white *toubab* investigator from the ICC with the long legs? Walking would be easier for him. It wasn't just the fatigue of the long distances that made it difficult for the women to get to their interviews. The main thing was, they didn't want to be seen passing in front of the compounds of families that still supported the insurgency. The younger men of these families, the outwardly dangerous ones, might now be camped out in the desert where their insurgency lingered, but that still left the older women. The insurgency's matrons weren't dangerous for this Canadian with the long white legs. They were dangerous to other women.

Peter had to admit, she had a point. The power of the matriarchs was in their words, creating alliances and dissolving them, building and destroying reputations. Even with the grief of their losses, with sons and husbands killed in battle, there were those who remained true believers, loyal to the movement. When it came down to it, behind their veils, the matrons were the supporting act, the whisperers in the ears of the men who wielded the AKs.

That left Peter and Goma in need of transport. It was a problem easily solved. Goma borrowed a motorcycle from a cousin for the afternoon. When presented with the Honda 250 as their mode of transport, Peter instinctively looked for a helmet, saw that of course there was none, and awkwardly swung a leg over to sit in the rear. His feet struggled to find the pegs and his legs splayed out sideways. Goma turned the throttle. The weight of the camera bag pulled Peter sideways.

"Now I take you to my marabout," Goma shouted over his shoulder.

"Shouldn't we be doing interviews?" Peter asked.

"This is an interview. You'll see."

The old man stood when he saw the motorcycle approaching. Even though he knew only a few words of their greeting in Tamashek, Peter understood that Goma and the marabout knew each other well. As soon as Goma had the kickstand on firm ground next to the house, he and the Marabout hugged and stood with hands on each other's shoulders. The old man brought the greeting to a close with, "*Al-hamd ul-Allah*," God be praised.

Goma introduced Peter to the marabout in Tamashek. His name was Muhammad At-Taher. Peter expected a mere handshake to follow, and was surprised when At-Taher held his outstretched hand in both of his. They were dry and thickly calloused, like the bark of a tree. He held Peter's gaze the same way he held his hands, without letting go, searching, to the point of discomfort. Peter squirmed inwardly and wanted to pull away, but knew that a simple gesture of refusal like that might cause offense, damage his connection with the old man irreparably. Maybe with Goma, too. The marabout's eyes stood out, framed by the green turban wrapped amply over his head and across his mouth and nose. They were dark and moist, a contrast with the deep, dry crevasses of his face. "*Bienvenue*," At-Taher said in French, breaking his gaze. "*Ijliss*," he added in Arabic with a gesture to the cushions arranged in a semi-circle on the straw mat. There was an open Koran on top of one of the cushions. Peter sat next to it. He wanted to be close to the old man, not relegated to the outside.

At-Taher had erected a comfortable desert encampment outside a modest *banco* house on the perimeter of the city. It had a canopy set on wooden poles with canvas walls on each side that could be rolled up and down, depending on the direction of the wind. There were straw mats laid out to cover the sand, an ample number of cushions, and next to them a loosely folded Fulani blanket, the kind woven in thin strips on a portable loom before being stitched together. The checkerboard pattern was black and white in the centre, then exploded outward in vibrant squares of blue, green, and orange.

This is a place of nomads, Peter noted. Should a sandstorm come, everything could be packed up and moved into the house in minutes.

Goma was a different person in At-Taher's presence. He seemed at ease, even with the inconvenience of translating the old man's Tamashek for Peter. He smiled and laughed before his expression became serious and he turned to Peter to speak At-Taher's words.

"The marabout talked about his love of the desert, the peace to be found there," Goma said. "What it means to be alone with your thoughts, taking care of your animals for days and weeks at a time. It isn't something he has to do. There are others who are herders. But it is sometimes good to be alone. He has memories from a long life and his Koran for company. Even here in the city, he prefers to sleep outside if he can. The *banco* house is good for shelter, but suffocating if one stays there too long."

Peter nodded. He remembered being with Tuaregs in the desert, but couldn't imagine wanting to be alone there.

Goma made tea while At-Taher talked. Peter wondered how much boiled tea it was humanly possible to drink. He already felt the onset of an involuntary twitch in the corner of his eye, likely from the caffeine. His stomach roiled ominously. His bowels were probably blocked up with the Imodium.

There was a lull in the conversation and a long silence while Goma and At-Taher looked vacantly to the ground. The silence made Peter uncomfortable, with the same feeling of a too-long handshake; of wanting to move on, wanting something else to happen.

Goma broke the silence by pouring the tea back and forth from the pot to a glass, raising the foam to the point that it spilled over the sides.

"We went to Sidi Mahmound this morning." Peter said. He spoke basic Tamashek, acquired during his days as a graduate student, but was rusty.

At-Taher nodded. His eyes narrowed.

"We'd like to hear about what you saw," Goma said. "When they destroyed it." He poured out three glasses of tea and handed one to At-Taher.

At-Taher sat pensively holding his glass. His eyes looked inward. Then he spoke in elegant Tamashek, too quickly for Peter to follow.

Goma turned to Peter. "He says it was just after the noon prayer. I think they chose that time so that people would be there. They brought picks, axes, sledge hammers and ladders on the back of their pickup truck. There was a young man who tried to stop them. He doesn't remember his name." Goma turned to At-Taher to indicate the translation was complete.

At-Taher continued. His voice raised and quavered. His eyes moistened with tears.

He paused and Goma translated. "They beat the man and tied him and threw him in the back of the truck. Then they went to work with their equipment. People wept. They fell on their knees. There was nothing anyone could say or do to stop them. It's as though they were possessed by evil spirits."

Peter asked, "Do you remember what they did with the man they tied up? Did they drive away with him?"

Goma translated.

The answer from At-Taher was brief. "They let him go when they were done."

"Was anyone in charge? Did anyone give orders?"

As At-Taher answered, Goma's eyes widened. They had a long exchange in which he forgot to translate for Peter.

"What did he say?" Peter asked at the first silence.

"He said the head of all the destruction was a man called Al-Mahdi. He was in charge of everything to do with destroying the shrines."

"Did he say anything else? Wait. Hang on." Peter brought his phone out of his pocket and played a video of a man shouting orders at men on ladders swinging picks at the wall of a shrine. He paused it when the exact image he was looking for came up, where the man stops shouting and turns to look directly into the camera, smiling, proud of his work. He handed it to At-Taher with the image on the screen.

At-Taher looked closely at the phone. He put his hand over it to get rid of the glare and nodded. "*Aiwa*, Al-Mahdi." He handed back the phone with a look of contempt.

They finished their tea in silence. Peter felt the thrill of a breakthrough in his work on the case. Now his investigation of the destruction of the monuments had a purpose. Not just photography and measurements. He was building a case. They had a perpetrator and a name. A man brought down by his own ego. Proud of making women weep. Glorifying in domination. With their use of video, they're indicting themselves! And now he had the beginning of witness testimony to back it up. He'd leave a message for Ferman at headquarters as soon as they got back to the house. Call Nora, too.

At-Taher was pensive. Peter sensed the mood and quieted his inner ebullience. Maybe it was the image on my iPhone, he thought. There were men with picks, axes and sledgehammers in the background. It must've touched a nerve. Maybe I should've warned At-Taher when I handed the phone over. He didn't seem fragile, but still . . .

Goma added sugar to the pot and waited for it to boil for the third pouring. They finished their tea in silence.

At-Taher brightened during their goodbyes. He stood next to his encampment and watched as they climbed on the motorcycle.

Peter spoke to Goma softly near his ear. "We should come back for a recorded interview. We need to make this official."

"Already done," Goma said. He reached in his pocket, held up his iPhone, and waved it for effect.

"You recorded it?"

"With his permission. Now I just need to write it up. I'll get his signature on the witness form tomorrow."

"Goma, you are an angel from heaven!"

Goma gave a dark glance back at Peter and kicked the motor to life. He shouted over the motor noise as he turned the throttle. "You shouldn't say things like that. I'm only a humble servant of God."

CHAPTER 11: THE RAPE OF TIMBUKTU

The more Peter learned about the interviews other team members were doing, the more he respected them. They followed such a clearly defined division of labor they almost never saw each other. Following the sexual segregation of conservative religion, the women only interviewed female victims and the men interviewed men. The boxes on the interview form (check one), male or female, acted as a guardian of faith. But the investigators' reasoning was different: to establish trust, avoid provoking the wrong kinds of memories, with the women especially. In this way at least, there was a match between local sensibilities and ICC protocols.

Then there were questions of investigative process; how to make things stick when probed and tested by the defense. This was a little trickier. Everyone on the team knew that the Office of the Prosecutor had a strict rule against translated witness statements. Defense lawyers were sure to single-mindedly pick holes in the statements, question the credentials of the translator, get their own language experts to find mistakes, mistranslations. Even a small inconsistency would throw everything else into doubt. Ostensibly, it was all about the rule of law, but in actuality it was something more. Reputation. Status. Not to mention, the prestige of their firm. Career. Money. They were motivated. To foreclose the possibility of a flaw in the testimony, the interviewer had to be fluent in the language and dialect of the witness and their notes had to be written in the language in which they were spoken.

The result, Peter learned, was an investigative team of polyglots. Aside from French, and in Goma's case, English, each investigator spoke at least two other languages, Tamashek, Songhai, Fulfulde, or Bambara. They did most interviews in people's homes, preferably in private rooms where the witnesses would be more comfortable. Some victims came to the office to give evidence, furtively, not wanting to be seen going in. There were eyes everywhere. Assumptions were twisted into convictions. Peter could easily imagine their voices, what they whispered. "Look, there she goes, talking to the investigators." "What do you think her story is?" "Do you think she went with the men willingly?" "Do you think it was a real marriage?" "Do you think she's telling them lies? Is she trying to make up for her lost honor?"

The people who stood in doorways or peered over walls watching and listening were open about their curiosity, almost advertising it. The hard-edged gossip of Timbuktu was a spy game, but without a pretense of casualness when tailing a mark.

***

Peter had the motorcycle to himself while Ibrahim drove Goma to the homes of men wanting to give statements. He was rusty. It'd been years since he rode. He stalled a few times before he learned to ease the clutch gradually.

He followed Goma's directions, got lost, and retraced his route. He nearly drove past the building a second time when he caught sight of the wooden tent pole propped next to the door as a marker. There was no sign, no placard in front, nothing proudly announcing the presence of the organization. The pole wasn't to hide the location of the office. It was simply to avoid the inflammatory effect of a sign. Almost everyone in Timbuktu knew the people working there were the ones talking to people, getting their stories. Many approved. A few, who felt strongly about it, didn't.

When he knocked on the sheet-metal door the sound reverberated as though he were conducting a police raid. The door opened a crack and part of Kella's face appeared, suspicious at first, then softening. She opened the door to let Peter in, then slammed it shut behind him and turned the key in the lock.

The room was lit from a single bare bulb. The electricity was working, for now. Probably an important factor in choosing the location. A woman with a brown headscarf sat at a roughly finished table. The adz marks and rough joints showed the furniture to be locally made by a craftsman using hand tools. In the middle of the table was a blank questionnaire, the same *formulaire* Vautour had gone through in Bamako. Next to it was a dogeared manilla folder. There were maybe a hundred pages inside it. The dossier was growing. It already looked like the beginnings of a case, if there ever was one. Yet, they weren't working with the energizing effect of an indictment. Everything was preliminary. Pending.

When Kella introduced them, Fatima held out her hand. It was soft, passive. Peter had to make a conscious effort not to hurt her with his grip.

Without thinking, she offered a greeting in her own language.

"*Aran kani baani*?"

She was Songhai, descended from the people who farmed the Niger's alluvial shores. Peter had done interviews in Songhai villages years ago as a student.

"*Baani Samey*." I am well, Peter responded.

Kella laughed. "*Wallahi*, where did you learn to speak Songhai?"

"I get around."

"We have no secrets from you," Fatima said.

Peter didn't want to admit the greeting was the limit of his knowledge of the language. He was relieved to see there was no tea on offer. Just water.

"I suppose you're curious about the interviews," Kella said.

"Absolutely."

"What we're finding, is that once the occupiers were secure in their power, they preyed on the women." Kella looked at Peter fiercely across the table.

"What do you mean by prey?" Peter asked.

"I mean that literally. The men who controlled the town took women and girls to satisfy their needs. It's what Goma said in the car, like hyenas hunting."

"They were systematically raped!" Fatima interjected. "There's no other way to call it."

Kella closed the folder on the table in front of her. "We're just getting started with the interviews, but things are already becoming clear."

"In what way?"

Kella sighed. "The leaders of Ansar Eddine promised every young man who joined their forces that they would get a wife. They made women and girls a recruitment tool."

"And not everyone agreed to their marriages?"

"Nobody agreed!" Fatima said.

Kella's eyes sparked with fury. "The men from Hesbah specialized in intimidation. They would drop in on families unannounced to get them to give over their daughters. They showed up with automatic rifles. Any girl who had her first menses was taken. Sometimes only eleven or twelve years old."

"So, the marriages were forced," Peter said. He felt blood rush to his face from anger without an outlet.

"Normally a marriage is something to be celebrated," Kella said. "There's feasting and singing. This is how it is with the Tuaregs, the Kunta, the Songhay, the Fulani. Everyone. The couple is joined in happiness. That's not what happened here." She tapped the folder.

Fatima reached for the folder and opened it. She leafed through the interview notes until she found the page she was looking for. She held it up to read. The top corners trembled in her hands. "Here. This one. The girl was taken away at gunpoint to satisfy the needs of a man who called himself her husband."

"Did you get a name?"

"No name. She was afraid."

"Afraid of what?" Peter knew the question was naïve, but asked it anyway.

Fatima sighed. "That if he was arrested others would retaliate. In her statement it just says the parents were forced, the girl was forced. He felt he owned—"

"I see." Peter realized he had interrupted only when Fatima fixed her gaze at him.

"Then when she came back to her family," she continued, "she'd lost her honor."

"Lost her honor?" This Peter found genuinely puzzling.

"They made all this seem normal by oppressing us with rules." Kella quickly moved away from Peter's question.

"What rules?" he asked. He'd keep things simple, return to the honor question later.

"I mean punishing women for not wearing the veil, or not wearing it properly, not covering their hands or feet, walking with a man who wasn't her husband, even being seen with a brother-in-law." Fatima paused. "Selling things in the market, too. They took away their livelihood. Kept them prisoners at home."

Kella reached for the dossier and leafed through it. "The Islamic Police constantly looked around for people to punish. Mostly women."

"What sort of punishment?"

"I was just going to answer that," Kella snapped. Peter could see she was on edge. "Here, I spoke to this young woman with her mother a few days ago. Her veil had slipped down while she was washing clothes. A man from Hesbah saw it and reported it to the Islamic Police. She was arrested and held for two days in prison before they took her to their court."

She wouldn't say what happened to her in prison, so we didn't get that part of it," Fatima said.

Kella flipped through the loose pages of the dossier without apparent purpose, distracted. "She was given a sentence of fifty lashes in the public market. By the end, she was unable to stand. She just hung by the ropes they tied her with."

"One of the worst parts of it," Fatima added, "is how the women were treated by their families afterward. Some said their families rejected them. They were suspected. They thought the girls didn't resist."

Peter nodded. Here it was again, the question of honor. He didn't have to bring it up. If ever there was a case, it would hinge on this. The defense would say the women and girls went along willingly.

With no signal between them, Kella put words to Peter's thoughts. "The Islamists are saying their so-called wives went with their so-called husbands willingly. No abduction. No rape."

Fatima slouched in her chair with her arms crossed, Peter couldn't tell whether from resignation or indignation. "So now people think of them as joiners. Responsible for everything that happened."

"What do you mean by everything?" Peter sensed that what Kella and Fatima had just told him was only the beginning. He felt himself torn between sympathetic revulsion at the stories he was hearing and a small spark of ardency. They could well have the makings of a war crimes case.

"The prison's another part of the story," Kella said. Sometime around six months into the occupation, they turned the bank into a women's prison. Some of the women held there say they were kept in cells two metres by two metres. No mattress. The guards didn't even give them anything for their needs. They sat for days in their own dirt."

Peter took a deep breath. It was the ultimate form of dehumanization. Force them into a condition of pollution. Then that state of inhumanity and degradation justified anything.

"We're pretty sure they were raped in the prison," Kella continued. "So far nobody wants to talk about it. The shame is too much."

"I don't want to think about what we'll find out when we talk to more women," Fatima said.

"I think you'd better prepare for the worst," Peter said.

"What kind of talk is that?" Kella snapped. "What could be worse than what these women have gone through."

"I didn't mean, I—"

"You and your monuments! Mud and bones! Listen to what these women have told us! Listen to their suffering! How will we ever recover from this?"

"But, I—"

"What does your court care? It doesn't! Go take your pictures. But remember the living. We too have been turned to rubble."

Peter understood her anger. He felt it, too. "I promise, I'll remember," he said.

* * *

Ibrahim drove Peter to Goma's house for the time of the *sieste*. With the change of season, the sun was getting hot and people took the midday break more seriously. Men walked home with the loose shoulders of their *boubous* draped over their heads for shade. Their sleep was sometimes deeper in the early afternoon than at night, full of dreams. To disturb someone in a *sieste* was tantamount to ringing a doorbell at three in the morning.

The house appeared empty. The women had retired to their rooms. Goma wasn't there, probably working or resting where he was a guest doing interviews. To Peter, the quiet house was welcome. It gave him a few hours alone; time to get his notes in order. He would transfer his pictures to an external hard drive, and, if the connection worked, call Nora. He wanted to hear her voice and feel the confused ache of loneliness and connection, like the itch of a healing wound. He'd start with the usual, "I just wanted to hear your voice. I miss you." She would reply, "Ooh, *schatje*, I wish you were here," and work toward something else. Maybe those simple opening words were what it was all about.

Once the photos were transferred, he called Nora. She picked up after two rings. The first part of their conversation was just as he imagined it. Then it became sombre. "I've heard so many stories about women being tortured and violated," Peter said. "I'm beginning to feel like a perpetrator. I can't get an erection in the morning without thinking about rape."

"That isn't you. You're good to me."

"I get that, on one level. But this is out of my control," Peter confessed. "The stories have power. I can't really explain. They take over the way you see the world."

There was only so much Nora could do to commiserate. She tried anyway. "The fact that it bothers you is a sign of your goodness."

There was a pause before Peter said, "I think this place is getting to me."

"It's the only reasonable response to being where you are."

Their back-and-forth was a contest between the despair closing in on Peter and the affirmation that Nora rallied against it. The forces were equally matched and they both felt themselves tire from the tug-of-war. Then Nora said simply, "I miss you, *guppy'tje*," and the world-weariness fell from Peter, and he was overtaken by thoughts of the future, of Nora and their lives together. They texted a few lines after saying goodbye, the ordinary things that millions of people text to each other, like how much they missed each other, the places they'd visit when Peter got back, the train versus a rental car. Without being fully aware of it, it was this simple company, this letting go of cleverness and instead saying the mundane, that pulled Peter out of his funk.

And, like so many of these other lovers, he and Nora ended with an exchange of ♥

CHAPTER 12: VISITORS

"You know," Aunt Julia began, "whenever I see something about the war on TV, it gives me nightmares." She paused with her blue eyes darting back and forth as she thought her way forward. "There's always something about war movies that doesn't seem right."

She and Nora were in Aunt Julia's living room. Toen was perched on Nora's shoulder, allowing her to stroke his head with the back of her finger. There was no coffee or tea, no biscuits or *spekulaas* cookies. Aunt Julia was all business today, with something to say. Nora's phone was on the table with the recording function on. Pushing up against Nora's finger as she petted him, Toen was the most relaxed in the room. He treated Nora as a familiar figure now, someone safe. The feeling was mutual. The softness of his head-feathers on the back of her finger calmed her while Aunt Julia struggled to find words.

Aunt Julia looked down at her hands in her lap. "What I really wanted to tell you about was New Year's Eve, 1944," she said. Her breathing came faster. "I came home from the market and we had unwanted guests. No warning. No car parked outside. The first thing I noticed when I walked in the door was the smell of leather. And then I looked up and there they were, three men from the Waffen SS. I thought about that little joke that cost my teacher his life. That's the first thing that came to mind when I saw them in our living room with their muddy boots and their fine, double-breasted leather greatcoats. I didn't tell you that story, did

I? Yes? About my teacher who told jokes and went on trial and disappeared early in the war. I did?"

"Yes, you told me about that."

"Good. So, there they were in the living room. 'Oh', I said to myself, 'Here are the *essen waf waf*—the Waffen SS, like hungry dogs. Which they were. And then I thought about my teacher and what those words could do."

"You were frightened."

Aunt Julia didn't acknowledge the comment. She spoke from somewhere deep. "It wasn't hard to see who the leader was. He was bald with his remaining hair cut short so you could see the skin, and with dark puffiness under his eyes that went down to his cheekbones. A real Nazi. Not everyone who wore the uniform was, but him? No question. I remember thinking his face matched the Totenkopf insignia on his uniform. He took up the whole sofa with his arms across the back of it, with his coat open and a big smile, and he said something like, 'Ah, here is the *meisje* home from the market. Let's see what she's brought us,' and he sat there and gestured for me to open my bag, and when he saw that all I had were two onions, half a head of cabbage, and a few sprouted potatoes, his smile went away. 'No, no no!' he said. 'This is not a day for cabbage and potatoes! This will be a year of victory! We have to celebrate the coming year of victory and glory!'"

Nora noticed Aunt Julia's voice shift toward a German accent, and, a flamboyant wave of the arms. Toen opened his wings in response to her movement, then re-settled.

"I remember thinking this man was clearly out of his mind from not enough sleep. We didn't get much news, but we heard from Radio Oranje out of London that the war had turned and the Canadians weren't far away. I thought, these men probably have weeks or days to live and they want to celebrate victory. But instead, he said, 'Ach, I'm forgetting my manners. These are my *Kamaraden*', and he introduced me to the others, but now I forget their names. I do remember that one of them was dark-haired and handsome in a swaggering way—when he kissed my hand, he lingered over it even though I was just fourteen—and the other was a blond Dutchman young and strong looking, but awkward, the way young men sometimes are. He had a large Adam's apple and his eyes kept darting away. The officer kept referring to him proudly as '*unser Freiwilliger*'—our volunteer. You see, toward the war's end, there was a shortage of soldiers and the Waffen SS opened up to recruits from some occupied countries. He's a good example of the Dutchmen who joined. He was quiet, as though I could see through him, one *Nederlander* to another. The dark-haired one was not so shy. From the moment I walked in the door, he kept staring at me up and down.

"Ma stood in the kitchen door in her apron, her lips pressed tight together. The officer said, turning to her, 'Please don't be alarmed, but my men are tired and hungry, we're low on ammunition, and they can't be running around chasing geese. I would ask that everyone please stay inside until further notice.' He and the Freiwilliger went through the kitchen door and a moment later two explosions shook the windows. They came back with a limp, white goose dripping blood from its wingtip. The officer was happy and said, 'Look what a fine specimen we have for our feast.' And to my mother he added more quietly, 'I regret, *Mevrouw*, that there are a few others that did not come out quite so intact. I hope you can still make some use of them later.' He casually tossed the goose on the counter for her to pluck. He then pivoted on the balls of his feet and said, 'I have something else,' and came back with a bottle filled with cooking oil. At that time, this oil was something more precious than cognac."

"You already had shortages then?" Nora asked.

"Well, yes. Not nearly as bad as later in the worst of the Hunger Winter, but everything was already in short supply." She paused, staring, then continued. "The officer said something like, 'Do you by any chance have apples in storage?' And when my mother answered that we did, he pounded the table. 'We shall have *Apfelklöße*!' He asked about other ingredients. One of the geese had indeed produced an egg that morning, the last of its time on this earth, and we had just enough flour left in the flour bin. Each item from the recipe produced more enthusiasm from him, to the point where he lost his Dutch and said all kinds of happy things in German, like '*Heerlich*!' and '*Wunderschön*!' I don't remember the exact words. The main thing is, he got worked up about the deep-fried apple-somethings, and as a result I had to get my boots on and fetch the apples. There'd been flooding in the barn that year, but we kept the apples high up off the ground, and they were still good except for smelling like the barn."

Toen flew from Nora's shoulder and landed at the open door of the cage. He hopped onto the trapeze and deposited a dropping on the newspaper laid on the floor. That done, he flew back to her shoulder and rubbed his head against her ear.

"What a clever bird! Did you train him to do that?"

Aunt Julia smiled as though the compliment was for her. "Oh, he's a smart little Toentje. He learned that on his own. Well, at first he pooped on me a few times, but I think he saw I didn't like that so well."

"Clever Toentje." Nora returned to stroking his head.

"Let's see. Where was I? I was talking about the Nazis and their visit. So, when I got back from the barn and left the apples in a bowl in the kitchen, I went to get my knitting and saw the officer find his way to the upright piano in a corner of the living room, sit at the stool, fold up the keyboard cover, and begin to play. He started with a few scales, then a few chords, and then a piece I recognized as a Beethoven sonata."

"Actually, that doesn't make him sound like a typical Hollywood Nazi. Or does it?"

Aunt Julia thought about that. "I'm not sure. Maybe a perfectly evil villain has to have a sensitive side, right? Brings out the evil all the more."

Nora nodded.

"Anyway," Aunt Julia continued. "He played with feeling, and then he made a mistake and hit the keys randomly and said to no-one in particular, 'I am sad to say that this piano is out of tune.' He went back to playing, but without commitment or completion, moving from one stanza to another. I turned to go back to the kitchen and he shouted after me, 'Remember to keep the apples in cold water with a towel on top!'"

"So, a cook, too," Nora commented.

"He had definite ideas about how it had to be done. I half expected him to give me pointers on my knitting."

Nora smiled, but without comment, not wanting to interrupt.

"Anyway, I was peeling apples in the kitchen when I heard Arie come home. At first, I didn't know for sure if it was him or Joop, but when I looked through the doorway to see who it was, there he was standing at the door with a shocked expression, his arms outstretched as the dark-haired one was finishing patting him down, searching around his ankles. The Freiwilliger was pointing a pistol at his chest. It was a good thing it wasn't Joop because Joop carried a pistol tucked in his belt at the back. You know, the one I told you about. He would've been executed on the spot. Or maybe packed off to the Oranjehotel to be shot in the dunes later. But this was toward the end of the war, so there wouldn't have been any ceremony. Anyway, while Arie was being searched, the officer sat exactly the same way as when I came home, as though it were staged, arms across the back of the sofa, legs crossed. The same pose, different meaning. This time it was saying, 'I'm the one in charge here.' I couldn't see if he was smiling. Maybe not this time. I did see—and I really noticed the smell because the tobacco was not very good—that they'd been smoking and playing cards. He said, '*Wilkommen*, come in and join us, won't you?' Arie stayed standing there looking nervous and the officer said, 'Come, come. You don't think we're in the sordid business of rounding up strong young men like you to work in the factories. That would be undignified. Come, join.' They made a place for him at the table and even gave him a cigarette."

"How nice of them."

Aunt Julia smiled, encouraged. "The goose started smelling good, and the heat from the kitchen warmed the house to the point that the soldiers took off their coats. I set the table, and the dark-haired one came to help and was—what's the word in English? —*onuitstaanbaar*.

"Insufferable?"

"Right. Insufferable, getting in the way, and then the officer said, "Heinrich," and he went back to playing cards. The *Apfelklöße* came out well and was set out to cool—we nearly used up the whole bottle of cooking oil except for some that Ma hid away in a little jar. We had goose with stuffing made from stale bread and onions and sauerkraut with fried potatoes. Ma sat at one end of the table and the officer on the other. She said a prayer, which the officer conceded was something necessary for these 'good Christian folk.' After the amen, he raised his glass—filled with schnapps that our neighbor had distilled from plums—and proposed a toast to the New Year and the coming victory and eternal glory of the *Herrenvolk*. We looked to Ma and finally she raised her glass with them, we clinked glasses, and as the Germans tossed back the schnapps, she put her glass down without drinking. I followed her and did the same, except touching the schnapps to my lips, wondering if that would count as a betrayal later on. If I was still alive.

"We filled our plates and ate in silence, with the dark-haired one and the Freiwilliger bent over their food, making those starvation noises people make when they eat after going a few days without, forgetting any manners they might have had. After a while, the officer said, 'This is not a time for eating in silence. We need conversation!' And at that the silence deepened and we all looked to Ma, who said, 'I certainly don't know what there is to talk about. Things are very quiet here. *Were* very quiet here.'"

"That was bold," Nora remarked. "It might've been taken the wrong way."

"True. And I was worried because the officer went quiet. It was a very tense moment. Nobody could tell if he'd taken offense. Then he smiled and said, 'Eat! Don't worry. There will be plenty again soon. Our victory is so close.' And he cut himself another piece of goose. I remember these words clearly because I suddenly realized how out of touch with reality he was—*they* were, all of them. Nothing to do with hope, but something closer to insanity. The war was already decided, and yet here he was talking about victory and imagining a glorious future. I realized we had at our dinner table some of the last, desperate fanatics of the war. His headquarters bombed, an army closing in, and his mind was full of parades and kissing girls and statues to be built. Funny, having such a clear memory about a thought. Not about something that happened in the world, but just in my head, and I remember it as though someone took a film. I remember feeling at that instant that we were in very real danger, beyond the feeling I had when I first walked in the door and saw them in the living room. We were under the power of deluded men with lugers on their belts, who'd just walked into our house and sat themselves down to dinner."

"That sounds awful."

"Well, yes, it was. But I was just a girl. What was I to do?"

"You felt powerless."

"I think we all did."

"Where was Corine during all this?" Nora posed the question as a loose end, without thinking there was anything sensitive about it at all, but it seemed to touch a nerve. Aunt Julia was startled at first, then stared blankly. Nora had the impression of an inner struggle as Aunt Julia tried to remember. "Right. Corine was there, too. She was wearing a pretty dress and her best Sunday shoes. The visitors didn't really pay her any mind. She helped cut the apples. Ma brought the *Apfelklöße* in from the kitchen, still steaming on the plate, her lips still pressed together in a straight line. For coffee she made chicory, *koffiecichorei*, which we used to gather by the river when there was nothing else. It was just fine if you didn't think of it as coffee. As she prepared it, there was none of the usual singing from the kitchen."

"I can only imagine what this must've been like for your mother."

"I can more than imagine it. I can feel it, right here." Aunt Julia pointed to a spot on her solar plexus, then moved it over her heart, as though unsure of where the emotion lay.

"What happened next?"

"At one point the officer put down his cup and said, 'You're all too quiet. I will tell a story.' He told a long, rambling story about how a little over a week previously he had a bad molar. There was no military dentist available. It was not an especially good time to go in search of someone to do the work, but he had to go anyway. The thing was keeping him awake at night in a cold sweat. The closest dentist was a ten-kilometre drive and when he arrived nobody was there. He asked at the neighbors, and they said they didn't know where the dentist might've gone. So—

and this part he got enthusiastic about—he pulled out his gun and suddenly everyone was so very helpful and within minutes the dentist arrived. He'd been visiting his daughter, the dentist said, and just as soon as he heard there was a German officer who needed him, well …

"He brought the officer into the examining room right away and looked at the tooth and touched it with his pic, which made the officer nearly leap out of the chair, and he shook his head. It had to come out. Ideally this would be a job for a surgeon, but under the circumstances they'd have to do their best. Supplies were short and there was unfortunately no anaesthetic. The dentist pulled and pulled, stopping when the pain was too much to bear or when there was blood to spit out, and finally out it came without breaking.

"He stopped talking long enough for us to understand that that was the end of his story. He looked at us one by one to see if we enjoyed hearing it and seemed disappointed at our downcast looks. Then Arie said, 'Show us the hole.' And the officer pulled back his lip to reveal the place in the back where his molar had been. And Corine said 'aaw' and turned away. The hole still had blood seeping. Corine's reaction seemed to encourage him. He told us about how the Fatherland's enemies are everywhere, trying to undo everything that is right and good. 'They need to be pulled out like a bad molar,' he said, and, enjoying the thought, he went on about how we have to first endure the pain of the extraction, and then will see the world in a new way. What I found most offensive is that he included *us* in his warped vision, as his brothers and countrymen, with the same blood in our veins. I couldn't really express it then, but I felt violated by this joining of our people, almost as though, in a mental way, of course, the dark-haired one, who had been staring at me all night, had pinned me against the wall and forced himself on me."

"I can imagine."

"Yes," Aunt Julia said matter-of-factly. She stared straight ahead, gathering her thoughts, then said, "I want share something else with you, and with Peter listening to this later, something I haven't told anyone else." For the first time that afternoon, her voice quavered with emotion. "Something that has to do with Arie and how he behaved with these fine people from the SS. I looked at Arie while the officer was holding forth about Aryan superiority and I didn't see the slightest trace of displeasure or disagreement, not a furrowed brow or a downturned mouth or anything to show he was bothered by this man's delusional ideas. In fact, he was, as far as I could tell, smiling and taking it all in. I might've thought this apparent sympathy for the Nazis was just my misunderstanding if something else hadn't happened. The officer went over to the piano, played a few chords, and said something like, 'After such a fine meal on this festive evening, what we really need is song!' And he looked at us again like a school teacher. His comrades, the Freiwilliger and the creepy one, said, 'Yes, of course' and '*natuurlich*' and they gathered round the piano. Arie joined them. I remember the music of the evening started with Heil Deutschland, which the teacher with the swollen ankles taught us in school. I remember it clearly, it was so drilled into us. *Deutschland du Land der Treue* . . ." Aunt Julia's voice shook and went off key. "They spent the whole evening alternating between Christmas songs and Nazi hymns. Arie got right into it. I really began to wonder about him. Was this man with his arm around one of our oppressors, singing their patriotic songs, my brother or was he someone alien that I didn't know? Was he in the resistance like Joop? Or was this just good acting to save his own skin? I still don't know. He seemed to value the company of others, even if they were officers from the SS, but as far as I could tell his attachments had nothing to do with any other sort of conviction. He was—what do you call it?—a reed, bending any which way. I never had these kinds of doubts about Joop. If anything, Joop was too reckless. He took incredible risks. And, by the way, he never did come home that night. He heard about the Waffen SS being in the area and threw his pistol in the water from a bridge and went into hiding. I think the whole purpose of their visit was to look for him and then they stayed for dinner and waited to see if he'd come home. Anyway, they sang and toasted the New Year and got drunk on the schnapps, and we all went to bed, the soldiers camped in the living room. I . . . I'm not sure how things ended. I remember I stayed close to Ma. I watched her take down her hair and let it fall to her waist, and comb it as she did every night. We slept together."

"Corine too?"

Aunt Julia's eyelids fluttered. "Corine too. She fell asleep right away. I lay awake the whole night. The next morning, they were already gone. Ma and I went out to check on the geese and there was nothing left except two grenade craters and white feathers here and there. The dogs must've eaten well. I looked at Ma to see what she thought and saw, for the first time in this whole episode, the tears running down her cheeks."

And in saying this, Aunt Julia's own eyes filled and a tear broke free and ran down her cheek. Nora gave her an awkward hug, taking care not to bump Toen off her shoulder.

Aunt Julia sniffed and wiped her eyes with the back of her hand. "Well, I think that's quite enough for now. Why don't you sit here while I make us some tea?" And she got up to bustle in the kitchen.

CHAPTER 13: THE BANK

Peter, Goma, and Ibrahim were in the Land Cruiser on their way to Goma's house at the end of the day when Peter had a thought. "The bank," he said, tapping Ibrahim on the shoulder. "Let's go to the Banque Malienne de Securité. The women's prison."

"We can go tomorrow."

"I think now would be better." Peter looked to Goma.

Goma shrugged. "Okay, let's go look."

Ibrahim did a U-turn. The Land Cruiser bogged down in a patch of deep sand before the treads found their grip.

The bank was the only multi-storeyed building on an open, unpaved boulevard. The powerline that connected it to the nearest pole was thicker than those running along the street and sagged just enough to provoke a worried thought just outside the realm of awareness that at any moment it might collapse in a shower of sparks.

Goma and Peter got out of the Land Cruiser. Peter walked to the main door and rattled it. The building was locked and deserted.

"Looks like they finished for the day. Maybe better tomorrow," Goma said.

"Finished what?" Peter asked.

Goma nodded toward a pile of concrete rubble next to the bank. It appeared there was construction work being done.

A man with deep wrinkles and dust in his hair paused to stare. Goma approached him, shook hands, exchanged a few words, and spoke some more. The man pointed toward a building behind the bank. Goma shook the man's hand again. He walked to the Land Cruiser and climbed in the front passenger side.

"Wait here," Ibrahim said to Peter with the window down. "In case anyone comes." The vehicle started with a roar and disappeared around the corner in a cloud of dust.

Peter paced, then felt the futility of the movement in the afternoon sun. He brushed sand from the bank's concrete stoop and sat. He was almost on his haunches, as though crouching over the fosse hole to defecate. He felt his stomach churn, but no urge. At least he was in the shade.

A boy rode by on the back of a donkey, hitting it rhythmically on the haunches with a short stick. He stared at Peter, looked ahead feigning disinterest, then stared longer as the donkey moved with quick steps down the street.

Shit, I really stand out, Peter thought. They shouldn't have left me here. Wasn't Ibrahim supposed to look out for me? His tongue stuck to the roof of his mouth. The thermos with water was in his backpack in the Land Cruiser.

Just when Peter was weighing the option of walking in search of something to drink, the Land Cruiser came around the corner. It raised a grey-brown cloud similar to that from its departure and skidded to a stop in front of Peter. The dust got into his eyes and made him blink. There was a third man in the truck besides Goma and Ibrahim. He was dressed in a richly embroidered light blue *boubou* and a close-fitting white cap. He stepped gingerly on the running board with a white slip-on shoe tapered to a point. Peter shook his hand in a cursory way as the man passed him on his way to the entrance.

"The new construction manager," Goma whispered to Peter.

The manager unlocked the door and gestured for them to enter. He shuffled with his elflike shoes through a coating of dust on the concrete floor. Bare bulbs hung from wires from the ceiling. The ceiling tiles, too, were in disarray, with gaps that reminded Peter of the window pattern at the headquarters in The Hague. There was the smell of dust and raw sewage. Peter fought back a gag reflex.

"I imagine what you came to see is back here," the manager said.

He led them around a concrete pillar to the rear of the main floor and stood in front of a pile of broken cinder blocks. A sledge hammer and a flat shovel lay on top of it at odd angles. Next to it was a dented wheelbarrow with a deflated tire.

"Where are the doors?" Peter asked.

The manager looked perplexed. "The doors?"

"The doors to the prison cells. Where are they?"

"Oh, those were the first things to go," the manager said. "They were metal. I think the workers had other uses for them."

Peter's dismay at the loss of evidence led into a feeling of powerlessness. Now there'd be nothing to prove what happened here. It would be the women's word against . . . The thought remained incomplete, something like a news clip, just nameless, faceless men in turbans. There'd be no way Peter could communicate this smell to the prosecutors. He felt his face flush with anger.

"Did anyone take pictures?" Peter couldn't suppress a tremor in his voice.

"Why would they do that?" the manager asked.

Peter blew up. "What the fuck! What is it with you people and your goddamned sledgehammers!"

There was silence.

Peter tried to read Goma's expression, but it was impassive, his eyes turned toward the rubble. Ibrahim looked in the same direction. The manager stared down at the floor. All his life, Peter had chafed against 'you people' statements as a weapon of bigots. Now one had come from him. It all felt out of control.

He turned on his heels and walked back to the Land Cruiser. It was parked in the sun and the interior was already hot. He left the door open, drank deeply from his thermos and poured the remaining water over his head. His stomach cramped. He struggled through the pain to stand upright.

When Peter walked back into the bank, he saw that Goma, Ibrahim, and the manager had moved away from the rubble and were talking in a three-person huddle. They stopped and turned to look at him. He approached the manager. "I'm sorry," he said. "It's been a day of disappointment."

They shook hands. "Quite all right. I understand."

Peter led the way back to the Land Cruiser. From behind, he heard the manager say quietly to Goma, "These Americans. Always know better. Always in a hurry."

Peter felt a wave of nausea. The voices of Goma and the manager came hollow, as though from the end a long corridor. His field of vision closed in.

He slumped to the ground, fighting with every particle of energy he had against losing consciousness.

This wasn't the time to die. He had work to do.

CHAPTER 14: JAN

Nora took the train and subway to the station in the outskirts of Amsterdam where Jan Achterberg, Peter's maternal uncle, had agreed to meet her. She could see better than usual because the weather was perfect—for her—overcast but not raining. She still had difficulty with signage if the print was too small. In the train station, where the signs were hard to read, she asked directions from anyone willing to pause long enough to provide them. She had her white cane at the ready as an excuse for stopping fast-walking strangers.

She exited the subway station through a long outdoor escalator covered with Plexiglas. At the top, she jumped when a voice too close to her ear said, "You must be Nora."

Jan Achterberg's volume was high in nearly everything he did. His handshake pumped Nora's arm up and down as though he were doing battle-rope exercises in a gym. His brusqueness was audible in the wiff, wiff, wiff of his raincoat. He walked too fast for her, made her struggle to keep up, and scarcely concealed his impatience when he had to wait. His wisps of hair blew upward as though trying to escape his head. Even his shoes staged a rebellion—his laces came undone twice along the way. Each time, he knelt and retied them with sharp movements while Nora took a few seconds to catch her breath.

Jan's apartment was a modest third-floor walk-up. The sounds from throughout the building concentrated in the stairwell: a television with the volume up, a kettle whistling, a baby crying, a dog yapping. Inside Jan's apartment, it was impeccably tidy. The boots and shoes in the vestibule were aligned in perfect symmetry. Magazines were stacked neatly on a shelf under the coffee table, and the few books on the bookshelf were carefully arranged among painted miniatures and family photos in stand-up frames. The orderliness of the apartment didn't jibe with Jan's abruptness. Or maybe it did. Maybe his excess energy went toward keeping things in their place.

A plump woman entered the living room wiping her hands on a checkered apron. Her very presence answered the question about the apartment's tidiness. She had her hair in a bouffant that gave extra height to her round figure. Jan introduced her as his wife Geertruida, which she corrected. "Geery," she said. The plump hand she offered was still damp. She was delighted, simply delighted, that Nora had come for a visit. She had just made *stroopwafels*, sugar waffles, for the occasion. There was coffee and tea of course, and, ooh, an éclair left over from yesterday if Nora should want it.

Nora didn't want the éclair for the moment, but *stroopwafels* and coffee sounded lovely.

Jan established himself at the dining room table adjacent to the sitting room. He folded his arms on the table. Sitting opposite, Nora could see knotted muscles in his forearms. Geery clattered teacups, plates, and cutlery in the kitchen.

"So," Jan said.

Silence followed.

"So," Nora replied after a pause.

Jan fixed her with his eyes and drummed his fingers on the table. He finally said, "*Ja*, you wanted to talk about the war, you said. About Arie."

"I was thinking—"

"That man's no good. The way he—"

Geery came in from the kitchen carrying a tray with a stainless-steel coffee carafe, china cups, a mug with teaspoons, and a plate heaped with small, thin waffles still steaming from the oven. She poured out coffee and placed a cup in front of Jan first, then Nora. Nora felt a twinge of irritation at this minor breech of etiquette, directed toward Jan more than Geery. She put the third cup on a side table next to a sofa and flopped into the corner of the couch. "Help yourself to a *poffertje*," she said, correcting her earlier manners.

Nora did. It was possibly the best she had ever tasted. She told Geery so and she smiled at the compliment.

Jan stopped drumming his fingers and folded his arms more tightly. "Peter should've called sooner. Why hasn't he come by for a visit?"

"I don't know," Nora said. "I can't make excuses for him. Except he was pretty busy with his first assignment. He's in Timbuktu now, as you know."

"*Ja natuurlijk*. Timbuktu. I didn't know that place really existed until you said Peter was there."

"It exists, that's for sure."

"It sounds so exciting, what Peter is doing," Geery said from the sofa. "The places he gets to travel. I'd love to go to an exotic place like that."

"You'd die," Jan snapped. "You wouldn't survive a minute."

Geery was crestfallen, then recovered. "I think I'd be just fine. I would ride a camel." She got up, went to the kitchen and returned with an éclair on a blue china plate.

"Is it okay if I record our conversation for Peter?" Nora held up her iPhone.

"Sure, sure."

"And maybe speak in English?"

"Fine. No problem, except I'm a little rusty," Jan said. "Wow, English. Been a while." He looked toward the ceiling. "Wow," he said again, feeling the shape of the language on his tongue. "Let's see. What were we talking about? The war, the war. I didn't know Arie so well during the war. It's when we came to Canada that I got to know him better. I really liked his sister Julia. She was a real looker, I tell you. And *nice*. I don't know how those two got along as brother and sister, but they were as different as night and day. Arie was . . . Well, for one thing, he married my sister Ida under false prefixes."

Nora resisted the temptation to correct his English. "What do you mean?"

"The thing is, she was the smartest in the family. The smartest in the *school*. It's just that, you know, being the eldest daughter and to take care of the family and everything. Well, the long and the little of it is, our parents took her out of school, even with her exam results."

"And Arie wasn't at that level. Is that what you're saying?"

"Right, exact. He *pretended*. And she fell for it. He was a pretender." Jan uncrossed his arms and tapped the table for emphasis.

"But wouldn't she have seen that in him?" Nora asked. "Wouldn't it be hard to keep that up?"

"I tell you, she made friends with a group of Frenchmen straight away. Out on the deck. They were talking and laughing, and that was the first time she'd ever used French outside the classroom. She just found the words."

"Pretty impressive."

"Yes, and Arie was jealous like you wouldn't believe. He sure let her know."

"In what way?"

"I dunno. She said afterward that he'd been jealous."

"Mmm."

"So, we arrived in Halifax and they dropped the crate from the crane with all our things. Well, not dropped really. Came down hard. Ker-pow! The Delft Blue China that was part of her, whaddya call it? The gifts from the family when you get married."

"Her trousseau?"

"Right. That. Everything smashed to smithereens. So anyways, we took the train across the country to Banff, near where our sponsors lived. They had a job ready for us building camp shelters in the park. Out in the middle of fucking nowhere. Our sponsors were in Crow's Nest Pass, also the middle of fucking nowhere. We got set up, shown our tents, you know, the ones with the wood stove and the stovepipe out the top?"

"Yes, I've seen pictures. I forget what they're called."

"Well, anyways, as soon as people heard where we were from, they started calling us DPs. DPs this and the DPs that."

"And that means?"

"Displaced persons. It was *years and years* after the war, and they were saying, 'fuck you, DP.' We were no more displaced than they were. In fact, we were *all* displaced there, every man jerk of us. But what they meant by DP was, made homeless and somehow lesser by the war. As though being bombed out of your house is a sin."

Geery chimed in from the sitting room. "It was terrible, *vreselijk*. So hard for Jan in those early days." She put her plate on the seat of her chair and got up to refill her cup from the carafe on the table. When she returned to her chair she sat on the half-eaten éclair. "Ooh. Now look what I've done!" She put the plate with the flattened éclair on the side table and tried brushing the cream and chocolate from her dress. She only succeeded in smearing it deeper into the fabric. For a moment she looked indecisive, then rushed out of the room, licking her fingers. The sound of running water came from the bathroom.

Jan sighed and relaxed in his chair as though he'd been waiting for Geery to spill something or make an inappropriate remark. Now that she *had* done something embarrassing, it was out of the way.

"Where was I? Oh, yeah. DPs. So, when the camps were done, we both found work for the Cominco mine in Kimberley. I was hauling timbers—you know, those beams they use to shore up the mineshaft—which was bloody hard work, I tell you. And when one of the guys couldn't keep up, I'd carry theirs for a while. Give 'em a chance to catch their breath. Arie was a carpenter, banging nails. Worked on this and that. Greenhouses one time, I think. Why a mine would need a greenhouse, I have no idea, but there you have it. Propaganda takes many forms. Anyways, one day I was home from work. Day off, lying in bed, resting my tired muscles. And Arie comes home. It'd been raining and he comes home and walks through the house with his muddy boots. And Ida had just finished cleaning the floors. Still on her hands and knees scrubbing the last corner. And she tells him to take off his muddy boots. She said it sharply, like, 'Hey, what're you doing coming through the house with those boots?'

And from the other room I hear him go clomping over to her and he says, '*Godverdomme*. Don't you ever talk to me like that.' And I hear, *smack*! You know, that sound when someone gets slapped. I didn't see it, but I heard it and that was enough. I got up. He looked surprised, eyes wide open like that, and he says, 'What're you doing home?' And I say nothing. Just, *bam*! I hit him on the nose. Blood all over the place. So now the floor has blood, too, mixed in with the mud. Like Vimy Ridge." He paused to savor his witticism and the memory behind it, then continued. "I pretty much broke it. He never got it fixed. Too embarrassed, I think. Even now, if you look at him up close, his nose is just a little bit sideways."

Jan leaned back in his chair. For the first time in Nora's visit, his serious expression softened into a smile. "Fucker had it coming."

CHAPTER 15: GOMA

Peter arrived at the Doctors Without Borders tent with shuffling steps, supported on Goma's arm. The doctor on duty sat cross-legged on a straw mat in front of a thin middle-aged woman. Her headscarf was tied loosely and hung forward in a way that kept her face in shadow. Her *boubou* was over her shoulders for the consultation and there were visible lumps near her armpits. She sat next to a younger woman dressed in kakis who translated between them. The doctor motioned for Peter and Goma to wait on an unoccupied mat. His accent was Parisian French, with his Rs coming from his throat. He was young, sandy-haired, not quite innocent, not quite coarsened by life and the suffering he witnessed day to day in a just-liberated outpost with no clinic and few supplies. He wore jeans and a dark blue short-sleeved shirt with a button-down collar; no white lab coat. His only equipment consisted of the stethoscope around his neck and whatever he had in a half-open medical bag. The doctor asked the woman how many children she had, and she answered nine. How old was the youngest? Three. Did she have a husband? No, he died two years ago. The doctor sighed heavily.

"You see," he said, "the cancer has metastasized." He caught himself and looked for another way to say it. "It's spread here and here and here and inside your body, too." He pointed to the lumps. "We could send you to Bamako for tests, but from what I can see it's already gone too far. Nothing we can do. Better for you to spend your last days here." When the translator finished speaking, she nodded, numb, understanding only that she was at the end. She stood, helped to her feet by the doctor, no tears, no words, and shuffled away.

"Now you," the doctor said sharply, looking at Peter.

Peter wanted to deny there was anything wrong with him. It was nothing, really. Just a fainting spell. Dehydration. After overhearing the consultation with the woman, he wondered what right he had to be sick and take the doctor's time.

"He fainted. We had some trouble getting him back," Goma offered.

Peter added that, yes, he woke up in the back of the Land Cruiser, but he already felt better after he drank some water.

The doctor asked him about medications and raised an eyebrow when Peter's mentioned that morning's Imodium tablets. Other symptoms? Fever? Fatigue? "Just a little diarrhea and then, poof, over you go?"

"Something like that," Peter said.

The doctor shone a light in his pupils, took his blood pressure, and listened to his chest through the stethoscope. "Okay," he said. "Here's what I think. It sounds like giardiasis, basically little critters living in your intestines. My guess is, from unfiltered water. I'm going to send out a blood sample to test for malaria. Meanwhile stop taking the Imodium. Rest at home. Drink plenty of clean water. Eat plain, simple foods like bananas, bread, rice, and porridge. Get it out of your system. You'll probably be a hundred percent in a week."

Peter opened his mouth to protest that he couldn't possibly stay off his feet for a week and thought better of it. Better just a day or two. See how it went.

The doctor drew the blood sample for the malaria test from Peter's arm, screwed the cap on the vial and said, "Okay, who's next?"

When he heard these words, Peter realized there were people waiting in the shade of a tree on the far side of the tent. A mother holding a gaunt-faced infant, a heavily pregnant woman with narrow ankles and bony feet, and an old man with open sores on his arms. Who knew what private suffering there was among those under the tree? And how had he jumped the queue and been seen ahead of them? Did Goma pull strings, make calls on the way there? How did it work?

Goma looked in the direction of Peter's gaze. "Don't worry," he said. "They have time to wait."

Peter wasn't easily reassured. "How did I get seen before them? Why me? I don't get it."

"You're thinking too much," Goma said. "It's been this way ever since the French. Just one of those leftover habits." After a moment he added, quietly, as though to himself, "We've never really been free."

***

The next morning, after a simple breakfast of *bouille* porridge and bread and studious avoidance of black boiled tea, Peter gave Goma instructions on how to use his Leica camera. He suggested leaving it on auto, given that the light was good. Then he went through everything in his camera bag, showed him where the tape measure was stored, instructed him on how to take notes. "Start with a heading with the name of the site, the geolocation, and note every photo you keep, with the date and time. Put the measurements here, in columns like this." Goma nodded.

Ibrahim announced his arrival outside the house with two gentle taps on the horn and Goma left with the camera bag slung over his shoulder.

With all his equipment in Goma's hands, Peter was left bereft and bored. He texted Nora. "Quiet here. Missing you," but didn't get a reply.

Even with the cautious breakfast, his intestines were in turmoil, and he had to go twice to the hole-in-the-floor fosse. The doctor's instructions were to drink plenty of water, but the cistern was getting low. Besides, the water was suspect, a probable source of his affliction. He went to the faucet in the courtyard. The water came out brown and sputtering at first, then ran clear. The pool of water he created by running the tap would attract mosquitoes. Using a piece of scrap cardboard, he moved sand from a corner of the courtyard to the faucet area until everything was dry. Filtering the water into his thermos and the cistern took time, but offered a feeling of accomplishment. It only partly made up for the day's losses. Searching for more to do, he took down his mosquito net and inspected it for holes. He found only one, which he patched using two small pieces of duct tape, one on either side. He then lay on his mattress and read the news on his iPhone, all of it depressing. He consoled himself by doing a crossword puzzle. It was too hard and required him to do Google searches to find answers.

He sat up on one elbow and texted Goma. "If you have any questions about anything, I'm here."

Three moving dots showed that Goma was writing a reply; then they disappeared. Possibly a bad connection. Peter wondered what Goma was up to.

He threw himself on his back and stared at the ceiling. The mud-clay plaster was coming loose from the beams. The beams themselves were riddled with holes, inhabited by termites. If he closed his eyes, he could faintly hear them at work, tik, tik, tik, busying themselves with the destruction for which they were programmed, their little hive brains each more complex than the computers that sent men to the moon.

The secret marvel of it wouldn't help whoever was underneath when the beam finally gave way. Peter wondered why, even though people know it's dangerous, they still lie under the beams. Too lazy or stubborn or self-destructive to move.

There's another marvel.

***

Goma returned to the house in the late afternoon accompanied by an elderly man with a jujube-tree walking stick. He wore a loosely tied white turban, jaunty in its informality, the equivalent of a flat-cap worn at a tilt. An intricately embroidered white boubou, miraculously dust free, gave an impression of high status, interrupted by a pair of plain cowhide sandals. He greeted Peter with a handshake and a smile that revealed a missing front tooth.

Goma led their guest to the upstairs terrace, followed by Peter. Once they were settled on the cushions, Goma introduced him as Cheikh

Muhammad Ag Brahim, a distinguished name that went together with the occupation of librarian.

"Not just any librarian," Goma explained. "A keeper of manuscripts. Ag Brahim was one of those who smuggled manuscripts out of his family's library for safe keeping in Bamako before the insurgents took over the city."

Ag Brahim smiled at the explanation of his role. But his smile faded quickly. In what he said next in a mix of Tamasheq, Arabic, and French, Peter recognized the words for 'criminals,' 'blasphemers' and 'apostates.'

"It's true, we did get some of the most precious manuscripts out, but others they burned to ashes," Ag Brahim said, despondently.

"Is the ash pile still there?" Peter asked.

"Some of the ashes are still there, but it happened more than six months ago. Most have blown away."

"We will get some pictures from the site. Goma, let's pay a visit tomorrow, shall we?"

"If it's photos you want, I have those," Ag Brahim said. "My nephew took them with his phone camera. Also, the fire burning."

"That's fantastic. Can you get your nephew to come by with those tomorrow morning? We'll get copies and make a record of the phone data." Peter was buoyed by the sudden progress in the investigation. "What do you think, Goma?"

From one moment to the next, Goma had disappeared. Peter heard him moving something across the concrete floor in the lower level of the house. He returned clattering in the stairwell with three stackable chairs made with roughly welded frames upholstered with wrappings of bright orange plastic string. The plastic had broken and been roughly tied in several places to keep them from unravelling completely. Goma arranged the chairs on the terrace so they faced one another. Ag Brahim left his cushion and sat spryly, out of keeping with the walking stick he propped against the arm rest. Peter moved into his chair more cautiously. The plastic string was flimsy and, with one's weight settled, gave the impression of sitting on a potato slicer. Goma established himself in his chair without fuss, one ankle across a knee, and lit a cigarette.

Peter turned to Ag Brahim. "Please tell us more about these books that were burned. What sort of books were they? And why did they offend the Islamists?"

Ag Brahim answered indirectly, starting from the beginning, with the first stirrings of Timbuktu as a hub of trans-Saharan travel, as an intellectual centre, as a clandestine and coveted prize of European colonists. The rumours of Timbuktu's splendour that reached the ears of European adventurers were not at all exaggerated. There was no way to overestimate the glories of this great city.

Peter grew impatient, wanting an answer to his question, but kept silent.

Ag Brahim, by slow degrees, moved his narrative toward Peter's questions. "The scholars here were dedicated to knowledge. About everything. The Sankoré Madrasa was a centre of Islamic learning that rivalled the great universities of Cairo and Shiraz. The scholars produced beautiful illuminated manuscripts and translated the great works of Plato, Aristotle, and Averroes. More than that, there were scientists, mathematicians, astronomers working here. They observed the heavens with a scholar's curiosity. There are books here, centuries old, on the movements of the planets with diagrams of their orbits. Scholars documented everything, even a great meteor shower. He recited from memory. "In the year 991, in God's month of Rajab the Godly, after half the night had passed, stars flew as if fire had been kindled in the whole sky, east, west, north, and south. It became a flame lighting up the earth and the people were stricken with terror."

Peter recalled the lines from Blake, which he quietly, almost to himself, recited. "When the stars threw down their spears, And water'd heaven with their tears, Did he smile his work to see?" He looked up and saw Goma staring at him blankly. "And that's what offended the jihadists?" Peter asked, returning to the topic.

"No, no. Not just that." Ag Brahim both denied the statement and gave it credence. "Their offense is that they're offended by *everything*. They are *jāhil*. Ignorant. They worship God by forbidding knowledge of creation, which is a rejection of the Creator."

"So they even burned the manuscripts that told about the stars on fire."

"They are uneducated men." Ag Brahim paused and then completed the thought. "They had no way of knowing *what* they were burning. They didn't read any of the books they threw on the fire. Only maybe just to see if it was a Qur'an. Those they didn't burn. Everything else—into the fire." He made a simple gesture that somehow pantomimed a book being thrown and a fire burning with increased energy. "But the thing that really got them were the books of magic."

"Magic?"

"Well, not really magic, but explorations into the mysteries of God's power. Things like the influence of numbers."

"Numerology?"

"If you want to use that word. And things like fortune telling with bones you throw, reading the marks on the ground or the waves in a pond from tossed rocks, summoning spirits of the dead, how to avoid the evil eye and the power of djinns, spirits that inhabit rocks and trees and whirlpools. Things like that."

"So, the occult."

This time, Ag Brahim ignored Peter's word choice. "There were also books about family life. Instruction manuals, if you know what I mean."

"I'm not sure I follow."

"There was once a book in my library called *Advising Men on Sexual Engagement with Their Women*." His eyes glinted with mischief. "A completely normal subject matter, if you ask me. There are sayings of the Prophet that discuss whether it is permitted for a man to look down toward the sexual organs during . . . aah . . . what shall I say? During the act. And this book went from there into, aah, more detail. Remedies for, ahh, flaccidity, infertility, winning women's hearts, how to live peacefully with your wives, things like that."

"And this book was burned with the others?"

"Ashes," Ag Brahim replied.

"Awful. I would've liked to read that," Peter said. His attempt to lighten the conversation fell flat.

Ag Brahim looked at his hands in his lap. "The book burning was one of the last things the ignorant ones did before the French and Malian armies came and forced them into the desert. So many gone. Gasoline and then . . ." His voice broke and trailed off.

Goma, who up to that point had been quietly attentive to his cigarette, said, "I once bought a manuscript from a tourist for fifty dollars and returned it to the library. Actually, to Ag Brahim's library. The one who sold it couldn't be trusted. When people are desperate, they'll do anything. I blame the government for keeping people so poor. If we had our own government, none of this would've happened."

Ag Brahim nodded. "We sent many manuscripts to warehouses in Bamako. Some came back as damp wads of mold. The only reason paper survived through the centuries in Timbuktu is the dry air. But we kept the smuggling operation going. If the ignorant ones caught us, who knows. We would've been accused of theft. They would have cut off our hands. But it was worth it. Every book that made it out, escaped their destruction. In the end, we saved a lot of them, *al hamd ul'Allah*."

In Ag Brahim's telling, the books were precious, independent lives, committed to the page for generations to follow. Peter understood him. Their burning was a form of murder, with no physical pain in the bonfires, but that left the survivors bereft and impoverished, without connection to their ancestors, every book destroyed an erasure, the death of a moment in the life of a mind. Yet, even before the Islamists came, some keepers were selling manuscripts to tourists. What was their motivation? Were the sellers desperate for money? Had the books lost their allure? Others went to heroic lengths to save the manuscripts from the threat of the Islamists. They risked everything, like those who in other times and places sheltered the persecuted and defied the will of their would-be killers.

Ag Brahim waved off Goma's offer to call Ibrahim to drive him home and took his leave with the same politeness with which he had arrived. His smile was open, oblivious to his missing tooth. His house wasn't far.

Peter walked him to the door. They shook hands. Ag Brahim looked both ways before he stepped down from the sill. Peter watched him saunter down the street, his jujube-stick swinging in time with his steps.

* * *

The sheet-metal door at first refused to seat properly in its frame. Peter wiggled it in place and turned the key. He found Goma still up on the terrasse in a chair where they had just finished their meeting with Ag Brahim.

"Did everything go okay at the sites? Camera worked all right?" Peter asked.

"Yes, yes."

Goma reached in the bag, switched on the Leica and handed it to Peter, pupil to teacher. Peter accepted it gingerly, unsure of what he would find. The images were perfect, no different than if he had taken them himself. Maybe better. There were more closeups of tool marks in the rubble than he would've taken. Peter felt a confused combination of appreciation of Goma's work, pleasure in the progress they were making and a twinge of jealousy, or maybe something closer to a comparative sense of his own vulnerabilities and failings.

"That's fantastic," he said. "Good work."

Goma smiled in a way that Peter understood to be saying, *Of course. What did you expect?*

They sat quietly for a moment in their orange-string chairs.

"Let me show you something." Goma scrolled on his phone until he found what he was looking for. "Here." He handed the phone to Peter.

It was a photograph of a desert scene with bones emerging from the sand, a long vertebral column, half exposed. There was nothing else in the image, so Peter had no sense of the scale. "It looks like bones," he said unenthusiastically.

"Dinosaur bones." Goma lit a cigarette and blew the smoke upward. "I used to play on them when I was a kid. These ones are from an enormous plant eater like a brontosaurus. Maybe bigger. Could be an undiscovered species. I can't be sure without seeing the rest of it."

Peter was surprised, not just by the bones, but Goma's knowledge of them, like a secret he carried and only now revealed. "That's incredible," he said. "I had no idea those were out there."

"Lots of them," Goma said. "Not just these. I went to university in Belgium to learn more about them. Got a master's degree. Did research at the Royal Belgian Institute of Natural Sciences. Worked on a dig in Montana. But I couldn't go any further without getting back to the desert. So, now I do research for the ICC. Instead of working on dinosaurs, I do forensics in mass graves. The only bones I work with are from war victims."

"So this assignment, what we're working on now, doing interviews, is different for you."

"Different, yes." Goma agreed. "I have to talk to people. Some of it's hard. The things people say aren't easy to listen to. Still, in some ways it isn't as bad as the mass graves. No more taking the smell home in my clothes."

Peter couldn't repress the feeling that Goma had in some ways surpassed him. It was more than the fact that this was his home and he was Peter's guide. More than the four languages he spoke fluently. Even in the things that mattered most, Goma had gone further. Paleontology. What boy of eleven didn't want that as a career? Even Goma's failures were more spectacular. A career pathway cut short by a war. What was Peter's excuse? When he was a student researcher, he'd been bitten by a mosquito. A malarial one, but still . . .

"Maybe you can still get back there someday. To the desert, I mean." Peter offered. "With the dinosaur bones. Pick up your career where you left off."

"Not any time soon," Goma said. He drew from his cigarette, looking up at the twilight sky. "Not with Ansar Eddine and Al Qaida out there. Can you imagine an expedition going there? It's hard enough keeping people alive in the desert without having to worry about *them*."

Peter noted that Goma's concern was about keeping *people* alive in the desert, not himself. For Goma, the desert was home, where he lived and traveled and, as a boy, played among dinosaur bones. He looked at the photo again and imagined the shrieks and laughter of children among the bones. He handed the phone back.

The ash from Goma's cigarette glowed brightly in the fading light. He blew the smoke upward, away from Peter. "Instead of bringing knowledge out of the desert . . ." He searched for the right words. "The only things coming out of there right now are bodies and the weapons the French sometimes find hidden in caves. The people who took over this city say they have a holy cause, but they're ignorant. Like Ag Brahim says, *jāhil*. They just want power, control. All they're able to read, if they read at all, are the instructions on their stolen rocket launchers."

After hearing about what had been done to the women during the occupation, Peter found Goma's contempt soothing.

Goma flicked his cigarette in a long arc across the terrace. It bounced in a shower of sparks, rolled and stopped against the *banco* wall on the far side. He stood and turned to leave.

"Ignorant," he said as he walked through the entryway to the stairs.

***

After Goma left, Peter moved his mattress outside to the open terrasse on the roof next to the chairs. The small room that served as his sleeping quarters was stuffy. There were no attachments on the terrasse for a mosquito net, but he tied a rope from one window shutter across to another and used it to hang the netting. He made sure his thermos was full and next to the mattress inside the net. The mosquitoes were diabolical. They could get inside the netting with the slightest opportunity, even something as simple and careless as a hand reaching under to grab a drink of water in the night. They'd sense him there, the heat from his body, his breath, buzzing and bumping on the netting, poking their proboscises through, searching for skin and blood. If he left an exposed elbow or knee against the net, he'd have a cluster of bites there the next morning.

His phone buzzed in his pocket. He had a series of WhatsApp messages from Nora. He hadn't noticed them coming through during his conversation with Goma. There was one long text telling him what a lovely time she had with Aunt Julia, how they had gone to a café called Victor or Victoria or something like that, and how Aunt Julia talked about her experience during the war. It was followed by a series of recordings.

Peter listened to them one by one, through to the end.

He had trouble deciding whether to first call Nora or his father. He was curious about something Aunt Julia said in the recording. Something about public hearings after the war. It was hauntingly similar to what he learned a short time ago about the jihadists and their court.

Arie answered on the seventh ring, just as Peter was about to hang up.

"Oh, halloo, Peter. Are you still in Africa—where was it?"

"Timbuktu."

"Of course, Timbuktu. How could I forget *that*?"

"Yes, Dad, I'm still here."

"And you're still working for that court? No time for a vacation?"

"I'm still working for the ICC, yes. Taking a break now. Had a bout of illness. Nothing serious, but it took me off my feet for a while."

"Ah, I know just what you mean. Strange food. Can throw you off. Happened to me once when we first came to Canada."

"Yes, I can imagine. Say, Dad, I heard some things about the end of the war in Holland and—"

"Must've been that camp food. We were living in a tent and building tourist shelters in Banff. Food did *not* agree with me. I had to shit in a hole we dug in the woods, sit on a board nailed across two trees. So, there I was with my guts all in turmoil and I went to sit down and I scared a grouse. Right underneath me with my pants down, the little bastard. The fright sure helped it all come out." He laughed hard enough to make Peter hold the phone away from his ear.

"That's funny. You never told me that story. Listen, Dad, I—"

"I've got lots of stories."

"I'm sure you do. I wish you told me more. But I wanted to ask you about one in particular. From when—"

"Good ones. There was this Hungarian once in the—"

"Dad, Nora's been talking with Aunt Julia while I've been in Africa. Some things have come up about the war. About the resistance. About the aftermath. The public tribunals."

"Who's Nora?"

"Dad, Nora's my partner. We're living together in The Hague. I told you about her."

"What the hell's a *partner*? Is that what you call her? You make a business deal, you shake hands, *that's* a partner. Are you fucking her or not?"

"Dad, that's rude. I know, it seems a little awkward, but that's the word we use. It's about new kinds of marriage and gender binaries and . . . Never mind. Listen, Dad, I—"

"What's this Nora character doing talking to Julia? Didn't I tell you? You can't trust what she says."

"Does that mean you *weren't* part of the tribunals after the war?" Peter knew that putting the question negatively was the best way to draw Arie out.

"*Yes*, I was at some of those." He rose to the bait.

"Presiding? I mean leading things?"

"Sure, a few times. But what's that got to do with anything? Better to forget about all that."

"Some things are important to remember," Peter replied. "Some stories are like sentinels. They stand as a warning." He knew as soon as the words came out that this was the wrong tone to take with his father.

"Sentinels? What the hell're you talking about? Why don't you try to make sense some time? Let me tell you a real story, about this Hungarian. He was—"

"Honestly, Dad. I don't understand why you're so resistant to talking about the war."

Silence.

"Dad? Are you there?"

"I'm here."

"So what's going on? I know it was hard and everything, but it's important to know what happened."

"You can't trust that woman. She lies."

"Who, Julia? Okay, let's grant that she hasn't told the absolute truth or the whole story. Doesn't that make it *more* important for us to hear things from you? Hear another version?"

"Except I'd rather not. Not now. Let's just leave it at that."

"Another time then." Peter put it as a statement.

Arie said cautiously, after a significant pause, "Maybe."

The line went dead, but Peter had the distinct impression Arie had put the handset back in the cradle gently.

CHAPTER 16: KURT

Kurt Achterberg gave the impression of a man of substance, not so much in the material sense, though he was wearing a tweed jacket on a Saturday and driving a high-end station wagon. Nora sized him up from the Audi's passenger seat. If she had to put her finger on it, she'd say he had poise, a straight back and sure movements, despite his eighty-something years. It was a sureness that made him seem at least a decade younger and made up for his thinning wisps of white hair and thick glasses. There was mental acuity, too in the way he held himself, an almost hawkish alertness (despite the glasses), the substance of someone who tries—sometimes struggles—to understand the world, even if they never fully succeed.

Kurt asked about his nephew Peter and his work in The Hague. Peter had called a while ago to say he was in the Netherlands, but they hadn't yet had a chance to get together. He said all the polite things. "Nel and I haven't seen Peter since he last came for a visit—when was it?—years and years ago. Must've been sometime while he was doing his studies at McGill and on a break, he did the European tour." When Nora mentioned Timbuktu, Kurt knew where it was and even knew a thing or two about the recent civil war. "I don't understand it," he said after they'd exchanged a synopsis of the conflict. "I don't understand any of it. Fighting over a desert. Forcing your religion on people, as though violence is a way to give them faith. All that's beyond me. And now killing UN peacekeepers. A total mystery."

Nora couldn't think how to respond and stayed silent.

Kurt navigated off the freeway and shared Nora's silence while he concentrated on the traffic. Once on a side road, he asked, "How's Peter doing? Does he like working for the ICC?"

This was within her ability to answer. She told what she knew about his assignment, a sanitized version that didn't dwell on the nights she lay awake worrying.

"How nice that the two of you met at the university in England," Kurt said. "We hope the two of you can come by to see us when he's back from Africa. Wouldn't that be nice?"

"That would be nice," Nora replied, and she meant it.

The gravel on the driveway crunched under the wheels of the Audi as they pulled up to the house. Nel met them at the front door. She stood on a portico with the door open behind her. Nora could see her short dark hair and a close-fitting green dress, hemmed just above the knee. She was younger than Kurt. By how much, hard to say. Maybe even thirty years.

"What a gorgeous house," Nora said on her exit from the car.

Nora's compliment provoked an instant tour of the house. Nel proudly took her through a spacious living room hung with abstract paintings. At least they seemed abstract, with bold shapes and bright colors. The kitchen had a gas range and an island with a deep, basin-like sink and high-arching faucet. Nel slid open a glass door, revealing an expanse of grass surrounded by a flower garden. Nora asked about the flowers and Nel replied with a full accounting. The roses were struggling with aphids this year. The irises were just coming into bloom. When Nora squinted to find the irises, she saw a white shape move in the grass. The sound of bleating revealed it to be a sheep or a goat.

"Oh, *wat leuk*! You keep animals?"

Nel expounded on the virtues of keeping a goat. The milk was wonderful once you got used to it. And, she explained, "why waste all that grass by mowing it and throwing it all away?" She had a point.

Interesting, Nora thought, how it takes money to pursue those sorts of ideals.

They went back inside. The highlight for Nel was the sewing room on the upper floor, loft-like with skylights, complete with a spinning wheel, a loom, and all the accoutrements for preparing the wool. She knitted mostly hats and wove wall hangings. She rummaged through a pile of woolens and retrieved a toque with iridescent greens and violets that she placed on Nora's head with the solemnity of an archbishop at a coronation, then pulled it over her ponytail.

"A perfect fit," Nel said.

Nora felt herself blush. "I couldn't possibly take this. You must've spent days working on it."

Nel insisted. "You'll do me a favor. This way I'll know it's being worn on a beautiful, smart head."

Nora relented. "After hearing you say something so lovely, how could I say no."

When they descended to the living room, Nora smelled coffee.

"Well, well," Kurt said. "That looks very fine on you."

Nora felt herself blush again. "Thank you. It's very kind. Almost too much, really."

"You're making Nel happy by wearing her hat. Nothing gives her greater pleasure."

"It's true," Nel said. "It feels pointless to knit a hat when there's nobody to wear it. I've already given them to everyone I know. *I* should be thanking *you*." She gave the toque a pat and tilted it slightly sideways. "There. Like that." She stepped back and smiled at her work. "And now I'll leave the two of you alone for a while. I have another masterpiece in the works, in the kitchen this time."

Nora sat in a leather chair, poured herself coffee and put a biscuit on the saucer. "This is really a very lovely house."

"Too big for us, now that the kids are grown." Kurt paused reflectively, as though following each of his children from their birth to their present station in life.

"I understand from Peter that you're an engineer," Nora said, knowing she was interrupting his thoughts.

"Engineer, yes," Kurt said, back in the present. "Civil aviation. I was lucky. Well, not lucky, really. I was able to file a few patents and they turned out pretty well. Here . . ." Kurt stood, went into an adjoining room and returned with a model plane. He gave it to Nora. "My design for winglets, you know, those vertical foils on the end of airplane wings. Cuts down on fuel consumption."

"You designed those?" She ran her fingers along the model, feeling the wing's elegant shape.

"Among other things. My other inventions would be harder to explain."

"My goodness." She handed the model back to Kurt.

Nora sipped her coffee while Kurt returned the model to its place in the adjoining room. "I was wondering . . ." she said, loud enough for him to hear. "I was hoping we could talk about Peter's father, Arie. I'm finding him something of a mystery."

There was silence. Kurt reappeared and said nothing. The chair's leather creaked as he sat. Nora was about to repeat her request when he said, "I'm not sure I have anything to say about Arie. I don't really know him that well. I only saw him once in all the time since he and my sister were married. At a family gathering, around the time of the fifty years since the armistice. He shook my hand and said hello and that was that."

"Did Ida ever say anything about him? In letters?"

"*Ja, natuurlijk*. But her letters were just—how should I say this?—updates. They did this and they did that. They moved here and there. The kids liked their new school. Merry Christmas, happy birthday. That sort of thing."

"Nothing very personal."

"No, not really. I always got the feeling from her letters that she was covering up what was actually going on with her. This I understood better when she died."

"When was that?"

"Oh, seven, eight years now."

"What makes you think there was something going on in Ida's life that she didn't want to write about?"

Before Kurt could answer, Nel came into the living room carrying a cardboard box. "Look what I found. Old pictures!"

She put the box on the coffee table, nearly overturning the coffee pot. It was filled with albums with red and tan covers in imitation leather, embossed in gold. Nora held one up. It said, *Foto's*, in florid cursive script. Inside were photographs in plastic covers depicting people she didn't know at dinner tables and outside in flower gardens.

Nel looked over her shoulder. "This one is from my visit to cousins in France."

Nora closed the cover slowly and returned the album to the box, careful not to cause offense by putting it away too definitely. "You have family in France?"

"No. Well, yes, sort of. They have a summer place. We pay them a visit now and then."

Nora picked up another album.

"Here we are in Tromsø," Nel said from behind her shoulder. "Kurt gave a talk at the university there. The scenery is breathtaking, don't you think?"

Nora took out her iPhone and opened a magnification app. She put the photo album flat on the table and steadied the phone in her hand. The album was full of postcard-worthy images of mountains and water.

"These are of the Arctic Ocean, seen from Norway. *Prachtig*," Nel said. She turned the page. "Here. This is a Laestadian village."

Nel pointed out the lack of curtains on any window—the rules of the Lutheran community called for everyone to make their private lives visible to everyone else. She explained how they took Protestant ideas to the limit, in ways that became visible. Sin happens in private, so no privacy, no curtains. She had a special fascination for this place. "When the Nazis retreated from northern Norway, they set fire to quite a few villages," she said.

"Why do you think they did that?"

Nel thought before she answered. "I don't really know. Because they could. Because they were defeated. Frustrated. Then the beast comes out. There was no other outlet for their loss of pride."

"They lost their humanity," Kurt added. "At a certain point, they became something else."

Nora reflected on that. Lost their humanity or became quintessentially human? There's a question for the ages. She left the thought unspoken. The talk about the war in Norway left an opening to shift the conversation. "Do you have anything in your photo albums from the war in the Netherlands?"

Nel took the photo albums out of the box one by one. At the bottom was a layer of letters and black-and-white photos, left there at random, as though too burdensome to be held, thought about, and assigned a place between plastic covers.

Nora put the letters in one pile on the table and the photographs on another. There were letters and cards from Ida still in their envelopes. Her handwriting was impeccable, with decorative loops and swirls on the capital letters. The photos were mostly old family portraits, the same kind Aunt Julia had on her wall. There was one of a rail bridge, destroyed by bombs.

Kurt held it far from his face and squinted through his bifocals. "Oh, dear. I think I'm ready for a new prescription," he said. He adjusted the length of his reach to bring the picture into focus. "Ah, yes. That's the ruin of the bridge over the Ijssel outside Zwolle, before it was rebuilt. After that you could only get across by boat. It left one part of the country cut off from the rest. That was one reason for the famine at the end of the war."

Nora held her iPhone over another image. It was of a crowd gathered around a car, a long-hooded convertible. It looked as though they were celebrating a football victory with smiles and sparkling eyes, their arms around each other. A German officer was tied to the front grille. You could see he was an SS officer by the uniform, once likely carefully ironed, but now dishevelled, torn in a few places, shirt untucked. His arms were behind his back and a long rope had been wrapped several times around his chest and probably passed through the grillwork behind. It was hard to see exactly how the rope was tied, but the creases in the uniform showed that it was tight. One celebrant, a man in his twenties with a hat cocked sideways, had his arms around the officer's shoulders in an ironic gesture of comradeship. The officer looked straight at the camera with an expression of defeat and resignation. Nora handed the phone to Kurt. He squinted and brought it into focus.

"Ah," he said, and put it on the pile on the table without further comment.

Nora waited for him to say more, but he stayed silent. "Taken just after the liberation?" she asked.

"It looks that way. I think my dad took this. He had a nice camera."

"I wonder what happened to the soldier." Nora's words were a distillation of questions and images that filled her thoughts. She wondered how fast they drove with him tied to the front of the car. She imagined what he might look like, with his hair blown back by the wind, the horn honking, the celebrants shouting. She had so many questions swirling, ones she dared not speak. How else did they torture him? Did they kill him and leave him at the side of the road? The instinctive revulsion she felt on seeing a playful, murderous mob made her feel sympathy for the officer. At the same time, she knew the celebrants weren't entirely wrong in making him an object of revenge. Behind his defeated look must've been an awareness of what he'd done to deserve this fate—the sadness of the perpetrator brought to account.

She picked up another photo. This one depicted a young couple holding bicycles and looking toward the camera. Her mouth was turned in a slight smile, as though taking pleasure in a complicity. The man stood erect with a steady and confident look.

She handed it to Kurt.

"Ah, here we are!" Kurt exclaimed. "This is Ida and Arie. Before they were married, I think."

Kurt passed the photo on to Nel. "They look happy," she said, and handed it back to Kurt.

He looked at it again, holding his arm out and squinting. "The happiness of a fox with a rabbit."

Nel straightened her back. "How can you say that? Just look. I think they were happy together. At least in the early days."

"If they were happy, it was as more about the future and its possibilities than about each other. She was in love with the idea of escape. I think they were already discussing plans to go to Canada."

"Can I borrow this to show Peter?" Nora asked.

"You can keep it. I have no use for it," Kurt said.

Nora found an empty envelope with the greeting cards in the bottom of the box. She put the photo in the envelope and tucked it into her purse. The three sat close to the table without speaking.

Nora broke the silence. "Some of these are worth keeping," she said. "There's history here."

"Do you think?" Kurt asked.

"Of course. Even this one of the bridge. It might look like just a blown-up bridge, but it was important at the time. It helps understand the famine. The problems transporting food in the last year of the war."

"Let's see what else we have," Nel said.

Together, they sorted out the photographs by subject, family, vacations, gardens, wartime. Nora looked at the images more closely through her magnification app. "Aside from the photos of the bombed bridge, most of these were taken during the liberation."

"A happier subject," Kurt suggested. "Who wants pictures of suffering and starvation for the family album?"

Nora tapped her finger next to the small collection assembled on the table. "You can take these to the National Archives in The Hague."

"They might already have something you're looking for," Nel suggested. "Who knows?"

Kurt jumped to his feet. "Let's have a look."

He led Nora into his office. It had a floor-to-ceiling bookshelf filled with books. Model airplanes took over every open space on the desk and side table. Every other space on the desk was filled with stacks of books and papers of varying height. The computer looked vintage.

Kurt typed slowly, hunt and peck, hitting the keys hard. The homepage of the National Archive loaded from the top down. Kurt typed again, each keystroke separated from the next by nearly a full second.

Nora repressed her impatience. "What words are you searching?"

"Arie Dekker, of course," Kurt answered.

The screen filled slowly. There were two thumbnails.

"What did you get?"

"Football teams. Group shots taken on a playing field. There must be an Arie Dekker who played football."

"Hmm. Try Waffen SS."

Kurt typed and waited for the result. There were twenty pages of images. "You want to go through all these now?"

Nora demurred. She could do it from home, take her time.

"I'd be happy to do it for you," Nel offered. Her voice came from behind. Nora hadn't noticed her enter the room.

"Certainly no harm," Kurt answered for Nora.

"Great!" Nel enthused. "I'll get started right away. But first, a little lunch. I made a soup. *Groentensoep met balletjes.*"

"Sounds lovely," Nora said. She didn't eat red meat as a rule, but would make an exception for Nel's vegetable meatball soup.

CHAPTER 17: INTERRUPTION

Peter could smell Goma's cigarette breath as he leaned over Peter's shoulder with his hand on the back of the plastic-string chair. Peter scrolled through the images on the Leica. He had his bare feet burrowed in the sand in a corner of the courtyard where it was deeper. The main outer wall cast a shadow that minimized glare on the camera's screen. Their collaboration was based on a simple binary question—keep or discard? The actual reasons for their decisions were complex and intuitive. There was usually a series of shots of the same subject. The differences between them were miniscule. Peter compared two images at a time and scrolled back and forth between them. With each comparison, they decided which had sharper focus, which had cleaner shadows, which was taken from the best angle. Using the editing tools, Peter cropped and repositioned some of the images closer to the main subject matter: a broken mud-brick with a tool mark, a pile of rubble, scatterings of ruined mausoleums, all to serve as evidence of the insurgent's destructive rampage. Rarely did they find the remnants of a wall still standing. The support beams, if there were any, lay where they fell. The trick was to capture the destruction in shadows and light.

Three knocks on the sheet-metal door resonated in the courtyard like thunderclaps. Goma sauntered over to answer it. Before he could answer, whoever was on the other side pounded the door again.

When Goma turned the key and opened the door, Peter saw two men standing in the street in front of the raised stoop. They were dressed in khaki tunics and pants hemmed midway between the knee and the ankle, and in every other way had the appearance of Islamists: hair short, crowned with white skullcaps, full beards and moustaches trimmed, and prayer-callouses in the middle of their foreheads from genuflections in the sand. One was older, his beard flecked with grey. Goma offered no greeting. The older of the two men said, "*Salaamu alaikum.*" Goma muttered something inaudible, which Peter first assumed to be the usual reply, "*Wa alaikum as-salaam,*" but it might've been something else, something that deflected or rejected the greeting. At least that would explain the raised voices that followed. They switched to Tamashek and spoke too quickly for Peter to follow. Goma was quieter than the two men, whose voices raised to the point of shouting. They furrowed their brows and their eyes glinted with anger.

Peter walked toward the door in imitation of Goma's relaxed gait. When they saw Peter approach they stopped and stared. His mere presence shifted an implicit balance of power. Or maybe it was because he was an unexpected sight: a tall European, out of place.

The younger man with the dark beard spoke in French, looking past Goma to address Peter directly. "Who are you? What are you doing here?"

Goma answered for Peter. "That's none of your business."

"Everything here is our business," the younger man said, turning his attention to Goma.

Peter stood above them, with the door stoop adding to his already imposing height. Goma raised his voice to match theirs. "You have no authority here. You should go hide in the desert with your defeated brothers. Don't ever come here again."

He tried to close the door and one of the men pushed against it from the other side. Peter helped Goma push. Together, they forced the door into its frame and Goma turned the key. Through the door, Peter heard the two men talk between themselves.

Peter's heart pounded, as much from the stress of the confrontation as from the exertion of pushing the door. They listened. The voices of the two men receded down the street. Goma nodded, a sign to Peter they weren't coming back. They returned to the courtyard. Peter sat heavily in the chair and felt a string snap, an elastic pulled beyond its limit. He'd tie the loose strand to the frame later. Goma eased into his chair carefully.

"Who were they?" Peter asked.

"Fanatics," Goma replied.

Peter waited for him to elaborate. The silence was longer than he expected. Goma finally added more. "They belong to Ansar Eddine. I think they were members of the Islamic police before the French came and they lost their authority."

"I thought they were all hiding in the desert."

"Not everyone. There's no proof against some of them. Not yet. So, they're allowed to stay, at least the ones who stopped fighting. The Malian state is broken. Coalition forces are out in the desert. Not much the UN peacekeepers can do either. It's a tricky thing, going after someone just because they're too pious."

"What'd they come here for? What business did they have with you?"

Goma snorted disdainfully. "Friday prayers. They're going around making sure everyone goes to the mosque. To *their* mosque. I told them I was a good Muslim and didn't make a habit of praying with infidels." He smiled at Peter with a glint in his eyes. "I guess they didn't like that very much."

Peter laughed, hard, releasing the tension of the confrontation. Behind his laughter was a combination of pleasure at Goma's bold wit and concern about what it might provoke. "Do you think they'll be back?"

"I worry," Goma answered. The object of his worry wasn't entirely clear.

Peter wanted him to say more. He was getting used to Goma's cryptic way of talking, but this was important, so he persisted. "In Canada we have people who go door to door trying to peddle their religion," he said. "But this felt different. This felt like they were, you know, like they still *were* religious police. Not wanting a conversation or a convert. Enforcing a rule."

Goma nodded. "I get that. Just a few months ago, they had all the power. They could do whatever they wanted. Beat people up in the street even. During the occupation, those two could've been jailors or they might've whipped women in the market for not wearing the veil. They might've been there for the amputation, helping out. Following orders."

"Or they could be rapists," Peter added.

"Not just could be," Goma said. "Very likely they *are* rapists. But not in their law. The law of Ansar Eddine gives them permission to do anything. Follow their desires. Maybe they're still married to a twelve-year-old they picked up during the occupation."

"Shit." Peter could think of nothing more to say. He wiggled his feet in the sand and watched it flow between his toes. "So, you think they'll be back?"

"Probably."

"Trying to get you to go to their mosque?"

"That? No. That fight's over," Goma replied. "I worry next time it'll be about you."

Peter was silent while he took that in. Then he said, "You mean, wanting to know more about what the tall white guy's doing here."

Goma's hands trembled as he tried to light a cigarette. On his first attempt, the match went out. The next one caught and he inhaled deeply and blew the smoke away from Peter. "Could be," he said. Or maybe they already know."

"You mean, know that we're working for the ICC?"

"They probably don't even know what that means. The thing is, we're poking around their shit. They have to know we're investigating them. We're not exactly keeping a low profile. We're out there at the sites all day. Fancy camera. Tape measures. Peacekeepers with checkpoints nearby. I'm pretty sure they have their eyes on us."

"And their spies on us." Peter remembered the boy on the donkey who passed in front of the bank. It might've been perfectly innocent, but then there was that long stare. There was no telling whose family he came from. Anyone could be reporting to the Islamists. "Let's say they have loyalists all over the place and they know what we're doing. Let's say they know we're collecting evidence against their leaders. What then? What can they do about it?"

Goma flicked an ash from his cigarette towards the base of the wall. "Well, for one thing, they could kill us," he said, without a trace of irony.

Peter couldn't think what to say. Or what to do.

Goma turned to look at him and waited for Peter to return his gaze. "Time's up, white boy," he said with a mischievous smile.

CHAPTER 18: RETURN

Peter Dekker's plane landed at Schiphol Airport at 4:36 p.m. on a Monday. A soon as the wheels hit the ground, he turned on his phone and texted Nora to tell her he'd landed.

Her reply came right away: On my way Guppy'tje! 😉

The border official lingered over Peter's recent stamps from Mali, especially the half-page of stamps and signatures from the gendarmeries in Mopti and Timbuktu. He looked at Peter, looked again at the passport, and stamped it vigorously before waving him through the gate.

Peter picked up his luggage and made his way through customs and the exit. Nora was nowhere to be seen. He felt bereft and worried. She said she was on her way. But what if she got lost? She'd text him. He checked his phone for a message. Then he saw her in the distance. He almost didn't recognize her. She was wearing a hat he hadn't seen before, a toque without a pompom. When she got close, he called her name. She smiled, and oriented toward him. Her eyes gleamed through the reflection in her glasses. When she got close, he pulled her toward him. They kissed and Peter could feel the rise and fall of her chest and the warmth of her breath.

"You ran," he said. "You shouldn't have. I'd have waited."

"I wanted to be here when you arrived, but the roads were too much . . ." She looked for the word, couldn't find it, and came out with "*fila*."

"Traffic jams," Peter said, translating. Nora's English had slipped, either from lack of use or the emotion of the moment. Peter felt a surge of warmth coupled with a sudden urge to kiss her neck. The swirl of people moving past them was inhibiting. He pushed the urge aside and said, "I like your hat. Where'd you get it?"

Nora told him about her visit to Kurt and Nel and Nel's knitting. As she spoke, Peter trailed his luggage and looked for signs to the taxi stand. They walked slowly and talked about Nora's recent visits to Peter's aunts and uncles. She kept things descriptive: Jan's mannerisms, Kurt's model plane, the two aunts and how different they were. Surely she had more to say. Impossible that she, of all people, would be satisfied with superficialities. It would have to wait. Maybe with a visit to Aunt Julia. Her apartment had a way of prying memories free from their moorings.

* * *

As soon as they opened the door to the apartment, Peter smelled smoke. "Something's burning!" He dropped his shoulder bag and rushed inside.

"No, no, it's okay," Nora shouted after him. "I had a little accident."

That afternoon, she explained, she had tried to bake a cake from scratch to celebrate his return, but made a mistake with the timer. The smoke detector didn't work. She got lost in her work. By the time she remembered, the cake was in flames. The firemen were very tall and very nice and their clothing smelled almost as strongly of smoke as the fire itself. They put the cake on top of the oven and extinguished the flames just by patting them down with their gloves. One of them looked through the kitchen and showed her where an extinguisher was kept under the sink in case, heaven forbid, something like that were to ever happened again. She tried opening all the windows to clear the smell, but it still wasn't gone. It would take a while.

"Why didn't you tell me all this in the taxi?"

She looked down sheepishly, her hands together. There was something girlish about her that way in her funny hat and summer dress.

Peter hugged her tightly. "Here I go off to Timbuktu and you're the one who has the adventure." He leaned down and kissed her neck just under her ear. Her skin was white and delicate. She pulled off her hat and turned her head to kiss him on the lips.

Peter felt her lips and her eagerness and thought how much he missed her and how long he had wanted this. Then his mind wandered unbidden to the rape files on Kella's desk in Timbuktu and the image they conjured of girls being taken away from their families, their eyes filled with terror. He wondered what happened to them on the so-called marriage bed. He felt a surge of passion, guilt, and confusion. For an instant, he couldn't tell if the desire he felt was for Nora or if it came from somewhere deeper and darker.

He stood straight and held her close. "Your kisses are sweeter than any cake," he said, smothering his thoughts, like the fireman's mitt.

She took hold of two of his fingers and led him to the bedroom, threw her glasses on the side table, flopped on the bed, lay on her back, and held both her arms outstretched with her fingers beckoning. He entered her embrace and they kissed. Her pelvis pressed into his abdomen. She wrapped her legs around him, pulling him tighter. He moved his lips to her neck, indulging the urge that he felt in the airport. They broke off and undressed quickly. From the light coming in through a crack in the curtain, he could see small blue veins under the pale skin of her breasts. He moved from kissing her breasts, back to her neck, then shifted his body higher up.

She reached down and he felt her hand on his unresponsive member. "Ooh, poor Guppytje, tired from his trip."

"It isn't that."

"What is it then?"

"I don't know." He was genuinely confused.

She pushed his head gently between her breasts and stroked his hair. "You've been through a lot these past few weeks."

"No, I haven't. Nothing happened. A stand storm. A bout of diarrhea. A couple of fanatics. Nothing."

Nora shushed him. "Silly nonsense. Your heart is hurting. I feel it."

As Peter lay with his head on her chest, he listened to her heartbeat and felt a rush of sorrow. He saw in his mind's eye the girl being taken away with terror in her eyes, but this time as though he were a father or a brother watching helplessly. He heard and felt Nora's heartbeat quicken—beat, beat, beat—like a soundtrack to his unspooling memories. His mind played images from the files on Kella's desk and the sound of her voice quavering as she read them aloud. He smelled the shit and urine of the women's prison. He heard the crack of the whip striking flesh in the market.

For the briefest instant, he heard his father's hand slapping his mother and saw her startled look—toward *him*—on feeling the sting.

Then the tears came, and his chest heaved with sobs. He wept for his mother and the powerlessness of his not-yet-manhood. He wept for all he had seen and heard in Timbuktu. He wept for all he didn't see or know, but that must've occurred for there to be so much wrong. His tears came from a deep well filled from the experience of centuries. He felt his cheeks wet from tears gathered in Nora's bosom and moved his head in small circles to spread them on the rest of his face, his forehead, his nose, his ears. Nora stroked his hair and kissed the top of his head. He moved higher up on her. The tears wet their bodies, as if they were sweating and lovemaking in a heatwave. They kissed and their passion grew together.

He moved inside her.

"All better now," she whispered in his ear.

CHAPTER 19: DEBRIEFING

"Hail the conquering hero," Rash said from behind his monitor.

There was something about the moment that made the cliché true. Peter felt an extra swagger in his stride as he navigated the return to his workstation at the west-facing window. His equipment bag still had a patina of dust from the sandstorm on the edge of the Sahara. It contained precious material, the photographs still stored on the Leica, the ledger, the notes and diagrams, the measurements taken with care. He'd risked his life for it, driving around in the Hilux without armor. Every time he'd gone out with Ibrahim and Goma, there was a risk of hitting an IED. It would've been a stray one, cleverly placed, one the sniffer dogs and sensor detectors somehow missed. That was how it happened.

"You're gonna like what I have in here." Peter patted the bag, sending some of the fine dust particles into the air.

Olga's head appeared above her monitor. "Hey, Peter! Welcome back!" Her hair was unkempt from a habit of holding her head in her hands as she looked at the screen. "How was it in the forbidden city?"

He wanted to say, *that would be the palace in Beijing*, but before he could answer there was the sound of someone vomiting and retching. Peter put his bag next to his desk and looked for the source. He found Evan leaned over the wastebasket next to his desk. Evan lifted his head and drew with it the smell of his sick. "Hi Peter," he said weakly, and turned back to the wastebasket, racked by another bout of heaving.

"God, Evan. Are you okay?"

"All good," he said. His voice sounded hollow from inside the wastebin.

"What happened? Something you ate?"

"Nope. Something I saw. Aww, man."

Rash and Olga gathered and created a presence of concern.

Evan got unsteadily to his feet and flopped in the chair at his workstation. The screen displayed his desktop, revealing nothing of what he'd seen. Even in his agony, he'd taken a moment to navigate away from whatever had caused his distress. "A side gig," he said. "I was looking at videos of police brutality in Iraq. Not a war crime per se, but you know . . . A state going after its own citizens. There this guy protesting. The video is shot right up close. He's mad as hell, shouting at the police. You can tell he's in the front lines. The people next to him are all mad as hell, too, pumping their fists in the air. There's tear gas, but not too much of it and they're fighting it off, tears coming down, faces all puffy, but they're still on their feet, not clearing away. I can't tell if anyone threw something at the police. The camera's really focusing on this one guy. Then all of a sudden his face explodes."

"Explodes?" Olga asked.

"Yeah, just like, pfff!" Evan opened his fingers in pantomime of an explosion. "No more face. Blood and brains, like . . ." He reached the limit of the capacity for words to describe what he'd seen.

"So what was it? A dum-dum bullet?" There was excited curiosity in Rash's voice. He blinked and looked down when he caught Olga's disapproving look.

"That's what I was trying to find out," Evan said. "I was slowing it down, going frame by frame. That's when it hit me. The nausea. It's like one part of my brain was doing the analysis while another part was living the experience without me knowing."

"Ugh," Olga somehow found the perfect word under the circumstances.

"Ugh is right," Evan said. "Oh, and by the way, it was a tear gas canister fired point blank."

"That would do it," Rash said.

"Yeah, but a useless piece of shit video. No context. Can't see who fired it, where it came from. Uploaded to a platform that stripped out the metadata, so I can't see when it was filmed. No geolocation. I could only take their word for it that it was a protest in Iraq in the comments before it was all taken down by content moderation. I didn't see anything that mentioned the city. Probably Fallujah. I still have to work that out. There's nothing, nothing, nothing of any use here except the blood and brains, and that I could've really done without. Fuck." Evan dabbed his mouth with the back of his sleeve and looked back toward the ceiling, his fingers interlaced behind his head and his eyes closed. "Fuck, fuck, fuck."

Peter looked over at his bag next to his keyboard and wondered what it'd be like, going over and over the material waiting for him there.

Rash put his hand on Peter's shoulder. "Who'd've thought. War trauma in an office. New adventures for everyone. Right, my dear friend?" He patted him amicably.

* * *

Ferman had his back to Peter and was looking out across the forest toward the dunes. Peter waited for his attention from the other side of the desk. The visitor's space was cramped. He had trouble finding a comfortable place for his knees.

"I'm happy to read in your report that the people we hired are doing such good work in Mali," he said. He turned to face Peter. "An excellent report, by the way. Given the quick turnaround. Well done."

"Thank you," Peter said. "Yes, the people working for us are excellent. Really talented."

Ferman sat and swiveled in his chair with it tilted back as far as it would go. Despite the relaxed gesture, he somehow didn't lose his military bearing. "So, tell me something," he said.

Peter waited for the second part of the sentence, but it didn't come. "Yes?" he said to move things along.

"So, tell me something that *isn't* in the report."

"Hmm." Peter wasn't sure how to respond. "Like what?"

"Anything. Like what didn't you expect when you got there."

Once he understood what Ferman was driving at, Peter appreciated the question, aimed as it was at a deeper truth. "Well, for one thing," he began, "I didn't expect just getting there to be so difficult." Peter told him about the sandstorm and the overland stretch of the trip from Mopti to Timbuktu. About how there were no soldiers on the road as expected. How it seemed exposed. Dangerous.

"Right," Ferman said. "Good."

For an instant Peter had trouble understanding what the word "good" applied to. Good there were no soldiers? He decided Ferman was satisfied with his initial observation and wanted him to continue. "Then there was the difficulty of daily life in Timbuktu," Peter continued. "I wasn't expecting everything to be so slow coming back."

"Like what, exactly?"

"Well," Peter drew from a collage of mental images. "Basics like electricity, water. The hotels all still shut for renovations. The bank."

"Yes, I saw what you wrote about the bank," Ferman said dryly.

"I know some of this is in the report," Peter went on, "but I was really surprised at the extent of the crimes during the occupation. I thought at first I was just going there to gather data on the destruction of shrines and mausoleums and libraries, but there was so much more."

Ferman nodded. He picked up a pencil and wiggled it distractedly. "I read that too. Anything missing from that part of your report?"

Peter noticed Ferman was skirting around the violence without putting words to it, as though the topic were taboo. He decided to go there: "One thing I didn't mention was the evidence coming out of the Malian army committing *rapes*. There's some evidence of them committing *torture* as well." He put emphasis on the words, "rape" and "torture" as a provocation. "Not to mention extrajudicial executions," he continued. "Shooting captives and leaving their bodies in the desert. There's pretty solid evidence of that, too."

Ferman looked at him over his glasses. "Yes, well. Very important, that. I'm glad you mentioned it. The defense might someday find a use for that information."

"The defense? What about the prosecution? Those are war crimes." Peter knew the futility of his objection, and posed the question anyway. "Can't the OTP open an investigation?" As he spoke these words, he felt the strangeness on his tongue of the acronym for the Office of the Prosecutor. It brought home to him his lack of experience. Still, the question rankled.

Ferman looked at his watch. "How about an early lunch? Beat the rush. What say you?"

* * *

"The thing is . . ." Ferman picked up on Peter's question from fifteen minutes earlier, as though no time had elapsed, no selection of entrees, no bantering exchange with the cashier, no casting about the nearly empty cafeteria looking for right table. Peter recognized this quality of his boss as a rare talent. Not just a good memory. A persistent mind. "The thing is," Ferman repeated, "we can't prosecute anyone in the Malian army. We're free to investigate the incidents surrounding Mali's role in the war in the north—in fact we should—but we can't issue any indictments in that direction."

There was a mismatch between his erect bearing supported by a crisp suit and the informality of the cafeteria. He and Peter were at one of the more coveted tables along the windows overlooking a honeycomb-pattered cement wall. At least there was light coming in, something to look at other than functional furnishings. Even at ground level, the semi-wild park that started at the top of the wall beckoned.

"Because, politics?" Peter said curtly, but meant it as a serious question.

"If you like. Or rather, even if you don't like. You see—and this is interesting—the only reason we're able to investigate the war crimes in

Timbuktu is because the Malian government put in a request. We were *invited*. That's important to remember."

"Invited by the very government that's ultimately responsible for its share of the war crimes during the fighting."

"I'll be the first to admit, it's distasteful. But, for political reasons more than anything else, we have to hold our nose and move on." Ferman took a large bite from a ham and cheese sandwich with a gusto that put the lie to his expression of distaste.

Peter poked at the fried potato in front of him with his fork, his appetite lagging. "I understand. Without Mali's support, no investigation into Ansar Eddine and Al-Qaida and the rest. And the people in leadership in those organizations are the worst of the worst. It's a matter of priorities. I get it. Still, it's interesting to lift the lid on the politics here, see what's there, don't you think?"

Ferman perked up. "Sure. Of course. What're you thinking?"

"For starters, the investigation takes some of the spotlight away from the Malian army's failure in the north. The fact that the French had to come to the rescue. There's a PR angle to the investigation."

"Right. Completely," Ferman agreed.

Peter pursued the thought, still unsure where it might lead. "The ICC's investigation says to the world, 'this is the kind of enemy the government of Mali has to deal with. How can you possibly expect us to do without international help?'"

"I can see that."

"And then," Peter continued, "it justifies total control of the north. It gives Mali the excuse to break its treaty with the Tuaregs. Everyone wearing a turban gets tarred with the same brush. Even the rights defenders we hired to do our investigation. It hardens everyone's position on regional autonomy and indigenous rights, and gives Mali access to the north and its resources. Minerals. Money. Power. That's the long and the short of it."

Ferman nodded in quiet assent. "Okay, that could well be part of it. I don't know. I haven't spoken with the president. But let's say our investigation indirectly supports Mali's control of the north the way you describe. Let's then think about the role of the Court in all this. Do we ignore the worst war crimes because there might be a political motive behind a government's request for an investigation? No. We go where we can. Right now, we're an orphan in the international system. We're a pariah, because we're a threat to all the states that commit mass crimes. And there are more than a few. Every case we successfully prosecute gives the Court more credibility, gives us a little more clout with unwilling governments. More funding, more leverage. At this point early on, we need some wins. Badly."

"So, what you're saying is, we start with cases we can win. Rebels who commit the worst atrocities. States want us to prosecute those rebel leaders because those are their enemies. Easy from our end because the insurgencies have no standing in the international system. Then, case by case, we build the legitimacy of the Court. Show how rigorous and fair it all is. Establish the rule of law. And slowly but surely, we extend our reach. Go after bigger fish."

"In broad terms, that's the picture," Ferman agreed. "A little oversimplified, but yes."

"And the destruction of shrines and mausoleums in Timbuktu in violation of their UNESCO world heritage standing is a relatively easy case to win."

Ferman furrowed his brow. "Let's not get too confident. We can't leave anything to chance."

"Of course."

There was a long silence during which Ferman revealed nothing of his thoughts. He looked out the window toward the cement wall and stirred his coffee. "How've you been keeping? Since you got back, I mean." Ferman's switch to something more personal was forced, but Peter accepted it as well-intentioned.

"Good, good."

"Mmm." Ferman stirred his coffee beyond the point of necessity, oblivious to the repetitive noise of the spoon against the mug. Peter pushed back his irritation.

"I've been looking into Dutch war history in my spare time." Peter switched topics as a way to put an end to the coffee stirring without causing offense.

"Oh?"

"It seems my family on my father's side was involved in the resistance. At some point, someone related to me was arrested." Peter brought out his phone and showed Ferman the picture of his surname scratched in the cell wall in the Oranjehotel in Scheveningen.

Ferman peered at it closely through his reading glasses. "Interesting."

"My partner Nora kept things going while I was away, talking to relatives. There's some evidence that a member of my family was a sympathizer, maybe even an informer for the SS."

Ferman furrowed his brow. "Be careful. When you start investigating family, you lose all perspective. You have to be detached. Just think about your work in Timbuktu. Photographing, measuring, doing everything carefully. It has to be like that."

"Even though you can't go back in time with a tape measure," Peter added.

"Right," Ferman agreed. "Your judgment has to be the measure."

"But don't these kinds of investigations not also have an element of intuition?" Peter drew from a mental inventory of TV police procedurals. "What about beginning with a suspicion and following through?"

Ferman looked at Peter over his glasses. "Sure, but that's where you have to be extra careful. Have your suspicion, your intuition, what have you. Then follow through carefully, step by step. Start with an investigation plan. Don't fall prey to confirmation bias just because you want a certain outcome. Or want to avoid it."

Peter nodded. "Seems reasonable enough."

"So, who's the person in your family you suspect of being a collaborator?"

"My father."

"Oh, good lord. You're *fucking* kidding me."

This was the first time Peter had heard Ferman use foul language. It was jarring. He couldn't tell if Ferman meant it as a reproach or if it a genuine expression of surprise.

"Well, there's nothing definite," Peter said, backpedaling. "At this point it's just suggestions. Indications."

"From what source?"

Peter told him about his Aunt Julia, her stories from the war, the Nazis in the house, the geese killed with grenades, and his father's suspicious behavior, his comradeship with the officer. And, not to forget, the name on the cell wall.

"Can I tell you what I think?" Ferman said when Peter finished.

"Of course."

"As far as your family's concerned, it's just an interesting story. Suspicions."

"I know," Peter said.

"But it's also a story of a war crime. They had an elaborate banquet and left the family without food, to face starvation. And there's likely much more to the story than that."

"That's right." Peter was encouraged.

"It'd be interesting to find out who this sonofabitch was, don't you think?" Ferman said.

"There's no way he could still be alive."

"For curiosity's sake." Ferman brought out a note pad and pen. "Here's the name of a friend of mine in the Netherlands Public Prosecution Service." He wrote the name and an email address. "He's a pretty special guy. Very good at what he does."

"Which is?"

"He specializes in finding war criminals." Ferman smiled knowingly and looked at Peter over his glasses. "Including a Nazi or two."

CHAPTER 20: THE CALL

Peter was at his desk analyzing a video from *France 24* of the destruction of a mausoleum when his phone buzzed. It was a message on WhatsApp from Ferman.

“Could you come upstairs a minute?”

“Be right there.” Peter typed.

In the elevator, Peter tried to think what might cause a summons like this. Ferman didn’t habitually do that. Most of his interactions were informal, polite conversations. Too polite.

Ferman opened the door right away in response to Peter’s knock. “Please, have a seat.”

Peter felt his heart beating in his chest. Maybe this was about another trip to Timbuktu. Or somewhere worse.

“I don’t want you to take this the wrong way,” Ferman said. “This isn’t really about you. Well, it is but . . .” He was having trouble getting to the topic.

Peter’s mouth felt dry.

“You see, well . . .” Ferman said, struggling to find the words. “I’ve been getting calls from your father.”

There it is. Peter, thought. My life is ruined.

“They go straight to voice messages so I’m not really bothered by them,” Ferman said. “Still, they’re rather interesting.”

"Oh, no. You're kidding. I'm so sorry." Peter felt more than sorry; he was mortified. His father had dared cross a sacred boundary between personal life and work, like a pestilence that attacked its host with sympathetic embarrassment. Now Arie's eccentricity would infect Peter's reputation.

"Nothing for you to be sorry about. It can't be helped." Ferman's looked at his phone sharply, undoing the words or reassurance.

Peter wondered whether his father's behavior really couldn't be helped. Maybe he could've expected something like this. Maybe he should've warned Arie off. "You said calls, plural. How many did he make?" Peter asked, afraid to know.

"Five."

"Good grief. How did he get your number?" Peter didn't think his father capable of such a feat of investigative prowess. It would've involved a spectacular hack.

"No idea. I thought you gave it to him."

Ferman picked up the phone on his desk. "Hello," he said. "Is this Ayodele?" Peter couldn't make out the voice on the other end. "Hi Ayo. Ferman here. I wonder if you might solve a mystery for me. Phone calls from a Mr. Dekker."

An indistinct voice reached Peter from the earpiece.

"No not that Dekker. His father."

Peter heard more sounds on the phone, but couldn't make out what the other person was saying.

"Oh, really? I see. Thank you. Thank you, very much. I'm glad we cleared that up."

Ferman hung up and looked at Peter. "Mystery solved. It seems I was away from my desk and the receptionist gave your father my private number to call back later by mistake. He introduced himself as Dekker and she thought it was you."

Peter felt a wave of relief. Arie getting Ferman's number was pure luck. An oversight by the receptionist. His father's capabilities were strictly limited, he assured himself. Then again, there was no telling.

"Are you at all interested in what he had to say in those five messages?" Ferman gazed at Peter above his reading glasses.

"I'm afraid to ask. What did he say?"

"Well, let's see." Ferman's eyes twinkled. He took off his glasses and twirled them adeptly. He was enjoying this. "He usually begins by saying he's an investigator, too. Lots of experience. I've no idea who he's referring to when he says, '*investigator too*'. There's a person of reference there, someone not explicitly identified. Setting himself up an investigator, just like you or me. Then he offers his services. Something about inspecting buildings. Very adept at looking for clues. Stress fractures in concrete, and such."

"Oh, gawd. His services. Of course. What's the point in being the world's greatest investigator if you've nothing to investigate?" Peter had to perform the delicate balancing act of deflecting the impact of Arie's calls without coming across as uncharitable.

"He occasionally mentions something unintelligible about Queen Wilhelmina. Of The Netherlands, I gather."

Peter nodded. "On her majesty's secret service. Except Dutch."

Ferman laughed. "That makes sense."

"Did he say anything else?"

"Nothing, really," Ferman replied. "A couple of rants about Nazis. To be expected from a man of his generation, I suppose, with his experience. He says things like, 'I was in a war. There were war crimes then, too.'"

"That's interesting. No details?" Peter was curious. Maybe his father let drop some fragment about his life during the war.

"That's about it. Do you want me to play one of them for you?" Ferman asked, playfully.

"No!" Peter objected louder than intended. He felt himself blush, and said more quietly, "No, thanks. That I can do without."

Ferman laughed again. "My, my . . ." he said, without completing the sentence. He looked at Peter fixedly with his blue-grey eyes. "It does get interesting and sad when our parents become our children, don't you think?"

"It sure does," Peter replied. "Except he's always been this way."

***

Evan and Peter approached one another from opposite directions in the workstation aisle. There was only room for one to pass at a time. Peter stepped aside between two desks, ceding the space. Rather than accept the gesture and move past, Evan said, "Why so glum, Peter? Bad news?"

Peter wasn't aware he'd been looking downcast. As far as he could tell, he was only wondering what might've motivated his father to call Mr. Ferman. Five times. The calls might just express eccentricity, the tendency of Dutch men of his generation to be forthright and oblivious to social niceties. Then again, there might be something calculated in his behavior. Perhaps Arie felt he had something to hide and decided to go towards the danger instead of run away. A bluff. No telling. That would call for understanding Arie, getting to his inner life. And that was an enigma beyond reckoning.

Peter told Evan about his father's phone calls to Ferman. "I've no idea why he did that. Or how to stop him," he confessed. "If I tell him not to, he'll do it more. It seems quaint and old-mannish, but it's actually sadistic. It's so embarrassing."

"Well, in that case why don't we give him what he wants?" Evan suggested.

"What do you mean by that?" Peter felt uneasy, not knowing what Evan was thinking. Before he could say anything. Evan called across the room, "Olga! Say, Olga! Come here, please. We've something for you to do."

"Oh, no." Peter formed a notion of what Evan had in mind. "No. Really, please don't. This is undignified. We have more serious things to do."

"Exactly," Evan said. "Serious, serious. Cluster bombs here, body parts there. Vicarious trauma. Puking in the wastebin. It's driving us all crazy. This is actually interesting."

Olga responded to Evan's summons by walking to his desk with shuffling steps, unaware of the fact that her hair was spectacularly askew. "Yes?"

Rash appeared behind her. "What's going on?"

Evan seemed to revel in the presence of his small audience. "My dear friends. In furtherance of Peter's inquiries into his father's sordid past and in response to his assaults on Mr. Ferman's voicemail and valuable time, I thought we would give Mr. Dekker the elder an opportunity to clarify what exactly he has to offer. It behooves us to reply to his importuning. But respectfully. As fellow investigators." He looked at his watch. "Let's see. Where does your dad live, Peter?"

Peter was stunned. He couldn't be sure if it was a guess or if Evan knew Peter was looking into his father's past. He decided Evan was guessing. "Kamloops, British Columbia," Peter answered.

"Okay, that'd be Pacific time," Evan said. "Nine hours earlier. He should just be finishing breakfast about now."

Peter covered his eyes with his hand. "This is so embarrassing."

"And since Mr. Dekker the elder is, from what I gather, especially inclined to open himself up to female interlocution," Evan continued, "Olga should do the honors." He unlocked his cell phone and handed it to Peter. "Peter, if you could . . ."

Peter hesitated. Even if he didn't give him Arie's number, Evan could probably find it in a matter of seconds.

"C'mon, now," Evan said.

Peter entered Arie's number and passed the phone to Olga.

Olga put the phone on speaker. It rang five times before Arie answered.

"Halloo."

"Oh, hello, Mr. Dekker?"

"*Ja*. Who's this?"

"My name is Olga Podporska. I work at the Office of the Prosecutor at the International Criminal Court. Sorry about the delay in getting back to you. Things are so busy here."

"Ooh, that's right. I called Peter's boss."

"Yes, you did, Mr. Dekker. Mr. Ferman is busy at the moment so I'm calling you. Is that all right?" Olga winked at Peter.

"Ooh, yes. That's just fine." Arie sounded alert, interested.

"I understand you have some experience as an investigator. Is that what you called about?" Olga looked over to Evan for encouragement. Evan nodded.

The question prompted a silence on the other end of the call. Peter imagined it was because Arie so rarely received affirmation of his fantasies. His mind must be racing, trying to catch up.

Eventually, Arie cleared his throat to indicate his thoughts were in order. "Ahem! Well, you see . . . erm . . . I was a building inspector for many years and . . . you know—"

"You were also a survivor of a war, weren't you?" Olga interjected. "You lived through an occupation by the Nazis. You must've witnessed war crimes yourself. This is exactly the sort of thing we look into here. I'd think that would be an excellent qualification for an investigator."

"Well, yes, I suppose so, but—" Peter could hear the uncertainty in Arie's voice. Olga was throwing him off stride.

"I'd be really interested to hear about that," Olga said.

Peter tried to picture Arie on the other end of the call. He faced a difficult choice: talk about himself and his great accomplishments as an erstwhile building inspector at the risk of losing his audience, or conform to the interest of the young and possibly attractive woman calling him and tell her something about the war.

"Well, what would you like to know?" Arie asked.

Olga tried mouthing something to Peter, but he didn't understand. He shook his head and shrugged in quick succession. She stood on her toes and whispered, "What do you want to know?"

Peter thought for a moment, then bent down and whispered in reply, "Ask him about forced labor in the German factories. How'd he get out of it?" Peter had questions about Arie's life in the later years of the war. He would've been older than sixteen and at constant risk of being sent off to Germany as part of the system of slave labor. Peter wondered how he'd avoided capture. *If* he'd avoided it.

"Mr. Dekker? Are you still there?"

"*Ja, ja.*"

"I was wondering, as one investigator to another, of course, how you eluded capture by the Germans who were looking for people to work in the factories." Olga looked at Peter. He nodded.

There was a long silence.

"Mr. Dekker, do you hear me?"

"Well," Arie said, finally. "A couple of ways. One was the church. There was a secret room upstairs in the church. If the Germans were waiting outside to round people up, the Dominee would call for a certain hymn." He paused. "I forget which one. Anyway, when that hymn was called the men who were older than sixteen would go upstairs to a little room behind the bookcase. There was a book in front of a lever." He paused again. "I forget what book. I did that a couple of times. Hid in a secret room upstairs in the church."

"That's very interesting, Arie. Can I call you Arie?"

"*Ja*."

"But, Arie, wouldn't it have been easier just to stay at home?"

"It was Augustine!" Arie exclaimed.

"Augustine?"

"The book," he said. "The one that opened the door. It was Saint Augustine. *The City of God*, or something like that. The Dominee never told us why. Maybe because it was a fat book and you could get your hand behind and find the latch. Then we had to be completely silent. No talking. No coughing or sneezing. I remember now."

"So you had this amazing secret room." Olga pursued her question. "But wouldn't it have been safer to stay home? Hide?"

"*Naturlijk*, yes. And we did. But, you see, the church was really important in those days. It was where everyone met. Got information. Helped each other out. And then, don't forget, you'd go to hell if you didn't show faith. That's what they taught. The church was like that in those days. Not very friendly, like today, with the empty pews. So we went. But we mostly stayed home."

"Never tempted to go out?"

"Ooh, it was so boring," Arie said.

Peter was hearing this side of him for the first time. It confounded him why Arie had said nothing like this to him growing up. And now, to a complete stranger on the phone, it was all pouring out. There was injustice to it.

"Nothing to do," Arie continued. "We weren't even allowed to play cards. The church was so strict. So, sometimes I'd go out. Visit my cousins."

"How did you avoid getting picked up by the Germans when you went out?" Olga asked.

"Simple. I dressed as a woman. It worked pretty well. Except, you know, I started getting the wrong sort of attention from the soldiers. I rode my bike and they whistled and made a fuss. Ooh, I was a beautiful woman! I was—what do you say?—a hottie! Ha! Ha!"

"Well, it's been a real treat talking to you, Mr. Dekker." Olga returned to formality, trying to move the conversation to a close.

"I wore my mother's old dress and put a scarf over my head and some lipstick and ooh, boy! I was really something! Ha! Ha!"

"I'm sure you were." Olga rolled her eyes.

Peter felt the blood rush into his face.

"I nearly got killed once," Arie said.

"Oh?" Olga was back to paying attention.

"I got distracted and crashed my bike into a German soldier. He was on a bike coming the other direction, sideways. We were both getting up and he started apologizing, and then he got a good look at my face, and he said 'Halt!' But he didn't have his balance yet and he said 'Halt! Halt!' again and I got on my bike and rode like hell. Man, I never rode so fast in my life. Standing on the pedals. He shot at me and I could feel the bullet go past my ear. Bzzz. Like that. You can feel it when a bullet comes that close, you know. I got away."

"That's very interesting, Arie."

"It's a good thing he was a lousy shot."

"A very good thing," Olga agreed.

"But me, I was a good shot. How do you call it? A crack."

"You were?" Olga's inflection expressed genuine interest.

Peter was again amazed at how much was pouring out of his father. All his life, the war years had been a blank. The embarrassment he felt at the beginning of the call was replaced by an uncomfortable mix of curiosity and indignation.

"Who taught you to shoot like that?" Olga asked.

Silence. After a moment Arie said, "Oh, you know. Country life."

Peter looked for a scrap of paper and a pen on a nearby desk. He tore a page from a book and scribbled a note to Olga.

Ask him about the resistance.

Olga read the note silently, looked at Peter and nodded. "So Arie," she said. She pronounced the two syllables of his name distinctly. "Tell me something, would you?" She was slowing down to get his attention.

"Yes?"

"Were you ever in the resistance?" Olga got straight to the point.

Peter winced. He could anticipate Arie's reaction.

"You know," Olga continued, "fighting the Nazis during the occupation."

There was silence from the other end.

"Did you ever know anyone in the resistance? Interact with them?"

"It was a complicated time. Better to forget all that," Arie said, confirming what Peter expected.

"Well, thank you so much, Mr. Dekker," Olga said breezily. "It was lovely talking to you."

Arie wasn't there to reply. He had already hung up.

The group stood silent for a moment.

"Wow," Rash said. "That was intense."

"Olga looked at the phone in her hand. "Did you get what you wanted, Peter? That felt really uncomfortable."

Peter nodded. "I think so."

"He's pretty ballsy, your dad, by the sound of it," Evan said.

"I'd give anything to know what he did in the resistance," Rash said. "I mean, from his reaction, there's obviously more to know. I think your dad's a badass."

Peter mulled over the words, *obviously more to know*. It was the impression he had, too.

CHAPTER 21: CORINE

Nora and Aunt Julia agreed to meet at the beach in Scheveningen at nine o'clock as it was nicest in the morning hours, between the crack-of-dawn joggers and the hardy late-April sunbathers. They'd have a little time together, just the two of them, while Peter was at work. Nora was glad she was on a summer schedule until Michaelmas Term in early October and she enjoyed getting to know Aunt Julia. The Pier—together with its Ferris wheel, tower, casino and restaurants—was a famous landmark, but to Nora that didn't matter in the least. It was their rendezvous point, not what drew them to this place. She loved this wide beach, the smell of the sea, the sound of the waves, the sense of space. And of time. With the wide expanse of sand in front of them, there came a feeling of slowness.

Nora met Aunt Julia at the entrance closest to the pier. The wind was minimal and the cloud cover breezed in languidly over the North Sea. Nora heard the waves crash on the beach, driven by the same swells farther out that made the ferry crossing from Hoek van Holland to Harwich a stomach-churning adventure. Especially for tourists who lacked sea legs.

They looked for a place to have their picnic-breakfast and realized neither had brought a blanket or beach towel. Their solution was to walk closer to the boardwalk to find an empty bench. There they emptied out their bags and displayed the Tupperware bins and Ziplocs containing their offerings to one another: biscuits, buttered toast, boiled eggs, thin-sliced edam, smoked herring. Together, they assembled an abundance far beyond their meagre appetites. And, like the expanse of beach, the food gave them a sense of things slowed down, an absence of hurry or urgency. They talked about nothing of importance. Nora took pleasure in the children shrieking with the onset of waves. "How brave those children are to go in the water this time of year," she said.

Aunt Julia agreed but added that the North Beach with its nude sunbathing was less suitable for children than the cold water. "Last time I was here I came with Aksel. We went in that direction, not knowing. When we came to that part of the beach, he wanted me to undress. Can you imagine?"

"Actually," Nora pushed back mildly, "I think that would've been lovely."

"Ooh, *vreselijk*! At my age! I mean, that would've been, what, nine years ago and even then . . ." She looked down critically at her perfectly trim bosom and belly.

"You know," Nora said. "You don't have to have a perfect body to enjoy the beach without clothes. I think Aksel was right."

"Of course, he was right," Aunt Julia said. "He was always right. He won the argument by taking off his pants."

Nora laughed. "I think he and Peter would've liked each other."

"I know so."

They stared silently toward the sea. Nora put both hands around her mug, felt the warmth reach into her hands. The steam from it moved across two little spots of blue and green, the bathing suits of two children playing in the waves. "I wonder . . ."

"What?"

"If Peter and Aksel went to the North Beach together," Nora conjectured, "who would've been the first to take off his pants?"

Nora expected Aunt Julia to laugh, but she took the question seriously. "Oh, that's easy. Aksel."

"Do you think?" Nora thought the question over more seriously. "I'm not so sure. Peter can sometimes be . . . What's the word? Surprising. Unpredictable."

She felt Aunt Julia's eyes on her. "Lucky you," Aunt Julia said, and they both laughed.

When they finished the picnic, they packed up the remains. There was some confusion about whose Tupperware bin belonged to whom. Aunt Julia resolved it by saying it didn't matter one way or the other. They took off their shoes, put them in their tote bags, not minding the sand mixing with the Tupperware, and walked arm in arm southward along the beach. The waves were loud closer to the water line. A few seconds after each crash, Nora felt the cold North Sea water run across her toes.

They shared a meditative silence broken only by the breaking of waves. Then Aunt Julia said, "There's something I've been meaning to tell you."

She left it at that, waiting for Nora to respond. She didn't, not right away. The beach had taken over her senses and Aunt Julia's words needed time to penetrate. Eventually, Nora said, "What is it?"

"I wasn't completely truthful," Aunt Julia said.

Nora scanned her memory for any falsehoods Aunt Julia might've told, and found none. "I'm sure it's not important," she said.

"It's very important." Aunt Julia gripped her arm tighter.

"Then tell me."

"It's about Corine. How she died," Aunt Julia said.

"Oh?" Nora didn't know what to think. Peter had once told her his aunt Corine had died in a car accident before he was born. For an instant, she wondered whether he, too, wasn't telling the truth. More likely, Aunt Julia's deception, whatever it was, extended to him and he didn't know the secret Aunt Julia was about to reveal either. "How did she die, then?"

"She was murdered."

This wasn't what Nora expected. The weight of it made her feet heavy and stopped her from walking another step. "Murdered! How? How do you know?"

"I was there when they killed her." Aunt Julia spoke softly so Nora could hardly hear.

They continued walking, but slower than before. "Tell me what happened."

"It was the Waffen SS. Remember I told you about the three Nazis who invaded our house on New Year's Eve?"

Nora nodded.

"They're the ones who killed her." Aunt Julia's voice barely reached Nora. "When I told you about it the first time, I said we all went to bed, but—"

A wave breaking up into foam made it impossible for Nora to hear the rest. "I'm sorry. What? What did you say?"

Aunt Julia raised her voice. "I said we didn't go. We didn't go to bed. They killed her."

Her grip on Nora's arm tightened. Nora found it odd to hear no tremor or waver in Aunt Julia's voice to go along with her tight grip. It was steady—almost too steady. She'd gone from a hushed voice to that of a seasoned orator.

"Oh my God, I'm so, so sorry." Nora could think of nothing else to say.

Aunt Julia steered them higher on the beach, away from the breaking waves. They looked for a bench like the one where they had just picnicked, but they'd walked to a wilder part of the beach and there were none. Without exchanging a word, they sat in the damp sand.

"You don't have to tell me about it if you don't want to," Nora said.

"I want to tell you," Aunt Julia replied. She stared toward the sea.

Nora waited.

After a long silence, Aunt Julia began her story. "I remember it so clearly. Sometimes I wish I didn't, but that's just how it is, I suppose. It's like a photograph. No, like a movie that plays in my mind. I can still see it. Sometimes it plays even when I don't want to."

She paused and Nora resisted the urge to prompt her.

Aunt Julia continued. "It happened after the dinner, after the singing. Suddenly the mood changed. The officer took out his pistol, you know, one of those Lugers with the little round thingy on the side. The kind they all carried. He took out a bullet, held it up. He said, 'Here, my friends, is the very last bullet we have between us.' Very theatrical. Like bad acting. I sometimes wonder what would've happened if Arie had tried to overpower him right then when he had the last bullet in his hand and no usable weapon. There were three of them and four of us, sort of. Arie was the only man, but Ma was there and she was pretty strong. I was fourteen and small for my age and Corine was still a girl, only nine or so. I guess they would've overpowered us. Still, after what happened, maybe it would've been better to fight."

"You shouldn't be too hard on yourself," Nora said.

"It doesn't matter now," Aunt Julia said curtly. "Anyway, Arie's the one who decided for us. He just stood there staring. The officer pulled on a little lever on the top of his pistol and put the bullet in and the lever came down and it made a noise, like 'click' and everything changed. The chance was gone. Ma just stood there, her eyes big and her hand over her mouth. Then the officer said, 'Let's play a little game.' And he put two chairs together against the wall and sat me in one and Corine in the other. Then he turned to Arie and said, 'You choose.' Arie didn't know what he meant. He just stood there staring. And the officer said, 'Come, come now, don't be shy. You choose which one.' And he put the—what do you call it? —the end of the pistol where the bullet comes out on our foreheads, first Corine, then me, then Corine again, back and forth. I thought, Please let it be me. Let Corine live. And Arie just stood there, not saying anything. The Freiwilliger was there, too. He didn't say anything, but I remember he grinned like he was enjoying the show. I don't know where the other one was, maybe off in a corner. He was always slinking around where I couldn't see him. The officer said to Arie, 'You think maybe if you don't say anything, the Fates will change their minds and I'll put this away.' He waved the gun and then put it back on my forehead. 'But no. It's already decided. One of them will die. And it's up to you to choose which one.' All Arie said was. 'No, no. I can't.' The officer put the pistol on my forehead and started squeezing the trigger and Arie shouted, 'No!' And that's when it happened."

Aunt Julia fell silent again. Rather than prod, Nora kept her company. Aunt Julia was not so much looking toward the sea as not looking at her. Keeping her emotions in check. She sighed over the sound of waves and gulls, gathering herself to continue. "The officer said, 'Not this one? That's your choice? Then this one.' And the gun went off. It was so loud my ears rang. Beeeeeep, like that. When I heard that bang and smelled the smoke . . ." Aunt Julia took a deep breath and exhaled in a succession of short, quick puffs. She put her thumb and index finger in close to the bridge of her nose, pressed against her tear ducts, pushing the tears back.

"Then a strange thing happened," she continued. "I was looking at a drop of blood on the officer's belt. I thought, 'why is there a drop of blood on his belt?' Like it didn't belong there and somewhere in my mind I thought the answer to that question was the most important thing in the world. Ma was screaming and that brought me back. She rushed over to me and gathered me up in her arms and pulled me away. She held me close and steered me out of the room. I looked back over my shoulder." Aunt Julia paused and said, "I don't want to tell you what I saw."

Nora felt herself shake as though she was there in that room. She stayed silent and waited for Aunt Julia to continue.

"Ma took me to the bathroom and scrubbed my face and pulled off my dress. I realized thinking about it later that I must've been covered in Corine's blood and Ma was cleaning me up. I was numb, like sleepwalking, just a little girl getting ready for bed and she was scrubbing my face with a facecloth and everything was normal. Corine was somewhere in the house playing with her dolls and pretty soon it would be her turn. I don't know how she found the strength, Ma. She put on my nightdress and took me up to her bed. We lay in each other's arms. I started sucking my thumb and we were both shaking and she said, 'shhh, shhh, shhh.' She didn't say 'everything's going to be okay' because it wasn't. Ma was honest that way.

"I remember hearing men's voices downstairs. Except I didn't hear Arie. Later that night I heard shovelling outside. There was a pick, going thump, thump, and sometimes hitting a rock and then a different sound, a shovel, the scraping and dirt landing where they threw it. Now and then there were men's voices—I couldn't hear what they were saying—and sometimes one of them would laugh."

Aunt Julia paused and pressed her fingertips together. Nora recognized the pattern. When she put her fingers together like that, she was thinking about something deeply, drawn by an idea or an image.

After a while, Aunt Julia said, "How is it possible for someone to laugh like that after they kill a little girl in cold blood?"

"I don't know." Nora was herself puzzled. "Maybe they don't see the person they killed as human. It becomes like shooting a pheasant or a rabbit."

Aunt Julia shook her head. "It makes no sense." After another silence, she picked up her story. "Anyway, now and then the digging would stop and I smelled cigarette smoke and there'd be voices and more laughter and then it would start up again. It must've been right outside the window. It went on for a long time. I heard it all so clearly. After a while, it stopped and everything was quiet. Ma and I were still shaking. I didn't know if they were going to come back, if it would be my turn next. Maybe the dark-haired one who gave me those looks would take advantage of the moment. Maybe the hole they were digging was big enough for both of us. Honestly, there was one part of me that would've been fine with that. But I was trembling like a leaf. I think the way my body was shaking was a way of not giving up, of wanting to live. If I clung so hard to life, it was because of Ma lying there next to me. I can't imagine what it would've been like without her holding me. It wasn't so much that she made me feel safe. There was no feeling safe with those men still in the house. They could've done anything to us. But she made me feel not alone."

Nora felt herself tremble as though transported to that part the story where Aunt Julia lay with her mother, listening to the digging and the voices. "But they didn't come upstairs, did they?" Nora asked. "Please tell me they didn't come upstairs."

"No, no, they didn't come. We lay there awake all night. Eventually the digging stopped and it was quiet. Not even the sound of wind in the trees."

Neither Nora nor Aunt Julia said anything for a long time. They both looked out to the sea. Nora heard voices of children playing in the waves.

"The next morning the house was empty," Aunt Julia continued. "Ma told me to stay in bed. Said she'd be right back. I heard her go downstairs. She came back and told me they were gone and started packing a suitcase. It was all such a rush, everything folded so carelessly. She was always so careful, Ma. I started sucking my thumb again and Ma came over and held me and told me we had to go. She led me out through the kitchen door, so I never saw what the living room looked like. I remember thinking that we'd forgotten Corine, but I never said anything. Funny that I thought about Corine and didn't wonder about Arie and Joop."

Nora reached her arms around Aunt Julia to hug her. Aunt Julia returned the embrace, but in a polite way that lacked warmth, like the comfort of a doll or a stuffed animal. They sat in each other's arms for a while. Then, without exchanging words, they stood and brushed the sand from their clothes and walked arm in arm northward, back toward the pier.

CHAPTER 22: UNCLE HERO

The sand was cold between Nora's toes. She looked down at their feet and it occurred to her that Aunt Julia must be feeling the same thing. Sand between one's toes must be good for telling a difficult story, a tether to the present while descending into darkness.

Aunt Julia seemed not to notice where they were. She was in neutral, back to the orator's voice. "Ma carried the suitcase with one arm and had the other around my shoulder. When one arm got tired, she would switch sides. Eventually it was my turn to carry it. Honestly, it was good for me, carrying that suitcase. My sore arms gave me something else to think about. Ma was always on the lookout for who was on the road. One time we hid in the tall grass waiting for a convoy to go by. With the gas rationing and everything, it was unheard of for anyone to be out for a drive in the family car. Ma must've been really desperate because she flagged down a car with a man in civilian clothes. The man was really surprised to see her jump out on the road like that. Slammed on the brakes, dust everywhere. He turned out to be a doctor driving back to Zwolle after making a house call in the countryside. I didn't really hear what he and Ma talked about. My ears heard the words, but they didn't go in, if you know what I mean. But I know he was a doctor because at a certain point he shone one of those lights in my eyes. He drove us all the way to Zwolle and dropped us off at my Uncle Hero's house, Ma's eldest brother. Uncle Hero was a big wig in the Dutch Reformed Church. I don't remember much about the early days when we first arrived. I just remember he had nine children, eight girls and a boy, and a row house that went up three floors. Ma and I had our own room on the top floor. With all the kids around, I started to get back to myself. It was especially good taking care of the little one, Marijke. All the chores were too much for Aunt Annie. Even the older girls were kept busy. They left me to take care of the baby. I can't be sure, but I think Ma had something to do with that.

"The house was full of girls, but I only really got to know my cousin Saskia. She was the eldest, a year older than me, and she taught me how to play checkers. Uncle Hero had a chess board and liked to play, but he only played with other men and wouldn't teach his daughters. Only checkers for the girls. Aside from that, we weren't allowed to do anything except read the Bible. No cards. No ball playing. No sports. There were some novels that found their way in the house, but Uncle Hero had to read them first to make sure they were okay. They were always about the same stupid thing: Girl coming of age, doubt, temptation, then rediscovering the Christian way. Happy ending, but never any kissing. Chastity till marriage. Then—miracle! A baby! Happy family! Church, cooking, children. Drivel like that. I was so bored, going out of my mind. Saskia and I suffered through the burden of that household together. The work and the boredom, both. Thank goodness she was there."

Nora wondered whether, in the manner of some old women, Aunt Julia was going to narrate her entire life story, chasing one tangent after another, grasping at memories with the first onset of decline, with words gathered while one had the strength, like stones on a cairn, building something to last beyond oneself.

As though reading Nora's thoughts, Aunt Julia said, "I know I'm talking too much. I think I'll stop there."

"No, no," Nora protested. "I'm in no hurry. This is important. I want to hear what happened."

Aunt Julia seemed satisfied, as though she'd been waiting for Nora's encouragement. "Uncle Hero was a large man," she said. "He had what you might call 'presence'. He was fat, well not exactly fat, but . . . you know—what's the word, like the Portuguese wine—portly, that's it, and bald on top and had little round glasses that he liked to polish. He looked at himself a lot in the mirror and liked what he saw. There'd always be someone wanting to use the bathroom, but he acted like he had all the time in the world, smiling at himself and patting his belly, not minding it at all. He had a big library with all the major philosophers and fancied himself one of them. Kant and Hegel and Spinoza and Kierkegaard, that sort of thing. We weren't allowed to touch any of the books on those shelves. He said they were dangerous. They would make you doubt. He said the only reason the books were there was so that he would know about the enemies of the Church and the Truth. Whenever we all sat down to eat at the dining room table, no matter how meagre things were at the end of the war, he would pray, tuck in his napkin and say, 'Ah, Epicurus.' The same way, every time. Except, as I learned later, Epicurus was all about including women and slaves in his school of philosophy, something Uncle Hero would never, ever agree to. We had our place, we women and girls. Maybe Epicurus was one of those dangerous thinkers he talked about, I don't know. But if he was, why invoke him after every 'Amen'? I thought there was something funny about it. And that thought was a sign I was recovering. Teenagers have a special ability to detect hypocrisy." She paused, thinking. "I think that sense fades as we get older."

"But Ma still had it, that sense," Nora interjected.

"Oh, yes. She and Uncle Hero argued. Never what you'd call a blow-up, more in the way of 'having words.' She found a copy of *Mein Kampf* on his bookshelf, in there with all the philosophers, and that got her started. 'What's this doing here?' she wanted to know. He was used to everyone being deferential and didn't like the question. He said something like 'How can you understand what's happening all around us if you don't explore the thinking of the man at the origin of it all?' And Ma said, 'Did I not tell you that one of those men killed Corine?' His answer was that she was paying too much attention to her particular circumstances and missing the bigger picture. He said something like, what happened to Corine was just because of one man. Fighting sometimes did that to people. It was to be expected. 'How can you say that?' she said. 'They killed my daughter. Your niece.' Uncle Hero was saying 'he' and Ma was saying 'they' and that was the essence of the argument. To him, Corine's murder was because of the insanity of one man. To her, it was the insanity of a whole country. She was right of course. 'There's nothing complicated about it,' Ma said. 'Nothing philosophical. That man—she could never say Hitler's name but just pointed to the book—is driven by hate and a lust for power, and it's infected the whole country.' Another time I heard her say, 'Are you blind?' Haven't you seen what they're doing to the Jews? Don't you know about the trains?' He just shrugged and said, '*Na ja*,' as though that was an argument. She used the word *machtslust*, the lust for power, again and again and talked about how the ideas in that book led to the trains and pointed out how worn the pages were.

"One day we had a visitor, a Nazi big shot. His name was . . . What was it? Something-something-Rauter. In German his last name means 'rougher' so how could I forget that. He was the head of the whole Waffen-SS in the Netherlands. The resistance ambushed his convoy, everybody killed except him, just a finger shot off. Later, I saw his picture in the paper with that missing finger if you looked close. After the war, he was convicted of crimes against humanity and executed by firing squad." Aunt Julia pointed toward the dunes in the distance. "Just up there!" She paused and let that sink in, that they were a short distance away from where the SS commander she was talking about was executed by firing squad. "I haven't a clue what he was doing in Zwolle, but I do know Uncle Hero was expecting him because there was all this fuss in the kitchen. I had little Marijke in my lap, so I was doing my part. I heard talking in the living room, you know men's voices, and then Aunt Annie came and said, 'The gentleman visitor would like to see the children.' We all came filing in, like we were soldiers on parade, all in a row. He had blue, blue eyes, a high forehead with short hair combed straight back and a very fine, carefully pressed uniform. I was shaking. I couldn't help myself. I was thinking, he must know that officer who killed Corine. The same uniform. What if they talked? What if he's looking for me?"

"But there's no reason he'd be looking for you," Nora interjected. "Were you shaking because he reminded you of that terrible night?"

Aunt Julia thought it over. "Well, of course. At one level I knew he wasn't looking for me. It was just what you might call a friendly visit. But at another level . . . I suppose I was—what do they call it now?—in shock. Like electricity running through my body. Back then, if a woman had symptoms, she was hysterical. But whatever you want to call it, I wasn't happy to be standing in front of this Nazi who looked so much like the one who killed my sister. And then Marijke started to fuss. Rauter looked at us up close, one by one. 'Such a fine family,' he said. And he stopped at the one boy—funny, still I forget my cousin's name. It isn't coming back to me, but he was around seven. He later died of scarlet fever. Rauter put his hand under his chin to make him look up and said, 'Such a fine young lad. I can already see the soldier in him.' And he came to me and my knees were shaking so hard I could hardly stand and Marijke was really crying, but Rauter didn't mind at all. He said, 'My goodness, healthy lungs on this one,' and he turned to look at Uncle Hero and laughed. Uncle Hero laughed along with him, except his eyes weren't laughing; they had a worried look. I noticed Uncle Hero's glasses start to fog and he took them off and polished them and said, 'The Lord has most certainly blessed us.' Rauter just said, 'Hmm.' After that, we were dismissed and I went back to the kitchen to prepare Marijke's bottle.

"Anyway, Ma and I were safe there, as it turned out. Judging by Rauter's visit, it might've been because of Uncle Hero's connections to the Nazis. We stayed there through the Hunger Winter till the end of the war."

Nora and Aunt Julia walked in silence for a while. When they were closer to the pier, Aunt Julia said, "That's it. That's how my sister Corine died."

Nora had so many questions, she didn't know where to begin. She went with the most pressing. "Where were your brothers Arie and Joop all that time? What did they do while you and your mother stayed with your Uncle Hero?"

"Ah, yes." Aunt Julia nodded. She was silent for a while, to the point that Nora had an urge to repeat the question. She knew better not to.

Aunt Julia eventually formed an answer. "I know Joop went into hiding. Where and with whom, I have no idea. Probably moving around, one place and then another. The resistance took care of that. Arie, well, him I was never sure about. I always imagined he was taken in by the SS and became one of their informers. That would explain everything. That's why they killed Corine. That's how he survived the war. Informing. I could never bring myself to ask and he would never tell me even if I did."

"Maybe that's something we can still find out from him, don't you think?" Nora posed the question as much to herself as Aunt Julia.

"Maybe," Aunt Julia said, curtly. Her tone made it clear she didn't want to talk about it. "I don't think so."

Nora changed the topic to something else she was curious about. "What did Joop do after the war?"

"He did what he was good at. He kept fighting in the resistance." Nora gave her a quizzical look and Aunt Julia elaborated. "The war was never really over for him. He went into the police. Eventually worked as a homicide detective. Always after something or someone. Never happy with partial success. The stress of it was too much for him. He drank too much and then died of a stroke in his fifties."

"I'm sorry to hear that. I'm sorry you lost the men in your life when they were too young."

Aunt Julia acknowledged Nora's sympathy in silence.

A pink ball rolled toward them. Nora noticed it first and kicked it back to a girl who said '*Dank u wel*' and picked it up and ran. It occurred to Nora that this was the first time in her life she'd kicked a ball like that. For an instant she felt proud. Then she thought of Corine being about the same age as this girl when she was killed and felt tears run down her cheeks. She wiped them away with the back of her hand.

"Oh, a funny thing," Aunt Julia said. "A little while before the liberation, that copy of *Mein Kampf* disappeared from Uncle Hero's bookshelf."

"Oh, that *is* interesting."

"Yes," Aunt Julia said. "But getting rid of it didn't help his reputation as a Nazi sympathizer. I remember the Binnenlandse Strijdkrachten came to the door and took him in for questioning. He was gone a whole afternoon and evening. Came home completely exhausted."

"But never any charges?" Nora asked.

"*Nee*, never charges." Aunt Julia fell silent.

Nora's mind drifted and she noticed the sound of the waves and their footsteps in the sand making an almost perfect contrapuntal harmony.

They continued walking in silence. Long after Nora assumed the conversation was over, Aunt Julia said, "Nothing criminal about having Nazis over for tea, I suppose."

CHAPTER 23: PETER'S DILEMMA

For reasons he was unable to fathom, when Nora finished narrating Aunt Julia's story of Corine's murder, Peter thought of an image he'd come across during a social media search at work. It was a photo from the Syrian war that hadn't yet been removed by content moderators. It had been taken just after an air attack that bombed a busy market. In the image, an old man is leaning over a leg severed at the thigh. He's holding a piece of cardboard from a disassembled box. The rest of the scene is deserted, just the dusty-turbaned old man and the leg lying in the sand where it fell. Probably everyone who survived is still taking cover. The old man is first on the scene, trying to give the leg some dignity. But the piece of cardboard he's holding is much too small and he looks puzzled about what to do with it. Does he cover the bloody part at the thigh, the indignity of the wound? Or does he cover the foot with the painted toenails, a remnant of the unique person? He is poised, caught in a moment of hesitation. There's nothing in the image to tell the viewer what he decided.

Peter felt like that old man. His world had just been bombed, pieces of it scattered in all directions, and he felt ill equipped to cover everything. He wasn't sure what part of himself to reveal and what to leave exposed.

CHAPTER 24: CLOCKWORK

Peter and Nora sat upright in bed. He had his laptop open and headphones covering his ears. She tried to snuggle up to him, was rebuffed by the hard edge of the laptop and the sound and vibration of Peter's clicks on the keyboard. She leaned over to see what he was doing. "What is that?" Nora asked.

He lifted the headphone closest to her. "What'd you say?"

"I said, what is that?"

"A video game," he replied.

"I know that, but which one?" Nora persisted. "You've got a few. What're you playing?"

"Oh," Peter said. "Minecraft. I'm just fooling around on creative mode. That way, no time pressure, no competition. I'm trying to build a model of Moore's Utopia. It's one of the few interesting games that won't melt my laptop."

"I see."

Peter put his earpiece back on and continued playing.

"You've been playing it a lot lately," Nora said.

Peter took the headphones off all the way. "Sorry, what was that you said?"

"I said, you've been playing it a lot lately," she shouted.

"I can hear you. No need to shout."

"Since you got back from Africa, you've been playing that thing constantly." Nora lowered her voice. "You never used to play video games."

"You're probably right," Peter admitted. "I guess I'm doing it to relax."

"How can you relax with that thing when you're staring at a screen all day at work?" Nora was more than curious. It worried her. She reached for his hand and ran her fingers across his fingernails. They were ragged. She held his hand to her face to look at it closely. "Ooh, look. You bit your nails again. Now they're all bleedy looking."

"I know." Peter withdrew his hand and put it under the covers, out of sight.

"Poor thing. You've been upset ever since you came home," Nora said. "I can feel it. It's like you're an animal, walking back and forth."

"Pacing," Peter said.

Peter used his English that way. He pulled out the right word when he needed an advantage.

"We should talk," Nora said.

"What do you want to talk about?"

The reply annoyed her, but she wanted to be constructive, like in the game he was playing. Create something. "Well, let's start with you. How you're feeling?"

"Me? I'm fine. All good."

"That's not true," Nora said. It was getting harder to repress her irritation. "I really need you to talk to me about what's going on."

"But I've already told you about everything that's happening at work." Peter sounded defensive, petulant.

"That's not what I mean," Nora said.

"What do you mean then?"

Now he was hiding behind questions. Nora decided to be upfront about what worried her. "You came back from Timbuktu with your mind full of the horror of war. All the stories you heard, the destruction you saw, the discomfort and danger you faced. You were only gone a few weeks, but you almost had the experience of combat. Those things you heard and saw, they had an effect on you. They must've."

"Sounds about right," Peter said.

"It's really been like this since Timbuktu. Since then, you've been escaping into that thing." She nodded toward Peter's laptop.

"Really? I hadn't noticed."

"Hours and hours. I'm starting to feel lonely."

"I'm sorry about that. I had no idea." Peter's voice was muted, contrite. "You're right. I should probably stop."

"I don't mean stop. Well, okay, cut down. But I mean talk to me."

"We're back to that. I don't know what you want me to talk about." The sincerity was gone. Peter had returned to being defensive.

"How about telling me more about you?" Nora suggested.

"Me? Peter reflected a moment. "I thought we'd covered that already. Sort of."

"Exactly! Sort of."

"What else is there? What do you want to know? You want to know more about what happened in Mali?" Peter sounded irritated now.

"Look," Nora said. "There are things I'd like to know about you. I'm curious. What was your childhood like? Your dad seems like such a character, but what were your parents like together?" This last sentence reminded Nora of the photo of Peter's parents his Aunt Nel had given her. She jumped to her feet and looked for her purse. It took a while, with Peter asking 'What are you doing?' but she eventually found it covered by clothes on a chair in the bedroom.

Peter sighed and closed his laptop. He used more force than usual. The sound was sharp.

"Here." Nora handed Peter the envelope with the photo.

"What's this?" He looked at the photo of his parents holding bicycles. "Where'd you get this?" Peter sounded resistant, as though Nora was showing him a piece of evidence that put his place in the world in question.

"They seem happy." Nora repeated Nel's words to see what they would produce.

Peter studied the photo, then put it gingerly on the bedside table, face down. "Who knows," he said.

"I'm assuming that wasn't the same couple who raised you. Something happened."

Peter took a moment to formulate his thoughts. "I never saw them like that. It must've been the distance from their extended families when they moved to Canada. A moral distance as much as anything. I think it changed everything."

"What was it like for you then?" Nora asked. "How were they as parents if you never saw them happy like in the photo?"

"Let's see," Peter thought about what to say. "I guess the best way to put it is, they competed for real estate in my mind."

Nora was confused. "That sounds like something people just say. What does that even mean?"

"You're right. It's one of those expressions," Peter said. "It means they each tried to persuade me. Convince me of their way of seeing the world."

"Can you give an example?" Nora asked.

Peter was silent. "Okay, here's one," he said, after what felt to Nora like a full minute. "They had completely different stories about the first year after I was born. Till I was something like twelve, I had no inkling my mom wasn't there when I was a baby. Then, all of a sudden, out come the stories. My father talked about how hard it was to be married to a woman with schizophrenia."

"Your mother had schizophrenia?" Nora was taken aback.

"Of course not," Peter snapped, then tried to soften his tone. "That's just how they diagnosed depression in those days. But it was also a way for my dad to avoid responsibility. Like, gee, maybe smacking someone in the face when your supper was cold might make them depressed. Not hard for anyone to see. Except him. He made himself into a saint. He talked about how when I was a baby, he hired a babysitter, a thirteen-year-old girl from the neighborhood to help out. But *he* was really my surrogate mother, my provider, the changer-of-diapers, no time for anything else, all sacrifices because *she* wasn't there. Because she decided to be schizophrenic. From him, I learned that my mother had been institutionalized shortly after I was born—committed was the word he used. That was the word of choice in psychiatry at the time. We're *committed*, so you should be too. Trust us, we'll take care of you. We're *committed*. Just take your pills. But that bare fact of her being assigned to the trust and care of an institution is the full extent of what their different accounts had in common."

"What was her version?" Nora asked. "How was it different?"

"My mother's story was so completely different, it almost made me lose faith in the possibility of truth. Things weren't helped by the drugs the doctors gave her. I think that explains her decline in the end. I swear, those pills will mess you up. The cutting edge of the psychopharmacological revolution. A bit of this, a bit of that, a dash of something else. Then the decline. First my sister Emma took her in when it was clear my dad wouldn't lift a finger. That lasted nearly a year. Then my mom needed professional care. The last thing she remembered was me and Emma. She stared at a picture of us next to her bed and repeated our names over and over. 'Emma and Peter. Emma and Peter.' Like a mantra."

"That's so sad," Nora said. "But it also shows how much she loved you."

"Yes, but still, because of all the drugs, I have trouble trusting anything she told me."

"Well, let's hear her side anyway," Nora said, coaxing out the story. "From when she was still able to tell it."

"In her version," Peter said, "her depression came just after my birth because she couldn't face returning to *him*, his control of everything, his insults, his outbursts. There was nowhere else for her to go. To the doctors, normality involved going home, being a good wife and mother. The minister told her the same thing. She had a duty to fulfill. This idea was pushed at her from the very beginning, since she was a girl. Arie's family was super religious. Repressive. Everything forbidden. I can't imagine how boring that must've been. From Canada, her family in the Netherlands was too far away. She didn't have the airfare, and couldn't ask him for it. I suppose her pride got in the way, too. Or she was afraid of what he might do. With him, she was in a prison, and the hospital was her only refuge. Anyway, her story was that there was a teenage girl who took care of me for the first few weeks, who'd sometimes have a small group of friends come over and fuss over me and take turns holding me. I was around fourteen when I heard this. It was my favorite memory I never had."

"That's a completely different story. It must've been confusing," Nora observed, as much to herself as to Peter.

"You're not kidding," he said. "So, my mother's story goes, after a while, *he* got tired of having a baby in the house and I was sent into the care of a foster mother from the church. My mom never told me the name of this good woman. As I thought about it later, she probably didn't want to be replaced. This woman took me into her home until my mother was declared well and my father pleaded with her to come home. He was incapable of taking care of himself, never mind an infant son. She acquiesced. As bad as it was with him, the hospital was no place to spend her life."

"How do you think this affected you, this difference in the stories about you from your parents?" Nora asked. "I mean later on."

Peter considered the question. "I think one effect was insecurity about who I was, where I came from. Who was this woman who fostered me in that formative age of infancy? Did she even exist? I never did find out. And how could the two stories about me be so at odds? Who was lying and who telling the truth? Or were they both lying, and I really came from somewhere else? Was I really who they said I was?"

"You know," Nora said. "It explains perfectly why you became an investigator. Why you're doing what you do. You became someone whose job it is to find the truth. Maybe the conflicting stories of your early life made it so you were drawn to law. Investigating to get at the truth. For the security of it. Plus, you want to contribute." She cupped her hands into the shape of a horn. "Toot tee toot. Peter to the rescue."

"Yeah, well, we all get disabused sooner or later," Peter remarked dryly.

"Okay, so you've got these conflicting stories about you from your parents," Nora said. "What do *you* remember? What actually happened?"

"How can I know what actually happened?" Peter answered. "We're all so good at inventing things."

"Okay," Nora conceded. "What memories did you *invent* about yourself?"

"One of my first," Peter began, "was a co-construction. My mother and I worked on this one together when I was around fourteen."

"Okay, that'll do," Nora said.

"My mom was back on Valium," Peter said. "She was getting some sleep. It was before she developed a tolerance and took too many. But there was a brief period when the Valium actually made her more lucid. We sometimes talked. She'd sit on the raised hearth of the fireplace next to a cup of tea and tell me about my early life. The odd thing about what she said was, unlike most stories told from the hearth of a fireplace, this one had a connection to what I actually, vaguely, remembered. So, I guess it counts as one of my first memories."

"Tell me," Nora said, encouraging him.

Peter reached into his memories. "My mom would sometimes start these memory-stories with, 'You were such a good boy. Never any trouble'. A few times, going further, she'd talk about how, at age four, I'd been the only one in the family spared in a flu outbreak, and went from room to room with water and aspirin.

"Peter the virtuous," Nora said. "Peter the brave" It sounded harsh and she added a sweetener. "It sounds like you. That's one of the things I love about you. You're caring. You're still that way. That's why you do the work you do. You're still that little boy with the water and aspirins."

"Except now I bear the healing gift of war crimes," Peter said.

Nora was uncomfortable competing with Peter to define his character, but she had to say something. "You're being too hard on yourself. You do your work with a generous spirit."

"I can think of something else." Peter put his laptop upright against a leg of the side table. "This one's not so nice."

"Let's hear it." Nora felt an ember of pride that she had encouraged Peter to open up, explore who he was.

"My mom and I once talked about an argument she had with my dad. A fight, actually. Even though she told it as a story about herself, I remember it clearly. I wasn't yet in school. I was sitting under the kitchen table. I was looking up at the plywood under the table, you know, the underneath part that wasn't supposed to be seen. I'd remember that table if I saw it today. It was covered on top with Arborite and had a grooved metal strip around the sides to hide the seam. I was hugging my knees, looking at their feet. My mother was in knitted slippers, my father in work boots. They were speaking Dutch—they always spoke Dutch when they argued—but somehow, I understood.

"What was it about? Do you remember?"

"It was about the kitchen clock."

To Nora, the idea was absurd. "Why in the world would somebody argue about a kitchen clock?"

"I have no idea," Peter said. "I guess it came down to my dad's material neediness. He was like a child that way. When he wanted something, he had to have it. So, he was saying they needed a new clock. He'd seen a good one in the hardware store when he'd gone to buy nails. It was a nice clock and he liked it."

"Was there anything wrong with the one you had?" Nora asked.

"That's the weird thing," Peter replied. "My mom said the clock they had was fine. It worked, even if it was ugly. Then she said something that made me listen harder. There wasn't enough money. Whenever she went to the Nabob, she had to know exactly what she had in her basket and how much it cost. Always doing mental math. And she couldn't get a proper cut of meat."

"So your family was poor." It was something about Peter she already understood. She saw it in how he behaved shopping. Hesitating. Looking at the prices on menus. Not wanting to spend money.

"My dad said we were doing just fine," Peter continued. "He had work. Cominco needed a greenhouse for their visitor's centre, enough carpentry for three months. There was money in his pocket. It was his. He would spend it any way he wanted."

"Right," Nora said. "Back to the narcissism thing."

Peter thought it over. "That's basically it," he agreed. "But it was a strange self-centredness, materialistic and egocentric at the same time, with the persistence of a Swiss guard in his erection and patrol of boundaries, defending the world as he saw it. He refused to believe we needed anything. His wants came first. My mom kept going back to the money. Harping on it, you might say. She was doing everything she could, knitting sweaters and mitts, but Emma and I kept growing out of our winter clothes. Coats and boots cost money, even at the Sally Ann. That's how they always were, my mom and dad. His was the voice of want, hers of reason."

"Ugh," Nora observed simply. She lay her head on Peter's chest.

"They were arguing back and forth like that for a while," Peter's voice came deep, through his chest and straight into her ear. "To give her credit, she wasn't taking any shit. Then my dad reached up and pulled the clock from the wall. I saw it hit the floor. The casing split open and the mechanism of it came undone. In the slow-motion replay—you know how the mind works that way, everything slows down—I saw the clock bounce and the glass cover fly to pieces all over the place. And here's the thing: I didn't make a fuss. I was quiet afterward."

"That's so, so terrible. I'm sorry, my Petertje." She kissed his cheek and stroked the hair on his chest. "It makes sense, too," she said. "You're still that way. Quiet when everything's going to shit. Observing. *Gereserveerd*, reserved."

"Anyway," Peter went on, without acknowledging Nora's observation, "my dad shouted, 'There! *Now* we need a new clock.' And his boots went clomp-clomp through the house, and fast down the porch stairs. Funny how the mind works. I even remember that the truck took two tries for the ignition to catch."

"See?" Nora said. "How could you invent that sort of detail?"

"Maybe." That was the extent Peter was willing to agree. He fell silent.

"Tell me the rest," Nora said.

"So," Peter continued, encouraged, "the clock lay there on the kitchen floor, the life gone out of it, springs and sprockets all over the place. And the glass. I remember there was a shrapnel-spray of glass all over the place. I guess that's a sign of how old I am. They didn't make everything with plastic yet. I came out from under the table when I heard my mother crying and wrapped my arms around her leg. 'Good boy,' she said. She stroked my hair. Then she lifted me onto a chair and went to get the dustpan and broom. I covered my eyes with my hands and heard the main piece of clock going in the trash—Pfump, like that—and the little sounds of glass-on-glass across the linoleum floor."

"That's a sad memory," Nora said. "It almost makes me cry."

"There's more," Peter said. "A while later, my dad came back. He had a new painter's hat on his head and was carrying a flat, square cardboard box. He said, 'See what I got for us?' He was super happy. 'Look,' he said. He opened the box, unwrapped the tissue and hung a new clock on the hook where the old one had been above the kitchen window. My mom didn't participate. He looked to her for approval. 'See?' he said. He wanted to win, but she wouldn't let him."

"*Klootzak*," Nora said.

Peter looked surprised. "Funny you say that. That's what he always called me. It wasn't in my mom's Dutch-English dictionary when I tried to look it up. What does it mean?"

"Ooh, sorry," Nora said. "It isn't a nice word."

"What?"

Nora was reluctant to tell Peter what the word meant, not because it was crude, but because of how it would pain him. "It means ball sack," she felt compelled to say.

Peter gave no indication he was hurt. "That makes sense," he said. "At least it fits the context in which he said it—the *way* he said it."

"You haven't finished the story," Nora said.

"Right," Peter said. "Anyway, I realized there was something worse in all this than the fight and the clock smashing to smithereens. You know what it was?"

Nora shook her head.

"After all this anger and fighting and destruction and pain and my mother crying, you know what? That fucking, goddamned clock he brought home looked exactly the same as the old one."

Nora thought it over. "That's really weird," she said after a moment. "To you at that age—what, four? five?—it must've made no sense at all."

"Actually, if you really think about it," Peter said, "it makes perfect sense. The new clock wasn't the same as the old one at all. You know how appearances can be deceiving. It *looked* like the old clock, but it wasn't telling the same time."

Nora was puzzled at first. Then she had an insight. "I see what you're saying. It was as though your father hung a different universe on the kitchen wall," she said.

They were quiet for a moment. She heard his heartbeat and felt the rise and fall of his chest.

She felt Peter stroke her hair and kiss her forehead.

"You're something else," he said.

CHAPTER 25: THE PROSECUTOR

"Mr. Ferman sends his greetings," Peter said. He shook hands with Willem Jansen across a desk littered with papers, folders, manilla envelopes, and a scattering of paperclips. Jansen was a small man with widely flaring ears and a receding chin. His clothes reflected his misfortune in the allotment of genes: a green tweed jacket and a spectacularly mismatching plaid shirt and red, white and blue striped tie. To Peter, he looked dressed to meet the office code, nothing more. A man who had other, more pressing things to do.

"Thank you," Jansen said. "I was very happy for Ferman when I heard he was hired to lead the investigations team at the Office of the Prosecutor. He's perfect for it." Jansen sat back down in a rickety office chair. It creaked loudly. "First, let me tell you a little about what we do," he said. "I don't know what things are like in Canada—Ferman tells me you're Canadian, is that right?"

"The two of you spoke?" Peter asked.

"Of course, of course." Jansen replied. He didn't wait for an answer concerning Peter's nationality, but continued. "As a Canadian, you're used to a different legal environment. My office deals with war crimes, something exceedingly rare in your part of the world. For one thing, we're still grappling with the aftermath of the German occupation, even though it's now over seventy years after the war. We did a pretty good job of what you might call cleaning house after the war. Now, there aren't nearly as many prosecutions as there used to be. Fewer witnesses, even fewer perpetrators. We're approaching the end of a very important era, an important generation. Here in the Netherlands, we take our role in international law very seriously. My office prosecutes war crimes that involve Dutch nationals in any capacity. We have accepted the responsibility of universal jurisdiction. That means if anyone on our soil is credibly accused of a war crime, even a foreign national, they can and will be prosecuted." He gave Peter a fierce look as though to underscore his prosecutorial determination and powers. "Another thing. All that nonsense you see on TV? All that, *ladies and gentlemen of the jury* talk? Throw it out. We work with magistrates. No juries. There's no involving your average Joe, as they say—or Jane—that everyone puts themselves into contortions to manipulate. Here, the model is inquisitorial."

At this last word, Peter couldn't prevent the intrusive image of a medieval torture room with the screams of a heretic under interrogation, even though he knew Jansen meant something completely different.

"Now, what can I do for you?" Jansen asked.

Peter told him the gist of Aunt Julia's story about the murder of Corine. As he spoke, Jansen looked meditatively at the traffic passing under the building. Peter paused and looked in the same direction. They were on the third floor of National Head Office of the Public Prosecution Service. The view was mesmerizing in its ugliness: The rear of The Hague's Central Station, the flow of traffic along Prins Clauslaan, with the cross street, Theresiestraat, passing directly under the building. It solved the need for urban space, typical of the more daring Dutch architects of the sixties: build a three-storey prosecutor's office on stilts over a busy street. That way, no expensive land to buy and ready access to the courts next door at the Paleis van Justitie.

Jansen spoke before Peter could pick up the thread. "That's a very interesting story," he said. "But at this point, that's all it is. A story. I can't tell you how many heartbreaking stories I've heard from people who suffered under the occupation. If there are enough of them pointing at a particular individual, we're sometimes able to do something. That's why so many of our prosecutions have to do with camp guards. A lot of cruelty in one place and a lot of witnesses. Plus, the Germans made our jobs easier. Fastidious record keepers, those Nazis. They kept everything. If I wanted to, I could find out who attended the youth camps in 1942. With photographs." He stopped as though mentally searching for something. "Where were we?"

"I didn't get to the part about the burial," Peter said.

"The burial?"

Peter finished Aunt Julia's story, as told to him by Nora. He emphasized the sound of digging. Aunt Julia was certain she heard digging from the upstairs bedroom.

Jansen leaned back. His chair creaked loudly in response. He lay his arm on his desk along a narrow corridor free of papers and drummed his fingers. "Hmm." He reflected, looking out at the traffic.

Peter waited, wanted to say something to encourage Jansen, but decided silence would be better.

"The mind is a powerful, creative, deceitful thing," Jansen said finally. "It has its own cunning. The sound of digging might be a result of trauma. An auditory hallucination. Maybe a memory constructed later." He drummed his fingers harder. His thick nails gave focus to the sound, to the point that he seemed to interrupt himself. "Or not. There may be something here. Not very often we get a case with a body to work with."

"I would imagine not," Peter said. There was something overwhelming about Jansen's manner, his tense combination of war-weariness and doggedness. More than that. It was the whole thing, the office and its powers focused on this small but powerful man, one of the leading figures in a sprawling national network of war crimes investigators.

In Mali, Peter's investigative work was predicated on a state wanting to pursue its advantage over a rebellion. It stopped where the state itself was implicated. Jansen's office represented something different, a quality of national character, a government pouring resources into war crimes as a matter of *principle*. Jansen's rickety office chair bespoke some cost cutting, but the priority was still there, manifest in a building next to the courthouse.

"Can I ask you a basic question?" Peter said at the end of his thoughts.

"Of course." Jansen was almost intimidating in his attentiveness.

"Well, it's more than one question, actually. Why do you do all this? I don't mean you personally, but why does your office go after war crimes so long after the events? Why invest in that when so many recent things need our attention? What reason is there to go so far back, arrest people now, what, in their eighties and nineties? What danger do old people pose when there are so many other crimes that need our attention? Like the ones that happened just last year in Mali?" Having posed them, Peter realized the questions had multiplied and run away from him.

"You're right. All that comes down to a basic question." Jansen paused to think. "I suppose it all has to do with what we want to stand for collectively. Ultimately, not prosecuting someone despite their advanced age means turning a blind eye to the worst atrocities humans are capable of committing. If we do that, the lessons will never be learned. Every time we prosecute a war criminal, we're sending a message. So, it's more than a criminal procedure. It's a form of public education."

"A civics lesson," Peter noted.

"A lesson in civility," Jansen corrected.

"And, if you'll permit a personal follow up," Peter said. "Is that what motivated you to go into this line of work?"

"Absolutely." Jansen moved his hand from the desk to his lap and swiveled in his chair. "I suppose I have a story, too. Well, not really me. You see, my grandparents risked their lives during the war. There was a roundup. German soldiers looking for Jews in our neighborhood. One of the Jewish kids, Jacob, was playing with my mother. You know, riding around on a tricycle. My grandmother told the Germans he was theirs. Lucky thing, he was blond. They called him Willem in front of the Germans. He didn't respond when my grandmother called him Willem because that wasn't his name, so she took him by the hand and said loudly so the Germans could hear, 'Come, Willem, time for some lunch.' And the boy looked at her, you know, like wondering what the hell was going on, but thank goodness he didn't correct her and just allowed himself to be taken by the hand. The Germans went away with the boy's parents and siblings, never to be seen again. That boy stayed with my grandparents' family as one of theirs for the rest of the war. Later, they officially adopted him. That's the story of my uncle Jacob."

"That's quite a story," Peter said.

They fell silent and stared out at the traffic. A heavy truck passed under the building and vibrated the windows.

"After the war, Jacob's hair turned brown," Jansen added as an afterthought. "As though he was blond only as long as he needed to be."

"That's very curious," Peter said.

"Also in there is the story of how I got my name, Willem. They passed the lucky name on to me." Jansen laughed in a short spasm. "Tell you what," he continued, as though the laughter gave him a sudden surge of conviction. "Ferman says you're good at what you do. Why don't you help us out with the first steps?"

Peter was eager to demonstrate his skill. "That sounds great. I've thought about this already. Very basic. I'll interview Aunt Julia again. Get her to help find the house where Corine was killed. I'll start with Street View images. Geolocation. Show her some likely farm houses."

"That sounds perfect," Jansen said.

Peter felt a burst of pride, as though he'd been offered a promotion.

"Once you find the house, if it's still standing, we'll get a team out there," Jansen said. "The ones we work with from the Netherlands Forensic Institute. See if we have a body."

Peter completed the thought: "Or a constructed memory."

CHAPTER 26: GROUNDWORK

Peter had trouble with the car he rented from Alamo at in The Hague. Aunt Julia met him at the rental agency and helped him choose a five-speed manual Opel Mokka, the only country-road capable vehicle in their inventory. Even before he climbed into the driver's seat, he had trouble locating the adjust lever to accommodate his legs. Then he stalled it twice trying to back out of the spot in the parkade.

"I'm fine, I'm fine," he said in response to Aunt Julia's critical, quizzical look from the passenger seat. He revved the engine too hard as he tried to ease into first gear. He felt his hands grip the wheel tightly to make up for his uncertainty with the clutch. With the car in motion, it was a matter of navigating with the GPS unit. He was too proud to change the directions to English.

At the instructions, "*sla rechtsaf voor de oprijd naar de A4,*" he heard "A4" correctly, but turned left instead of right. He had to find a cloverleaf to enter the highway in the right direction. Aunt Julia said nothing. Occasionally she glanced over at him, her fingers interlaced nervously in her lap.

Once they settled into a comfortable speed on the highway, Peter asked the question that had occupied his thoughts ever since the possibility of finding Corine's body became real. "How do you feel about going back to where it happened?"

Aunt Julia turned her head farther toward the passenger side window and enclosed herself in silence. "It feels strange," she said after a minute of silence. "My first thought was, leave her where she is. Why unsettle everything. Then I decided I want to find her. Her bones. I want to bring her home."

"There's a good chance we will. Soon." Peter felt unsuited to a parental role with his elder aunt, but added, "Not today, but soon."

"What happens today?" Aunt Julia asked.

"Today we're going to meet some forensic anthropologists, help them set up the search area," Peter replied. "I also want to introduce you to the owner. It's a nuisance for him, the work we're doing. This isn't an official police investigation. Not yet, anyhow. The head of the Special Prosecutor's Office just agreed to a preliminary search. So the owner is volunteering, letting us on his property without a warrant. Under the circumstances, I thought it'd be good for him to meet you."

"I thought you were a war crimes investigator. Isn't this a war crime?"

"Well, yes. Yes, it is." Peter had some difficulty with this question. "But you see, the International Criminal Court was established in 2002. We can't investigate crimes that happened before that. Retroactively. *Ex post facto*."

Aunt Julia shook her head. "I don't understand. Does that mean no more war crimes from World War Two, from the occupation?"

"No, no. Those are still war crimes, but it was different." Peter was struggling with the nuances of international criminal law. He was glad he didn't have to teach it.

"How was it different?" Aunt Julia was persistently curious when she found a topic she wanted to know more about.

"There was no such thing as war crimes just after World War Two," Peter explained. "But it was such a terrible war with such terrible crimes that the tribunals looked backwards to what the customs were among nations at the time of the offenses. Courts like Nuremberg and the Dutch special tribunals were based on the idea of a universal public conscience.

That way it wasn't just a victor's justice. The law of war that applies to World War Two is based on what was accepted at the time."

Aunt Julia turned toward the window. "What was accepted at the time was people killing each other all over the place. Resistants were called terrorists. People were rounded up, executed in the public squares. What happens if every country does that sort of thing and accepts it as custom? It sounds like packs of wolves making law for the deer. Customary law of nations. Huh. Why do we need to make this all so complicated? Murder is murder."

Aunt Julia's fulmination put an end to the discussion. They continued in silence.

When they approached a town marked Hoogland, the navigation system said, "*Sla na vijfhonderd meter rechtsaf om in te voegen op de A28*."

"Shit, shit, shit," Peter said. "I turn right here to get onto the A28, is that right?"

"*Ja, ja*," Aunt Julia said. She smiled. "Your Dutch is getting better. You just need to relax."

She took over the directions when they left the highway at Zwolle, chiming in at the same time as the GPS. When the navigator said, "*Uw bestemming bevindt zich aan de linkerkant*," she corrected it and pointed to a dirt road on the right. "This way. I remember the tree."

A sequoia dwarfed all the other trees on the property. Peter was surprised to see it here. He thought they only grew in North America. "If you'd told me about that tree, we wouldn't have had to go through so many pictures from Google to find this place," he said. It was a species he associated with wilderness. The property was well kept, with an open yard—aside from the one major tree and a few others of little note—and trimmed hedges along the perimeter. The grass had gone to clover, but it was actually a sign of fastidious care. The inattention to the lawn perfectly matched where they were in the countryside.

Peter noted something else: The evenness of the ground would make their work easier.

Aunt Julia gave no reply to Peter's remark about the tree. He looked over at her. She stared straight ahead at the house.

It was a classic Dutch farmhouse with a sloping tile roof that reached halfway down the ground floor on either side, leaving almost no room for windows. Part of it sloped in the front as far as the second floor. Taken together, the roof gave an impression of a hunter's hat with ear flaps. The dark wooden door of the main entrance was flanked with two tall windows, but all the other windows were small and square.

Peter thought of Aunt Julia's story about the night the SS came to the house. He tried to match what he remembered of the story in the recording with the house standing before them. Aunt Julia would've come through that door and smelled the leather of their uniforms.

It wasn't yet ten-thirty in the morning. They were a few minutes early. There was no sign of the forensic archaeologists. Peter turned off the ignition and released the clutch too fast. The car lurched. He pulled the parking brake and looked over at Aunt Julia. She seemed not to notice his gaffe with the clutch. Her hands were in her lap. She looked down. The ends of her fingers were trembling.

"All okay?" he asked.

She nodded.

A man appeared at the entrance wearing unlaced work boots. He had a shock of dark hair that stuck out in different directions and thick eyebrows. He looked somewhere in his thirties, tall and lanky, with a prominent Adam's apple. As soon as Peter got out of the car, the man said, "Hallo, I'm Hans," he said. "You must be Peter." As he approached to shake hands, Peter noticed how tall he was, almost eye level.

"I'd like you to meet my Aunt Julia," Peter said in Dutch. He looked toward the car, where Aunt Julia was silhouetted in the passenger seat.

"So happy you brought her along," Hans replied in only slightly accented English. Peter was disappointed. Hans's switch to English was a sign his Dutch still had a long way to go.

Aunt Julia was startled when Peter tapped on the passenger side window. He opened the door and helped her to her feet. "This is Hans, the owner of the house," Peter said.

Hans bent, straight-backed and shook her hand. "I'm pleased to meet you. I was really shocked when I heard the news. When I bought this old house, I never imagined . . . Anyway, I'm very sorry for your loss."

Aunt Julia looked confused. "My loss? My loss? Oh yes, my sister. That's very kind of you to say after all these years."

"A terrible event like that is always a loss," Hans said. "I'm sure it doesn't go away with the years."

"No," she said. "It certainly doesn't. Especially not now that I'm here. At this place." She looked closely at the house. The three stood in silence—no one knew what to say next. "You added skylights," Aunt Julia finally noted.

"Yes," Hans replied. "These old farmhouses with the small windows are pretty dark. We wanted to add some light to the upstairs."

Aunt Julia nodded approvingly.

"You'll see we made some other changes," Hans continued. "We turned it into a tourist rental. So, no need for the cow shed next to the house."

"No, certainly no need for that," Aunt Julia said, deadpan. "Not many tourists with the knack for milking cows."

Peter marvelled at Aunt Julia's sudden self-possession. Kella and Goma had mentioned the same thing about one the survivors in Timbuktu, interviewed even closer to their trauma. People respond to loss in different ways. Some were destroyed by it. Others were better able to return to their agony, give words to it. Not necessarily coming out of their memories unscathed, but at least intact. Peter remembered the Mothers of the Plaza de Mayo in Argentina who volunteered to work uncovering the mass graves of their "disappeared" sons and daughters. They told jokes and laughed as they wallowed in the filth and bones, not to make light of their loss, but to lighten the burden of it. It was their sense of community that gave them the strength to do that terrible work. The force of being alive with others in a quest for justice that overpowered the stench and sorrow. Aunt Julia was like that, it seemed to him. She talked to the owner with no sign of the awful memories that must be filling her mind. And like the Argentinian mothers, Aunt Julia must feel some of that same sense of injustice. She's on a mission, Peter decided.

A white panel van pulled into the driveway and turned around on the ungroomed lawn, leaving a deep, muddy scar. The words Geosystems Detection were written on the side above an image of what might've been intended as radar waves, drawn as thin black squiggles.

"Ah," Hans said, "here come the ground detectives."

A burly man with a dark, close-cropped beard stepped onto the van's running board and hopped to the ground. Peter approved of his physical preparedness for outdoor work. He wore a mackinaw coat, unbuttoned to reveal a black denim shirt with mother-of-pearl snaps. There was a slight sheen to the patina of soil that stained his jeans. The only thing about him out of keeping with the stereotype of an archaeologist was a new pair of black Nikes.

He introduced himself as Rolf Beemsteboer. He didn't introduce his assistant, a mousy, bespectacled man in his early twenties, who already busied himself at the back of the van.

"Are you associated with the Netherlands Forensics Institute?" Peter asked.

"*Nee,* they contracted us," Rolf explained. "Our work is too specialized," he said. He proudly, almost theatrically, thumped his chest with his fist.

"True," Peter acknowledged.

"Well, I guess we better get right to work," Rolf said. "Did we confirm the search area?"

"Aunt Julia," Peter said. She stood staring at the house. "Aunt Julia," he repeated louder to get her attention. "You told Nora you heard digging. Was your room in the front or the back?"

She was startled. "Back," she said.

"Okay," Rolf said. "Off we go to the back. See what lies beneath."

It occurred to Peter that if a stranger were to overhear this exchange, they'd never guess the grim purpose of the work they were doing. They were, after all, looking for the remains of a child murdered more than seventy years ago.

Rolf and his assistant plotted out a grid in the back of the house that extended from the wall to a low hedge at the property line. They measured it out carefully using a long tape on a spool of the kind Peter used at the sites in Timbuktu. The grid quickly took form as they tied fluorescent yellow string to tent stakes at ground level.

With the search area carefully demarcated, they lifted the radar unit from the back of the panel truck. It looked strikingly like a lawn mower. It had six-spoked wheels, a red metal box in place of a grass-cutting blade and cover and a display screen on the handle. Their lifting efforts were lopsided, with Rolf clearly the stronger of the two. His assistant staggered under the unit's weight and he struggled to regain his balance. Once the unit was safely on the ground, the assistant pushed it into position on a corner of the grid. He moved his head from one side to another like a boxer—trying to put his shadow over the glare on the screen, Peter guessed—and then threw a few jabs at the touch pad. Rolf sat on the tailgate of the panel truck, took off his Nikes and replaced them with a pair of dirt-stained wooden shoes.

"What're those for?" Peter asked.

"I don't need them at this stage, but I have to walk the same speed both times, so I put them on now," Rolf answered cryptically.

At a signal from his assistant, Rolf took hold of the handle and walked slowly behind the ground penetrating radar unit. He followed the strings laid out on the lawn, back and forth. So much did it resemble a lawnmower, Peter found it odd there was no noise. The grass and clover, granted a reprieve, sprang back up behind it unscathed. Once he passed over the grid, the assistant changed a setting and Rolf repeated the process. With the survey completed twice (different frequencies? Peter wondered), Rolf parked the GPR unit behind the truck and lit a cigarette.

"Now we go magnetic," Rolf said. He took off his jacket and hung it on the back of the GPR unit. Then he undid the snaps on the front of his shirt with one motion, pulled his arms out of the sleeves and threw it in the back of the van. The undershirt he wore underneath exposed his pudgy shoulders and pulled tight across his belly. He had a tattoo on one shoulder that looked like ghosts intertwined in a macabre dance. Peter tried to imagine what would motivate someone to get a tattoo like that—not just to pay an artist and endure the pain of the procedure, but to make an image of horror indelible on one's body. He drew a blank. It was beyond comprehension. Maybe he'd been working on genocides too long. Maybe he was getting out of touch.

Rolf slipped his feet out of his dirty clogs and hopped on one leg to remove his pants. He now wore a pair of loose-fitting boxer shorts with red stripes.

"I assume all this undressing is for a reason and isn't a striptease," Peter remarked wryly.

"Because of the magnet," Rolf answered. "A little like an MRI in the hospital, except I use a rod that points the magnetism downward, underground." He pointed with his lips to a pole with black straps long enough to serve as a yoke. Next to it lay a small black backpack, which Peter assumed to be a battery pack and processing unit. "You don't want anything metallic anywhere near this thing," Rolf said. "Things like snaps on your shirt or a zipper on your jeans are a big no-no. It's cold this way, but problem solved."

"And shoes? That's why the clogs, right?" Peter associated wooden shoes with porcelain figurines in tourist shops. Like the ones in Aunt Julia's apartment.

"Absolutely," Rolf said. "You never know what ordinary shoes are made of, where they might be hiding metal, so I make a habit of working with these." With a downward look he slipped his feet back into the dirt-stained clogs. "Back to basics, my friend. Good old-fashioned *klompen*. The one brand of footwear guaranteed to be metal free."

Rolf repeated his back-and-forth along the grid. This time, he held the magnetic induction rod with both hands spaced wide apart. As before, he shuffled in his wooden shoes. "I'm trying to keep the same pace as when I pushed the radar unit," he shouted through one corner of his mouth, a cigarette skilfully clamped in the other. The sight of Rolf in his underwear, a cigarette dangling from his lips, ambling along in wooden shoes, prompted Peter to take a video with his iPhone. He'd ask Rolf's permission to post it later. Or at least share it with Nora. It'd give her a laugh.

Peter turned to Aunt Julia to ask what she thought of it all, but she wasn't there. It was one of those "funny, she was just here a second ago" moments. He glanced over at the Opel, but there was no one visible inside. He opened the passenger side of the panel truck. The assistant was in the driver's seat with a sandwich in one hand and an iPhone in the other. He scrolled with his thumb and didn't look up.

"Did you see my aunt? The old woman who was here with me a minute ago?" Peter asked.

The assistant shook his head and said "*Nee*" with his mouth full, still staring at the phone.

Peter walked up the gravel path to the farmhouse and rang the bell. Hans opened the door. The sill added to Hans's height and Peter found it momentarily disconcerting to be looking up to someone who stood a few inches taller. "By any chance did my aunt come in the house."

Hans shook his head. "No. I wonder where she could be?" He led the way around the back of the house where Rein continued to walk on the grid. There was no sign of her. "Sometimes people play hide-and-seek like that, looking at one place while the person they're looking for already went somewhere else. I'll bet she's on the other side of the house," Hans suggested.

Peter and Hans walked around the house in opposite directions. They approached one another at the front stoop.

"Nothing?" Peter asked.

"Nothing."

On a hunch, Peter walked back to the Opel to have a closer look. Through the rear window, he saw Aunt Julia curled in a fetal position in the back seat. She was startled and blinked when he opened the door.

"Aunt Julia! What're you doing here? Are you okay?" Peter asked.

"Just tired," she replied.

"Let me take you home," Peter offered. "There's nothing more for us to do here."

"That would be nice," she said. She sat upright and looked toward the house. "Too many memories there." She paused and moved her eyes rapidly back and forth the way she did whenever she explored a thought. "It's funny how grief can feel so much like fear. Nobody tells you that when you're young."

* * *

Peter's phone vibrated two days later. He was having lunch with Rash and Olga in the cafeteria at the ICC headquarters. (They hadn't been able to pry Evan from his desk; he was attached to the screen like a limpet.) Rash was engaged in a passionate complaint about how tall Dutch women were. It was making it hard for him to find anyone suitable. "I just think, you know, a man should be taller. It's just how I feel. I'm not saying for everyone, but for me it hurts to have a woman look down at you. And here, they're all so damned tall."

Olga had her arms crossed. "You just need to get over it," she said. "It isn't like everyone's two meters like Peter here. You can keep looking for the ideal petite little thing or you can be open, go out with someone an inch or two taller than you."

Peter brought his phone out of his pocket and looked at the number. It was Rolf. "Sorry. Gotta take this." He stood abruptly and looked for a quiet place to talk. There was an empty table in a windowless corner with no one sitting nearby.

He answered on his way to the table. "Hello, Rolf."

"We have some preliminary results for you," Rolf said without preamble.

Peter sat and leaned on his elbows. He fought the urge to bite the corner of a fingernail, then put his hands to use by pressing the palm of one hand against one ear and the phone's speaker against the other. "Preliminary, meaning . . ."

"Nobody's digging. Yet."

"Ah."

"It's only when you pull things from the ground that you really know what's there." Judging only by Rolf's voice, Peter couldn't tell if the simple statement was a jibe or an explanation.

"Of course. So, what're your initial findings?" Peter asked.

"First, I should tell you honestly, the ground penetrating radar was pretty shitty." Rolf's voice was animated. An expert with a willing audience. "It usually works better than the other methods, but not this time. Might be because of the soil composition. Too much clay, not enough sand and silt. Too little porosity, so we couldn't get a sharp picture. Just a few anomalies that could be one thing or another. Setting the antenna to different frequencies only helped slightly. Against expectations, we got slightly better results at two-hundred-fifty megahertz instead of five hundred. We did find what looks like a filled-in latrine. Pretty clear. A square, deep hole. My guess is it was filled in way more recently than seventy-whatever years ago, which is when you said your person was buried. After three years or so, a hole that's dug and refilled starts to get indistinguishable from the surrounding soil. Tough to find. The latrine was probably filled with dirt trucked in from somewhere else, rocks and building rubble and whatnot with a cap of topsoil, which is why it turned up so clearly. In short, definitely not your burial site."

He'd half expected it, but Peter couldn't help but find this information discouraging. "Okay, good. Thanks all the same."

"Wait. I'm not finished," Rolf said. "I haven't told you about the electromagnetic induction. We use a dual sensor approach, remember?"

"Oh, right." Without knowing why, Peter felt his heart beat faster in his chest. "And?"

"First of all, horseshoes. Lots of damned horseshoes. Fine if you're superstitious, I suppose," Rolf said.

Peter understood the game Rolf was playing: build up his expectations and then deflate them. He was enjoying it. "Of course," Peter said, playing along. "You can expect that, it being a farm. Or used to be."

"Yes. And a large item," Rolf added. "Really lots of iron there. We think it's an old plough."

"Again, consistent with the history of land usage," Peter said.

"Yup. And then the good news. Or not-so-good news, depending." The levity was gone from Rolf's voice. "There's a strong likelihood we found the burial site you were looking for."

"What? Really?" Peter tried to stay calm. He wasn't going to allow himself to get strung along and then disappointed again. "How can you be so sure?"

"Can you think of another reason why we would find the steel shanks of a pair of size thirty or thirty-one children's shoes spaced seven centimetres apart at a depth of one-and-a-half metres?" Rolf asked.

CHAPTER 27: FIRST EVIDENCE

Peter drove the Opel flawlessly the second time. He had no trouble with the clutch starting out of first, his shifting was smooth, and the navigation system made sense. The traffic was light in the late morning between rush hours. He felt the ease of it as an affirmation of his ability to learn.

When he pulled into the driveway and heard gravel crunch under the tires, he imagined himself driving into the set of a police procedural, which, in fact, he was. There were two police cars, a panel van with the logo of the University of Leiden, and a minivan marked with an image of a book with a stylized flame emerging from the cover and the words "Politie" and "Forensisch Technische Onderzoeken." Peter assumed from these words it was either a special forensics team or from the coroner's office—or both.

He kept his foot depressed firmly on the clutch when he turned off the ignition. With the Opel properly parked, he felt the small satisfaction of a simple task well done.

The house owner, Hans, was talking to a uniformed policeman wearing a yellow vest. When Peter emerged from the car, Hans looked over at him, waved and resumed his conversation. The policeman, it seemed, wanted access to the house. Hans opened the door and invited him inside.

There was a crime scene ribbon stretched around the rear of the property at the place where Corine's likely burial site had been discovered by magnetic imaging. Jansen was there exuding authority among the uniformed policemen, even with his back turned. One of the policemen looked in Peter's direction and nodded with a gesture intended for Jansen, who then turned, took note, and ducked under the tape. He looked down at his feet as he approached. His face was serious, drawn. They shook hands and said hello the usual way. Jansen thanked Peter for taking the time to come, then added, "I wonder if I might ask whether you and your aunt . . . What's her name again?"

"Julia."

"Yes. Right. I wonder whether I might ask the two of you to provide us with a DNA sample. Third party DNA testing is entirely voluntary, of course. I'm afraid you'll have to do it at the station. We'll establish your identity first so please each of you bring identification. We have a little form for you to fill out. Consent and such. Then we'll have our experts take the saliva sample from your mouth. All very routine."

"It's call third party because?"

"You're not a suspect." Jansen answered on autopilot, his thoughts clearly elsewhere.

"Thank goodness for that," Peter said. "And, of course, you need our DNA to identify the body here."

"Right," Jansen said, businesslike, to the point. "Actually, either one of you would do. Then, if you're related to these bones, the story from your aunt holds together."

Peter felt it strange that Jansen saw him as *related* to Corine's bones. It made him somehow kindred with death.

"I'll take care of it right away," Peter said.

"Oh." Jansen pursued another thought. "Something else. I know we've already heard the story from you, second hand. But we also would like your aunt—Julia—to make an official statement. Recorded. Enter it into evidence."

"That shouldn't be a problem," Peter said. "I'm sure she wants this looked into as much as we do."

"Good," Jansen said. "Now let me introduce you to your other aunt," Jansen said. "Or the person we think is your aunt."

By way of invitation onto the crime scene, Jansen lifted the perimeter tape as high as he was able. Peter ducked underneath, bent low. The excavation hole had the sharp, clean corners of a military bed. A person—who Peter assumed to be a woman from either the university or police forensics—was hunched over in the hole. A long braid protruded from the back of her sun hat. Peter approached the edge and saw the object of her attention: a half-buried skeleton. The bones of an upper arm and part of the ribcage were already exposed. The hole was wide enough for the researcher's feet to be off to one side, putting her in a position to work on the area around the skull and jawbone. She took out small amounts of soil with a trowel, deposited them in a bucket and brushed off the bones. An assistant stood next to the hole, close to a sifting screen with a pile of fine soil underneath, looking for evidence in the soil taken out of the hole. A bullet maybe. Buttons from her dress. They'd be the only parts left after all these years. A photographer stood nearby, ready to take a picture of the bones *in situ*.

The forensic anthropologist stood for a moment, giving Peter a better view of the burial site. The skeleton was positioned in the grave face down with the head sideways. Corine had been thrown in without ceremony. Dumped there. All that effort to dig a metre-and-a-half hole, and they couldn't be bothered to show the least bit of respect. Not that shooting someone point blank in the head at the beginning of their life was an act of respect. At least in that they were consistent.

"You're here at the moment of truth," Jansen said.

While the researcher worked, the skull came more clearly into view. First the eye sockets and brow ridges, low and soft, with a high forehead, consistent with a nine-year-old girl. Then the nasal cavity. Finally, what they'd all been waiting for: a small hole in the left part of the forehead. According to Aunt Julia's story, the SS officer changed suddenly from pointing the pistol at her head to Corine's just before he fired it. That might be why the hole was a little to the left. If the officer was right-handed, Aunt Julia would've been forced into the chair on his right. That would be a good follow-up question for her. Peter wondered if he should share his thoughts with Jansen. He kept quiet. Jansen seemed competent enough.

"Well, there you have it," Jansen said. "Now we have a murder investigation."

The woman excavating the skeleton looked up at him with a serious expression. "Such a young little thing to have a bullet wound like that."

The excavation hole was stepped to make it easier for her to climb out without disturbing the excavation. She walked a short distance away and stretched her back.

For the first time, Peter saw the full length of the skeleton. On Corine's feet were the shoes that had shown up on the magnetic imaging and led them to her. They were browned and cracked, but still recognizable as pretty girls' shoes.

The photographer approached and snapped photos.

"You see the entrance wound?" Peter couldn't tell if Jansen was talking to him or the anthropologist or both. "It's consistent with a Luger P08 firing a nine-by-nineteen-millimetre parabellum round. Lower velocity than some handguns. That's why you get a slightly ragged entrance wound." Jansen and Peter stood shoulder-to-shoulder silently staring into the hole. "*Si vis pacem, para bellum*," Jansen added.

"What does that mean?" Peter asked.

"It means 'if you want peace, prepare for war.' It's the Latin motto of the Deutsche Waffen-und Munitionsfabriken. That's the company that produced so much of the German war machine. It's where we get the term nine-millimetre parabellum. For the round."

"That's interesting," was all Peter could think to say. After a while, Peter remembered something relevant. "A few days ago, I saw some graffiti on an electric box. It said, bombs for peace is like fucking for virginity."

Jansen smiled. "I guess there are two sides to everything."

"Not really." Peter looked into the grave site. "There weren't two sides to that."

"You're right," Jansen said. "Not by any stretch of the imagination."

The skeleton was a perfect prop for performing mentalism, like a crystal ball, lending focus to one's thoughts. For Peter, it brought vividly to mind the circumstances of Corine's death. The sadism of it. He went over it in his imagination in minute detail, then tried to push the thoughts aside, but they intruded.

The researcher clambered back into the hole with a large see-through bag. She carefully lifted the exposed right arm of the skeleton and slid it into the bag. In the process, two of the fingers fell off.

"That happens every time," she said to no one in particular. She gathered them from the soil and deposited them in the bag. "Fragile ligaments in the phalanges. Especially with time. Especially with children."

Peter looked sideways at Jansen. "What's all this for?" he said. "Why go to all this trouble? Aren't we sure whoever did this is long since dead? My aunt described him as looking middle aged already at the end of the war."

Jansen nodded. "That's right," was all he said.

"So, are we doing this just for closure? For the sake of history? To close the book on a war crime without a living perpetrator?"

"Oh, we have a suspect all right," Jansen said.

Peter was taken aback. "What? Really? Who?"

Jansen looked up at him. There was something raptorial in his eyes, out of keeping with the gnome-like arrangement of his features. "I'm grateful to you for all your help, Peter, but I'm afraid I can't answer that. Even one investigator to another. I'll be sure to keep you informed when the time comes."

He turned and walked away.

CHAPTER 28: DOUBT

Peter was in the grave, in the same spot where the researcher had been, digging next to the bones. Rain began to fall and he had nothing with which to cover the skeleton. He tried taking off his jacket, but it was too small to cover all the bones. Either the skull or the feet with the half-decomposed shoes would get wet. He chose to cover the skull, the seat of the soul—when she was alive. The ground was already muddy. The grave filled with water. It ran down the sides and gradually submerged the bones; the water level covered the fingers first, then rose up the sides of the skull.

Corine appeared above, at the edge of the hole. She wore a yellow dress with a matching yellow bow in her hair and white knee-highs and shiny black shoes. She looked down at Peter with a serious expression. Despite her children's attire, there was nothing at all little girlish about her. "Peter, stop," she said.

Peter was confused. "Stop what? What do you want me to stop?"

The rain fell harder. Corine's dress was soaked. Her hair came undone and stuck to her face and water dripped from her fingertips.

"You're hurting her," Corine said.

"Who? Who am I hurting?"

Then Peter felt something move next to him. It was the bones. They stirred in the water. He felt a bony hand clutch his wrist under the muddy water. A face appeared, half submerged. It was Aunt Julia. She was barely recognizable because her face was partly decomposed and she had only one eye. Her mouth opened. It was full of water. It gurgled and flowed out and she gasped for air. She tried to say something to him, but the words didn't form. What was it? Was it his name?

"Peter! Peter! I'm here Peter. Everything's okay." It was Nora's voice.

Peter brought her face into focus. He felt his heart beating hard in his chest and heard his pulse in his ears.

"You were having a nightmare," Nora said.

"Oh, gawd." Only when Peter flopped his head back on the pillow did he realize he'd been sitting half upright.

"What was it about?" Nora asked.

Peter told her about his dream. As he spoke, Nora pulled his head onto her shoulder and stroked his hair.

When he finished, he lifted his head and looked at her. "What do you think it means?"

"You don't know?" She sounded incredulous.

"Not a clue," he answered. "About the bones, okay, I get it. That was from yesterday at the site, but why was Aunt Julia in the dream? I don't understand."

"Oh, Peter, Peter, Peter," was all Nora said.

"What do you mean by that? Did I say something wrong?"

"No, it's just that it's so obvious," she said. "And you're so clueless." She said it affectionately, as though his cluelessness were something she found endearing.

"Explain it to me then."

"All right," Nora said. "If I have to explain it to you, here it is: The dream is giving you a warning. It's telling you that digging up Corine's body—and beyond that, the search for perpetrators—is hurting your Aunt Julia."

"But Aunt Julia told me she wanted to find Corine's body. She's helping us."

"Sure," Nora said, "but that doesn't make it any easier for her. You've got to be careful. Look at the effect just listening to stories from the war in northern Mali started having on you. And with her, it's much closer to home. It's about her little sister. It's an experience she suffered. Starting an investigation into it, digging things up—literally—must be unbearable to her."

Peter thought that over. "I suppose you're right. I have to admit, when I found her curled up in the back seat of the car, I was a little worried. But then she seemed okay."

"*Seemed* okay," Nora retorted. "But you have no idea what's going on with her. What she's experiencing. The same goes for you, by the way."

He felt her stroke his hair. The movement of her fingers along his scalp was pensive, abstracted.

"You should sleep more," she said. "Part of you understands what's going on. You need to let it out, give your deeper thoughts room to guide you."

Peter felt his heartbeat slow, his breathing calm. Nora was right. He was pushing too hard. Aunt Julia seemed solid, formidable even, but there was fragility when you went deeper. He had to be careful with her. Not force things. Not make her remember and relive the worst experiences of her life.

"We should check up on her," he said. "Bring her some dinner, maybe. I'll take the day off."

"Good idea. Let's give her a call."

Peter rang Aunt Julia's number. There was no answer.

* * *

Aunt Julia finally picked up when they were in the Opel on their way to her apartment. Nora had a casserole in a Pyrex dish covered with tinfoil on her lap. Peter's phone was connected to the car's sound system.

"*Met* Julia," Aunt Julia said.

Peter had to steer around a parked delivery truck. Nora answered from their end. "Hello, *Tante* Julia. This is Nora and Peter. We didn't hear from you and were a little worried. We're in the car Peter rented. On our way to your place. We won't stay. We just wanted to drop something off. We made you some dinner, thought you might like some help."

There was a long silence.

"Julia? Are you there?" Peter said. He was worried, thought about his dream from the night before, then felt guilty about Aunt Julia's distress. This wasn't really about solving Corine's murder. She was the star witness for his sense of self. He lost perspective in his will to uncover the past. Maybe it was too late. Maybe he'd already pushed her over the edge.

"*Na*, well," Aunt Julia said at last. "Of course, come by. I'll just tidy up a bit."

"No, no," Nora said. "No need for that. We'll just meet you at the door."

"*Doie*," Aunt Julia said.

Peter glanced at his phone and saw that the call had ended.

"Bye," he said to no one in particular.

***

Aunt Julia opened the door to her apartment a crack. She looked at Peter and Nora with one eye. "There you are," she said. She opened the door wider, but not wide enough to let them in. "So glad you came."

Something was wrong. Aunt Julia's hair was unkempt. Until now, Peter wasn't aware she wore makeup, but its absence was notable. Her skin was sallow and there were dark circles under her eyes. "We brought you a casserole," he said. He held up the dish.

"How very thoughtful of you." Aunt Julia reached through the door to accept the casserole.

"Is everything okay?" Nora asked.

"*Ja*," Aunt Julia said. "*Alles goed*."

"Waf, waf!" Toen said from the other room.

"Ooh, little Toentje!" Nora exclaimed. "How is he? I missed him."

Peter saw a flicker of doubt in Aunt Julia's eyes. He imagined her to be torn between defending the redoubt of her privacy and allowing Nora past the gate for a visit with her beloved parrot.

"He's not been doing so well lately," Aunt Julia admitted. "Maybe he'd like it if you said hello." She opened the door wide to let them in.

Nora rushed in and was the first in the other room. Peter put the casserole dish on the kitchen table on his way through. Aunt Julia followed.

Toen was in his cage perched on the uppermost part of the climbing limb. He was bedraggled. His feathers were patchy; some were broken.

"He's been eating his feathers," Aunt Julia explained.

The confirming evidence was there in a scattering of broken feathers mixed with droppings on the bottom of the cage. It hadn't been cleaned for some time. There was a musty basement smell. Peter opened the cage door and reached in to unclip a nearly-empty water bottle from its attachment. Toen took his extended arm as an invitation and hopped onto his sleeve. When Peter withdrew his arm from the cage, Toen flapped his way over to Nora and perched on her shoulder. He nuzzled her ear. She stroked his head with her finger.

"Would you care for some tea?" Aunt Julia asked.

"I'll get it started," Peter said. On his way to the kitchen, Peter noted the disarray in the apartment. There were books and old newspapers and magazines scattered haphazardly on the coffee table, kitchen table, even on the couch and chairs. Half the books had been taken down from the shelves. (The shelf with the collection of books from the war was empty.) There were mugs—some empty, some half full of tea or coffee—in various places: between piles of books on the table, on the bookshelf, on the carpet next to a wing chair. In the kitchen, the sink was piled with dishes. There was uneaten toast still in the toaster. The counter was littered with crumbs and a smear of jam. The sponge reeked. He threw it in the trash, found a clean one under the sink and set to work. Armed with a new sponge and dish soap, he scrubbed the water dispenser for the birdcage. He put water on to boil, gathered all the mugs he could find around the apartment, scrubbed and rinsed them over the unwashed dishes, then filled the sink with soapy water and left the dishes to soak. The fridge was almost bare, with only wilted celery, lettuce, an overripe avocado, and a pint of milk. He smelled the milk before he added it to the tea. It seemed fine.

"Bravo," Nora said as Peter entered the living room.

He carried a tray containing tea, biscuits, and a filled water dispenser lying sideways with an air pocket moving back and forth like a bubble level. He had nowhere to set down the tray. Nora quickly moved some books and magazines into a pile on one end of the coffee table to make room. Once he put down the tray, his hands were free to attach the water cylinder to its clip in the birdcage. Toen signaled his approval from Nora's shoulder by bobbing his head.

"Thank you for the tea, Peter." Aunt Julia was perched on the edge of the sofa with a pile of magazines behind her. She left her tea on the tray.

"It looks like you've been busy," Nora observed. "Been doing research, have you?"

To Peter it didn't look like research. The disarray suggested something else, something more frenetic.

Aunt Julia picked up her tea mug and held it tightly in her hands. "*Na*, well, not really. Just reading. A little of this and a little of that."

"Anything worth sharing?" Peter was curious.

"Remi . . . Reminis . . ."

"Reminiscences," Peter finished for her.

"Yes," Aunt Julia said. "I'm reminiscen-cing."

"Mmm." Peter wasn't convinced, but he didn't want to push.

They fell silent. Each occasionally sipped their tea. Toen joined them. He flew to the open door of his cage, hopped inside and took a drink from the dispenser.

"It must be hard," Nora said. "Going back to the war. Remembering."

Aunt Julia nodded. "Finding Corine was . . ." She struggled to find the right word and left the sentence unfinished. "This is hard in a different way." She nodded toward the books. "I'm trying to find out *why* she died. I can't find an answer."

"The origin of evil," Peter said. "If you find an answer to that, let me know. You'll be the first."

"I'm just trying to make sense of it all," Aunt Julia said, face contorted with sorrow. "I mean, why her and not me." She put down her tea and covered her face with both hands. Nora moved to sit beside her and put an arm around her shoulder.

"She would've been seventy-nine by now," Nora said.

Aunt Julia turned her face toward Nora, then buried it in her shoulder.

Peter felt awkward, not knowing what to do or say. He went to the bathroom to find her a tissue.

Aunt Julia accepted the tissue from Peter with her face still in Nora's shoulder. She covered her face with it and only showed herself when her tears were dry. "I'm sorry," she said.

Nora kept a hand on her back. "No reason to be sorry."

"I've been thinking," Aunt Julia said. "About why we're doing this. Uncovering the bones and memories. It hurts so much. What good does it do?"

She and Nora both looked toward Peter.

"Well, I . . ." He found himself unable to form a cogent thought. "I suppose," he said, "the first thing is, remembering helps the same way all these do." He gestured toward the books amassed on the end of the coffee table. "The personal stories come together to give us a sense of what actually happened. Not what people *want* the story to be. They undo the lies people tell for their personal advantage. To escape responsibility." He paused to think, then added, "Those truths are like the dunes next to the shoreline. They protect us from the encroachments of evil. Every grain of sand matters."

"That all sounds well and good," Nora said. "Except . . ." She patted Aunt Julia's shoulder. "What good does it do the truthtellers? What's the cost to them of remembering? What happens to the stones where the sand comes from?"

"Well," Aunt Julia said. "Enough nonsense about grains of sand and stones and pebbles or whatnot. I've made up my mind." She left it at that.

"Made up your mind?" Nora asked.

"Let's go in, shall we?" Aunt Julia turned to Peter with a hollow smile. "To the police. I think I'm ready to tell them what I know."

CHAPTER 29: STRUCTURES

The office in the converted warehouse in London couldn't be missed. The numbers were over a foot high in a column running down one side of the double-doored entrance. "STRUCTURES," was bannered above the doors. Peter had taken the train that morning, planning a quick overnight trip. Ferman had insisted. He wanted Peter to follow the digital evidence every step of the way.

Peter rang a bell connected to an intercom.

"Hello?" came a static voice.

"Peter Dekker here. I have an appointment to see Trevor Jakobsen."

Instead of a buzz and lock release as Peter expected, the door opened a crack, manually. The face of a man with tousled reddish-brown hair appeared. "Hi Peter, I'm Trevor. Pleased to meet you. Just to let you know, Lola is very friendly."

Before Peter could answer, Trevor opened the door wide to reveal a large dog with half-erect ears wearing a martingale collar with chains and a thick strap. Lola approached Peter with something like a wide, mischievous grin, put her nose between his legs, and looked up at him with her muzzle in his crotch. She wagged her tail vigorously from the hip.

"She likes to do that when she meets people for the first time. I haven't the slightest idea why," Trevor said, apologetically.

Peter realized he was holding his elbows out sideways in a position of surrender. He willed himself to reach down and give Lola a pet. She seemed happy with that and scampered back into the room with a click of toenails and a slight skid on the linoleum flooring. “Nice dog,” Peter said. “What breed is it?”

“She’s a Staffie,” Trevor said. Peter must’ve given him a blank look because he added, “A Staffordshire terrier. With a smidge of something else. Something taller.”

Entering the room, Peter was suddenly at ease. The sound of keyboards clicking rose above a maze of monitors and potted palms. The usual open office design of digital investigators, same as the ICC, except with a generous number of decorative palms. More attention to ambience, to how design influences emotions.

Covering an entire corkboard wall was a series of photos of a building complex, a mock-up of a project-in-progress, Peter guessed. He matched the images on the wall against an intricate wooden model occupying a large table. “Work in progress?” he asked.

Trevor followed the direction of Peter’s gaze. “A new Facebook office,” he answered. “Can’t tell you where it’ll be. It’s one of those, ‘if I tell you, I’ll have to kill you’ situations. These are just some preliminary ideas.”

“So, you still do traditional architecture.” Peter knew the word “traditional” was wrong as soon as it left his mouth.

Trevor deflected the gaffe gently. “If you want to call it that.”

Peter looked closely at the photos on the wall. One stood out. It was at the top of the display, where most people wouldn’t get a good view of it. It was of a rustic, domed building among trees with the faint outline of a glass and steel structure in the background. “You have a yurt in the middle of a Facebook office complex?”

“With a fire pit,” Trevor said proudly. “I’m especially happy with that. A gas fire with an on/off switch and cedar shavings you can add to give it an authentic wood-burning smell. It meets fire regulations as an incense burner.”

“And that adds a rustic element to a Facebook office?” Peter asked.

Trevor looked at the mock-up wall with admiration. "A place for thinking, meditation, reconnecting with nature. The kind of retreat that helps people generate ideas. But instead of having to drive somewhere or take vacation time, we have it right here in the courtyard."

"Genius," Peter said. He gave the yurt another look before turning back to the room. He judged this to be the right time to get down to business. "Tell me more about what you do. The sort of thing you're doing with digital investigations. Forensics."

Trevor was ready with a response to a question he must've been asked often. "The main principle is pretty basic. Architecture nowadays is heavily into software and digital design. So, we—I mean me and a few others in my cohort—decided that if design can look toward building the future, it can also look to the past, reconstruct events that've already happened. We apply the principles of architecture to forensics.

Peter nodded.

"Let's say you have a video of a shooting," Trevor continued. "You can't see the shooter, just the victims. We can tell where a bullet was fired by reconstructing the area, digital modelling, then going back to the video—or videos—frame by frame to follow a fatal shot in a series of images, how it bounces off the pavement or travels through someone. Through a victim."

At this, Peter grimaced. He imagined an investigator watching a bullet pass through someone's flesh, taking measurements with every millisecond before the analysis was complete.

"By starting with a reconstruction of the entire scene," Trevor said, "we can show exactly where a sniper was positioned, this spot on the roof, or this balcony. Using video taken from a completely different angle."

"And with that information, you begin to build a case," Peter followed up. "You undo the narrative of self-defense or measured response."

Trevor nodded. "Exactly." They both looked toward the image of the yurt on the wall display, even though their conversation was elsewhere. "The data don't tell a story by themselves. We have to put the data together in such a way that the story comes out."

"That's interesting," Peter said. "When I think of architecture I don't think of storytelling."

Trevor jumped on Peter's gap in knowledge. "Ah, now that's where you're wrong," he said. "Even a bridge or a high rise tells a story. Or, better, this yurt here. The appeal of it, the way it helps with creativity, how it stimulates the imagination."

"Well," Peter said. "It took a real act of storytelling to put it in the middle of a Facebook complex."

Peter meant it as a compliment, but saw Trevor wince. He tried to redirect the conversation: "I'm curious to see how you're telling the story of the case from Timbuktu."

"Of course," Trevor said. "Come this way." He led Peter into an office with thick glass separating it from the main room. Even the door was glass with a brushed steel handle and frame. There were the usual three linked monitors on the desk and a larger curved monitor mounted on the wall. Trevor switched on a computer under the desk and the wall monitor came to life. Only two folders were displayed, one labeled "Projects," the other "Al-Mahdi." Trevor clicked open the Al-Mahdi folder, followed by an identically-named file. It revealed a detailed aerial view of Timbuktu with labeled pins locating the main sites of destruction. A side column with the title "Case Against M. Al-Mahdi," comprised a numbered list of the sites. "Here's where we put the links," Trevor explained. He brought the cursor above the one labeled "01. Sidi Mahmoud."

"This is the first one we finished. The rest are in various stages of . . . Well, I'm not sure what. Incompleteness. Disarray. Whatever. But this one's pretty much ready. It'll show you what the platform will look like when its finished." Trevor clicked on the link. It revealed a series of still photos next to a navigable satellite image. To the left side was a column comprising three circles labeled *Before, During,* and *After*. He clicked on the *After* circle to reveal a series of images of the ruins of the mausoleum. It invoked in Peter a flashback to the day he, Ibrahim and Goma went past the UN checkpoint and he took the measurements and photos.

"This is your work." Trevor turned to Peter. "You and Goma. We have you to thank for the *After* images." He paused. "No pun intended."

It took Peter a moment to find the double meaning of "after-images." "You made them look great," he said. He was genuinely impressed. "Better than I imagined."

Trevor looked more closely at the work-in-progress. "That's a nice, clean shot. You used an amazing camera. Interesting to think, the strength of a case can come down to the number of megapixels we're able to assemble." He moved the cursor too quickly for Peter to connect its movements with any train of thought. "Some of the 'During' videos we have to work with are better than others," Trevor said.

Peter had to agree. He couldn't help but feel responsible for the uneven quality. "For some of the sites, there's nothing at all. Not yet. But the ones we do have are pretty damning."

"I've seen them," Trevor said. "Basically, unsolicited confessions uploaded to social media. Great, fist-pumping stuff."

"You'd be surprised how often that happens," Peter said. Some people are so proud of their atrocities, they want to share them with the world."

"War crimes for likes," Trevor remarked as he turned off the computer. The monitor went dark. "I wonder what the Nazis would've done in World War Two if everyone had smart phones and social media," he said.

Before Peter could respond he was startled by Lola licking his hand. The door hadn't been closed all the way and she had soundlessly found her way in. She nudged his hand with her nose and he obliged with a firm scritch behind the ears. Lola's tail beat a tattoo against the side of Trevor's metal desk.

"Interesting question." Peter spoke over the boom, boom, boom of Lola's tail. "Probably with social media, the Nuremberg trials would've been a lot bigger. More complicated. Or less. Justice was swift back then. One thing's for sure: a lot more people would've swung from the gallows or been marched to the firing squads at the dunes instead of spending quiet lives as civilians."

Trevor nodded. "Imagine all the video we'd have of the deportation trains."

In his mind's eye Peter saw a montage of the black-and-white images he remembered of Jews being forced into cattle cars. "We'd probably have been able to reconstruct every inch of their journeys," he said. "All the way to the death camps. Maybe even video smuggled out. The question is, what good would it have done?"

Trevor picked up a stray pen from the desk and expertly twirled it, something he must've practiced over years of sitting at a desk. He nodded, abstractedly. "Disinformation. Propaganda. Fanaticism. Megapixels only get us so far," he said. "And they aren't worth a damn if the public will isn't there."

Lola turned and left the office, then gave a backward look from the main room, as though leading the way somewhere. Asking for a walk.

Trevor looked at his watch. "I'm parched. How 'bout a drink? I want to hear more about what you did in Timbuktu."

CHAPTER 30: TRUTH TELLING

Immediately on his return to The Hague, Peter reported to Mr. Ferman on the progress Structures was making. He also re-occupied his place on the margins of another war-crimes investigation, this one involving his Aunt Corine. Or the girl who would've been his aunt. His real Aunt Julia was also a victim, albeit a surviving one. For the purposes of the state and its system of justice, though, she had to serve as a witness, a victim with a purpose. She was a source of information, her mind a vessel of evidence that had to be coaxed out, separated from lapses and lies, assessed for truth value, and compared with the testimony of others as the process fumbled toward facts, the raw material of judgment. For this, there was a process for pulling facts away from emotional truth, isolating them from their context, like a centrifuge separating components according to density.

It began with an appointment at the office of the public prosecutor.

It occurred to Peter as odd that both he and Aunt Julia were called in to give their fingerprints, ID check, and cheek swabs for the DNA test. Either of them would've done nicely. It was probably Jansen who'd arranged that. He wanted the elderly witness to have some company, make her feel better, improve conditions of compliance. People don't like being fingerprinted alone. Makes them feel like perpetrators, isolated from the group. Peter was there, not to give his DNA, but to prep Aunt Julia for her interview.

He sat with his thoughts in the hallway of the Public Prosecution Service in a chair upholstered with grey Naugahyde, still feeling the effects of his trip to London. His head was thick, his eyelids heavy, but the chair was a torture device, not designed for dozing. He noticed a rip with stuffing coming out on one side. The wooden armrest was loose. It was stained with the accumulated sweat and whatever was on people's hands—he could only imagine what—rubbed in over the years to replace the original finish.

He was about to nibble a fingernail, but remembered the residual ink on his fingertips. The baby oil and tissue the policewoman had given him and Aunt Julia to remove it worked only so well. He'd have to be careful not to stain his suit jacket or pants.

A woman with an armful of file folders approached. Her hair was done up in a tight bun and her high heels clicked on the floor. Peter had to pull his legs in to keep them from being in the way. She smiled wanly as she walked by.

The door in front of him had a sign in a metal slot that said, *INTERVIEW AAN DE GANG*. Peter heard voices through the door of the interview room, but not individual words. Jansen and Aunt Julia took turns talking at first, then it was mostly Aunt Julia. He wondered what she was saying all this time. He looked at his watch. It had been over an hour. Close to an hour-and-a-quarter.

After nearly two hours, Jansen flung open the door so hard it bounced against the doorstop. He was burdened with a folder thick with papers, a ring binder, and a professional recording device. Peter reached instinctively to shake his hand, but the objects Jansen was carrying prevented it.

Jansen smiled broadly. "An excellent interview. Your aunt is a remarkable witness. Thank you for bringing her here."

Before Peter could answer, Jansen bustled down the hallway and disappeared around the corner.

Peter saw Aunt Julia through the open door of the interview room. She sat with her elbows resting on a metal table, her hands covering her face. He walked in and stood next to her. He wanted to put his hand on her shoulder, but didn't want to stain her clothes with residual ink.

"Aunt Julia," he said. He wanted to ask if she was okay, but he knew she wasn't.

When she looked up at him, he saw a row of dark smudges along her forehead—she had stained her face with ink from the fingerprinting. Her eyes were pained.

"*Alles goed*," she said.

The woman who had passed him in the hallway while he was waiting, approached them holding a brown manilla envelope. "Mr. Jansen asked me to give this to you," she said, handing it to Peter. "Nothing urgent. Just for your interest."

***

In the car on the way to Aunt Julia's apartment, Peter's phone rang. He glanced down and saw it was from Arie.

"Do you mind if I put Arie on speaker?" he asked.

Aunt Julia waved her hand dismissively. "Do what you want."

Peter waited for the next stoplight and called him back.

"Haloo," Arie said.

"Dad, I just got your call. I'm here in the car with Aunt Julia."

There was a long silence.

"What're you doing with her?" Arie spoke as though she wasn't there.

"We're just coming from the prosecutor's office," Peter said. "She gave a statement. About Corine."

There was another long silence. Then the call disconnected.

"See?" Aunt Julia said. Then she turned her face to the window and wrapped herself in silence.

***

That evening, alone in the living room, Peter opened the envelope. Without understanding why, his hands shook. He opened it raggedly with his index finger under the flap. The document he pulled out was dated May 1945 and titled *Arie Dekker v. The Public Prosecutor*. He read quickly until he found the words, *cruelty, torture, rape, and other inhumane acts in respect of civilian populations*. He skimmed to the end and found the words, *In the absence of evidence other than the sworn testimony of Mevrouw Mariam Visser, the court finds the accused not guilty of all charges*. Peter had never heard the name Visser before. Of course, Arie would've been exonerated or his personal history would've been different. Even so, there had to be some truth to it. There had to be. Otherwise, why keep this episode a secret all these years? All these decades?

He called Arie from the bedroom with the door closed. Arie would have to talk this time. No excuses.

It rang eight times before Arie picked up. He was getting slow.

"Halloo," Arie said.

"Hi Dad. Peter here."

"I hope you're alone this time." Arie's tone was clipped.

"I'm alone. You needn't worry," Peter reassured him. "Listen, Dad, I've come across this document and—"

"I really hope you're not with that woman."

They were seconds into their conversation and Peter already felt a tight mass of irritation in his chest. "I don't know why you keep calling Aunt Julia *that woman*. She's your sister. I've gotten to know her over the last little while. She's actually very nice." Peter paused. "And, by the way, you've got to stop hanging up on me. It's very rude."

"A man was here," Arie said.

Peter sighed. He recognized the ploy. Arie changed the topic whenever someone said something he didn't like.

"What man?" Peter asked, playing along.

"From the police," Arie replied. "Two men actually. But only the *Nederlander* talked. We spoke some Dutch to say hello, but mostly English so the other one could understand."

If there was a Dutch-speaking policeman there, it had to do with the investigation into Corine's murder. Maybe a Mountie who spoke Dutch or—who knows?—someone flown over from the Netherlands for the purpose. The two police forces cooperating.

"When was this?" Peter asked.

"Yesterday."

"What did they want to know?" Peter was brimming with curiosity.

"I'm an investigator, too, you know," Arie said proudly. "A woman from your office said so. It must've been her who recommended me."

No matter how often it happened, Peter continued to be astonished at Arie's talent for turning a conversation toward his personal obsessions. His *self*-obsession. "Where was he from, the Dutch-speaking policeman? Do you remember?"

"I helped the police with their investigation," Arie replied with another non-sequitur, but at least this time closer to the subject. "We went through some photos. SS officers. Waffen SS. Lots of them. I never knew there were so many Dutch people in the Waffen SS. Did you know that? Hundreds of them. They had their own uniforms. Shame on them. Bastards."

"Were the police asking you to identify someone?" Peter's curiosity about Corine's case undid the original reason for his call. Finding out more about Arie's indictment after the war would have to wait. He'd try his best to be patient. Things came more easily that way.

"*Ja*. Yes."

"And? Did you? Did you identify someone?" Peter asked.

"They said I had a very good memory," Arie said. "A doctor tested my memory a few weeks ago. I did puzzles. He said the same thing. My memory is like in my twenties. That's what he said. I'm still really sharp."

"Dad, what did you tell them about the photographs?"

"I get . . . you know, *up* too," Arie said proudly.

"Dad—"

"Just like when I was young. What's the word? Vi- . . . vi-tal. That's it."

"Dad—"

"I bet I could still do it with a woman."

Peter finally lost patience. "Dad, for crissake! Would you please listen to me? What did the police want to know?"

"No need to get upset." Arie's voice was calm, as though to underscore the point. "I just told you. They showed me photos. Of people from the SS."

"And? Did you find anything?" Peter asked.

"Of course, I did," Arie said. "Didn't I just tell you that, too? What's the matter with you? My memory is like it was in my twenties. What's the expression? A trap. No, a steel trap. That's it. I remember, see? A mind like a steel trap. That's what the doctor said. How could I forget a face?"

"Whose face? Who?"

There was a long pause. Peter looked at his phone to see if they were still connected and saw the seconds still ticking over. "Whose face?" he repeated.

"That bastard who killed Corine," Arie said somberly. "And another one of the Nazi *klotzaks* who was there with him."

"You were certain? You were able to identify them?" Peter asked.

"The third one I couldn't find." Arie's voice had lost its joviality. "He wasn't there in the photos."

"That's great. Dad, about this court document from after the war, I—"

"Peter, I'm going to go now.

"Dad, I have one more—"

"Because I don't want you to get upset when I hang up."

"Okay, Dad."

"Goodbye, Peter. All the best."

"Bye, Dad." Peter removed the phone from his ear.

His thumb was poised to disconnect when he heard Arie say, "Oh, Peter, one more thing."

Peter returned the phone to his ear. Maybe his father wanted to offer a compliment. Some kind words before ending the call. "Yes?"

"Don't you think I'm a great investigator? Didn't I do a good job?" Arie asked.

Peter felt deflated. "You're terrific, Dad."

"Thanks. I thought so. Goodbye."

"Bye, Dad."

CHAPTER 31: PRESS RELEASE

A text message came from Jansen eight days after Aunt Julia had given her interview at the prosecutor's office. Peter's phone buzzed and lit up next to his keyboard at work. The text read simply, "Check your email. Call if you have any questions."

The email message from Jansen was no less cryptic. "Please read below. It hasn't gone out yet, but will shortly. I thought you and your aunt, Mw. Julia Olsen, should be the first outside my office to know."

Peter scrolled down and read:

6 May 2013

Dutch Prosecutor issues indictment of a Dutch citizen suspected of war crimes during the Nazi occupation of The Netherlands.

News item / 06-05-2013

The Netherlands Public Prosecution Service today issued a warrant for the arrest of a Dutch citizen suspected of committing war crimes during the Nazi occupation of the Netherlands.

The 87-year-old defendant was a volunteer in the Waffen SS, an elite branch of the occupying German armed forces. In this capacity, the defendant is accused of active participation in Operation Silbertanne, a murder action by which members of the Germanic (Netherlands) S.S., in collaboration with the Security

Police, shot civilians in reprisal for attacks on agents of the occupying German forces, the perpetrators of which were ostensibly not discovered. This operation consisted of systematic terrorism against the people of The Kingdom of the Netherlands and is already well established as a policy instrument of war crimes. As a volunteer member of the Waffen S.S., the suspect is accused of willingly and intentionally assisting in the commission of these war crimes.

In issuing its warrant of arrest, the Public Prosecution Service bases its analysis on witness interviews; corroborating evidence from the scene of a murder; and internal orders and documentation of the Waffen SS. On the basis of this evidence, the Public Prosecutor has reasonable grounds to demonstrate that the accused was a co-conspirator to the war crime of murder, namely the murder in her home of a Dutch female minor, and fifteen counts of accessory to the war crime of the torture and murder of Dutch citizens, all committed under the command of Hauptman Walter Berka, now deceased.

The case will be heard in the District Court at the Schiphol Judicial Complex (JCS) in Badhoevedorp.

The only question that occurred to Peter was why no names were mentioned. It was still a mystery who did it. The people reading this won't even know it was Corine who was murdered in her home. The prosecutor's office was sheltering its suspects behind privacy laws. But this man they accused, whoever he was, was no juvenile. His life was lived. Why not tell us something about him?

Peter tried calling Jansen, but only got as far as his answering service. When he tried Aunt Julia's number, he had more success. She picked up on the second ring, as though expecting his—or someone's—call.

When she answered, she surprised him with, "Hallo, Peter."

"How did you know it was me?" Peter remembered her old flip phone, incapable of identifying incoming callers.

"The nice woman told me I should get a new phone, one that tells you who's calling. She said I might need better security."

Peter had a sudden feeling in the pit of his stomach of things happening beyond his control. It was good advice, but it didn't come from him. Advice about threats of which he had no knowledge. Why would Aunt Julia need better security on her phone? Why now? Probably for the same reason the press release didn't reveal any names.

"What woman was this?" he asked. "From the prosecutor's office?"

"*Ja, natuurlijk.*"

"So you know about the arrest? The press release?"

"Peter, Peter," Aunt Julia said, not answering. "You're very sweet."

He wondered if she meant to be condescending.

"But they have things well under control," Aunt Julia said. "They made an arrest, did you hear?"

"Yes, Jansen just told me. How do you feel about that?"

There was silence on the other end.

"Happy and afraid," Aunt Julia said eventually.

"Happy about what?" Peter asked. "Afraid of what?"

There was another pause before Aunt Julia said, "Happy they found one of Corine's killers after all these years. Afraid of everything else."

She turned the subject of conversation to her new phone, how the nice man at the store was, how he made everything big so she was able to read it. Then they said goodbye cordially. That was one of the marvels of Aunt Julia, Peter thought as he looked at the phone in his hand. She keeps her fears to herself better than anyone he knew. Almost too well.

Left to themselves, these fears multiply, ferment, and pull toward dark imaginings. This he knew from experience.

CHAPTER 32: THE PHOTOGRAPH

The crunch and pop of the gravel under the tires of the Opel as Peter pulled into the driveway at his Uncle Kurt and Aunt Nel's home made him think of the farmhouse near Zwolle where Corine's bones lay buried for three-quarters of a century. Nel had called the day before and left a message, something about a photograph. Arie, with a Nazi. Peter had long suspected his father of being a war criminal of some sort. At least a collaborator, maybe an informer. There had to be a reason for his silence. Now the evidence was coming together.

Aunt Nel opened the front door to the house before he exited the car. They said hello as he walked across the gravel driveway and kissed once on each cheek when he arrived at the stoop. They were eye-to-eye with her standing on the raised landing. Even so, she seemed smaller than when he last saw her, with the same bird-like quality as Aunt Julia.

Kurt was away at the university, she explained. Some meeting or other. She didn't always know what he was up to. Aeronautics, of course. Heavens knows what that was all about, so much math, it made her head spin. Then there were professional things, things that had to be decided among the professors. Meetings about department administration. Graduate student supervision. Funding for a new wind tunnel to test their model planes.

She then abruptly changed tack and asked Peter if he'd like a quick tour of the house. He wanted to see the photo she'd found, to the exclusion of all else, but it could wait. Social niceties were a priority.

They did the tour of the house, starting with the goat in the back garden. Peter remarked on the goat, what a fine goat it was, such a shaggy coat, the epitome of what a goat should be. All the while, he was thinking about the photo, wondering what she could possibly have found, this aunt of his with her goat. The spinning room came next, with its colorful wool and finished woolens. Peter said all the right things, how lovely it was she had learned to card and spin wool like that using the ancient methods. Not to mention the dyeing. How did she get such bright colors? The indigo was particularly iridescent. He was on social nicety autopilot. Meanwhile, in the front of his mind was the photo, the photo, the photo.

When the house tour was over, he waited in the living room while Nel made dishwashing and kettle noises in the kitchen. There was a book on the coffee table about airplanes, with an image of a yellow single-prop mustang on the cover. Nel came in carrying a tray with a teapot, mugs, and *speculaas* cookies. Cinnamon and nutmeg, mood enhancers. Something the Dutch would need, with their drizzly weather and flat landscape. No mountains, hardly any hills, no relief. It sent the investigators at the ICC scurrying to the Alps during snippets of vacation time to recover their sanity. Until then, the cookies were a small consolation.

"You found a photograph," Peter said, stating the obvious.

"I know I should've sent it to you by email, only I don't know how. I barely know how to use my phone. I guess I haven't kept up. Let me get it." Nel hurried into Kurt's office and came out carrying a shoebox. "It's this one here on top." She put it in front of Peter, proudly, like a hunter returned to camp with quarry.

It was an image of Arie with an SS officer, black-and-white with a wavy white border—a decorative option at the time it was developed. Peter recognized the SS uniform, but not the individual wearing it. It wasn't someone Jansen had identified as one of Corine's killers. Dark hair. Not the Aryan ideal. There were trees in the background, too many for it to be in a city centre. Maybe a suburb with a park. The officer had his hand on Arie's shoulder in a gesture of friendliness, smiling, showing his teeth. Arie was neither smiling, nor scowling. Intent. An intent look toward the camera, hands behind his back.

"Could you tell me again where you found this?" Peter asked.

"Oh," Nel said. "That is a long story." She spoke with her T-sounds almost too distinct, the sign of a good English-language education. "After Nora visited us, you know, when you were in Africa, I started to looking. None of the museum archives had anything, like Nora said. But I checked anyway. You never know. Then I asked around to friends and family, see if anyone had their own collection. This photo was with your dad's cousin, Cor. I mean with his children. He died about five years back. Maybe seven. The daughter said there was a collection in their attic. She inherited the house and moved there with her husband and kids. Nobody had looked at the photos for years and years. She fetched it down for me. It was there near the bottom, with a bunch of others from the war. None as interesting as this one."

"Were there any others with Arie?" Peter had no faith that Nel hadn't overlooked something important.

"No," Nel said. "Just this one. I'm sorry to say, but it looks like your father was friendly with the SS."

"It does look that way," Peter said. "But you can't really know for sure."

Nel was suddenly downcast. It seemed she wanted Arie to be a perpetrator.

"I agree, though," Peter added as a salve. "It doesn't look good,"

She looked at the photo more closely and scowled. "No," she said. "It doesn't look good at all."

"May I keep this?"

"Yes, of course. I found it for you."

"I'm very grateful," Peter said. He meant it.

With their business completed, both were momentarily at a loss for words. Peter found it difficult to converse with someone whose considerable talents were given over to domesticity. When the awkwardness approached its limit, Aunt Nel suddenly brightened. "Would you like some soup?" she said. I made a delicious vegetable soup with meatballs. With vegetables from our greenhouse."

"I'd like that very much," Peter answered. He slid the photograph carefully into his breast pocket.

* * *

"What do you think?" Peter said, looking down at the photograph he'd placed on Evan's desk.

"Who is that?" Evan asked.

"My dad with an SS officer, as yet unidentified." Peter tried to report the facts, without betraying emotion.

"What the fuck," Evan said.

"Looks pretty bad, right?" Peter said.

"Not necessarily," Evan was quick to reply. "Look. Your dad has his hands behind his back. Was he just holding them there relaxing or was he a prisoner in handcuffs? Did he work for them as an informer? Was he on his way somewhere when they pulled him off the street for a photo-op? Part of their propaganda campaign? We can't tell. There's no context. It could be anything."

"Hmm," Peter said noncommittally.

They stood in silence for a while, joined in camaraderie by the mystery of the photograph.

"Well, can you?" Peter gave voice to an unformed thought.

"You mean can I geolocate this?" Evan deduced Peter's meaning. "Probably. Actually, sure, no problem."

"How? It's just two men in front of a bunch of trees."

"That's the point. How many forested areas are there in Holland? It's all cultivated. And you mentioned it was in all likelihood taken around Zwolle, so that narrows it down. Gives us a place to start."

"Still, it seems impossible."

Evan bent closer to the photo. "Look," he said. "Look here in this corner where there's a clearing. See that?" He hovered his index finger over the right side of the image.

Peter looked closely. "A cross? It looks like a tree branch."

"No, it's a steeple with a cross. It's at a slight angle from the position of the photographer, about forty-five degrees if you draw a straight line. Look here. There's the very top part of it, scarcely visible."

"Damn," was all Peter found to say.

"I could do it for you, but I've got quite a lot to do. Under the cosh, as it were. Might be a few days before I can get around to it."

"No need, thanks," Peter replied. "I've got this." He snatched up the photo and rushed toward his desk. "You're amazing," he shouted over his shoulder as an afterthought.

Peter heard no reply and looked over at Evan. He was already back at work, his mouth open, concentrating on his monitor.

***

The challenge was where to get satellite images of the Zwolle region from the war period. The time slider for the Netherlands on Google Earth Pro only went back as far as 1984, which was pretty good compared to other parts of the world, but still made it all but useless for geolocating a photo from the war period. So much had changed in the decades just after the war. The Marshall Plan, reconstruction, people on the move, roads built, bridges repaired or replaced, entire villages abandoned or built up into towns. Almost nothing stayed the same.

Peter began with a stroke of luck. Within moments of looking, he found an online database of aerial photographs taken by the Royal Air Force, in a special collection housed at the University of Wageningen. According to the collection's website, something like 95,000 images were taken by RAF pilots from Spitfires or Mosquitoes making sorties between September 1944 and May 1945. Once their wartime purpose was over, the images were used by the Dutch Institute of Soil Mapping. Repurposed to make better dirt.

Amazing creativity, Peter thought. Something to be said for such ingenuity. It marked a transition from war to peace—violence to forgetting. Soil science used to cover over the past, make the country prosperous, get past the trauma.

It took Peter close to three hours of combing through the aerial images until he found a likely series from the outskirts of Zwolle. The photos overlapped by about sixty percent, which was helpful when one was blurred or obstructed by a low-lying cloud. He was looking for a church. Not a cathedral, but a small parish church with a plain cross. From an aerial view, there'd be nothing obvious to tell it apart from other buildings. No, there'd be the pitch of the roof split down the middle and a square indicating a steeple. Maybe an adjoining cemetery. He found several possibilities, but none anywhere near what the Dutch might call a forest.

Then he found it, lined up about the right distance from a wooded area and at a forty-five-degree angle from it. This part of the reconnaissance imagery must've been taken by an RAF pilot following up on a bombing raid because next to the woods were the blown-up remains of a building, nothing left of it but scattered stone, a fragment of what looked like a roof, the outline of a foundation and a few adjacent bomb craters that had missed their target. There was a clearing between the bomb ruin and the woods. That was where the photographer had likely stood when he took the photo of Arie and the SS officer. It could've been taken anytime between a few days or a few years previous to the bombing raid. One of the only targets in and around Zwolle would've been the regional headquarters of the Waffen SS. Aunt Julia would be able confirm it for him.

He took a screenshot and sent it to Evan.

A few seconds later he heard, "Well done, my friend!" shouted from across the room.

CHAPTER 33: BEARING WITNESS

Peter meticulously followed the Opel's GPS directions to the Schiphol Judicial Complex in Badhoevedorp. Once on the highway, he couldn't suppress the uncomfortable feeling that there must be some mistake and it was taking him to Schiphol Airport instead. He needn't have worried. As Peter soon discovered, the Dutch had it all figured out. The Judicial Complex was an off-white, shopping-mall-sized prison-and-court-in-one, surrounded by a major international airport. One-stop shopping for any arrest and prosecution of a smuggler caught in the act by airport security across the street. Practical. Everything in place for post-arrest lockup, a speedy trial, and the year or two of incarceration almost inevitably to follow. Plus, there were secure facilities and a press building for anything out of the ordinary: sensational murders, acts of terrorism, war crimes. Crimes like Corine's murder by the Nazis all those years ago.

Peter had booked a place online to attend the hearing, but the web registration didn't allow a place for Nora. He called the number at the bottom of the page to find out what was going on. The woman on the phone told him no, almost everything was booked, so no room for anyone who wasn't next-of-kin. No place for Nora, sorry. She advised him to get there early. There was interest in this case. They were going to have to turn people away. Given he was a relative of a victim, she was happy to confirm his place. Just him.

When he'd called Nora to explain the situation, she took it well and added, "You might find Dutch courts different from what you're used to. But you're trained as an anthropologist. You'll be fine. Just bring your notepad and pen."

Before Peter could get to the courtroom, he had to go through a passport screening and a security checkpoint, much like at an airport. On the other side, the courtrooms were arranged along a hallway with a vaulted roof, cathedral-like, except without frescoes on the ceiling, only fluorescent bulbs recessed behind metal grates.

The public gallery of Courtroom D was at the top of a flight of cement stars, painted grey. The stairs didn't lead directly to the gallery, but opened onto two vending machines (one for coffee, another for chips and candy) and bathrooms—the essentials for people at long events with nowhere else to go. Peter entered the gallery through a heavy glass door. There wasn't much to see: Six rows of fold-down seats, tiered like in a theater, headphones hung on the backs. Pot lights in the ceiling illuminated the gallery evenly, without shadows. Oddly, there was no odor at all, not even of germicide or rug shampoo. Sterile, yet without a whiff of disinfectant.

Peter was the first to arrive. As a good anthropologist, he chose a seat in the middle and toward the back where he'd have a view of both the courtroom and its audience. Everybody was a legitimate subject of observation, including mere attendees.

A glass wall in the gallery's front ostensibly gave a view onto the court, but the scene below was blocked by a blind—curtains down until the show began. A TV monitor in the upper right corner showed only the classic image of Lady Justice, scales in her left hand, a sword in her right. No, the sword *appeared* on her right side. You couldn't see her hand on the hilt. If the logo were visual evidence, you'd have to leave open the possibility that her hand was hanging down at her side and the sword was wielded by someone else. Most likely an assassin.

A group of nine people entered the gallery and arranged themselves in the first two rows of seats with 'media' labels taped to the backs. Without the labels there'd be nothing to set them apart as members of the press, no cards on lanyards, nothing identifiably professional about them. Notepads in their hands, sure, but anyone can take notes. Mostly thirtyish, casually dressed, loose around the edges, the women with plain, practical hair, the men in jeans and unbuttoned jackets. They must have all known each other and were in the hallway gabbing before they came in. Once inside the gallery they fell quiet or talked in whispers.

As the gallery filled, the latecomers—relatives of the victims, Peter assumed—faced the problem of separation that sometimes happens to theatregoers without reservations: a seat here, a seat there, but none together. At nine-thirty am, with a few minutes remaining before the start of the court session, the gallery was full.

There was a mechanical click and the blind rose slowly, accompanied by the hum of an electric motor, revealing the courtroom scene below. Everything was made of smoothly-planed white oak. Each place in a row of desks was equipped with a computer monitor—recessed to give the occupants a view of the court over the top—a microphone with control panel, a water pitcher, and a drinking glass.

A few people were already at their places wearing the black robes and ascots of officers of the court. A woman with tied-back hair and half-moon reading glasses sat in a place labeled '*Griffier*'— clerk—to the right of the judges' desks. A woman next to her, with well-coiffed grey hair and reading glasses on a chain around her neck, sat behind the word '*Stenograaf*'.

There was Willem Jansen with an assistant at a row of three desks off to one side, labeled '*Officier van Justitie*'. Peter noted there were only two prosecutors this time around, with one of the desks empty. But why were they off to the side? Was the prosecution imagined as somehow neutral? Peter recognized Jansen's assistant. It was the woman who'd given him the document about Arie's trial after the war. The white ascot made her look pale and her hair was in an even more severe bun than before. On the floor next to her was a leather briefcase with its accordion sides expanded to the limit. Papers already cluttered the surface of her desk. Peter discerned passages highlighted in pink and green. Why would she use different colors? He supposed it could be anything, arguments to be emphasized, weaknesses in the defense's case, topics to be avoided. She had come prepared.

Three judges entered the courtroom from a door behind their desks. Peter stood, along with everyone else in the gallery. The judge in the lead bore herself with confidence walking ahead of the other two. At forty-something, with straight blonde hair, she broke the stereotype of a judge. Peter found it both impressive and incongruous that a youthful judge had been chosen to preside in this case—it meant the defendant was accused of committing crimes decades before she was born. The judges who followed her were not so well preserved. One was balding, with dark pouches under his eyes, the other dramatically stooped with a full mane of white hair pointing in the direction of his steps. Lifetime appointments. The judges took their seats, the cue for the audience to sit, and arranged papers on their desks like birds preparing a nest.

With the blind now up all the way, Peter saw no-one else in the courtroom. Where was Aunt Julia? The other witnesses? The defense? Was this it? Then, by following the turned heads of the press corps toward the TV monitor, he realized that everything else in the courtroom was out of the line of sight of the gallery and was being broadcast instead. The members of the media who'd been given the honor of a front row seat had to crane their necks to see the screen. Not every courtesy came with advantages.

Most of the courtroom was actually beneath their feet. It meant the public's view of the court, aside from the judges and prosecution, was subject to the manipulations of camerawork and recording. There were high-definition cameras with zoom lenses in each corner of the courtroom. The technicians were behind a glass booth on the opposite side to the translators where they controlled what the world saw. Faces could be blurred, voices disguised, witnesses' identities protected. Everything accountable and controlled at the same time.

From the TV image, of which Peter had a fantastic view, everything fell into place. Opposite the judges' dais was a row of desks labeled *Verdediging*—defense. Testimony went in the direction of the judges sitting opposite, another sign *they* ran the show.

A man sat at a desk facing the judges, the lawyer for the defense. He had every sign of being court-appointed. Peter surmised he was in his early thirties, so not long out of law school, seemingly uncomfortable in the head-to-toe robes of the court functionary. Judging solely by his manner, he looked more like the stereotypical murder accomplice than the elderly man he'd be defending. His eyes flitted from one part the courtroom to another without fastening onto any one thing. Taking it all in. Nerves, very likely.

Maybe the guard sitting at the wall a few feet away made him nervous. Perhaps he was put off by the proximity of a twenty-something woman in a police uniform, with a bullet-proof vest, shoulder communication unit, handcuffs, sidearm, and pepper spray, not to mention her thick, smooth arms with muscles not so much defined as built into her manner. Her hair was in a long pony tail with the bottom half dyed blond. She alternated between pinching off split ends and lifting her eyes to glance at different parts the room.

There was Aunt Julia, second from the end of a row of desks behind the defense. Peter lifted his hand to wave, then realized his view of her was through the camera. How could he have not seen her sooner? Too much to take in at once. A woman with wisps of hair falling in her face said something inaudible to Aunt Julia from her desk on the end of the row. Aunt Julia nodded, but said nothing. She was in her own world. There was a walker in the aisle, canes resting against other chairs and desks. The 'victims' row established an age-divide from the rest of the court—except for a young man in the middle desk, bent over a sheaf of papers. His full head of brown hair stood out from the white and grey wisps, incongruous dyes, and bald pates of the elders on either side of him. A state-appointed victims' representative, no doubt.

The rest of the courtroom toward the back was filled with reporters. At least it looked that way from their appearance, which was identical to those in the front row of the upper gallery. Notepads and pens at the ready; the warrior class of truth.

If Peter had to give a few words to describe the scene, it would be controlled chaos, not in defense against mobs on the outside, but protection from the *inner* experience of violence. There was a carryover effect from the adjacent prison like fumes under a doorway. It was all part of a beautiful, terrifying design, intended not only to control bodies, but to imprison emotion. Too much weeping from the victims and their state-appointed representative was there to step in with a tissue and maybe a hand on the elbow toward the exit. One little untoward noise or signal from the gallery and the curtain would come down. Not to mention the guards.

Finally, the presiding judge looked up from her workstation, apparently satisfied her papers were in order, and adjusted her microphone. Everyone in the gallery had already put on their headphones. Peter quickly put his over his ears, just in time to hear the judge say, "*Goedemorgen iedereen.*"

There was a muted murmur of *goedemorgen* in response.

The judge looked up at a translation booth to her left, on the same level as the gallery. "*Is de vertaler klaar, ja? Goed.*" The translator gave a thumbs up from behind the reflected glass.

Peter missed something else the judge said. The plug for his headset was on his armrest and the connection was loose, probably from years of people just like him hitting it with their elbows. He wiggled the plug, restored the connection, and put his left arm in his lap.

"You can bring in the defendant," the judge announced. The guard let go of her ponytail, stood, and used a key card to open a side door next to where she was sitting. Groendyke, the defendant, came through the door, accompanied by another guard, tall, masculine, twenty-something, with tattoos on his forearms. Handsome couple, Peter thought, but as far as he could tell, there was not so much as a glance between them. Once the guard deposited the defendant next to his lawyer, he went to sit in a chair on the other side of the room.

Peter barely recognized Groendyke from the ID-photo image from the war years circulating in the press, nothing left of the strong, gangly youth sporting the Hugo Boss-designed SS uniform. He was frail looking, with dark-rimmed glasses and wisps of white hair pulled across his mostly bald crown. His suit was ill-fitting and wrinkled, a size or two too large, likely pulled out of a box in an attic and worn without the ministrations of a dry cleaner. All eyes were on him. Hard looks had followed the old man as the guard accompanied him to the seat next to his lawyer facing the judges' bench. Now, the victims and their representatives sat in a row behind him. He must have felt their presence, their eyes on him, burning holes in his back. Even from the TV screen, Peter felt a palpable force of hostility in the room.

The presiding judge again adjusted her microphone, getting it just so. "I am Justice Teuling," she said. "To my left here is Justice Kubascha and to my right Justice De Groot." The translation came through as a strong female voice, well matched to the original. "Well then," judge Teuling said, "let's get started, shall we? Would the prosecution please call the case? Mevrouw Torenbeek?"

The woman Peter had assumed was Jansen's assistant stood and faced the judges. "This is the case against Aloysius Groendyke. The Special Prosecutor's Office has decided to proceed with the charges of one count of co-perpetrator of the war crime of murder and fifteen counts of the war crime of accessory to torture and murder. Some of the survivors and descendants of these crimes are here in this court. All are crimes that allegedly took place during Meneer Groendyke's service as a member of the Waffen SS from 1944 to 1945, the last year of the Nazi occupation of the Netherlands." Torenbeek sat back down behind her desk.

"Thank you," Justice Teuling said. "Before we begin, a few observations about these proceedings. It should be obvious to everyone here that this is an unusual case, with a most unusual defendant. The accused faces charges of exceptional severity. Under ordinary circumstances, I do not allow media in my courtroom. But there is a special public interest in this case, so for the moment I will allow members of the press to attend. To take notes only. No photographs or videos. Is that clear?" She looked at the reporters in the back of the courtroom sharply.

Some nodded deferentially. Others stared blankly. Some in the upper gallery squirmed in their seats.

"Good." She paused looking out over the courtroom. "Now, to continue on the subject of procedure, I have already informed myself thoroughly about the facts of this case. I have read the materials assembled by the prosecutor and have interviewed the defendant. I have also spoken with several witnesses, including, at length, a key witness in this case, Mevrouw Julia Olsen."

Peter looked at the image of Aunt Julia in the TV screen. She sat impassively at her desk.

"What I would like to do today," Justice Teuling went on, "is begin to inquire further into the various perspectives on the case."

For reasons Peter couldn't discern, she swiveled in her chair and looked up to the glassed-in gallery before the translator finished the sentence. Even from the second-to-last row, Peter felt exposed.

"For those of you from the foreign press, today we will hear statements from the first of what looks to be a considerable number of witnesses," she continued. "Later, I hope after not too many days, I would like to hear from the defendant and then the closing statements by the Officer of Justice and the defense. At a later time, I will call this court into session to render our verdict. Is that clear to everyone?"

Everyone in the court nodded except the two elder judges, who looked impassively over the assembly. The word Jansen once used—inquisitorial—came to mind.

"Good," Justice Teuling said. "I call upon Mevrouw Julia Olsen to make a statement."

This announcement surprised Peter at first, but then it made sense. Everything had already been investigated. The facts had been amassed in documents stored and accessible on everyone's computers—everyone except the public. Statements from the victims of the crime were the centerpiece of the public process. Aunt Julia rose from her seat. The podium raised soundlessly until the microphone was at the proper level. Someone, somewhere was watching, pushing the buttons. Surveillance with a practical purpose.

"Mevrouw Olsen," the judge began. She spoke while staring attentively at her computer screen, then raised her eyes to Aunt Julia. "In your deposition, you said you were present at the murder of your sister Corine Dekker, is that correct?"

"Yes," Aunt Julia said.

"You identified the person who murdered Corine Dekker as an officer of the Waffen SS, Hauptmann Walter Berka, is that right?"

"Yes, I found him in the pictures you showed me. I'm certain that's who it was."

"And you identified two other members of the SS who were there at the same time, did you not?"

"I did."

"And one of those you identified from the photographs was Feldwebel Heinrich Zufall.

"I'll never forget," Aunt Julia said, vaguely.

"For the record," Judge Teuling looked from one side and then the other toward her fellow judges, "Feldwebel Zufall died of natural causes in nineteen-ninety-two in the German city of Halle-an-der-Salle and was never prosecuted for his actions during the German occupation of the Netherlands." The judge returned her gaze to Aunt Julia. "You also identified the photograph of another of the SS members who participated in the murder of Corine Dekker, Meneer Groendyke, the defendant. Is that right?"

Aunt Julia's turned toward Groendyke. She raised a trembling hand, but extended no fingers, hesitating to commit. That she did with her words: "It was him." Her voice shook. Peter couldn't tell if it was from fear or anger or another emotion for which there are no words. "I recognized him in the photographs. I recognize him now." She let her hand return to the podium.

The judge continued her questioning. "Could you please tell the court, as though you were telling a story, how the man you just pointed out, Meneer Groendyke, reacted to your sister's murder. What he did after it happened." Torenbeek said.

"I don't remember."

"You don't remember?" Torenbeek seemed taken aback by the answer.

"No," Aunt Julia said. "I heard the pistol go off and knew I wasn't dead, but wasn't looking at him when she was shot and I don't remember anything about the time just after."

"Do you remember how the defendant reacted before the pistol was fired? How he reacted to the way you were threatened by Hauptmann Berka?"

"Yes," Aunt Julia said. "That I remember clearly. He smiled."

"He smiled? Did he say or do anything else?" Justice Teuling asked.

"No, he just smiled. Like he was enjoying watching it."

"Thank you, Mevrouw Olsen," the Judge said. "Since I have taken the liberty of asking some questions, I suppose I should give the defense an opportunity to do the same. Meneer Haas, do you have anything you would like to ask Mevrouw Olsen?"

"Yes, thank you, Your Honor." Haas stood and looked in Aunt Julia's direction. Peter couldn't understand the reason for the delay. Composing his thoughts or trying to make her uncomfortable? One or the other. No, both. Dutch courts do have theatrics, even if they rarely influence the judges.

"Mevrouw Olsen," Haas said finally. "When you say Meneer Haas smiled, do you know what he was thinking at the time?"

"No, I don't, really. I don't have that ability."

"Might he have been smiling in pain?"

"No, you can tell the difference. When someone's smiling in pain and when they're enjoying something, it's very different. He was enjoying it."

"But you can't be a hundred percent sure, can you? Not having that ability."

"I suppose not," Aunt Julia admitted.

"Thank you, Mevrouw Olsen. Your Honor, that is all."

"Thank you, Meneer Haas. Mevrouw Olsen, I imagine there is something you would like to say to the court. A statement." Judge Teuling said.

It surprised Peter, first, that the judge had taken the lead in asking questions, then that she would ask Aunt Julia for a statement. She kept looking down at her computer screen and at the papers next to her keyboard. The questioning was just a preamble, to confirm a few facts before the witness statement.

"Thank you, Your Honor," Aunt Julia began. "I just wanted to say, I know that what this man did was a crime. A war crime, as you say. I know he was one of my sister's killers. He took some pleasure in seeing her killed. Anyway, that's what I saw. He certainly took no care of her body afterwards. But he was also a teenage boy. He was just a few years older than me. I don't know how he would've turned out like if the Germans hadn't invaded our country. Would he have been a killer in times of peace? Almost certainly not. He's not any different from most of us who survived the war. My sister's actual killer, Hauptmann Berka, the one who pulled the trigger, was one of those people who thrive in times of violence. They thrive on bloodshed. Groendyke wasn't—isn't—one of those people. Is he a war criminal just the same? Maybe. Probably. You are the ones who know the law, not me. But I ask that you treat him appropriately. Please don't give him a prison sentence. Prison only makes people worse. It would be so much better for us all if you found some other way to punish him. Something like community service, talk to the youth today. Let him work to undo some of the culture he helped create. That is all I have to say."

"Thank you, Mevrouw Olsen, for your wise observations and words of counsel," Justice Teuling said.

She's being dismissive, Peter observed. Very subtle sarcasm disguised as neutrality. Aunt Julia seemed to feel it, too. She wore a dark expression as she sat back down. Once in her seat, she crossed her arms in sterile defiance.

Peter listened with half an ear as the next witness was asked to give a statement, an elderly woman with a four-tipped cane visible next to her desk. His thoughts were in turmoil. What just happened? Groendyke's smile, the smile Aunt Julia remembered so clearly, was the mark of a sadist. Then for her to follow that with an appeal to clemency? It made no sense.

He returned his attention to the court. The woman rose at her chair and insisted on standing, despite her infirmity. There was something familiar about her testimony as she recounted the arrest and execution of her father. The terror the old woman described of the knock on the door made him think of the Islamic police who came with their summons to prayer. If he had stayed in Timbuktu, there was no telling what would've happened to him. And if the insurgents were so sure of themselves after defeat, imagine what it must've been like under their rule—when they had total power.

This witness too pointed to Groendyke as her tormentor. Of that she had no doubt. She was fifteen at the time. They came to the door, three of them. At first, Groendyke stood behind the officer who held the piece of paper. She couldn't be sure it was an arrest warrant. Groendyke was the one who used force. The one who took her father by the arm. She looked through the window from the second floor. Her father didn't resist, but Groendyke took out his baton anyway and hit him hard between the shoulder blades. It knocked him to the ground. Groendyke was the one who did that, and then forced her father to his feet before he was ready. Unspeakable cruelty and cowardice. Later, they made her watch while her father was shot with the other prisoners. She forced herself not to scream or cry because she knew that was what they wanted. She refused to allow herself to be used as an instrument of their terror. To this day, she hadn't allowed herself to cry, to give in. Yes, Groendyke was there. Yes, he pulled a trigger. He killed another prisoner, not her father. She didn't remember who killed her father. Just someone in an SS uniform. That was all she remembered.

It took a while for all this to come out. By the end, her body shook and swayed and she leaned heavily on her cane. She was determined to endure, to stand until her testimony was given.

The judge called a recess for lunch. The image on the screen switched to Lady Justice with her scales and sword. There was an electric motor sound as the blind lowered and obstructed the gallery-view of the court.

CHAPTER 34: INTERLUDE

Peter was caught in the flow of reporters and relatives descending the stairs from the gallery into the hallway and lobby of the main floor. Aunt Julia was nowhere to be seen. Then she appeared, walking briskly toward Peter down the hall. When she caught up to him, she took him by the arm and kept walking toward the exit. A reporter in the crowd spotted her and said, "Mevrouw Olsen!" but she and Peter were already through the glass security door.

Aunt Julia took Peter up to a bus stop sign at the street and stood close to it even though the building had a portico and a broad sidewalk in front with a clear view of any approaching bus.

"Why a bus?" Peter asked.

"For lunch," In response to Peter's blank stare, Aunt Julia added, "For lunch at the airport. There's no cafeteria in the court building."

"Weird." Peter felt another of the little nudges of strangeness that never quite allowed him to recover his balance. "I could fetch the car," he suggested.

"And park at the airport?" Aunt Julia had it figured out. Maybe from a briefing by the state-appointed victims' representative.

Before the bus arrived, a group of five reporters exited the building and approached them at the bus stop. They wanted to know more about Aunt Julia's testimony. Why did she want clemency for a man responsible for the death of her sister? Was she inspired by a Christian ethic of forgiveness? Did she feel sorry for the defendant? Peter couldn't hear everything she said in reply. He'd been pushed aside and there was the sound of an airplane taxiing not far away. From what he did hear, Aunt Julia answered patiently. No, she wasn't making a statement about criminal justice in the Netherlands. It's just that she thought, for this crime, at least, the punishment should be more fitting than a prison cell. If this old man needed a correction to reflect on his life, it should be in the company of people harmed by violence. The judges could do what they wanted.

The bus arrived, its doors opened, and it lowered with a hydraulic hiss. Aunt Julia turned to the reporters and ended her impromptu press conference with, "*Bedankt, dames en herren*, now I really must get something to eat."

One reporter, a woman with carefully coiffed blonde hair, shouted after her with an American accent. "How did you feel when you saw your sister lying in her own blood?"

Aunt Julia's face turned white and her lips compressed, then she raised her hand above her head and waved dismissively. She stepped inside, followed by Peter, and the doors closed.

***

After a three-minute bus ride past the judicial complex and over a maze of highway overpasses, Peter and Aunt Julia got off at the main entrance of Schiphol Airport. The multi-directional bustle and noise of a combined airport departure hall, rail station, and shopping mall was disorienting. Peter gathered himself, navigated through the crowd with Aunt Julia in tow, and, without considering alternatives, chose an Italian-themed café serving paninis and salads. He waited for their order while Aunt Julia sat at a stool between two people eating hurriedly at a counter. When their food was ready, tray in hand, Peter looked for somewhere to sit just outside the café. There was the confused din of the airport hall and the only two places were at the end of an already occupied table. Peter received a nod of permission to share the table from a middle-aged man with heavy eyebrows. Peter recognized him as one of the next of kin from the court. He was with a stout middle-aged woman and two frail-looking elderly men. Peter recognized the old men from the court too. They'd been sitting near the end of the row farthest from Aunt Julia. The plump woman he didn't recognise. Maybe a latecomer. Maybe watching the livestream from somewhere nearby. Peter guessed the group had gotten to the airport sooner by taking a taxi. In unison, they glanced over at Peter and Aunt Julia, then quietly resumed their conversation with their heads inclined toward one another.

Peter and Aunt Julia sat opposite one another without words, surrounded by the din of the airport, for what seemed like a full minute. Aunt Julia took a few bites, then left her sandwich on her plate.

"Your food okay?" Peter asked, his voice raised.

"*Ja, ja. Lekker*." Aunt Julia looked at him with a faint smile that quickly disappeared. She was somewhere else.

The two victims and their offspring stood and gathered up their trays filled with dirty dishes and sandwich wrappers. The stout woman stood and approached Aunt Julia. She came uncomfortably close with a protruding bosom and belly, then released a salvo of prepared words: "What you said in the court today. I want you to know, I didn't like that." She turned on her heels without waiting for a reply, took one of the frail old men by the elbow and dragged him, more than supported him, on the way to the taxis outside.

Peter looked to Aunt Julia. She ignored the comment, picked up her sandwich, and ate with greater gusto than before.

"What the hell was that all about?" Peter asked.

Aunt Julia swallowed a half-chewed mouthful and shrugged at the same time. "It's exactly what I expected," was all she said.

CHAPTER 35: DER FREIWILLIGER

Over the next three days, the court heard more victim statements about the roundups and executions of Operation Silbertanne. The audience in the public gallery was diminished. Most of the reporters had come the first day to cover the story of the trial's beginning. They had less to say about the actual testimony, that much was clear from their absence. Only a handful stayed the course, picking up scraps here and there, but only the most poignant, with their notebooks already replete.

A pattern soon established itself. Witness after witness remembered Groendyke as the one who came to the door with a superior, made the arrest, administered beatings, pulled a trigger, and loaded the bodies. He seemed to enjoy his power. He expressed no remorse. He revelled in it. They spoke with trembling voices at first, and gained confidence as their stories emerged. Unlike Aunt Julia and the witness who had followed her, they struggled to control their emotion. Each of them battled against their tears, some with more success than others. Most had to pause at some point in their testimony to regain their composure. A few wept openly, usually when they remembered their parent or grandparent taken away or shot in the public square. There was the sound of repressed sobs and sniffling in the audience as they spoke of their loss. One said, "It felt like I was in a sea with high waves and I couldn't get enough air. I couldn't breathe." Another, after describing the execution of their father, reflected, "It seemed strange to me that the sun was still in the sky. The world was going on, but without him." It was as though the early testimony from Aunt Julia, dry-eyed and clear, made room for the release of emotion that followed.

One elderly witness was so stricken with grief, he was unable to utter a word, try as he might. Justice Teuling seemed unprepared to encourage him, posed another question, and received only sobs by way of reply. The judge was patient at first and gave the witness a moment to recover, then excused him with a glance at the clock when no words rose through the dam of his distress. He sat back in his seat, still bent and convulsed with grief.

As the hearing went on, several boxes of tissues were depleted and replaced. A wire-mesh wastebasket next to the desks of the victims gradually filled with the detritus of sorrow. At the start of each day, it was empty.

All this time, Groendyke sat with his back to the audience. There were no tissues on his desk. He didn't move in his seat. There was no sign from him of discomfort. Occasionally his balding head inclined toward the coiffed hair of his lawyer. Words exchanged. Peter could only guess what they were saying. Strategizing. Be patient, you'll get your chance.

And his chance came. One afternoon, when the court reassembled after a recess, Justice Teuling reconvened with the words, "In Dutch courts, we always give the last word to the defense. I now call upon Meneer Groendyke to give a statement." The court filled with voices, just shy of loud enough for a call to order.

Then a hush descended as Groendyke adjusted the microphone at his desk. He chose to sit rather than stand, probably to draw attention to his frailty. He found a comfortable position with his arms on the podium, his fingers interlaced.

"Meneer Groendyke," Justice Teuling began, and then stopped. Her eyes went to the monitor in front of her, then back to Groendyke. "Your testimony is exceptionally important, for reasons that go beyond this court. I would first like to ask you to confirm some things for me and fill in a few details. Is that alright?"

Groendyke nodded. "Yes, of course."

Justice Teuling continued. "You voluntarily joined the Waffen SS as a young man, is that correct?" She began with an established fact, taking control.

"Yes, that is correct," Groendyke replied. He pronounced each word with care.

"Could you tell the court the German word given to people in your position, who volunteered?" Justice Teuling asked.

"We were often called *Freiwilligers*, if that's what you mean."

"Which basically means those who *freely willed* their services, is that correct?"

"About so, yes."

"And as a freely enlisted member of the Waffen SS, what were your duties?"

"I beg your pardon?" Groendyke blinked rapidly and shifted in his seat.

"I'm curious," Justice Teuling said. "What were the things you might do in a typical day?"

"A typical day. Oh my." Groendyke looked to the ceiling. "I don't think there was any such thing as a typical day. Everything depended on what my superiors wanted done."

"Can you give an example?"

"Well, for the longest time," Groendyke said, "I was in charge of shooting pigeons. With a shotgun."

"Shooting pigeons? Can you clarify why your superiors wanted you to shoot pigeons?" Justice Teuling leaned forward.

"Well, you see," Groedyke began, "the resistance was using them to send messages. So, we shot them. As many as we could, to interrupt the communications. Maybe intercept them if there was a message on one."

"Did you ever find a message attached to one of these pigeons you shot?" Justice Teuling asked.

"No."

"And how many would you shoot in a day?"

Groendyke paused for a moment, trying to remember. "Maybe fifty or a hundred."

"What did you do with the dead pigeons once you killed them?"

"We took them to a field and poured gasoline on them and burned them."

"Interesting," Judge Teuling remarked, then added, "Meneer Jansen, would you care to continue the questioning?"

Jansen leaped to his feet. "Yes. Thank you, your Honor." He looked down at the papers next to his keyboard, then looked up. "Mr. Groendyke, in the course of your duties did you kill anything or anyone else?" He looked at Groendyke fixedly.

Groendyke returned his look, defiant. "I was *ordered* to take part in executions." He put heavy emphasis on the word *ordered*.

"Executions." Jansen let the word sit for a moment before continuing. "Executions of people, I assume."

"Yes."

"And were these people criminals, the ones you executed? Were they previously tried in a court of law like this one?" Jansen asked.

"No."

"They were civilians." Jansen said it as a statement.

"Yes."

"Could you please tell us how these innocent civilians were chosen for execution?"

"Well, some were already in custody," Groendyke answered. "They were suspected of resistance activity, but we didn't really have much evidence."

"So, you executed untried suspects?"

"Some, yes."

"You said some. Who were the others?"

"Just people."

"Just people? What sort of people?"

Groendyke reflected for a moment. "I don't really know. It was my superiors who decided. They seemed to just pick people randomly. Go into their homes or offices and put them under arrest. You have to understand . . ."

He looked up at the judges as though asking for permission to continue.

"Do please go on." Justice Teuling refused him the consolation of a smile.

Groendyke returned to the microphone. "You see," he said, "things were very difficult at the end of the war. Confusing. We couldn't tell friend from foe. The orders came telling us we had to put an end to the resistance, and we did. Or at least we tried. And during the war, especially after the Allied landing, trying to do something like that, well, it got messy. I suppose that's what led my superiors to the point they were taking people out of their homes. We arrested them to put pressure on the resistance."

"Then you shot them?" Jansen said. He wasted no time getting back to the topic of violence.

"Yes."

"In a public square."

"Yes."

"And you participated in these killings." Jansen again put his question as a statement of fact.

For a few seconds, the TV monitor cut to a camera zoomed in close. Peter saw Groendyke blink behind his glasses. His brow was deeply furrowed. "Under orders, yes."

"Was there anything you wouldn't do under orders?" Jansen asked.

"I'm sorry, I don't understand the question." Groendyke looked confused and ill at ease, as though Jansen had just called on him to perform handsprings.

Justice Teuling leaned toward her microphone. "Meneer Groendyke, as a young man, how did you feel about being given orders to kill non-combatants, people who you and your fellow members of the SS were taking from their homes?"

"I felt really terrible about it. My superior officer, Hauptmann Berka, was cruel. Sadistic. He enjoyed the killing. Once when we were making arrests, I saw him tear an infant from its mother's—" His voice caught. "I couldn't stand being under his command."

Justice Kubascha roused himself, glanced at Justice Teuling, received a nod from her, and pressed the button on his microphone. "What did he do with the infant?" he asked.

"She wouldn't part with it when she was being arrested so he killed it. He strangled it with his hands and threw it on the paving stones."

A moan rose from the court. Some of the witnesses in the front row sobbed, one louder than the others.

Justice Teuling activated her microphone. "Did you at any time ask for a transfer?" she asked.

"No. That was unheard of. Nobody did that." Groendyke replied.

Justice Teuling leaned closer to her microphone. "But you could have, if you had wanted."

"I suppose it was formally possible, yes."

"Thank you, Meneer Groendyke," Justice Teuling said. "Meneer Jansen, you may continue."

"Thank you, Your Honor. Meneer Groendyke, do you remember the events of New Year's Eve, 1944, at the home of the Dekker family."

"Yes, I do. It would be hard to forget."

Peter looked closely at the screen to find Aunt Julia. Her eyes were fixed on Groendyke, her face hardened. He wondered whether she would still feel the same about restorative punishment after hearing his testimony online.

"Could you please tell us what took place that evening?" Jansen asked.

"Well, to begin with, we killed some geese and had a fine dinner," Groendyke replied. "To celebrate New Year's."

Jansen flipped through some papers on his desk, looking down. "In my report it says you killed the geese with explosives. Grenades. Could you please explain the reason for that?"

"Well, our headquarters had been bombed and we were low on ammunition, so we made do, I suppose."

"And by we, you mean yourself, Berka and . . .?"

"Feldwebel Zufall."

Jansen looked up from his papers. "Were the three of you invited onto the Dekker's property to blow up their geese and enjoy a fine dinner?" Jansen asked.

"No, it was Hauptmann Berka who decided that."

"Please tell us what happened after the dinner."

"Hauptmann Berka killed a young girl." Groendyke said. He stopped there, refusing the invitation of a story, and spoke without inflection, as though killing a young girl was something ordinary, like tying one's shoelaces.

"He shot her in the head, did he not?" Jansen asked.

"Yes."

Jansen's face hardened. "Did you enjoy witnessing this act? Did it make you smile?"

Groendyke remained impassive. "I didn't enjoy it. It disgusted me."

"Was it part of your regular practice, as members of the Waffen SS, to murder innocent children?" Jansen asked.

"No."

"Did Berka ever say anything to you about why he committed this act?"

"I don't really remember." Groendyke paused for a moment, then said, "I think it had something to do with the resistance. He used the girl as a way to get one of the suspects to cooperate."

"Was that suspect Arie Dekker, Corine's older brother?"

"I think so. I'm not sure."

"Please tell the court," Jansen continued, "What happened after Berka murdered Corine Dekker."

"We were ordered to dig a hole and bury her."

"And by, *we*, you mean . . .?"

"Me and Feldwebel Zufall."

"The two of you dug a hole in the back garden."

"Yes."

"And you put the body of Corine Dekker in the hole that the two of you dug, correct?"

"Yes."

Jansen paced a few times behind his desk and returned to the microphone. "Can you explain to the court why her body was found lying face down?"

"I'm sorry, could you repeat the question?" Groendyke's fingers fidgeted on the podium in front of him. He interlaced them and got them under control.

"I am hoping," Jansen enunciated slowly, his voice cracking with emotion, "that you can explain to us, why the body of the girl, Corine Dekker, was found lying face down in the grave you dug. Did you give no care as to how you lay her body in her final resting place?"

"We were in a hurry, I suppose," Groendyke replied, curtly.

"You were in a hurry." Jansen repeated, unable to conceal his distaste.

"Yes," Groendyke snapped. "Hauptmann Berka wanted it done quickly. We had little time."

"You had to leave. You needed to get away. Is that it?"

"That's what I understood about our situation, yes." Groendyke spoke more calmly, returning to his impassivity.

"Because the three of you knew that what you had done was a crime," Jansen stated.

De Groot, the judge with the bald pate, scowled and stirred as though he were about to speak.

Jansen corrected himself. "Let me put it another way. In your hurry, did anyone express regret about killing the girl, Corine Dekker?"

"No, not really," Groendyke said. "I was certainly aware it was irregular. I took my orders from Hauptmann Berka."

"Thank you. I have no further questions." Before he sat, Jansen turned to the audience with a hard-to-read expression, something between anger and world-weariness.

"Meneer Haas," Justice Teuling turned to the lawyer for the defense. "Do you have any questions for the defendant?"

"I do, Your Honor."

"Please proceed."

"Thank you, Your Honor. Meneer Groendyke, we have established that Hauptmann Berka was an extremely violent, even sadistic, man. Did you at any point fear for your life when you served under his command?"

"Well, I knew for certain that if I didn't obey any of his orders I would be dealt with severely."

"Could you please be more precise?" Haas asked. "What do you mean by, severely?"

"Well, I would have been court martialed."

"By that you mean tried in a military court, for insubordination." Haas bent toward his desk. He was reading from prepared notes.

"Yes."

"And what would be the consequence of such a court martial?" Haas asked.

"Well, I would really be in trouble if I didn't do what he said. I might have been executed for desertion."

"Thank you. No further questions, Your Honor." Haas returned to his seat.

"Thank you, Meneer Haas. This is important testimony and I want to be thorough. Meneer Jansen, do you have any follow-up questions?"

"I do, Your Honor." Jansen stood sharply. "Meneer Groendyke, were you aware of any colleague in the SS court martialed for insubordination?"

Groendyke shifted uncomfortably in his chair. "No," he replied. "People just obeyed orders. Even to kill civilians."

"So, you don't actually know what would have happened if you had refused to obey orders to commit war crimes, do you?"

"I'm sorry, I don't understand." Groendyke looked confused. His eyes roamed without fixing on anything, looking everywhere except at Jansen.

"Do you have any example, any basis in fact, for your assertion that you would have been court martialed for refusing to obey orders to kill civilians?" Jansen struggled with minimal success to control his voice.

"No, not really. It was something I just assumed," Groendyke answered.

"No further questions, Your Honor." Jansen sat with the same vigor that had brought him to his feet.

"Thank you, Meneer Jansen," Justice Teuling said. "Meneer Haas, is there any line of questioning you would like to add?"

Haas shook his head. "No, Your Honor."

"In that case . . ." Justice Teuling looked at her watch, as though deciding whether to continue or announce a recess. She looked to the other judges. "Let us take a recess. This court is adjourned until . . . three-thirty."

Voices filled the room. Peter couldn't quite identify the mood. It was something between anger and sorrow, like the first stirrings of a mob.

* * *

Justice Teuling appeared refreshed after the recess. The weight of the testimony had lifted. Her voice was stronger when she said, "The court will now hear a concluding statement from the Officer of Justice in this case, Meneer Jansen."

"Thank you, Your Honor." Jansen arranged the papers on the table and adjusted the microphone. "The Public Prosecution Service made the decision to prosecute this case because of the severity of the crimes for which the defendant stands accused. There is no statute of limitations for the crime of murder or co-perpetrator or accessory to murder. There is no statute of limitations for war crimes or crimes against humanity."

Jansen turned to look straight at Groendyke, who didn't return the withering gaze, but instead stared down at his hands folded on the empty desk in front of him.

"Some might say that we in this country have had enough of coming to terms with our wartime past," Jansen continued. "Those who committed crimes during the war are either deceased or well advanced in age. The defendant is now eighty-five-years old. Some might have sympathy for him because of that. He was living in quiet retirement in the village of Kapelle. Not a threat to society, some would say. But impunity *is* a threat to society, even if the individuals enjoying it are not. How can we leave the past behind when the crimes that took place continue to haunt us? We pride ourselves on the fact that justice is a core value of our democracy. How can we have justice when we leave those who willingly participated in mass murder to live out their lives in peace and dignity, without ever answering for their crimes?"

The monitor's point of view switched briefly to Aunt Julia—she looked down at her hands in her lap, sorrowful, concentrating—then back to Jansen.

Jansen took a deep breath and continued. "Your Honor, the accused was a youth when the alleged murders took place."

Peter noticed he used the plural—murders. The executions were murders, too. Of course they were.

"This is why we find ourselves in your court," Jansen continued, "He was sixteen when he joined the SS and eighteen, an adult, when he volunteered to participate in the gruesome work of the Silbertanne, the Nazi operation to suppress the resistance. He signed up for it. And at the age of eighteen, he was old enough to know that his superiors in the SS had exceeded all bounds of human decency. He witnessed their depravity first-hand. He took part in it as a brutal enforcer. At the same time, he was free to go. He could have requested another detail. Something boring perhaps, and not as violent. He did not. He chose to willingly participate in the summary executions of innocent people. And even if it happened at the hands of his superior officer, he volunteered to take part in the murder of nine-year-old Corine Dekker."

Aunt Julia looked up when she heard her sister's name.

"He chose to actively involve himself in killing innocent civilians. He beat them when they didn't resist. He took a rifle in his hands, aimed, and pulled the trigger to execute them. In the Nuremberg Trials just after the war, the judges repeatedly heard the excuse of prominent Nazis, *Befehl ist Befehl*, orders are orders. It was not accepted as an excuse then and should not be to this day. An order to commit a heinous crime does not make it any less a crime. And that, Your Honor, is why the Public Prosecution Service is charging the defendant as a co-perpetrator and not as an accessory to the war crime murder of Corine Dekker. He buried her body, intending for it not to be discovered in the chaos of war. He pulled a trigger when his SS detail executed innocents. And he knew full well they were not guilty of any crime. The old man sitting before us was young when he did these things, yes. But make no mistake, we have before us a war criminal. And war criminals, no matter their age when they committed their crimes or when they stand accused of them, are in this country punished to the full extent of the law. Thank you, Your Honor."

He sat back in his chair and adjusted his ascot.

"Thank you, Meneer Jansen." Justice Teuling wrote something in a notebook. She put down her pen and looked up. "The court will now hear from Meneer Markus Haas, with a few words on behalf of the defendant."

Haas stood and put a sheaf of papers on the table in front of him.

"Thank you, Your Honor." He rearranged the order of the papers.

Peter saw the judge growing impatient. "Meneer Haas, you have the floor."

"Er, um, Yes, I'm ready." He tapped the microphone to make sure it was on. "Your Honor, my client, the defendant in this case, was fourteen-years-old when Germany invaded the Netherlands. He came of age when the Nazis occupied this country. To a fourteen-year-old back then, their presence among us was as natural as that of a baker or a street sweeper. They were a part of daily life. More than that, they reached out to him as he got older. They told him stories of glory. They gave him purpose, lectured him in school about good and evil and how they were the ones protecting the world from evil. Later, they offered him a stylish uniform. They fed him an illusion of virtuous manhood. And, as a young man from a broken home, he succumbed. He made the biggest mistake of his life. He looked to the Waffen SS as a replacement, in a way, of the father who abandoned his family when he was seven years old.

"Your Honor, Meneer Groendyke does not deny the basic facts as represented by the Special Prosecutor. As a young man, he was a volunteer member of the Waffen SS. He was present when the criminal activities ordered by his superiors took place. For his membership in the SS, the biggest mistake of his life, he has already been punished. He was imprisoned for two years in Camp Vucht, without charges and without rights of *habeus corpus*. It was, even by the standards of justice at the time, an illegal confinement in appalling conditions. Since his release in 1947, he worked as a custodian for the Netherlands Railway. A menial occupation. One of the only jobs available to him. With respect to my esteemed colleague, it is simply not true that he has gone unpunished for his enlistment with the SS. He has paid dearly for it ever since the end of the war.

"A final point, Your Honor, before I conclude. My client made the terrible mistake of putting on the Nazi uniform, of formally aligning himself with our occupiers. But the line is too starkly drawn between those who wore the uniform or joined the party, and those who were good and faithful Dutch citizens, loyal to queen and country. Many more Dutch citizens than we care to admit were collaborators in one way or another. We like to hear the stories of courage, of Jews hidden in attics and basements, Jewish children adopted, and so on. That's the sort of thing we told ourselves after the war. But let's be honest with ourselves—"

There was a murmur from the audience that grew steadily louder as Haas spoke and reached a crescendo with these words.

"*Dames en heren, stilte alstublieft*," Justice Teuling said, shouting. The words came through the window of the gallery, untranslated. When the courtroom was quiet, she said, "Please continue, Mister Haas."

"Thank you, Your Honor. I am nearly done. What I am trying to say is, there were many more Dutch people who were complicit with the occupiers than those who formally joined their ranks. The landlady who denounces her Jewish tenants because she wants to be rid of them—and this happened more than once—is guilty of using Nazi policy as an instrument of murder. My client, who wore a uniform that made him stand out more clearly, is guilty only of a young man's obedience to his superiors. And for this he has already paid his debt. Under these circumstances, I ask for this court's clemency. Thank you, Your Honor."

"Thank you, Meneer Haas, for your very edifying discourse."

The translation came several seconds after she spoke and by the time he heard it, Peter couldn't tell from Justice Teuling's expression if she was being sarcastic or not.

"This court is adjourned," Justice Teuling said. She struck her gavel sharply against the block. "We will reconvene when we are ready with our verdict." In movements choreographed by repetition, the judges stood, adjusted their robes, and passed through the door behind their desks.

The blind closing the scene began its descent down the gallery windows.

CHAPTER 36: ARIE

Peter looked out from the airplane window as it descended for landing at the rural airport in Kamloops, BC. The town lay in an arid zone between the Coast Range and the Rocky Mountains that extended up from Washington State into the interior of British Columbia, Canada. The surrounding hills were dotted with sagebrush. All the trappings of dry-country life passed below him: barns, feed lots, cattle penned in their range with split-log fences, pickup trucks. As the plane flew over the city, he looked for changes since he'd last lived there. There was the strip of hotels and bars in the town centre. He remembered the hard living that came with the back-breaking labor of ranching, evidenced in broken bottles and vomit littering the sidewalks downtown on weekend mornings. That likely hadn't changed. If work was slow for the ropy-muscled men in the ranches, there was always the Domtar pulp mill. There it was, its smokestack still the most prominent landmark, halfway up a sparsely treed hill, painted the red and white of a coral snake as a warning to air traffic. Peter remembered the emissions from that smokestack, not just the innocent white plume at the top, but an invisible rotten-egg smell that sometimes carried down to the city. For this, the company, via the local news, sometimes made formal apologies, while blaming weather inversions.

The plane circled for its final approach. There was the Brocklehurst Estates, the trailer park where Peter once lived when he went to junior high school. The idea his parents agreed to was that a building inspector might have to move when the project was done, so a mobile home was the answer. To the Dutch way of thinking, those little houses all in a row, with the possibility of a flower bed and tool shed and kitchen garden in the back, was close to ideal. He saw the railroad track clearly, the straight line through the town from one end to the other like a delete mark. Peter remembered lying awake, waiting for the 11:05 night train before he could sleep. He never did figure out where that train was going.

There was the refinery next to the tracks with its natural gas flare and oily rag smell. Its proximity helped make the trailer park affordable. (His parents probably got a discount for the spot next to the railroad, too.) Alongside the refinery was the road to Tranquille, a dead end five-kilometre highway to the suburb with a 'facility' for the mentally disabled. The guys in senior high liked that road, straight and rarely patrolled. He often heard the phrase, "Open 'er up. See what she can do!" Almost every kid with a driver's license was a would-be street racer.

Arie had chosen well. It was a working town, inward looking. Europe was far away, the Second World War even farther.

His secrets would've been safe here.

***

Emmy was there to meet Peter at the airport. He spotted her easily next to a group of denim-shirted men in work boots. She was wearing flats, but still had the runway walk of the Miss Kamloops Daily News beauty queen, second runner-up in the city-wide contest.

"Hi bro." Emmy said it casually as though he'd just come back from the corner store. They hugged. He traveled with carry on, so there was no need to wait at the luggage conveyors.

Emmy drove confidently, a sign she'd lived in Kamloops her whole life. There was permanence to her existence. Peter admired and was repelled by it at the same time.

"The doctor said he has two or three weeks," she said. "Some sort of blood condition. Not making any more white cells or something. No treatment. Just keeping him comfortable 'til he's gone." She said it without emotion, like describing a chore on her to-do list.

Peter looked out the window. They drove past a shopping mall with a Save-On Foods, a Shoppers Drug Mart and a BC Liquor Store. All of life's necessities in one convenient location.

"I haven't told you how he is with the nurses," Emmy said.

"How is he with the nurses?" As he posed the question, Peter already had an inkling of the answer.

"Well, at least we know for sure he's hetero."

"You're kidding."

"Whenever he has a . . . you know, he has to show them. So proud. 'I'm ninety-one and look!' Then he pops open the bathrobe. Ta-da!"

"Oh, dear God."

"Yeah. Nothing they can do, really. How do you deal with something like that? Ninety-one. So now he gets his own room and only male nurses."

"Serves him right."

Emmy looked at Peter sideways and had to correct her steering when she looked back at the road. "In a weird way, he's having fun." She paused, thinking. "With his body falling apart and weeks left to live, it's the only power he's got left."

* * *

The door opened and Arie entered the hospital room in a wheelchair pushed by a man wearing a blue nurse's smock. There was no sign of the playful pervert Emmy had described in the car. The decline must've been steep. Arie was slumped in the wheelchair looking toward the floor. Peter saw him for the first time with his goatee fully white. Rather than an old-world patriarch, it gave him the look of a frail ascetic. His green plaid bathrobe was open to his navel, revealing a bony white chest with a few straggling hairs. He seemed aware of his loss of vitality, ashamed of it in the way he looked down. He only raised his head when the nurse said, "Here we are. I hope you two have a nice visit."

"Oh, hello Peter." Arie said it matter-of-factly, without a smile, as though to say, "This is Peter. I know him."

"Hi Dad," Peter said with his on-the-phone voice, imitating his father's emotionless tone.

The nurse overheard the greeting and intuited the right distance to put between patient and visitor to keep them at ease. His foot came down on the wheelchair brake with a sharp movement that snapped Arie's head backward.

On his way out, he turned halfway through the door. "I'll leave you two alone for a bit. I've got to come back in fifteen minutes or so for his bath."

There was a long silence. Arie's head slumped forward. His eyes were half closed.

Peter felt the urge to start off with a comment about Arie and the nurses, but he checked himself. Instead, he said the expected, "How are you feeling today? Are you in any pain?"

Before Arie could answer there was a faint knock on the door and the nurse reappeared. "Sorry to interrupt." He walked briskly to Arie's wheelchair and unclipped the urostomy pouch from its place underneath. "He'll be more comfortable with this in a different position. He complained about it pulling when it was underneath." He put the bag half full of urine in Arie's lap.

Arie looked down at the bag with its tube reaching under his bathrobe. He patted it reflectively, then weakly shifted the bag to a position between his thigh and the side of the wheelchair. From the other side, he brought out a newspaper, *de Volkskrant*. He pulled on the chair's collapsible tabletop, but didn't have the strength to lift it. Peter reached over and unfolded it for him. The newspaper's presence on the tabletop in front of him seemed to rouse him. Without noticeably moving, he sat straighter in the wheelchair.

"Keeping up with world events, are you?" Peter said.

Arie didn't reply. His eyes were distant. "I went on a trip," he said after a long silence.

"Where'd you go?" Peter was curious to see where Arie's mind was taking him.

"To a farm."

"A farm? What farm?"

"We flew."

"Who's we?"

Arie ignored the question, lost in his literal flight of imagination. "We flew over the Ijssel River. I could see the farm where I spent the summer."

"When was this?"

"We flew," Arie continued. "There was the farm and the river where I played along the shore. Ooh, I was so, so happy."

"How old were you then?"

The question intruded. Arie's eyes lost their distant look. He turned to Peter intently. "It was just before the war."

"Do you have any memories from later on? From during the war?" Peter wanted to steer the conversation toward his questions.

Arie waved his hand dismissively. Peter noticed for the first time how bony it was, how splotched with liver marks and freckles, how his blood vessels were prominent in the absence of flesh. The habitual gesture, made when he wanted to be assertive—or as a warning—was undone by a tremor at the end. "Better to forget all that. No point bringing it up now."

Peter was torn between compassion and the urge to know more about Corine's murder. Get Arie to narrate, finally say something meaningful. Not so much to solve it as resolve it. "You've said that many times before. But there is a point. Especially now."

"What? Now that I'm dying?" Arie fixed Peter with a gaze from under his eyebrows.

The intense look threw Peter off stride for a moment. He felt the presence of the tyrant, still there under the cracks and hollows. He recovered his composure and said, "Yes, now that you're dying. It means we don't have much time. I'd really like to clear some things up. Things Aunt Julia mentioned. Testimony that just came out."

"Oh her."

"Yes, oh her," Peter said. "She told the prosecutors how Corine died. She didn't die in a car accident before I was born, did she?" Peter felt the urge to confront his father with his lies, but suppressed it.

Arie unfolded the newspaper and turned his attention to it as a last line of defense.

Peter waited him out. They sat in silence while Arie read the paper, or feigned to. He became aware of a clock on the wall with a scarcely audible mechanism ticking away the seconds.

Eventually Arie folded the newspaper, surrendering. "Your mother lied, too," he snapped. "We thought it would be better that way. We both wanted to leave the war behind. Start again. We didn't think those memories would be good for the children."

Peter bristled inwardly at the phrase, 'the children.' He felt the sharp edge of his irritation. By returning to it a few times in his thoughts, he came to understand it had more to do with the secrecy of suffering. That decision to close off the past and start again—to leave even the language behind—drew a curtain across an earlier life.

Peter realized for the first time he wasn't solving a crime so much as inquiring into himself.

"Isn't there more to it than that?" he said. "Weren't you there when Corine was killed?"

There was a long silence. For an anxious moment Peter couldn't tell if Arie's wide-open stare was provoked by a deep reflection or the final act of dying.

"I didn't mean to," Arie said, still distant. "They killed her."

"What do you mean, 'I didn't mean to?'"

"I didn't mean to."

"What—"

"I wasn't the one they wanted and they killed you." Arie was again at the edge of another world.

Peter wasn't sure what to say.

"I told them things that weren't true," Arie continued. "I tried being nice, having fun. It didn't stop them. They killed you anyway."

"You lied to the SS, so they killed Corine?" Peter knew his questions were going into a void, but he couldn't help himself.

"If only the war had ended sooner. If only he'd been killed a few weeks earlier."

"Killed? Who? Berka, the one who murdered Corine?" Peter couldn't stop his questions from spilling out.

Arie looked at him, returning. He raised his hand slowly. It trembled as if afflicted by palsy. "He was targeted by the resistance. Someone got him. Someone, I don't know who. They found his body in the woods near the headquarters."

Peter thought back to Aunt Julia's story about collecting firewood. In his mind's eye, he could picture the very spot. "Who do you mean?" he asked. "Are you talking about Berka?"

"They shot fifteen people in retaliation," Arie continued. "The Germans went hard after the resistance. Rounded them up. All innocent. Three old men. Whoever killed that bastard must've known they'd do that."

"Why do you think they did it, the resistance, knowing there'd be retaliation? Was it the fact that he killed Corine?"

"He was out of control. Lost his mind. He would've killed way more than fifteen."

"So you think the resistance made a rational decision that this guy in the SS, Berka or whoever he was, had to be stopped."

Arie said nothing.

Peter brought an envelope out of his breast pocket, pulled out the photo of Arie and the SS officer, and put it on the wheelchair's folding tabletop.

"What's this?" Arie was confused, then angry. An impotent anger. "Where did you get this?" was all he could muster.

"This was taken next to the SS headquarters in Zwolle. Do you remember it?"

Arie nodded.

There was a tap on the door and the nurse reappeared. "Sorry to interrupt," he said cheerfully. He looked at father and son more closely and said, "I'll give you two a few more minutes." He closed the door in a way that made audible the latch clicking into place.

Peter shifted his chair closer and took hold of Arie's hands where the table wasn't in the way. He felt the bones and sinews like a tactile anatomy lesson. Arie looked down at their hands together.

"Dad, this is really important. Is there anything else you remember from that time?"

"What's it to you? Why does it matter?"

"Dad, please."

Silence.

Then Arie said, "They took me in after they killed Corine." His voice was barely above a whisper. "The SS. They mistook me for Joop."

"They were after Joop?"

Arie nodded. "I was never in the resistance. They were okay after they realized their mistake. All friendly. They posed with me for pictures outside. I don't know why. Propaganda maybe. They took my identification. Everything I had. Kept it. Then the British bombers targeted the SS headquarters. Up in flame. I have no idea how that photo survived. Everything else about me was gone. For all anybody knew, I didn't exist anymore. What a mess."

There was something about this that made no sense to Peter. The SS had just murdered his nine-year-old sister and his killers were "friendly." Then Arie's main concern was the loss of his identification papers. The priorities were out of kilter.

Peter decided to press. He pulled the indictment document out of another envelope, *Public Prosecutor v. Arie Dekker*, and put it in Arie's lap.

"What's this?" Arie said, reading. "What are you doing to me? You're treating me like some kind of criminal. I was never found guilty. You've got no right to do this." If he had the energy, he would have shouted. As it was, Arie croaked and sputtered his defense.

"Who was she?" Peter asked.

Arie gave no answer.

"It says here she was being held in a basement as a collaborator. You were part of the public tribunals. Is that how it started?"

Arie said nothing. He kept his gaze downward.

Peter straightened in his chair. "Dad, I have to fly back tomorrow. This might be the last time I see you."

Silence.

"Is there anything you want to tell me before I go?" Peter had thought to say, "before *you* go," but stopped himself.

"She was a *moff*," Arie said.

"A German sympathizer?"

"*Ja*, Yes."

"And you questioned her?" Peter decided to assemble the pieces, present them, see from Arie's response if they fit.

Arie nodded.

"And things got out of hand."

Arie looked up. His eyes were lucid. "She wasn't just any *moffenhore*. She was *his*."

"Who, his?" Then it occurred to him. "Berka's? The one who killed Corine?"

Arie nodded.

"You were questioning her and you found out she was the girlfriend of the one who killed your sister?"

Arie nodded again. "That bitch. She was proud of it. I had to teach her a lesson."

"So you raped her?"

Arie smiled, a slight curl of his lips in one corner of his mouth. "She deserved a spanking. That's all I did. Put her over my knee like a naughty girl. That's what she was, a naughty girl. No control. She just did what she wanted. Had to be taught a lesson." He looked at Peter with eyes dancing with mischief. "How was I supposed to know she'd like it?"

"Oh, Christ." Peter buried his face in his hands. He rubbed his face up and down, then looked at Arie from above his fingertips. "Then what?"

"We fucked of course." This time, his smile was full. He had control of the story. He revelled in it. "She liked it when I slapped her. It got her going. She really was a naughty girl."

"Dad, that's just—"

"Let me tell you, she was really something. I never told anybody about that. You're the first. Well, you and the judge after I was arrested. How was I supposed to know she was so, what do you call it? Connected. That's what got me in trouble. All the people she knew."

"Dad, you raped a prisoner."

"I didn't. It was, what do you say, con-sen-su-al. I got off. I wasn't guilty. That's what the judge said."

Flickers of what Peter had seen and heard and smelled in Mali pushed him over the edge. "Jesus Christ, Dad, everybody gets off for that sort of thing!" Then he realized that shouting, losing control, was just what Arie wanted. What he was trying to provoke. By an act of will, Peter calmed himself, felt the pounding in his chest abate. "Dad." He spoke as calmly as possible, but there was still a tremor at the edge of his voice. "She was a prisoner. Under your power. It couldn't have been consensual. Don't you see that?"

"That woman had some fire, I tell you. Man, I wish your mother had been a little more like her."

The words went into Peter like a knife, just as they were meant to. He stood to leave.

But then there was doubt. Maybe, just maybe, Arie was only a foolish, selfish old man, living his dying days. Maybe his effort to shock was defensive. Or it wasn't efforted at all. Maybe he just said the first things that came into his head. No filter. It sometimes came across as manipulation, but it was only desire put into words. The people who found Arie "interesting" or "quirky" might have gotten him right.

Peter had no way to tell if his father was truly, deeply, darkly evil or just a charming simpleton.

Peter sat back down. Now at least he had an inkling of what had happened in the last year of the war. Arie wasn't the one the SS was after; it was his brother Joop. It somehow fit. Arie wasn't the type to risk his life for a greater good.

Having found some answers, he was looking for and thwarted definitively in others, Peter was done with his father. Now he was torn between the unabated fury he still felt over Arie's warped confession and pity for the man whose life, with all its moral ambiguity, was at an end. Maybe the visit had gone off the rails because he'd pushed too hard. He should at least try a normal conversation before he left. Before saying goodbye for the last time.

"There were times you tried," Peter said. "To be a good father, I mean." Listening to himself, it sounded awkward. "You took me fishing a few times. I liked that."

Arie stared straight ahead.

"I remember mostly the small disasters," Peter continued, undeterred. "Like the time you cast a lure from the boat and you accidentally snagged a seagull in mid-flight. You had to reel it in to get the lure out and it fought back. Before that happened, I never knew their beaks were so sharp."

"I'm not a criminal," Arie said. He turned his head away from Peter.

Peter softened. "No, Dad, you're not a criminal. The judge said so."

"That's right." He looked at Peter sharply. "The judge said I wasn't guilty. That means I'm not."

They sat in silence for a while.

Then Peter stood and leaned forward to give Arie a hug. Arie received it rigidly, raising his arms with some effort to pat Peter's back. Peter kissed him on the forehead. "Goodbye."

Arie gave no answer. His eyes were vacant, his mind elsewhere. "I wish I had a map for where I'm going," he said.

Peter said nothing in reply. What was there to say? Best not to interrupt. He walked out the door and looked back to see the old man silhouetted by light from the window, slumped in a wheelchair, waiting for his bath.

CHAPTER 37: SENTENCE

The verdict caught Peter unawares. He'd lost track of the court and its schedule of sessions while he was in Kamloops. Now his head was still thick from jetlag, worse going west to east. There'd been no announcement, nothing he could find online. Nora was no better informed than he. He wondered why Jansen had said nothing about it. Maybe he'd told Aunt Julia and she'd gone to the court alone. Without him.

The press had been there, though. Journalists knew through their networks when things were going to happen. But there were no headlines reaching out from the kiosks. Their stories were relegated to a corner of the first page. "Four Years for One of the Last Second World War Criminals," or buried inside on page three like a human-interest story, "Court Sentences Eighty-Five-Year-Old to Four Years."

Aunt Julia answered after the first ring. Enamored of her new phone, no doubt.

Peter tried to broach the question of the verdict gently, but she beat him to it.

"They sentenced Groendyke to four years," she announced.

"I heard," Peter said. "Were you there in the court when they did it?"

"Oh, yes," she said. Then, anticipating his disappointment, she added, "It was nothing really. It took just a few minutes."

"Why didn't you call me?" Peter heard himself. He sounded peevish.

"Oh, nothing to bother you about, really. I knew you'd probably be sleeping after your trip."

"That was good of you," Peter said. "How did Groendyke look when they read the sentence. I'm curious."

"Not so well. He shouted something I couldn't hear when the man took him away. I think he was expecting some form of community service. An improvement to his social life. I might've planted that seed. Maybe I shouldn't have."

"I've come around to thinking you did the right thing," Peter said. "It was something the judges had to hear."

"You're sweet, Petertje."

Aunt Julia had softened now that the verdict was announced. She used the diminutive, made Peter a child after he came around to her opinion. He couldn't tell whether she'd just expressed the love of a close relation or a subtle put-down. Maybe she wasn't so soft, after all. Kind-hearted, maybe, but direct. Polite, but with barbs at the ready. Qualities almost expected of Dutch women past a certain age.

They said goodbye after arranging to meet at the beach later that week.

She didn't ask about Arie.

CHAPTER 38: MEMENTO MORTUIS

The coffee table in Aunt Julia's apartment had been moved closer to the living room window and converted into an impromptu altar. A blurry portrait of Corine in a stand-up frame stood next to an urn and a bouquet of white roses. Peter stood transfixed looking at Corine's image while Aunt Julia's guests mingled and bustled and looked for places to sit. The photo was from the same sepia print hung on Aunt Julia's kitchen wall. In it, Corine was smiling with her lips, looking straight into the camera. The way it was cropped called attention to the absence of others. Her hand rested on Aunt Julia's shoulder, but the only way Peter could tell the shoulder belonged to Aunt Julia was from the photo in the kitchen, the master portrait. Julia was the older sister, just coming into her beauty. Was there a tinge of envy in those fingers? Peter pushed the thought aside. There was a tuft of hair, a loose strand from his *oma's* bun, no doubt. But this silver-framed image had been prepared for Corine's day, so everyone else had to go, even Corine's Ma. Why is it that in funerals, we have to make individuals of the dead? How fortunate we are, those of us who don't have to live within those frames.

"What are you thinking?" Nora whispered in Peter's ear.

"I'm thinking how lucky we are," he said. He knew it was a platitude, not a genuine reflection of his thoughts, but no less true.

Peter looked around the room. It was standing-room only. Aunt Julia hadn't thought about practicalities when she sent the invitations. There was Hans from the old farmhouse and a woman next to him—his wife?—with the same lankiness minus the Adam's apple. There was Ferman from work, standing erect in an impeccable Italian-cut suit. And farther in the back near the bedroom door, the inseparable Evan, Olga and Rash, talking in a triangular huddle. Jansen was there, too, in his signature tweed and mismatched tie. An older man with the same ears but a better jacket sat next to him in a kitchen chair. Jansen's father? There was the Torenbeek woman from Jansen's office, the one who did so much of the prosecution's work in court. Peter didn't recognize anyone else. Oh, there was Uncle Jan, the amorous one who liked Aunt Julia's church entrances. The rest were strangers.

Then there was Toen. He was in his cage keeping a wary eye on the goings on from the other side of the wires. He looked better. His feathers were already growing back. Far from appearing agitated, he seemed to enjoy the presence of so many people. Energized.

With his thumb, Peter felt along the smooth, half-moon edge of his fingernail, manicured to perfection. It was a point of affinity with the bird, both of them recovering from inclinations to self-injury in response to stress.

Peter wanted something to occupy himself. He leaned toward Nora and spoke over the noise. "I'll go ask the neighbors if they have any extra chairs we can borrow," he said.

"Good idea," she said.

He returned a few minutes later accompanied by an old man, each of them carrying two kitchen chairs. As soon as the chairs were set down in a row facing the altar, the old man sat in one of them.

And people kept coming, with guests answering the door to let in other guests. Soon the apartment was full to capacity. There were photojournalists, too, two of them. Peter watched them at work. The table with Corine's haunting image must've made a good subject; a way to hook the stories they'd soon write. They focused on that for a while, then let their cameras hang from their straps. Peter imagined the titles soon to follow: "Justice at Last for Corine Dekker." Maybe a feature story about Willem Jansen: "The Man who Won't Let Us Forget," or something overblown like, "The Demon Hunter: A Dutch Prosecutor Hunts the Last Nazi War Criminals."

A man in his late twenties wearing a grey suit approached the front of the room and faced the audience to command attention. He was smooth-skinned with dark hair and matching dark-rimmed glasses. Even within the variety of human shapes and manners in the room, he was out of place. He seemed not to know what to do with his hands. He put one in his pocket, as though to appear relaxed, then changed his mind and folded both hands behind his back in the military at ease position. Maybe did a stint.

"Who's that?" Peter bent to ask Aunt Julia.

"The Dominee," she said. "Well, a new one from the seminary in Kampen. He's still in school." Then, by way of excuse, she added, "For the ladies from the historical society." She nodded to three elderly women perched on the sofa. One of them waved with her fingers in response to Peter's glance in their direction.

"*Dames en heren,*" began the Dominee-in-training. The room gradually quieted. Someone in the back coughed. "*Dames en heren,* ladies and gentlemen. We are gathered here today to honor and remember Corine Dekker. A mere girl when she died. Rather, when her life was taken. Nine years old. She hadn't yet made her contribution to the world other than through the gift of her presence. And yet, I see from this full room, that her life had great importance. That her contribution was considerable. Jesus Christ our Savior died that we might live. In this way of Christ, and following his example for mankind, so did the child Corine."

"Waf, waf!" Toen said from his cage.

The Dominee-in-training was momentarily flustered, but pushed forward with his over-prepared discourse.

"We cannot know the designs of the Almighty," he continued, "but we do know the fate that at His hands befell those who took Corine's precious life. We can see glimmers of God's intent for us in the way He wields justice in this earth. There is nothing inscrutable in—"

"Waf, waf!" Toen said again, this time with emphasis from a vigorous wingbeat.

The Dominee-in-training was thrown off stride. "Er . . . Um . . . Where was I?" he stammered. After an awkward silence, he gave up trying to recover his train of thought. "A homily will now be presented by Julia Dekker, Corine's beloved sister," he said. He stepped backward, red-faced, to cede the speaking-space to Aunt Julia.

She seemed prepared for his signal and in a few brisk steps approached the spot designated for her, the way she might once have walked down the church aisle.

"My dear friends," Aunt Julia began. "Thank you all for coming. I'm really very touched." She looked toward the urn and photograph on the table. "Corine would have been surprised to see so many of you here today. She would've said, 'Who, me? All this fuss about me?' And, in a way, she'd be right. She was an ordinary person, like so many supposedly ordinary people. Who would she have been, had she lived? What kind of person? I don't know for sure, but I do know one thing about her: she loved the year we spent on the farm, loved animals. I don't mean in the abstract. I mean, she loved them with all her heart, connected with them, mind to mind. If you saw her cuddle a rabbit, it wasn't for the sake of holding a cute rabbit, see the pretty bunny, in the way of little girls. She got to know that rabbit, enter its thinking. She would know any animal she touched, and it would know her. That was her special gift."

She took a slow, measured sip from a glass of water on the table beside her.

"What strange symmetry that a person who cared more about life than anyone I know should have her life ended by those who cared the least."

She paused. Her brow furrowed. Her eyes were almost drawn closer together in concentration.

Peter watched her eyes move, tuning in to that mind of hers. The silence in the room became uncomfortable. People shifted in their chairs or moved on their feet to another position.

"I'm not sure about Corine's sacrifice to the world," she said finally. "No disrespect to the Dominee here."

He blushed a deeper pink.

"But . . ." She searched her thoughts again. "I think she was just a little girl, yet to become a woman. She was my sister. A light in the darkness. The war never seemed to reach her. Not until the day she died. It may be true, what our friend here said. Corine made it possible for others to live. She gave our family strength. She lifted our spirits when they most needed lifting. But the idea that she sacrificed herself for others is utter nonsense. The rest of her gifts to the world were yet to come. She was taken . . ." She paused again, this time longer than before. She wiped the tears from each eye with her palm. "Where's the justice in that?"

Then, she said, so quietly her audience leaned into her voice. "Revenge is a terrible thing." She struggled to find more words. As though to bring her discourse to a dignified conclusion, she blurted out, "A toast to Corine!" She reached for the water glass on the table beside her and raised it to the audience.

There was immediate consternation in the room. A murmur rose in volume. No one had a glass of any kind. Peter overheard their voices. "Do you have anything to toast with?" "Me? No. Does anyone?" "What do we do?" They looked to one another and shrugged.

Peter rushed into the kitchen and found the bottles of white wine in the fridge, placed sideways on the bottom shelf, half hidden by a large tray of canapes. He pulled one out. It was three quarters empty. Aunt Julia got a head start, he noted. He reached for an unopened bottle. Three rows of wine glasses were at the ready on the counter, placed there for the reception afterward. In his haste, he splashed wine over the glasses and onto the counter. Evan, Rash, and Olga began an impromptu relay between the kitchen and living room. Before long, everyone had a glass of wine in their hands.

Olga took the water glass from Aunt Julia's hand and replaced it with wine.

Aunt Julia raised it and said, "Corine, my beloved sister, I think of you and I miss you every day. To Corine." A tear slipped out of one eye and ran down her cheek.

There was a contagion of melancholy in the room. Most members of the audience looked down at the glasses they held, torn between sombre thoughts and the festive object in their hands. Then social propriety took over. Someone in the back of the room said, "hear, hear." Glasses clinked and voices rose. Toen squawked and beat his wings. Peter watched Nora approach the birdcage and touch her wine glass to the wire. He had to be included in all things human. Toen moved to the back corner of the cage in apparent disapproval of the foul-smelling, noisy object suddenly thrust toward him. Nora then offered her finger for a scratch, which he accepted by clambering toward her and nuzzling it with the top of his head.

Watching her, Peter suddenly thought a term of endearment for Nora. She was his *Vogeltje*, a little bird.

Evan and Olga circulated with trays of the canapes Peter and Nora had prepared that morning. There were *kroketten*, croquettes fried with ragout centres; shrimp-cucumber sandwiches cut into small, crustless triangles; and three-piece mini skewers of Indonesian chicken satay in peanut sauce. Rash should've been helping, but was deep in conversation with a member of the historical society whose twenty-something chaperone—a granddaughter perhaps—hovered nearby looking bored. The sly dog, taking the oblique approach by talking up the granny.

Aunt Julia was perched on one of the neighbor's chairs. The chair's owner, the neighbor, was on one side of her and Jansen's father—or the dapper gentleman who looked like his father—on the other. Survivors. They find one another. Without words, they understand one another. They give their testimony, tell their stories, and people nod and express sympathy, but no one else quite seems to understand. There's a look they give one another that goes deep, like a secret handshake.

Peter was startled by a hand suddenly clapped firmly on his shoulder. It was Ferman. He held a wine glass in one hand and looked sorrowful.

"I'm very sorry to hear about your father," he said. "We're here for your late aunt of course, but let's not forget about your other loss." Ferman was momentarily at a loss for words. "Or rather, your . . . what shall I say?"

Peter muttered his thanks, and added, "My dad's doing okay, thanks. He seems to enjoy the attention."

"Still," Ferman said. "In a way, it's a loss in waiting, having a close loved one in hospice."

The words, 'close loved one,' landed awkwardly. They invoked in Peter's mind a counterpoint-word, *klotzak*, Arie's preferred expletive, invoked countless times over the years to express frustration with his children, sometimes followed by open-handed blows. Peter responded the only way he felt would be appropriate. "That's very nice of you to say."

With these words, Ferman was released from duty and his expression brightened. "We've got Al-Mahdi in custody," he said. "You know, the one we've been waiting for. The extradition from Mali, all that."

"That's great." Peter felt less enthusiasm than he expected. He heard the words come out flat. "When can we expect to go to trial?"

"We might not," Ferman said. "Other than for the formalities. The evidence is pretty strong. He basically convicted himself with those videos. The defense is making noises about a plea."

Peter nodded. This was what success looked like. Perpetrator in custody. Plea negotiations. Or noises about them. Yet it was somehow unsatisfying. Al-Mahdi would likely spend years in a Malian prison for destroying buildings, while the ones who tore down people's bodies and spirits were living in freedom. Some still with the twelve-year-old wives they'd captured at gunpoint.

"When can we expect a result?" Peter asked.

"Probably a few years yet." Ferman said it without visible awareness of anything out of the ordinary. "We still need to finish building the case. Every detail. Brick by brick."

Peter nodded, feigning agreement. He wasn't new at his job anymore. That made it worse. No more excuses for not knowing the basics. "I know one shouldn't make excuses," he said in pursuit of that thought. "I just wanted to say, I realize I haven't been there a hundred percent. You know, since they found the body. The trial and everything."

Ferman smiled and put his arm paternally on Peter's shoulder. "My dear friend," he said, "we'll be prosecuting cases from that war for the next seventy years. Relax. You can take a week off." Then he seemed embarrassed by his expression of warmth, muttered something indistinct into his wine glass that sounded like "really must be going," and melted into a knot of people in the kitchen near the exit.

***

"What do you think, how'd it go?" The question was a banality, but Peter was genuinely interested in Nora's answer.

They were at the kitchen sink washing up after the reception for Corine. Toen watched everything they were doing from Nora's shoulder. Toen was fascinated by the suds and occasionally clambered sideways to get a better look. Aunt Julia, had gone to bed, suddenly overcome with fatigue just before seven o'clock. Despite her considerable means, she didn't have a dishwasher. It was one of those things about the war generation. So many didn't allow themselves luxuries. Especially if it came with an unfamiliar technology.

Peter put his question another way. "What do you think, *Vogeltje*?"

Nora looked at him sideways and smiled. She must've assumed the question was directed at the parrot.

"I think it was a huge success," Nora answered.

It wasn't what Peter expected. "I thought it was a disaster," he declared. "What about her speech? Calling out the seminarian like that? That crazy toast before anything was ready?"

"That's what made it a success," Nora said. "It was real." They were silent for a moment, paused in their work. "The missing of her sister is now a spoken thing," she added. "Your aunt's not carrying it by herself anymore. It must also reassure her that when she dies, she won't be alone. She will matter."

Peter continued washing plates. Nora dried and put them in a stack in the cupboard. Toen bobbed his head to the motion of Nora's dishtowel.

After a long silence Peter asked a question that had long occupied his thoughts. "Do you think she did it?"

"Did what?"

"Killed that SS officer. What's-his-name. Walther or Walter or Wilfred, whatever, Berka. The one found dead in the woods near the SS headquarters."

Nora paused in her work. She put a wet plate on a dish towel spread over the counter to catch drips.

"Of course," she said.

To Peter, that came as another surprise. "What do you mean, of course? There's nothing certain about it at all. If you were preparing an indictment it would fail. She'd only be a suspect."

"You're just thinking about it like a prosecutor," Nora said. "If you think about it like a person who loves her, you'd see it. There'd be no doubt."

Peter was mildly incensed. "Are you saying I don't love her?" He handed her another plate. She stacked it on top of the one on the towel.

"No, I'm not saying that at all. I'm just looking at it another way." She dried and put away the accumulated plates in silence. Peter waited. "Maybe if you took your mind outside the courtroom, you'd see it, too," she said finally.

"I'm sorry, I need more than feelings before coming to a conclusion like that." Peter wasn't ready to replace his reality with hers.

"I understand," Nora said. It didn't mean she agreed, he knew that. She stood tiptoe and kissed his cheek. He leaned into it.

"So, if your intuition is right, what do you think happened?" Peter asked.

"If I follow my intuition?" She paused in thought. "I think your Aunt Julia is one of the bravest people I know."

Peter was hoping for something more. "And?"

"And, after seeing Corine killed the way she was, your Aunt Julia found a purpose. It wasn't revenge. Not purely. It was more like a sacrifice. Berka was a dangerous sadist. Left alive, who knows how many more innocents he'd kill before the war was over? She was just a girl, really. She'd never fired a gun, but she had relevant practice with the soldiers when she collected firewood, seeing how easily they could be lured into the woods. I think it must've been her brother, Joop, who showed her how to use the pistol. Maybe one of his friends. Without actually firing it, of course. Just to get her used to how it worked, how it felt in her hands. Then she waited for the officer to walk by on his way to or from the SS headquarters. Allowed herself to be seen. Got him to come in after her. Lust or power, who knows what motivated him? The main thing is, he fell for the trap."

"I have to admit, it sounds plausible," Peter said. "As a story."

"Her guilt still gets to her. It comes out now and then," Nora said.

"You think Aunt Julia feels guilty about killing that Nazi?"

"No, not him," Nora explained. "The fifteen innocents. The executions afterward. The retaliation. That's what she struggles with. Corine's murder, she couldn't do anything to stop it. Killing the Nazi near the end of the war, okay, that was tough, but still nothing on her conscience. But the fifteen executed later, that had to get to her. If I had to say, that's what my overwrought intuition is picking up on. Her guilt."

Peter, as always, wanted more certainty. "There's one way to find out for sure." he said. "Why don't we ask her?"

"We could, but it isn't likely she'll want to talk about it."

"Why don't we at least try?" Peter insisted.

Nora paused with her dishtowel in mid-circle. "It might relieve her to be able to say it." She put the towel back in motion. "Okay," she said. "Let's ask her." She turned to the bird on her shoulder. "What say you, Toentje? Shall we ask her?"

Toen nodded and nuzzled her ear, as though in affirmation and consolation.

CHAPTER 39: THE BEACH

It was the first warm day of summer, a Saturday afternoon, and the pier, boardwalk and beach at Scheveningen were crowded. The three of them took off their shoes and walked in silence. Peter tied the laces of his running shoes together and hung them over his shoulder, a technique learned from carrying ice skates. Aunt Julia carried a bag with room enough for Nora's sandals and hers. The sand was moist and compacted and cool under their feet.

To Nora, whose vision was poor on this bright day, the sounds in the air were festive. Dogs barked, children shrieked, rollerblades and strollers bumped along the regular gaps in the boardwalk. There was the sound of gulls, drawn to the commercial area near the pier, pursuing the scent of grills and deep fryers. She heard voices in every direction: negotiations over ice cream, whether to walk, how far to walk, where to spread the towels, and fussing, "But I don't like sunscreen," and, "Mommy, I'm hungry."

Even the children's complaints and tears, empty of real suffering, added to the spirit of joy. As they got closer to the incoming waves, there were shrieks and shouts as the North Sea waves broke and washed in to shore. It reminded Nora of family vacations in the Spanish Costa Dorada. Funny how the sound of children playing in water is the same everywhere, no matter the language.

Aunt Julia put Nora's arm through hers and guided her around obstacles on the beach: trenches dug with plastic shovels, carrying water up from the wash through canals and moats, games of soccer with just-bought balls glinting in the sun, couples sunbathing, some marking their own space, your towel and mine, others in intimate embrace. Scheveningen in the summer was quite possibly the happiest place in the Netherlands—the perfect setting to raise the delicate topic of Aunt Julia's part in a revenge killing in the last year of the war.

Farther along the beach, away from the boardwalk and pier, the crowds on the beach thinned. Sounds of outward exuberance were replaced by the calm of an unobstructed expanse of sand and the sea's regular pulse of breaking waves. It was calming. A wide beach was, for Nora, synonymous with freedom and release from care.

"Julia." Nora searched for how to begin and only got as far as her name.

She felt Aunt Julia look at her quizzically. "Yes? What is it?"

"It's hard to talk about. I don't quite know how to begin."

"Goodness gracious," Aunt Julia said, without impatience in her voice. "Don't be so serious. Just come out with it."

"Well," Nora hesitated. She spoke softly, aware she was next to Aunt Julia's ear, and saw Peter move closer to better follow the conversation. "We were wondering, Peter and I, about who killed Berka. The one who murdered Corine. Whether you remember anything about who did it." She was careful in her choice of words to distinguish appropriately between killed and murdered.

Aunt Julia turned her gaze back to the expanse of beach with the expression of someone given an inappropriate gift. "It was a long time ago," she said. "Everything was so . . ." She searched for the right word and couldn't find it.

"Does that mean you had something to do with it?" Peter asked.

Nora put her arm around Aunt Julia's shoulder, partly for her own comfort and partly to compensate for Peter's bluntness.

"We're no better than so many of them," Aunt Julia said.

Peter moved closer to Aunt Julia, pressing her between her interrogators. "What do you mean by that? Was it planned? Did Joop help you?" Peter was dogged, a hound on the scent.

Aunt Julia stopped walking, broke free of Nora's embrace and turned to face Peter. She looked up at him, grabbed his attention the way she did with her active blue eyes, and said, "Listen to me carefully. A lot of us did things that in another time we could never have imagined ourselves doing. Things that disturbed our sleep the rest of our lives. Things we never did since." She paused, without letting go of her gaze. Peter shifted on his feet uncomfortably. "I've said all I want to say about that," she said.

Something in the way she uttered this made Nora aware of a door closing. There was finality in it.

"I'm sorry," Peter said. "I didn't mean to push. Well, I did, actually, but I didn't mean to, you know. . ." He didn't finish. Peter was sometimes stymied by the effort to understand his own intentions.

Nora slipped behind Aunt Julia, nimbly like a dancer, to take Peter's hand. She linked her other arm with Aunt Julia's, for closeness, but also to keep her from thinking the move was a shift in allegiance, even though it was, in a way. She wondered how Peter would take Aunt Julia's silence. Her refusal. He'd likely be put off by it at first, wonder why she had to be so stubborn, but he wouldn't be compelled by it. Not for long. No reforming answer lay hidden behind her privacy, nothing of real consequence, just a salve to his curiosity. He was drawn to other kinds of questions, the ones with possible correctives at the end. His indignation was bigger than hers, a great roiling thing that took on the ills of the world.

Peter would say there was no telling with Aunt Julia. He'd reassure himself that someday, probably not for a while, she might find the will to reach back and remember. Until then, she would hold on to her memories. The story of how Berka was killed would still be there, locked away.

They walked in silence.

There was the shadow of a seagull flying low overhead.

Peter shortened his stride to match Nora's.

"Now let's enjoy this beautiful day," Aunt Julia said.

AUTHOR'S NOTE ON SOURCES

Although a work of fiction, *The Memory Seeker* is inspired by actual events and experience. I drew, first, from the ten months I spent in northern Mali during my years as a doctoral student in social anthropology at Cambridge University. The subject of my PhD research—a nascent Islamic reform movement—later morphed into something more sinister and violent, the armed insurrection that occupied Timbuktu in 2012-2013. My connections and friendships with Tuareg people have continued through several decades of work in the international movement of indigenous peoples, participation in two annual gatherings of the Tuareg Diaspora in Europe, and co-hosting (with Sarah Federman) a series of Peace Dialogues with the Center for Human Rights and Legal Pluralism in the Faculty of Law at McGill University.

The International Criminal Court in The Hague did, in fact, begin to use digital methods of investigation around 2013, roughly when the events I describe in the novel took place. To better understand the world of digital forensics, I undertook training in open-source investigation methods at a week-long workshop hosted by the Netherlands-based NGO Bellingcat, another offered by Berkeley's Center for Human Rights, and an advanced course at the Institute for International Criminal Investigations in The Hague. One of the main threads of the plot in *The Memory Seeker* is closely modeled on an ICC investigation into the destruction of world heritage sites in Timbuktu following the city's occupation by Ansar Eddine and Al-Qaida in the Islamic Maghreb. This eventually led to the ICC's indictment and prosecution of Ahmad Al Faqi Al Mahdi, along the lines I describe in the novel. (For more on this case, see *The Prosecutor v. Ahmad Al Faqi Al Mahdi*, https://www.icc-cpi.int/mali/al-mahdi.) The systemic sexual assaults and other forms of violence committed by Ansar Eddine during the occupation of Timbuktu are the subject of an ongoing trial at the ICC, *The Prosecutor v. Al Hassan Ag Abdoul Aziz Ag Mohamed Ag Mahmoud* (https://www.icc-cpi.int/mali/al-hassan).

Peter Dekker's struggle to piece together events of the past is based on the memories, now faded or lost, of my own family members. Now and then, my mother, usually over cups of tea, talked about things like her experience as a girl having to testify against her teacher after he was denounced and arrested for telling jokes about the Nazis. My father wrote several stories about the war, which he intended mainly to highlight the humanity of ordinary German soldiers, printed in the Victoria Legion's newsletter. I set these family stories more centrally in the context of Operation Silbertanne, a Nazi war effort in the occupied Netherlands aimed at repressing the resistance. Hanns Albin Rauter, commander of the SS in the Netherlands and the architect of this operation, was tried and executed in The Hague shortly after the war. (Dutch-language excerpts from his trial and footage from the occupation of the Netherlands can be found at: https://www.youtube.com/watch?v=-4SzZPjr9Zs.)

My account of the more recent prosecution of war criminals involved in Operation Silbertanne follows Dutch prosecutorial roles, institutions, and court procedures. Here, I relied more on a pastiche of sources, including visits to the Schiphol Judicial Complex and guidance from livestreamed trials, including that of the MH 17 disaster in the District Court of The Hague. The trial of Oskar Gröning, a former SS accountant at Auschwitz who was indicted for complicity in the murder of 300,000 Jews in Germany in 2014, was another source of inspiration. This trial highlights a renewed determination by some European governments to prosecute war criminals from World War Two in the first decades of the twenty-first century, a final effort against time and mortality to bring Nazi war crimes suspects to justice. A feature of the Gröning case I noted was the unusual position taken by Eva Mozes Kor, a Holocaust survivor who, with her twin sister, was subjected to cruel medical experiments at the hands of Josef Mengele in Auschwitz. Despite the horrors she endured, she conversed with and hugged Gröning after she gave testimony and later expressed disappointment at Gröning's sentence of four years in prison. For her, community service in the form of speaking out against Nazis would have been a more fitting and socially responsible sentence. This argument caused controversy among Holocaust survivors. In *The Memory Seeker*, I attribute Kor's courageous position to the character of Aunt Julia.

ACKNOWLEDGMENTS

Besides those I just acknowledged in my Note on Sources, I wish to specifically thank those Tuareg people who shared with me their more recent memories of war and displacement. I had important conversations with Mariam Aboubakrine, chair of the Permanent UN Forum on Indigenous Issues and co-founder of the Timbuktu-based women's advocacy NGO, Tin Hinan. Dr. Adal ag Roubeid, President of the Movement for Democratic Renewal (MDR) Tarna in Niger, and Special Advisor to the President of Niger, was generous with his insight and inspiration. I am grateful to the Organisation de la Diaspora Touarègue en Europe Odte-Tanat for including me as a fellow camper in two of their annual gatherings in the countryside near Evreux, France. The participants' stories of life in their desert homeland and of forced displacement and immigration have stayed with me.

Special thanks to Brian Thom and his archaeological research team at the University of Victoria, who gave me insight into ground penetrating technology, specifically as it existed at the time of the story. No mean feat.

My writing coach / editor, Darcy Nybo, gave great advice to me as an author making a transition from academic writing to fiction. Susan Steckler, Ian Kalman, and Molly Quell each offered useful impressions and corrections on an early draft. Then I benefitted from the expertise of Reagan Rothe and the folks at Black Rose Writing, who offered creative book production and media savvy, everything one could hope for from an edgy indie press.

Special thanks to A.R., who many years ago gave me a personal introduction to the work of the Canadian National Institute for the Blind (CNIB) and educated me about how she saw the world differently.

Sarah Federman was a fellow traveler with our Tuareg friends and a supportive and loving part of the writing process. I dedicate this, my first novel, to her.

ABOUT THE AUTHOR

Ronald Niezen is a Distinguished James McGill Professor in the Department of Anthropology and Associate Member of the Faculty of Law at McGill University. He previously held positions as a professor of anthropology and of social studies at Harvard University. He completed a doctoral degree in Social Anthropology at Cambridge, for which he spent ten months living and traveling in northern Mali. Niezen has published ten nonfiction books on human rights and social justice activism. For his recent work on digital activism, Niezen received training in open-source investigations in workshops sponsored by the NGO Bellingcat, Berkeley's Center for Human Rights, and the Institute for International Criminal Investigations. *The Memory Seeker* is his first novel.

NOTE FROM THE AUTHOR

Word-of-mouth is how books travel. If you enjoyed *The Memory Seeker*, please leave a review online—anywhere you are able. Even if it's just a sentence or two. I'd appreciate it enormously.

Thanks!
Ronald Niezen

CPSIA information can be obtained
at www.ICGtesting.com
Printed in the USA
LVHW092043270123
738018LV00013B/489

9 781685 131401